Th

The Missing Years
Part I

Brian T. Seifrit

A Tyrell Sloan Western Adventure.

The Missing Years – Part I

Published by
William Jenkins
2106-1200 Alberni Street
Vancouver BC V6E 1A6 Canada
williamhenryjenkins@gmail.com
http://www.williamjenkins.ca
Telephone: 604-685-4136
Edition 1
ISBN: 978-1-928164-08-1
Copyright Brian T. Seifrit © 2014
All rights reserved.

Without limiting the rights under copyright, no part of this publication may be reproduced, stored in or introduced into a retrieval system, or transmitted, in any form, or by any means (electronic, mechanical, photocopying, recording, or otherwise) without the prior written permission of both the copyright owner and the above publisher of this book.

Thank you for respecting the author's work. An ebook is licensed for your personal use only whereas a paperback edition can be given away or re-sold. The ebook may not be re-sold or given away to other people. If you would like to share the ebook with another person, please download an additional copy for each person with whom you share it. If you are reading this as an ebook and did not purchase it, or it was not obtained for your use only, then you should obtain your own copy.)

Dedicated to:

All my past and present readers.

Special Acknowledgements:

This work would not have been possible without the dedicated editing of **William Jenkins**.

The Missing Years – Part I

Chapter 1

It was late September 1890 when Tyrell left Willow Gate. The pain he felt from the gunshot wound made him dizzy. He was grateful Emma was able to staunch the flow of blood. In a way, he was saddened at the fact that, only minutes earlier he had taken the lives of two men. They were scum; there was no arguing that point, still he felt withdrawn. Indeed, they drew on him first, and the better man won. Tyrell heeled Pony's flank, whistled for Black Dog and off into the distant horizon they went.

"Damn! Wish that hadn't happened, Pony ol' boy. I swear to God though I'm most certain Heath Roy and the no good Ollie Johnson were behind Grandpa Sloan's slaying. Even if they weren't, they got what was coming to them. They should have never drawn their pistols. Stupid asses. I wish I knew where to go from here." Tyrell looked over his shoulder and back the way he came. Sighing in relief that no one was following him, he cut northeast toward the Rocky Mountains.

In time, he would head towards Hells Bottom leaving behind a false trail that he headed to the Rockies. When he got to Hells Bottom, he would gather any remnants of his belongings that he left behind when he headed to Red Rock in the first place. He left the old homestead his father finally bought before he died in the hands of an old friend. God willing the place still stood. Bannock, as everyone called, him, wasn't the most dependable sort, but he was honest and a good friend. Tyrell reminisced about how he and Bannock first met. It was while he was in his late twenties; he was sitting in a saloon, playing cards and drinking whiskey, not very good whiskey either from what he could remember.

The Missing Years – Part I

Bannock strolled in as the saloon was closing, and Tyrell was in a drunken stupor. He couldn't even help himself as three men beat him, accusing him of cheating. They were plain mad, because they lost a month's wage each, to Tyrell. Bannock stepped in though and tossed the men off, cursing them for beating up on a drunkard. He wasn't a big man, but he knew how to fight with or without a gun, his bald head was sunburned as though he hadn't worn a hat in days and he walked bow-legged, dressed in old denim pants and shirt. The rawhide vest he wore was a bit tattered but it suited him. One of the men spoke with aggravation as he accused Tyrell of cheating.

Now finally able to catch his breath, Tyrell slurred out that he never cheated in cards a day in his life, that they were all mad as polecats because he won. "No damn way can a fella win that many hands in a row without cheating!" The man hollered back as he pulled his gun.

Bannock slapped it out of the man's hand and planted his fist into his face. "You gonna pull a pistol on an unarmed man, that there is pure cowardice. Now step away and get out of here!"

"Wait," Tyrell slurred once more, "yous think I was cheatin'," he started as he moved over to the table they were all once sitting at. "Come back tomorrow, I'll be sober then, and we'll play again. One hand wins all. How is that you bastards?"

"My cards, not yours," the man replied with anger.

"That suits me fine. Hell, better yet, we'll buy a brand new set. One hand, winner takes all." Tyrell repeated as his body slumped forward, being as drunk as he was, and his head bounced with a thud onto the round table. When he finally came to, he was upstairs lying on his bed in his room in the saloon. Shaking his head, he looked around. There wasn't much he remembered about the night before,

The Missing Years – Part I

but sitting in a chair there was Bannock. "Who are you?" Tyrell questioned as he tried to sit up. His head pounded relentlessly and his hands were shaking.

"Name is Bannock, I stopped you from taking a beating and a bullet last night. There weren't any more rooms available, so I helped myself to this chair after I laid you on your bed."

"Beating? Bullet? What are you talking about?" Tyrell asked.

"You were in a bit of trouble when I wandered into this saloon. Seems some unpleasant men accused you of cheating in cards. They was beating on you pretty good. Can't you feel the welts on your face?"

Tyrell brought his hand up to his face and rubbed it. "Ah, I see. Damn. Okay, well thank you. What did you say your name was again?"

"Folks call me Bannock. You can too."

"Nice to meet you Bannock, I'm Tyrell Sloan." Rising from his bed, he walked the few paces to where Bannock sat, and reached out his hand. "Guess I owe you a drink."

"Nope. You owe me nothing." With that, Bannock stood to exit Tyrell's room.

"Maybe I can buy you some breakfast."

"That you could do. I'll meet you downstairs. You best splash some water on your face and wash off that dried blood." With that, Bannock left and made his way to a table near the bottom of the stairs. A few minutes later Tyrell met him and their friendship started. They rode together for a few months, gambling and fighting. Then, one day, Bannock was gone. Tyrell finally met up with him again months later in Hells Bottom. Bannock had taken a position with a local rancher as a cowhand and once again, their friendship was rekindled. So it was as the years came and

The Missing Years – Part I

went, and when Tyrell left for Red Rock to take over his grandfather's estate, he convinced Bannock to stay at the little homestead. That was a year ago, and as Tyrell sat there looking toward the north, he reminisced. "Yep, sure hope Bannock ain't burned the old place down, Pony. In a few weeks, we'll find out, I suppose. Come on, let's get moving again, it's gonna be dark soon."

Meanwhile back at the saloon in Willow Gate, old man Roy was trying to make a deal with two of the town's best-known trackers, Eli Furgeson, and Noble Bathgate to track down his son's killer. "You bring me my son's killer or his head, and I will give you $2000 hard cash. Emma ain't been much help, only thing she did say was she thought his name might have been Tyrell something or other, she ain't sure though. What we do know is the direction in which my boy's killer is travelling. We ain't got much time before the law gets involved, I can hold them off for bit, but sooner or later it will be in their hands."

"I played cards with a fellow named Tyrell, I think that's what he said. I don't recall much about his looks, too many shots of whiskey if you know what I mean. What do you say Noble, think this is something we might be interested in?" Eli asked as he looked over to his friend.

"Could always use $2000 cash bucks. You got any recollection what he looks like at all, Eli?"

"Nope, not really, maybe something will come to me once I have a clear head. Still, I reckon he can't be that hard to follow."

"Humph, well we ain't got nothing else to do. Sounds like it might be an easy $2000. Yeah, I'd be interested." So it was that Noble and Eli left Willow Gate in search of Heath Roy's killer, and of course, their ultimate deaths, but neither of them could have known that.

The Missing Years – Part I

As the sun set that night, Tyrell, Pony, and Black Dog sat around a small fire, his mind racing with ifs, whatnots, and should have's. As his coffee pot began to perk and hiss, he poured a cup. Blowing on it gently he brought it to his lips and took a swallow. The tin cup warmed his hands as he looked into the darkening wood. Out there, somewhere, he knew men were looking for him. He had no intentions on letting his guard down, not yet, not until he was well on his way, and even then, he knew he'd have to be alert. The last thing he wanted was to hang from a rope, or worse, take a bullet in his back. Perhaps he should have stuck around and faced the law, at least then they'd have his side of the story. Even so, chances were that old man Roy would buy off the law and his side of the story wouldn't make a difference. For now, he'd keep moving, avoiding all confrontations with the law and with strangers.

Adding another piece of wood to his fire, Tyrell rested his head on the saddle and looked up to the sky. He thought about Marrisa and Grandma Heddy, he thought about Fry and old Wilson, and now wished he never left Red Rock Canyon. Nevertheless, he was tired of the charade. He wasn't and never would be a cattleman, nor was he a prospector. Hell he wasn't even sure what he was. One-thing for certain, he wasn't a cold-blooded killer. For now though, that is exactly what some folks thought. He looked over toward Black Dog who was lying comfortably next to him. "I've been a lot of things in my time Black Dog, always had the same name. Tonight I'm Travis Sweet, nice to meet you," he chuckled as he contemplated. *Yep, gonna introduce myself to anyone who don't know me as Travis Sweet. Perhaps that will slow down anyone looking for Tyrell Sloan. Once I get this mess sorted out maybe I'll go back to Tyrell, maybe I won't. Only time will tell. Now, I*

The Missing Years – Part I

wonder what a fellow named Travis Sweet does for a living, Tyrell thought.

It was while drinking his second cup of coffee that he heard the sound of horse hooves. He stood up and looked in the direction he heard the sounds come from. It was dark and he couldn't make anything out. Cautiously he pulled his rifle from the saddle he was using as a pillow and set it beside him. If someone was looking for trouble, Tyrell was going to oblige. Instead, though, he heard a voice in a deep English accent. "Hello there. May I join you at your fire?" The voice asked.

Tyrell squinted and could finally make out a man and a horse a short distance away in the undergrowth. The horse and rider approached closer and Black Dog began growling, finally, he relented and lay back down near the fire. "I suppose you could join me. I ain't got much to offer in the way of food, but I do have a pot of coffee. Sure, c'mon over," he gestured to the man, keeping the rifle in his hand and waited for the man to approach.

"Thank you very much. I have been on the trail for a week now and am not quite sure where I am," the man said as he swung off his horse.

"A foreigner huh?"

"You could say that, yes. My name is Dr. Harold Pike. I'm from England. Am looking for the town of Willow Gate, would you know where that is?" The man asked.

"Nope, not off hand." Tyrell lied. "I've heard of the place though."

"Hmm, yes well perhaps I'll find it eventually."

Tyrell reached out his hand to shake the Dr.'s. "My name is Travis Sweet. So, you are from England eh?"

"Yes. Three months on a ship that was scattered with rats, it is nice to be on solid ground, even if I am a little bit misplaced. I have business in Willow Gate, going to be starting up a medical office, if I can ever find the place."

"You are travelling from England without a map?"

"Well, yes, London actually. I did have a map but have somehow lost it."

"What I know of Willow Gate is that it is southwest of the Rocky Mountains. The Rockies are about a three maybe four days ride from here, so I'm guessing you head westerly and you might come across it, and if not I'm sure you'll run into someone who knows for sure." Tyrell said as he poured the man a coffee and handed it to him.

"Thank you very much," the doctor said as he took it.

"Going to start a medical office there, are you?"

"That is my intent, yes. I see you have a bit of a cut above your eye. I have some salve that will help the healing process if you care."

"Nah, ain't no point in that, the wound is about five days old," Tyrell lied again. "I reckon it is well on the healing side of things. How's your coffee?"

"Very good indeed, I do not usually drink coffee at night, I prefer tea, but this is very good."

"It is all I got. I ain't got any tea. Was never expecting to run into an Englishman," Tyrell chuckled.

"It is okay, here in the west I might have to get used to coffee as a preferred beverage."

"Yep, you'd do yourself a favour if you did. Not many folks in these parts drink tea. I ain't saying they don't, just that they like coffee better."

"Tea or coffee I guess doesn't matter during these cool nights." The doctor set his cup down on the ground next to him and held his hands over the fire to warm them. "I have some English sausage we could cook, if you like.

The Missing Years – Part I

They are well smoked and dry, so we can eat them cold if you'd prefer." The Dr. pulled a package of sausage from his saddlebags and smelled them. "Yes, they remain on the good side. Quite surprised they have lasted this long. I guess we can thank the preservatives-for that."

"No use eating them cold, cook them up. I ain't ate much today. Besides if they are little bad, the flames will fix them up. Do you need a frying pan?"

"I thought here in the west people cooked them on a stick. That is how I have been cooking them. They are quite delectable that way. A frying pan works too though. How would you prefer to cook them?"

"It don't matter any to me. Using a stick works and saves me from doing dishes."

"All right then we shall cook them on a stick." The doctor pulled out a knife from his waistband, and cut off two sticks from a nearby willow bush and handed one to Tyrell. "Here you go," he said as he sharpened his own and slid one of the sausages onto it.

Tyrell followed suit and before too long both were enjoying some English sausage. "Those are pretty good sausage. English type you say?"

"Yes, they are made in a little butcher-shop in Cambridge England. They are said to last without freezing for a few months, I guess that is true."

"So, why would a fellow like you want to live here in the west. Is there no need for doctors in England?"

The truth was, Dr. Harold Pike was not a doctor nor was that his real name. He did spend a few months in medical school that was true. However due to his malevolence he was eventually ejected by the head Doctor of Medicine who happened to be one of the first female doctors of the time. Eventually he found himself in London, where he took on the persona of one Jack the

Ripper. His new goal in life then was to lay waste to all the whores that reminded him of the wench who expelled him. For months he went on a murderous rampage slaughtering street-walkers of all ages, no woman was safe, but his preference were whores that he knew he could con into the dark alleys of London and where he knew he could kill without being noticed. The year then was 1888. He continued killing long after that, but, finally after some years of running and hiding from the law he left London and headed west. His desire was to continue with his cleansing of all whores in the west. However, he would never get a chance.

  After Tyrell and the doctor conversed for a few hours and as the moonlit sky became darkened by a setting fog and the two newly acquainted travellers settled in for the evening, Dr. Pike, while Tyrell slept, pulled a knife from the scabbard of his saddle and approached Tyrell with a desire to kill him. It had been a long while since he felt the warm blood from a victim pool over his hands, and this man Travis would be the first man he killed. Right from the beginning Black Dog, found something to be a little bit off about the doctor, and since they met did not take his eyes off him. Now as the doctor crept closer to Tyrell with a knife in his hand and blood lust on his mind, Black Dog acted. Tyrell, was woken by the ruckus and screams of horror, as Black Dog made quick work of Dr. Harold Pike.

  "Jesus Christ! What are you doing Black Dog?" Tyrell asked with alarm. It was then he saw the knife in the doctor's hand. "He... he... was going to kill me?" he asked in shock as though Black Dog would answer. "Thanks Black Dog, I owe you one. You did good. Now what do you suppose we ought to do with the body?" Looking around he decided he'd simply drag it off into the bushes, he didn't have the time or desire to bury the corpse, after all

The Missing Years – Part I

the man had tried to kill him. "There, the wolves and critters can have him. Damn, that was something else Black Dog. I'm sure glad you were alerted, otherwise it might be my carcass in the bush waiting to feed the animals. We'll go through his things in the morning, we can keep his horse and gear I reckon. I might have use for a pack horse."

Tyrell sat down at the fire and tossed a few more pieces of wood into the flickering flames, his mind scattered with what took place only a few minutes earlier. Eventually, he knew someone would find the rotting corpse, but it would matter little he would be long gone. Besides, it would look like a simple animal attack. *That is a couple dozen times now that the dog has saved me from the cold dirt,* Tyrell reminisced as he sat there numb from the day's ordeals. First the killing of the two no good for nothing men that drew on him and now the death of a man he shared a coffee and sausage with and whom he had been introduced to only hours earlier. He was glad that the day was over. What tomorrow might bring he had no idea, except that he would have to keep moving, and that is exactly what he intended to do at the first sign of daylight.

Chapter 2

It was early morning when he finally woke. Making sure that Dr. Harold Pike's horse wore no brand, Tyrell took some time going through the man's saddlebags, choosing carefully what he would keep and what he didn't want, he didn't bother with a coffee that morning nor did he toss any wood on the low burning embers of the past evenings fire. Instead, he saddled up Pony, whistled for Black Dog and leading the good doctor's horse, he headed east towards the Rocky Mountains. Four hours later, at mid-morning, he decided to stop for a short break. "Well, fellows," he started as he looked at Pony, Black Dog and the doctor's horse. "I figure we'll rest here for a bit. The doctor never told me your name horse, so I'll call you Horse for now."

He removed his canteen and took a long swallow from it. "It was quite the thing that happened last night. Who would have thought that Dr. Pike wasn't the friendly sort?" Tyrell shook his head. "Makes me wonder if he might have been on old man Roy's payroll, I don't imagine anyone could've caught up to us that quickly, so I doubt he was. I guess we'll never know will we?"

That evening, as the travelling companions made their way closer to the Rocky Mountains, two men, who were in fact on old man Roy's payroll were making their way closer to the body of Dr. Pike. It was the remnants of Tyrell's earlier fire, which drew their attention to the spot.

"Looks like this might have been where someone, maybe even the fellow that shot Heath Roy may have bedded down here last night." The one man said as he looked around and kicked the ashes hoping for a spark.

"I don't know Eli, looks like there were a couple folks here, a couple horses too. Weren't that fellow travelling alone?"

"He was indeed. Could be he may have bumped into another passerby."

"Could be means *'shit'*, I ain't so sure this is where he bed down or not. Either way, I say we hold up here tonight ourselves. I'll get a fire going."

"Yeah, might as well. We'll pick up the trail in the morning. I'm a bit tired and getting hungry too. You got anything in your saddlebags we can eat? I know for sure I ain't got nothing."

"Got some flour and jerked meat, probably got some coffee too. Go have a look see Eli, bring whatever is in them. We'll manage to cook something up I'm sure."

"Alright Noble, will do." Eli said as he traipsed over to their horses and dug through Noble's saddlebags. "Hey Noble, come over here, there is a dead man in these bushes. Hurry up Noble, Jesus Christ." Eli said as he pushed some bramble out of his way to get a better look at the man lying on the ground covered in blood.

"What do we have here, Eli?" Noble questioned, as he looked closer to where Eli was standing.

"I ain't sure he's dead Noble, got a bit of movement in him still. Give me a hand let's get him up near the fire."

"Yeah, yeah. Good idea. You don't suppose this here is that fellow we is looking for do you?"

"Ain't sure until we get him speaking I reckon." The two men wrestled with the doctor's limp body as they moved him closer to the flames of their fire. "He's in damn bad shape. Looks to me like he was attacked, by one thing or another, it smells as though, he soiled himself too. Whew." Eli waved his hand in the air. "Let's get some warm fluids into him. If he ain't that fellow maybe he saw him or something." The two men laid the Dr. near to the flames, and covered him with a horse blanket. "That ought to keep him warm for now. If he turns out to be that fellow we is looking for, we'll shoot him and collect our pay." Eli said in a sombre voice.

"Only time will tell if he is or isn't. Looks like he's starting to breathe a bit easier, moving some too. Maybe he'll come around soon."

The doctor rubbed his eyes, "Where, what happened? Who are you?" he questioned in an accent both Noble and Eli had not often heard.

"You's an Englishman, ain't you?" Noble asked, as he crouched down next to him.

"I am indeed. Where is that other fellow?"

"What other fellow?"

"The one with the dog," the doctor stated as he once more passed out.

"Huh. There ain't no one here except us. Damn, he's out cold again. What do you suppose he meant by that Eli?"

"Only he knows I reckon. Was that fellow who shot Heath Roy supposed to have a dog?"

"I ain't sure." Noble shrugged. "Humph, I guess we let him rest some. Leastwise he ain't dead."

"Not yet anyhow. Don't know how anyone could live through what looks like he has, tore up pretty good ain't he?"

"Yep, he's lost a lot of blood too. I don't know if he'll live through the night. Should have left him in the bushes Eli. He ain't our man."

"No, I don't think he is either. If he dies, I guess he dies, ain't much we can do for him."

"We'll see how it goes throughout the night. Maybe he'll share a little bit more about what happened here and to him. I don't know. Either way, we're here until morning; a lot could happen between now and then," Noble commented, as he tossed another log on the fire. "We'll keep him warm leastwise."

"Ain't much else we can do Noble." Eli sat next to the fire and rolled a cigarette. "You want one of these?" he asked as he gestured to Noble with his pouch of tobacco.

"Nah, maybe later. Right now I want a hot coffee and maybe a biscuit."

"It ain't going to make itself. You making it or am I?"

"I'll make the biscuits. You go ahead with the coffee." As each man went about their business preparing the coffee and biscuits, Dr. Pike slowly opened one eye and looked around. The two buffoons were going to find their throats slit before morning came that much was certain. He glanced at the wounds to his arm and chest, then cautiously raised his hand, making sure the two men weren't paying any heed to him. He felt the wound to his neck. The wounds he knew were superficial, there was no doubt that he would make a complete recovery, and when he finally managed to kill the two strangers, he'd make haste in the direction he knew Tyrell travelled, until then he'd be a possum. As he lay there his mind filled with excitement and desire, it had been a long time since he dragged the blade of his knife across the throat of a victim. He killed eleven women back in London and the stupid London Police blamed him for only five. He chuckled to himself as he thought about that. It didn't take long for him to realise how easy it was to kill woman up close and with a blade. Men, he knew, would be a different challenge. That is why he wanted to do it so badly - for the challenge.

"The coffee is done Noble, come and get it while it's hot." Eli said as he poured himself a cup.

"Be right there. Got to shake it off." Noble commented as he finished his business and zipped up his fly.

"You know, I was thinking," he commented as he came closer to the fire. "I was thinking that maybe Heath Roy deserved that bullet from that fellow we is chasing. He has been getting out of hand for years now, ever since he found out how damn rich his old man is. Many a time I thought about shooting him dead myself."

"Shit, ain't one man living in Willow Gate ain't thought the same thing. He probably did deserve it, but our business is with his old man. $2000 hard cash goes a long way to making a man happy, even split two ways Noble. So, whether or not Heath Roy deserved it or not makes no never mind to me, I want that $2000 cash."

"A $1000 cash you son-of-a-bitch, the $2000 split two ways." Noble chuckled. "You ain't trying to jip me are you?"

"Would never have considered that," Eli teased back. Dr. Pike was paying close attention to the words the two men were sharing. What he was able to discern was that, the two of them were on the trail of some fellow who shot some rich man's kid. He wondered then if that maybe he had been face to face with the killer the night before, as odd as that would seem. For the next couple of hours as day turned to night, the two men sat near the fire conversing back and forth. Dr. Pike remained silent and only listened to their idiotic conversation. People in the west he was beginning to realise were not very well educated.

"Well, Noble, it is getting on to darkness, if we want to get an early start tracking we best get our bedrolls out," Eli said as he stood from the fire and retrieved his bedroll. "That fellow," he began as he pointed to the man lying on the ground, "ain't said two words about nothing

The Missing Years – Part I

since he spoke the first time. He is breathing though. What we going to do with him in the morning?"

"Ain't sure Eli. If he don't come to soon or before morning, maybe we'll leave him here. I'd rather get the cash then sit around here waiting for him to say one thing or the other. I think he was attacked by a critter of some sort. Hell, his horse might not be too far away. Maybe it'll find its way back, and he can carry on by himself. That is all I can figure. Don't want to lose the trail of $2000 cash dollars."

"Yeah, I'd agree. Anyway, I'm done for the night. Eyes is tired. See you in the morning Noble." Eli said as he covered himself up and closed his eyes.

"Yep." Noble replied as he now gathered his own bedroll and turned in. Once the sounds of snoring by the two men could be heard, Dr. Pike gently rose from where he had been lying as not to wake the two men. Making sure he hadn't disturbed them, he slowly reached into his waistband and withdrew his knife. The blood from the first man as he drew his razor sharp blade across his throat spewed out onto his hand and sprayed him in the chest. The man only gurgled and opened his eyes briefly to see who his slayer was then he fell silent. It was the same result with the second man. Now covered in the dead men's blood, Dr. Pike added another piece of wood to the fire, and using the light from the flame, he wiped his hands clean on their bedrolls.

"So you fellows were going to leave me here. Now it is I who will be leaving you," Dr. Pike half chuckled as he looked over to the two as their blood began to coagulate on the cold dirt. "I wonder if all you westerners are as stupid as you two." Looking into the fire he smiled, it would be light soon and he would gather the men's meagre possessions and their horses and head in the direction he

The Missing Years – Part I

knew the man from the night before had travelled. Maybe he would gather the $2000 reward. Either way, the man from the night before who travelled with a dog had not seen the last of him. In Dr. Pike's mind, he'd be the third man he killed since stepping onto western soil.

Twenty miles away, Tyrell was adding wood to his morning fire and brewing coffee. Black Dog, Pony and Horse lolled next to him. "I slept well last night. How about you?" he asked of his entourage. Of course, neither animal spoke. Black Dog only licked himself and Pony snorted. "Well, leastwise we're in for a nice warm day. The sun looks like it is going to be hot today." Tyrell blocked the rays of bright light as he looked up to the clear blue sky. "Yep. It is going to be a good day to travel," he added as he poured a coffee. "We'll certainly make good time and be that much closer to the Rockies before the sun sets tonight. Ain't sure how many folks might be following us and want me dead, we best keep our smarts as we travel."

An hour later Tyrell, the two horses, and Black Dog were on their way, and travelling in their direction was Dr. Pike with nothing more than vengeance on his mind. He managed to doctor his own wounds and was now feeling a lot better. The two horses he took from the dead men were nothing special and their meagre supplies were not of much value, but his desire to track down and kill Tyrell outweighed any inconvenience of the horses and the supplies. Had he spent a few extra minutes that morning looking around he would have found some of his own that Tyrell had tossed into the bush when he left the doctor and took his horse. The doctor, though, was in a hurry and he had no time to waste. He knew that the man he was chasing would be some distance ahead. The sooner he got going the better his chances were in finding him.

The Missing Years – Part I

By mid-day Tyrell and his companions were taking a quick break. He shared jerky with Black Dog and let the horses graze as he rested. The sun was warm and the gentle breeze that blew was pleasant, so far, his day had been nothing more than spectacular he could tell by the terrain they were getting close to the Rocky Mountains; close though, didn't mean he was safe. He had a few days of travel before he could feel safe enough to turn north and follow the mountain range into Hells Bottom, which might easily be a week or two ride from the Rockies. He sighed. "Humph, we would not have to be running if I had spoken to the law on my own regarding what took place in Willow Gate. Ah," he waved his hand through the air, "I guess it don't matter much; it is what it is, I suppose. Ain't no use in harping about what could have or should have been. All that is left, I guess, is playing the cards we were dealt. Ain't that right Black Dog?" Black Dog licked his face as though assuring him. "Yeah, you're right, I guess we have been sitting long enough, come on, let's get."

Early evening found them near a creek and they settled for the night. The fire that burned was small and Tyrell had to sit close to keep the mosquitoes at bay. *Maybe we should have found a better spot,* he thought as he swatted at a handful of the pesky insects. With his bedroll wrapped around his shoulders he stood from the fire and relieved himself. In the distance and near the spot where he camped the night before, Dr. Pike was also settling for the evening. His fire too was small, and the mosquitoes that were plaguing Tyrell were also plaguing him.

"Damn blood thirsty critters," he said as he swatted at the swarm around his head. "Go on, get away," he repeated as he tossed another piece of wood on the fire, quite unexpectedly the flames grew high and ignited the bark of a nearby birch tree, they danced up the trunk spreading then to another and so on. The forest lit up like a coal oil lantern as he tried to extinguish them, but they continued to spread. "Oh my God!" he clamoured as the scorching flames encompassed him. The horses managed to skirt around the flames and falling ash to freedom, he however was not as lucky, and no one would ever know the true fate of Dr. Pike, aka Jack the Ripper.

Tyrell could smell and see the thick smoke that shrouded the deep forest like a halo. "We better get out of here! Someone has let their fire get away from them, goddamn it! We're gonna be caught up in a forest fire if we don't get moving." Tyrell said in a quick breath as he loaded up his gear, doused his own fire, and headed in the opposite direction. As they fled, he could see the flames dancing across the treetops, although they looked small from where he looked on, they were not by any means small.

The flames filled the air with a putrid smoke that spread far and nigh, only tapering off as the wind that made them dance dissipated. Finally feeling safe enough to rest, Tyrell pulled Pony to a halt and looked back. He could no longer see the flames and he noted that the smoke had cleared. "Looks like the fire has been snuffed, damn, that was close though. We'll stay here tonight, I think we're safe enough." He wondered as he set up for the second time that evening, if the fire had been ignited by someone who might have been following him, trying to flush him out. One thing was for certain, he'd never know. Eli and Noble were both dead due to the Dr.'s handy work, and Dr. Pike himself was nothing more than a burnt corpse on the forest floor. Had Tyrell known that, he would have sighed in relief, two of the men that were on old man Roy's payroll and hired to track him down were dead, the one man that

The Missing Years – Part I

knew for sure what he looked like was a pile of smouldering embers. *Lucky for him.*

Early next morning he was up and at it before the sun crested the eastern horizon, and an hour later he was once more on the trail. For the next three days, he travelled in the direction of the rising sun. On the fourth day, he could see the peaks of the Rocky Mountains come into view. Snow covered as they were, being as it was the early days of October, Tyrell rested as he looked on. "We're getting closer, Pony. It shouldn't be long until, we can turn north." It had taken him longer than he first anticipated, but he was making the distance. In a sense, he was relieved, and at the same time, he wasn't sure on why he was even running. All the things he had done in his life-never once did he have a need to run. He was a fugitive now and his life would never be the same. It came with the territory though, and he knew that. He also knew that he was innocent of cold-blooded murder. The law however wasn't going to see it that way, eight days had come and gone, and in that time old man Roy and all his wealth had found a way to pay off the law. Tyrell had no way of knowing this, but he did take Emma's advice to run and to get as far away as he could as quickly as he could.

For two more days, he headed east, and then turned north. Anyone following him he hoped would turn back the way they came. He couldn't imagine many folks would want to continue onward, into the Rockies, the snow would be knee deep by the time anyone picked up his trail.

Only thing was, a single horse-man known as Riley Scott, had gotten wind of old man Roy's reward to bring in his son's killer. Riley was a bounty hunter and one of the best in the Canadians. He made his own deal with old man Roy, and got the reward bumped up to $5000. He had the credentials to prove that he was worth every dirty dollar too, and so old man Roy agreed to Riley's terms of fifty-percent then and the rest when he brought in his son's killer. Although Riley was a week behind, he was hot on Tyrell's trail and getting closer every day. He missed the burnt up forest and the dead men that scattered it, by travelling first northerly and then he headed east, he finally came across an old camp some twenty miles from the Rocky Mountains which he deciphered to be that of a single man, a dog, and two horses, he decided to continue in the same direction.

By now, Tyrell already turned north himself and was only a few days ride away from Hells Bottom. Riley lost the trail shortly after that, and only because Tyrell crossed a rock bluff, which was clear of snow and dirt leaving behind no evidence of which way he travelled. He spent three nights in the cold without so much as a fire to keep warm, and by doing so, knew that his trail grew cold. Riley Scott however, had travelled to Hells Bottom a time or two and guessed that was the direction the man he was following headed. He smiled as he looked northwest- *I ain't going to lose you that easily my friend,* he thought as he rested.

Twelve days of riding the trail and running was beginning to take its toll on Tyrell. He had run out of food the day before and was now feeling the pangs. He knew that he had at least two more days of hard riding before he'd make the distance to Hells Bottom, but two days without food was going to make him even weaker than he already felt. For now, there was nothing he could do about that, unless, of course, he came across a deer or something. If he did, he would take the opportunity to replenish his strength. So far though, he had not even seen a game trail or track, nor did he want to waste any time in trying to find one, instead he continued on, miserable, cold, and hungry.

The Missing Years – Part I

It was only by coincidence that he ran into a passerby, who noted his lack of provisions, and who offered him a meal. At first Tyrell wasn't sure if the man he saw was even there, the forest was so thick. As he drew closer he could see him. "Hello there," he said as he approached.

"Hello back." The man answered. "Didn't expect to see anyone up in these parts, are you lost?" the man asked.

"Not at all, I'm heading to Hells Bottom."

"Well, you're going in the right direction. Two more days of riding will get you even closer. You look cold and hungry. Come and have a sit down. The fire is hot and coffee is on, you're quite welcome to join me."

"Thank you very kindly," Tyrell said as he pulled Pony to a halt and swung off his back. Tethering him and Horse to a tree, he approached the fire and held his hands over the flames to warm them, Black Dog stayed back and hid in the undergrowth. "My name is Travis Sweet," he lied as he reached out his hand to shake the man's hand who sat on the other side of the fire.

"Nice to meet you, my name is Ed McCoy," the man said as the two of them shook hands.

"Nice to meet you too, Ed," Tyrell held his hands over the fire.

"Where are you coming from?" Ed asked as he poured Tyrell a coffee.

"The prairies, been traveling for a few days now." Tyrell lied again as he took the coffee Ed offered.

"The prairies, well ain't that something, that is where I'm heading."

"Really?"

"Yes sir. I was over in Hells Bottom turning in a bounty. I'm a bounty hunter."

"Interesting, who did you bring in, if you don't mind me asking."

"No not at all. Turned in a fellow by the name of Ray Jackson who was wanted for cattle rustling and a few other ungodly deeds. He'll hang, might already be hung." Ed took a swig from his coffee. "What about you, what is it you do Travis?"

"Mostly work as a cattle hand, in between jobs at the moment though, hoping to find something in Hells Bottom."

"You couldn't find any work in cattle on the prairies?"

"Probably could have, but, I was getting tired of the flat lands. Thought it might be worth my efforts to see what might come about in Hells Bottom. I hear there are a few cattle ranches in that area. I've always been one who likes new scenery." Tyrell smiled and nodded as he took a drink from his own cup of coffee.

"I have a friend in Hells Bottom, who has a ranch. It ain't much of one though, but look him up, tell him I told you to do so. He goes by the name of Roger Jones, owns the RJ Black Angus Ranch. His operation is six or seven miles west of Hells Bottom. He might give you a few days work, maybe even longer."

"Well, thank you very much Ed. I will indeed look him up." Truth was Tyrell knew Roger, but, he wasn't about to tell Ed that. After all, Ed was a bounty hunter. The type of person he wanted to avoid.

"You are most welcome Travis. Say, you want to join me for some beans and biscuits?"

"Sure would. Thank you again, Ed."

"No problem, was about to fix myself some anyway." Ed stood from the fire and retrieved from his horse a pot and pan, and a couple cans of beans. "I noticed you seem to be traveling light. A lot of folks seem to make the same mistake." Ed said as he sat down and began fixing their meal.

"Yeah, I should have been better prepared. Thought what I did have was enough to get me over the Rockies and into Hells Bottom. I won't be making that mistake again. Been a day or two since I last ate, so, this here is greatly appreciated."

"Ah, I'm sure you'd have done the same for me." Ed commented as he opened the cans of beans and poured them into the pot.

"I would indeed Ed, if I could and was prepared a little better, otherwise I'm afraid we'd both be hungry."

"Live and learn, I suppose." Ed cracked a smile. "Here you go," he said as he handed Tyrell a plate of beans. "The biscuits will be ready soon. Want another coffee?" he offered.

"Sure, thank you again, Ed," Tyrell said as he handed his empty cup over. "These are damn good beans, by the way."

"I reckon they'd be good even if they weren't. Two days without any food is quite the spell. Most anything would be good, after that period of time."

"Yeah, I reckon so." Tyrell continued eating. It was then that for one reason or another Ed's horse reared up and pulled back on his tether, as though something spooked him. It stumbled back between two rocks and fell, breaking his leg as he did so. Neither man noticed that from the get go. They both stood quickly and tried to help the horse onto its feet, but the horse couldn't stand and each time they tried to help him he stumbled and fell again. "Shit, I see his problem Ed he seems to have popped out a leg bone."

Ed looked down to where Tyrell was pointing, "Jesus Christ almighty! How did he manage that goddamn it! There ain't nothing, we can do for him now." Ed shook

The Missing Years – Part I

his head as he contemplating his now dire situation. "Got to put a bullet in his head. Damn it!" he repeated as he stood and retrieved his rifle. The sound of the rifle as it echoed scattered a dozen or so crows that were in the area waiting to eat any leftovers the men threw out. "I am so sorry about that old boy," Ed said as he looked down to his now dead horse. "Well, looks like I'm horseless now. Damn it."

"Shit, Ed I don't know what to say. So sorry that happened." Tyrell said as the two of them covered up Ed's horse with some rocks and debris. "You are welcome to my pack horse. He ain't packing anything but a saddle bag. He's a good horse and I'm sure will get you to wherever it is you're heading." Tyrell walked to Horse and untied him from his tether, leading him to Ed he handed him over.

"You sure about that Travis?" Ed asked as he took the horse by his lead.

"Sure am. Go ahead, take him, he's yours."

"Maybe I should carry on with you into Hells Bottom, I could get myself a new horse there."

Tyrell didn't know what to say about that. If he and Ed both headed into Hells Bottom, Ed would certainly find out, that his real name was Tyrell Sloan, and that he'd been lying to him the whole time. "Well, that is up to you Ed, I can't say *'no'* to that, but I can tell you that the Rockies aren't going to hold back the snow, by the time you got turned around again from Hells Bottom chances are the snow will be knee deep by then. I know, because I came from that way, and already it was getting pretty messy."

"That's a good point, and I am due back soon. Leastwise let me pay you for him."

"I don't see any point in that. You did me a favour by feeding me. I'm returning the favour. Who knows maybe one-day we'll meet again, and if you have the horse I'll take him back then."

The Missing Years – Part I

"You're gonna give up your packing horse for a plate of beans and biscuits. That is mighty kind of you, but I'd feel better if you let me pay you for him."

"I'll tell you what, if you got any provisions that you can spare to get me through into Hells Bottom, that'll do fine, and like I said if we ever meet again and you have the horse, I'll take him back then."

"You sure about that?"

"Indeed. It is a fair trade. I ain't got any food whatsoever, and you ain't got a horse."

"Alright then, I'll agree to that. If you ever make it into Fort Macleod, east of the Rockies, look up McCoy's Bounty Hunting Service. Your horse will be there. Ask anyone that lives there and they'll point you in the right direction. Better yet, if you don't find any suitable work in Hells Bottom, I could likely put you on the payroll."

"I ain't sure what the legalities are in becoming a bounty hunter, and I ain't ever done anything like that before." Tyrell responded.

"That makes no never mind to me, I'm the boss. I can hire and fire anyone I want," Ed replied. "If you ain't wanted by any law and you can handle a gun, you can be a bounty hunter. There really ain't much to it, you find folks wanted by the law and you take them in. Simple."

"I would have never thought it was that easy."

"Now you know. There is some risk of course, but there ain't a job on this earth that doesn't come with risk."

"Who knows, Ed. Maybe I will take you up on that offer one-day, until then though I'll stick to being a cattle hand. Cows don't carry guns," Tyrell chuckled.

"Good enough, I guess we ought to finish up our meal then, and I'll gather up some gear and food for you. It is early enough that we can part ways here and both of us could make some distance to our destinations." Ed said as he and Tyrell made their way back to their beans and biscuits. Finishing up and having one last coffee together, the two men shook hands once more and Tyrell headed north while Ed headed east.

"That was quite the encounter wasn't it Black Dog?" Tyrell mentioned as the dog caught up to him and Pony. It was easier travelling now that he no longer needed to lead Horse, and he felt good about his meeting with Ed. His stomach was full and he made a new contact and one that even offered him a job, which he knew in time might even consider. *Me a bounty hunter,* he half chuckled at the idea even though it wasn't too farfetched. *Maybe that is what Travis Sweet ought to do,* he thought. For now though his intent was to make it to Hells Bottom and gather any remnants of his life he once had there. He would stay clear of town though, and only make his presence known to Bannock. The fewer people knew of his whereabouts the better off he would be. Bannock, he knew, wouldn't speak a word on whether or not he'd even been seen him.

As the day came to an end, Tyrell, Pony, and Black Dog headed to lower altitudes where the evenings wouldn't be so cold. He set up his evening camp on a grassy knoll that was within spitting distance of a creek. Although it was October, at that altitude, it was warm and he wasn't plagued with the bitter cold he had been dealing with for the past few days. That evening as he sat around his fire, he thought about Marissa and how badly he wanted to apologise to her for the way he had left. It had been well over a month and he wondered why he even cared. Perhaps it was the guilt, perhaps it was the fact that deep down he knew there was a chance he may never see her smile or feel her touch again. Like most good things in his life, that too he tossed away. It was better for him and anyone that was ever acquainted with him, that he simply disappear, *no ties, no regrets,* he thought.

On the trail again by early dawn he criss-crossed this way and that, hoping it would prevent anyone's attempts to follow. By mid-day he made his way into higher country, crossed a few more rockslides and through a couple of creeks, satisfied now that he had done a good enough job in hampering any possible followers, he headed due north. He was getting closer to Hells Bottom. The terrain he was in was familiar, and he knew that by early next evening he would be only a few miles from his father's homestead and the life he once had there.

Meanwhile, in the opposite direction two old acquaintances, Ed McCoy and Riley Scott were sharing a coffee over Riley's fire, and conversing on how odd it was that they had met up, way out there in the middle of nowhere. They hadn't seen each other in a few years and were both quite shocked at the coincidence. Their conversation was about who they were following, who they had taken in, and so on, and so forth.

"So you've been following a fellow named Tyrell?"

"Yep. He shot and killed Heath Roy and Ollie Johnson over in Willow Gate. I've been following him for a few weeks already. He always seems to get ahead of me one way or the other. He's travelling with two horses and a dog as far as I can guess. You haven't run across anyone like that have you?"

"Nope." It was then that he thought, *maybe he did come across the fellow that Riley was tracking.* Although he offered the name of Travis, Ed, though wasn't about to tell Riley, as far as he was concerned, if Travis was Tyrell, then he had done the world a service by killing Heath Roy and his garbage mouth friend Ollie. Besides, Travis or Tyrell was now only travelling with one horse, and that, he knew would certainly throw Riley off his trail. "Those two no-good for nothing sons-of-bitches, Heath and Ollie likely deserved it." Ed mentioned as he took a swig from his coffee.

"I ain't saying they didn't, but, I've been paid to find their killer, I got a good bounty from Gabe for it too." Riley replied.

"You do know that Gabe Roy is a swindler and a liar? That son-of-a-bitch has taken more land from homesteaders and the like than God's got apples."

"I know all about Gabe Roy and his uncouth way of doing business, you're right he's a swindler and liar, throws his weight around like a ton of spuds in a wagon. But, I don't care. Shit, I'm a bounty hunter no different than yourself."

"Well, I'd never take a penny from him, for no reason. That son of his, Heath, killed four men in cold blood that I know of, and I'm sure took advantage of more than one woman too. The law wouldn't touch him though due to Gabe's money. I say he deserved the bullet that killed him. In fact it should have happened a long time ago," Ed commented.

Riley chuckled. "Yeah, I reckon you are right, still, murder is murder. And men like you and me get paid to track those type of men down, to kill them or take them in."

Ed shook his head, "I ain't denying that. But, if this fellow Tyrell has fooled an old bounty hunter like yourself for this long, then I reckon he's long gone by now."

"Nope he ain't long gone, I'm betting he's heading into Hells Bottom, and I aim on finding him, if not for the challenge; then for the dirty dollars Gabe has paid me already and the rest that he'll owe me when I do find him."

"You're as cocky as you were the last time we met, you know that Riley." Ed dumped out the remainder of his coffee and stood. "Well, it's getting on in time and I'd like to put some more miles on before it gets to dark. It was nice seeing you again Riley, and good luck in finding that Tyrell fellow. I'll talk to you again some time. Take care my friend." he said as he swung onto his saddle and headed east.

"You bet Ed, you take care yourself and keep the bullets from hitting home." Riley said loud enough for him to hear as Ed ducked into the bush and out of sight. Pouring what was left of his, coffee and what remained in the pot into the fire, Riley swung onto his own saddle, and headed north, hoping to come across the trail he had been following. A few hours later as it was turning dark, he realised that he had lost the trail completely. For now, Tyrell had once again fooled him.

I think I have been swindled here by Ed, he thought as he continued on for a few more miles and came across a recent campfire that showed signs of three horses and two men. Tying his horse to a tree, he looked around he wasn't stupid; but he had been fooled. He scratched his head as he looked on, one horse and rider headed north, and whom he thought could have only been Ed headed east. It was confusing. There was no third horse, or dog track, that he could find leaving the area, but there had certainly been three horses there at one time or another, the tracks he did see proved that. *Hmm, well, maybe in the morning I'll see something that I don't see now,* he thought. Using the same campfire, he set up for the evening.

Fifteen miles north of where Riley was, Tyrell was setting up his evening camp. He had been running now for about two weeks give or take he guessed, and had made good time to be where he was now. Grateful as he was that so far no bullets had ripped into him, he didn't feel completely safe though. He knew that the law would be involved in the search for him, and God only knew how many other men were hired by old man Roy to track him down. The thought of hanging from a rope only heightened his desire and anxiety to continue to run. Where would he run to, where would he go and when would he be able to stop running? These questions and many others impaled his mind as he sat there warming his hands above the flames of his fire.

One thing was for certain he had made his bed and would now have to lie in it. *Things could be worse, I could already be dead,* he thought, as he stood from the fire and looked around at his surroundings. He felt as though something was watching him from a distance; looking he saw nothing. The telltale sign that nothing was awry was the way Black Dog simply lolled near the fire. "I guess I'm feeling a little jittery, Black Dog, I thought maybe there was something watching us." Tyrell sat back down and poured a coffee. "By this time tomorrow, we'll be in the company of an old friend of mine named Bannock. That is, of course, if he's alive." he chuckled as took a swig from his coffee and reminisced about Bannock. "He's going to be some surprised when we pull up to his stoop," he added as he reached over and scratched the dog behind the ear.

Chapter 3

By noon the following day, he was at an altitude where he could faintly make out the town of Hells Bottom. Not much had changed in the year he had been gone. The two streets that ran their distance from one end to the other had very few people walking about that he could see from that distance. He was relieved that in only a few hours he would be knocking on Bannock's front door. Turning Pony in the direction of his father's homestead where he hoped Bannock still resided, he carried on. Staying undercover so as to not be noticed, he followed the brush line keeping the town in his view. Soon he would turn west and cross the Stagway river. It wasn't much of a river and he knew he could cross it at its shallowest point without too much of an effort. By doing so, he wouldn't need to cross the bridge, and would be able to avoid anyone that may be crossing it at the same time.

Heading deeper into the forest in a northerly direction, he finally turned west, and made his way to the part of the Stagway where he could cross. Cautiously, he looked around making sure no one was along the shore. Noting it was clear, he reined Pony into the water, whistled for Black Dog, and the three companions waded over to the other side. Ducking again into the bush he once more headed north, leaving the town behind, and any possible encounter with someone who may know him. He had a few miles to go before he would reach his final destination, and staying hidden was a big part of his effort. The fewer people that saw him, the better off he would be in the long run, and the safer he would feel.

Riley Scott had picked up Tyrell's trail earlier that day and he wasn't too far behind, unfortunately he lost it for the final time near the Stagway river shore. He looked upstream and down, wondering if Tyrell slipped from his grasp. *Could be he went upstream or down, might even have crossed here,* he thought as he sat on his horse studying each possibility. *Guess, I'll cross, maybe luck will be with me and I'll find the trail again.* Making it to the other side some hundred feet from where Tyrell cut back into the bush, Riley looked for any signs, but somehow managed to miss the tracks that headed north. He swung off his horse and looked around but Tyrell's tracks eluded him.

"Damn it! Back to the other side I go, I don't think he crossed after all," he said to himself as he swung back onto his horse. Riley had come close. He spent the next few hours traipsing up and down the shore on the far side where he first lost Tyrell's trail, but found nothing that would point him in the direction that Tyrell travelled. Now he reined his horse in the direction of Hells Bottom. Maybe someone there could give him the heads up, on whether or not any strangers passed through town, or if anyone knew the name, of someone named Tyrell.

Tyrell was a mile or so away from his destination. The bush he was travelling through was hindering his progress, but it was in his opinion the safest way to go. Finally, he broke through the bush and was now on Sloan land and he sighed in relief. "This here is Sloan land Pony, up and over that hill and we'll be within shouting distance of my old home. C'mon giddy up," he said as he heeled Pony's flank. At the top of the hill, he looked in the direction of his father's house. "There it is, still standing too by God. That is always a good sign." He noted smoke rising from behind the house as he grew closer, and without warning Bannock appeared from around the corner. In his hand was a knife, and skewered to it, was a piece of fire-roasted pig.

The Missing Years – Part I

"That there is one ugly looking horse, Tyrell." he said as he approached the horse and rider. "How have you been old friend?"

"First off, how did you know it was me?" Tyrell asked as he slipped off Pony's back. Bannock hadn't changed one bit he looked the same, with his bald head and whiskered face, still walked bow legged as though it were him that had been riding for well over two weeks nonstop.

"That was easy, you have that same damn little pea shooter strapped to the horses back. I would have thought by now, that, you would have gotten rid of that .32-20, and would be packing something with more of a punch."

"That's horse shit Bannock, you didn't know it was me by that rifle." Tyrell chuckled as he tied Pony to the horse pole. "So how did you know it was me?"

"Lucky guess I suppose. Come on over here and let me look at you. It sure has been a long while. You're looking fit. So, how have you been?" Bannock repeated as the two shook hands.

"Been on the trail for a while, but I'm alive. That chunk of meat on that old knife sure looks good," Tyrell hinted.

"Well, there is plenty more out back. I roasted up a pig on the spit, ain't no way I can finish it off by myself." Bannock put his arm around Tyrell's shoulder and the two of them made their way to the back of the house and the fire that was dancing in the wind. Bannock sliced off a big piece and handed it to Tyrell. "That is some of the best hog meat I've ate in a long time, Tyrell. Hope you enjoy it."

"I'd have eaten a damn ground squirrel, Bannock." Tyrell took the meat and began eating it. "Yep, I'd say that is some damn good hog. Are you raising squealers or what?"

"Sure am. Good market for pork these days."

"You don't say."

"Say what," Bannock teased.

Tyrell only shook his head and smiled. "So, other than raising hogs how have you been getting on Bannock?"

"Like you, I'm alive. What brings you back to Hells Bottom? Did you give up on your granddads estate?"

"Something like that, I guess. More like, I gave it away."

"Gave it away? What for?" Bannock questioned as he sliced off another piece of roasted hog.

"It is a long story."

"Well, I have a bottle of whiskey that ain't been opened. Whiskey is always good with long stories." Bannock rose from the fire and entered the house, returning a short while later with two tin cups and the bottle. Pouring each of them a shot, he made a toast, and the two of them downed their drinks. "All ears now, Tyrell; go ahead fill me in," Bannock said as he poured them another shot. It was then his eyes got a glimpse of Black Dog who now approached Tyrell's side. "That your dog?" he questioned as Black Dog lay next to Tyrell.

"Sure is. His name is Black Dog."

"It wouldn't have made any sense if he were white." Bannock downed his second shot of whiskey. "Go ahead, fill me in on your escapades Tyrell, I ain't heard a good story in a long time." He poured himself another shot of whiskey and waited for Tyrell's story. By the time, the bottle was half-empty and the two were a little bit drunk, Tyrell spilled out the entire story. He told Bannock about Marissa, Grandma Heddy, how he bought Pony-the type of horse he was and the attitude he had. He explained the history of Black Dog, he told Bannock about Wilson, Fry, and the gold he found on the Sloan 1, 2, and 3. He told him about hiring the Wake Up Jake, meeting Emma and why he was now on the run- there wasn't anything that he left out, other than the one hundred or so satchels of gold he left behind. That would always be his secret, no one needed to know, not even his good friend Bannock.

"Shit, sounds like you have had a good time. I been stuck here, and you've been out shooting folks and getting rich." Bannock joked.

"It ain't been all that fun Bannock. I get caught and I'll likely swing from a rope."

"Ah, you ain't ever gonna get caught Tyrell. When we was running together we made a lot of enemies and were still kicking, I reckon that ain't about to change, for me or for you."

"The thing is I ain't sure I want to keep running, getting too old for shit like this." Tyrell poured himself another shot of whiskey. "Anyway, I only came back here to gather a few things and to make sure you ain't burned the place down." Tyrell chuckled as he downed the drink in his hand. The two of them by now were a little bit more than drunk, they were both pretty much done for. "I figure I'll hit the trail again in a day or two, ain't sure where I'll go next, but I can't stick around here for too long."

"Why not?"

"I reckon there is a bounty on my head, and as I said earlier, I don't want to hang from no rope, for simply protecting myself, over there in Willow Gate."

"Well, I ain't about to spill any beans that you was here, you can rest easy knowing that."

"I know. Still, if I've been followed someone might come poking around. I ain't sure Emma, over there in Willow Gate gave up my name or much of a description. She did tell me though that the man I killed was some rich bastard's son, and that he'd likely hire a posse, maybe even a bounty hunter, and would most likely buy off the law. I don't know, I think it be best if I keep low for a while, whilst I figure out what to damn do." Tyrell looked over to Bannock, who was sitting there oblivious to the last few words he had said, passed out drunk and drooling like a baby. Tyrell chuckled as he tried to stand, his own legs though gave him a fight, and he slumped back down. "Shit." he said as he too now passed out. It was the smoke, from the burning pig, that brought the two of them back to the here and now. "Hey, Bannock, looks like we forgot about that damn pig." Tyrell slurred as he and Bannock worked together as best they could in their state to douse the flames.

"I reckon it is over done now, Tyrell." Bannock slurred as the two of them began laughing at their blunder. "I reckon your dog can have what is left, once it stops smouldering and cools down some." He added in between catching his breath and laughing. "That whiskey sure hit the spot, ain't been this lit up in a long time. We'll be paying for it though come morning."

"As long as you have coffee, I reckon we'll survive." Tyrell said as he threw what was left of the burnt pig carcase onto the ground near Black Dog. "Well, Bannock, I'm tired from the riding reckon we ought to go inside and catch some shut eye."

"Yeah, she's getting late, pretty damn nippy out too. C'mon Tyrell, let's get inside and you settled."

"Right behind you." Tyrell said as he followed Bannock indoors. The house hadn't changed much, some of the same pictures, knick-knacks and patty-whacks hung on the wall and sat on the mantle of the wood burning fireplace. Even the minimal amount of furniture that was scattered here and there, and had always been in the house since his old man bought it, remained the same. The only thing that had changed, really, was who was living there

The Missing Years – Part I

now. Tyrell stumbled into the kitchen and sat down at the table. "What part of October are we into Bannock; what's the date?" he asked.

"October 15th, I think." Bannock scratched his head as he contemplated, and looked at his calendar. "Yep, 15th of October it is, according to the calendar. How long is it you say you've been on the trail?"

"Left Willow Gate at the end of September or there about, I think." Tyrell ran his fingers over his unshaved face, and smelled his armpits. He was filthy there was no doubt about it. By his own stench, he guessed that he had to shave and clean up.

"You've certainly been on the trail for a spell."

"Yeah, I didn't think it had been that long- but damn I guess it has been. No wonder I smell like an old bear den. Need a shave too I reckon. Is there still a bath house in Hells Bottom?"

"You ain't contemplating that are you? Shit, you could clean up here, without no folks asking questions."

"Yeah, I reckon so. Ah," he waved his hand through the air. "I'll clean up tomorrow. One more night in my own stink ain't gonna make a difference."

"Nope, we'll have to air out your room in the morning is all," Bannock chuckled as he sat down. "So here we are a year later from when you left. Damn, time sure flies don't it. I can't believe how fast it went."

"It did come and go pretty quick didn't it?"

"It seems that way, yep." The two of them grew silent as they contemplated the past year.

"I ain't gonna be sticking around much longer though, once I get my head on straight and gather some of my stuff, I reckon I'll be gone again. Not sure where to, but, I might head further north, or head down south to Montana."

The Missing Years – Part I

"Won't be long before the snow flies you know."

"I have thought about that, but, I reckon if I can put more distance between here and Willow Gate, the better off I'll be. Might drop in on our old friend Little Brown Bear, ain't seen him in two or three years. He'd give me sanctuary until spring, I reckon."

"You best take some rifles, tobacco and whiskey with you if you want sanctuary from him. He's getting old and grumpy, from what I last heard. Whiskey, rifles, and tobacco though go a long way in making deals with him nowadays."

"Hell, he's always been grumpy, but yeah, I'd bring along one thing or the other to make him happy. I figure it will be a good place to hold up for the winter, but if he's gotten grumpier than what he used to be, then maybe it ain't such a good idea. There is always the Yukon. A lot of mining camps and the like are popping up in that area."

"If it were me, I'd head for Montana, find a gambling saloon, and settle in. By the time spring rolls around you'd have a good cash kitty to take you wherever you wanted to go. You're still good with the cards ain't you?"

"I reckon I could bluff a hand or two," Tyrell replied with a smirk.

"I happen to have a deck of cards around here somewhere we could play a couple of hands, before we hit the sack. What do you say?"

"Sure, deal them up." Tyrell replied as Bannock went hunting for his cards.

"Here they are. I knew I'd find them." Bannock returned to the table and sat down. "First Jack deals," he said as the two of them started flipping over the cards from the deck. It was Bannock, who flipped the first Jack.

The Missing Years – Part I

"My deal I reckon." he said as he began shuffling the deck. With the cards now dealt out the two reacquainted friends began to play. They played ten hands and Tyrell won six out of the ten. "I reckon you do still have it, Tyrell. You always were good at cards I don't think you've lost a step."

"I got lucky a couple times. You ain't seem to have lost your touch either. Maybe we should go on together down to Montana and do some gambling?" Tyrell joked. He knew Bannock had sworn to give up that lifestyle, the last time they were a gambling duo.

"I wish it were that easy. I got over a dozen hogs that need my attention now. However, if you decide to go that way, I'll follow behind this spring. We could meet up in Sweetgrass at the old Gold Nugget saloon. Remember the last time we were there?" Bannock began to chuckle. "Shit, we both almost ate lead, but damn, we were good weren't we?"

"Indeed we were. I think though, those times have come and gone for the both of us. You're better off raising your hogs. I on the other hand have to keep moving until I know I'm in the clear. For now Bannock, I say let's hit the hay. Tomorrow we can talk a bit more. I'm tired and that whiskey you forced on me didn't improve my wakefulness." Tyrell smiled. "I'm hitting the hay. Talk to you in the morning Bannock."

"You bet Tyrell. I'll see you then." He replied as Tyrell made his way into his old bedroom and closed the door behind him. Bannock sat at the table reminiscing about the time he, and Tyrell rode together, the shit they got into and the good times they had. *Yep, we're a little bit old for those kind of shenanigans now,* he thought as he made his way into his own room.

The Missing Years – Part I

Riley Scott by now was feeling the effects of the whiskey he too had taken in. He had booked a room for the night at the White Owl Saloon in Hells Bottom. He managed to talk to a few folks if they had seen any strangers pass through in the last day or so. Most said no, they hadn't seen any strangers except for himself. When asked if anyone knew of a man named Tyrell, again most said no. Tired and drunk, Riley finally made his way to his room, in the morning when he was sober, he'd ask around a bit more, until then or until he found some answers, it appeared as though Heath Roy and Ollie Johnson's killer may have eluded him, for now. He slumped onto his bed and looked up at the ceiling, *might just have to turn around and head back to Willow Gate, I hate the thought of that, I ain't lost many bounty's in my time... but I might have lost this one. It'd be the fourth in all the years I've been doing this shit,* he thought as his eyes grew weary and he faded into sleep.

The Missing Years – Part I

Chapter 4

On the morning of October 16th, Tyrell and Bannock were sitting at the table drinking their first coffee of the day. They both looked like crap, but it was appropriate for how they felt. "I know now why I shy away from the whiskey." Tyrell said as he took a drink from his coffee.

"I know now why I ought to." Bannock replied. "I was thinking last night that I can help you some in disappearing- least wise Tyrell Sloan, that is."

"How is that?"

"There a few folks around here, that know you and knew your old man. It wouldn't take much for me to tell folks that I heard, you was killed. It might slow down any posse or bounty hunter looking for Tyrell Sloan, if that is who they are looking for." Bannock took a swig from his coffee. "A rumour like that would spread like wild fire in these parts, and I reckon it wouldn't take long for others to hear it as well. Spew a line of garbage like that to old Hathway, and rest assured, Tyrell Sloan will be dead. He is quite convincing when he's telling tales of truth, or telling lies. I'll make sure he believes me. He'll get the word out."

"Damn right he would." Tyrell smirked, he knew old Hathway quite well, and in a sense, he felt badly about using him to spread rumours about himself, but, spread them he would and that is exactly what Tyrell wanted. He looked across the table at Bannock. "That is a fine idea, Bannock. I met up with an old bounty hunter a few days ago. He went by the name of Ed McCoy. He didn't seem like a bounty hunter though, in fact I didn't have an inclination whatsoever to suspect that he was, that is until we got to talking, said he was coming from here, he was a burly old guy probably pushing his late fifties or early sixties, brought in that fellow Ray Jackson. Anyway, I introduced myself as Travis Sweet, in case he may or may not hear about a fellow named Tyrell that killed Heath Roy and his idiotic friend over there in Willow Gate. I reckon Travis Sweet will be the name I'll be using once I leave from here. If Tyrell Sloan is dead, it will certainly slow anyone down from looking for him. I like that idea." Tyrell winked at Bannock as he brought his coffee cup to his lips and finished it off.

"Consider it done." Bannock replied as he stood up and poured himself another coffee. "Want another?" he questioned Tyrell as he held the pot in his hand.

"Indeed, thanks." Tyrell reached out his arm with the empty cup and waited for Bannock to fill it. "By the way, are there any of my old man's belongings in the shed, his leather stitching needles that type of thing? I can't remember if there are or not."

"All his stuff is there indeed. Even some of his work, a few belts, a couple pair of boots, which, by the look of yours you'll likely need."

"That is good news, because you're right I'm in terrible need of a new pair. We'll finish up with these coffees and then go have a look see."

"You don't need me around to do that. I'll head into Hells Bottom and break the terrible news that I heard about Tyrell Sloan and his demise. No use waiting to get something started like that, the quicker you're dead the easier it'll be for you to avoid any confrontations, from the law or bounty boys."

Tyrell nodded. "Good point my friend." Twenty minutes later the two of them went about their day. Tyrell walked over to the old workshop his old man used while he was amongst the living. Even the old faded sign on the door that read *'Sloan Leatherworks,'* was still there. Tyrell

The Missing Years – Part I

smiled in respect as he opened the door and stepped in, waving to Bannock as he headed into town to break the news that Tyrell Sloan was dead.

He conjured up the lie, and what he would say as he made his way into Hells Bottom, a simple lie he knew would be best. By now, Tyrell was looking through wooden crates, cardboard boxes and drawers of his old man's shop, gathering up leather mending tools, pieces of rawhide, things he knew he would have a use for as he travelled to wherever it was he was going. Finding two pairs of boots that fit his feet, and a couple of belts as well as a new gun holster he threw all of it into the mix. He didn't want to pack heavy, but he didn't want to leave anything behind that he might have a use for. Finally satisfied with all he gathered, he carried it over to the fire pit, sat down and pulled off his old boots tossing them into the smouldering coals.

The small pig carcass from the night before that he had thrown to Black Dog, he noticed as he slipped his feet into his new boots, was nothing more than bones strewn this way and that. The dog had certainly feasted on it. He looked around to see if he could spot his travelling companion, but, Black Dog was nowhere in sight. *Maybe he took off with Bannock, humph, oh well, he'll be back, he always comes back,* Tyrell thought as he stood up and walked a few paces making sure the boots were a good fit. "Yep, a perfect fit," he said quietly to himself as he walked around to the front of the house and checked up on Pony.

"Morning Pony, going to be here for at least one more day, so, we might as well get you settled in the corral." Tyrell took Pony by the reins and led him into the horse corral. "The water trough is right over there," he pointed, "and I'm sure Bannock's old horse ain't gonna mind if you help yourself to some of that hay. I'll stop by

The Missing Years – Part I

later and check in on ya. See you later." Tyrell walked around the yard, more or less to give his boots a work out. They sure felt good on his feet it was too bad that he never made it back to Waldie and to Horst's place to pick up the boots he had asked the old Russian to make for him. There was always next time, and Tyrell was certain there would be a next time, he didn't know when, or if Horst would be alive. Nonetheless, he'd check it out the next time he made it back that way.

Riley Scott was hung over as he sat down with a heavy sigh at the table. He was waiting for his breakfast and coffee at the Maple Leaf eatery, across from the saloon that he spent the night at. His head ached and his stomach was as sour as three-day-old milk left in the sun. He knew that once he ate and had some coffee, he would start to feel better, but it sure seemed to be taking a long time to get. "Any chance I can get that coffee and eggs soon?" he questioned the young woman behind the counter.

"It won't be much longer now. A few more minutes is all."

"All right." Riley responded as he looked around the eatery. "By the way miss, you ever heard of a fellow named Tyrell in these parts?"

"The name doesn't ring a bell. I'm kind of new here, only been here six months or so," she shrugged her shoulders. "Oh, looks like your breakfast is ready." She turned and gathered the plate of eggs and coffee and set the plate in front of Riley. "There you go sir, hope you enjoy it."

"I will. Thank you kindly." Riley said as he looked at the food in front of him and then dug in with gusto. Finishing the last of his coffee, he asked for another as he finished his eggs and sausage. The woman returned and removed his empty plate as she warmed up his coffee. "The

The Missing Years – Part I

meal was very good by the way; give my regards to the cook."

"I will," she said, as she poured the coffee into his cup. "Our cook might know someone named Tyrell, he's been cooking here for a few years, and knows a lot more folks then I do. Would you like for me to ask him?"

Riley thought for a moment. "Nah, once I finish up here I'll ask him on my own, thanks for letting me know."

"You're welcome." She nodded politely then strode off to the sink and began washing dishes. Riley stared at her for a few minutes, wishing that he was twenty-years younger. Finally, he rose and paid his bill, he didn't bother asking the cook if he knew anyone named Tyrell, so far those he did ask never heard the name, he assumed he'd get the same result. Instead, he retrieved his horse from the town's stable and headed back to Willow Gate. For now, Tyrell was in the clear from Riley Scott. There would be others though, with a $5000 reward being offered for his capture, it wouldn't be long before someone else took on the hunt.

Riley headed north out of town, he wanted to take one last look at the spot where he lost Tyrell's trail, maybe something had changed, maybe he, did miss something. It was while he was making the distance that he came across Bannock, and behind him trailed a dog. It seemed conspicuous to him and he halted his horse as he watched Bannock get closer. "Hello there," he said as Bannock pulled up next to him.

"Hello back." Bannock responded. He knew the look. He knew the fellow who offered him a friendly *'hello'* was either a bounty hunter or the law. "Nice day out for a ride ain't it?"

"Sure is," the man responded. "It is going to get cooler though as fall approaches."

"Yep." Bannock nodded as he averted his eyes to the dog following him, he had no idea that Tyrell's dog was even there until he saw him. For a moment he felt uneasy, that is until Black Dog simply carried on right by the two men. He noted Riley's change of expression as he watched the dog pass.

"I'm guessing that isn't your dog." Riley gestured with his chin.

"Nope, he's a stray, been around these parts for a while."

"Kind of strange in a sense that I've been following somebody, that has been in the company of a dog." Riley looked deeply into Bannock's eyes as he said that, trying to decipher if he was lying or at the least knew the dog. Bannock though didn't show any emotion or attachment to the dog whatsoever, and that led Riley to believe that indeed the rider in front of him, had no idea who the dog was or who may or may not own him. "You know of anyone in these parts that travels with a dog? Might go by the name of Tyrell?"

Bannock contemplated for a while making it look as though he was thinking about it. "Nope. I ain't never heard anyone called Tyrell in these parts, been here most of my life." Bannock lied. "There are a couple folks that have a dog or two, but, ain't sure any of them travel with a dog."

"Humph," Riley muttered, he was convinced now that he was following a lost trail. "Well, anyway, I ought to be going. Nice talking to you." he said as he turned his horse now easterly and headed out of town.

"Yeah, nice talking to you too." Bannock said as he watched the rider disappear down the dirt road that led out of town. *That was close, don't think he was the law he wore no badge, but, I'm betting he was a bounty hunter,* he thought as he continued into town. He would let Tyrell

The Missing Years – Part I

know about the encounter once he made his way back home later that day. Bannock pulled his horse up to the horse rail outside the Pony Express Station and tethered him. With a heavy heart, he entered and made his way up to the counter hoping old Hathway was on duty, and sure enough- he was.

"Good morning Bannock." Hathway said before he noted the sullen look on Bannock's face. "What is a matter boy?" he asked now with concern.

"I got word that Tyrell is dead."

"What? Jesus Christ, were did you hear that. God damn it! That is some bad unwanted news you're bringing me Bannock."

"I know." Bannock lowered his head to show distraught. "I know it is Lester but, that is what I've been told."

"Who told you?"

"Was an old fellow from Red Rock, a friend of Tyrell's I reckon, rode all the way up here on his way to the town of Chase to tell me, said Tyrell was shot. I ain't got no reason not to believe him either, he was quite sincere. He claimed Tyrell told him about the homestead he owns up here and the fact that I've been watching over it for him."

"Shit. That ruined my day. Is this fellow still around? I'd like to talk to him."

"Nope, he headed to Chase early this morning."

"That is a damn shame even more of shame is what you're telling me about Tyrell, I reckon he's the last Sloan in these parts. First, his old man goes and dies, then his granddaddy, and now him. God damn it, sometimes the world isn't fair."

The Missing Years – Part I

"Yeah... I know." Bannock responded. "I reckon I ought to let the others know as well, you seen Tim and Jay lately?"

"They were kicking around here yesterday. I haven't seen them yet today though."

"Humph, well I ain't in much of a mood to stroll over to their place. I'm gonna head to the saloon and wet my whistle some. If they show up in the next hour or so, send them over there. Otherwise I'll be home if anyone wants to stop by."

"Yeah, will do Bannock, if they don't come around today, I'll let them know about Tyrell." Lester Hathway had one more question. "Did this fellow tell you when this happened?"

"Said it happened about two months ago, or there about, August, I think he said." Bannock responded.

"That's the problem with folks we've known in our lives who move away, we're always the last folks to find out bad news like this."

"Two months I reckon, are better than never knowing, wouldn't you agree?"

"Yeah, I suppose. I'd liked to have known a lot sooner." He shook his head as he thought about Tyrell. "I'll tell you one thing, I'm gonna miss him."

Bannock nodded solemnly as he stepped out of the station and onto the street. *Whew, that wasn't easy, almost convinced myself,* he thought as he made his way over to the saloon. He wasn't too surprised to see that it wasn't overly crowded. Sitting at his table, the one he always sat at, he waited for the barmaid to bring him his usual as he scanned the few tables looking for anyone that he and Tyrell knew. He was relieved in a sense that he saw no one he knew very well, or any close associates of Tyrell's. It would make his visit there a lot quicker, and the sooner he could get back home. It took the barmaid a few more minutes to finally, bring him his Draft beer, he thanked her as she set it down.

"Are you going to want another when you are empty," she asked, while Bannock fished in his pocket for a dime.

"Not today, Kate. Just going to have the one, I got work waiting that won't do itself." he winked at her as he handed her the money. "Keep the .2 cents change," he added as he brought the cold beer to his lips.

"Thank you very much Bannock. That is kind of you." She responded as she tossed the money into her apron's pocket.

"You've always been good to me Kate, I think I've asked only two or three times for a Draft since the first day I started coming in here, ever since then, you've always brought it to me, without me even asking." he smiled.

"Yes, and since those first few times, you have always sat here. Some things never change." She replied as she wrinkled up her nose and smiled back. "I got to get Bannock, I have work to do that won't do itself," she chortled as she quoted him.

Bannock chuckled. "Well then you best get at it. Talk to you the next time, Kate."

"Sure will." She replied as she darted off to the next table and so on. Bannock watched her as she made her way back and stood behind the bar and waited for the next drunk to make an order. Finishing his drink, he stood from the table, waved across the room to Kate and headed for home. An hour and half later he was crossing the Stagway river bridge, and to his surprise tailing close behind was Tyrell's dog. Bannock slowed his horse down and waited for the dog to catch up. "You know what dog you almost made a mess out of my lie. You should've stayed back with

The Missing Years – Part I

Tyrell." Black Dog though sauntered by paying little heed to Bannock's complaining. Bannock sat there on his horse, and watched as the dog took the lead, and crossed the bridge before him. He chuckled as he caught up. A few minutes later, horse and rider as well as Black Dog walked through the gate opening of home.

Tyrell was sitting on the front porch, admiring his one and only true home. He reminisced most of the day, about the time he and his old man spent there, the good times and the bad. He was saddened that for now he'd have to let it all go, but, that was what he had to do, and so, do it, he would. He rose now from where he sat and made his way over to Bannock and Black Dog. "How did it go in town?" he asked.

"Ran into a fellow on my way in, was asking questions. When he saw your dog tailing me, he asked a few more, said he'd been following you. Or least wise a fellow named Tyrell who was travelling with a dog, my best guess is that would have been you. I reckon he was a bounty hunter, he wore no star."

"Shit. Did he give you his name?"

"Nope. I didn't give him mine either. It was friendly chit-chat mostly. A way for him I suppose to question me, if I knew anybody of the sort. Rest assured, I don't figure it was that fellow you met on your trip here. This guy wasn't burly, and weren't too old neither mid-to-late-forties, I suspect."

"Well now we know that folks are looking for a fellow named Tyrell who travels with a dog in these parts, the only thing that is ever going change is the name Tyrell."

"I wouldn't get to worried. The dog strode right past us as we conversed. I convinced him he was a stray. At first I thought I was going to get caught in a lie, had he stopped

The Missing Years – Part I

I likely might have." Bannock chuckled, "as if that would have been the first time eh?"

"Yeah right," Tyrell responded, more concerned about what else might have, been exchanged. "Did this fellow say anything else?"

"Not really, once the dog was gone, he headed east out of town."

"Towards, Willow Gate I reckon."

"Could be, I honestly don't know. Most likely though. You seem a bit worked up about this Tyrell."

"I reckon I have the right to, it's my neck not yours," he chuckled. "But, I ain't going to worry about it much. Was curious is all and wanted to be clear on what was said and what wasn't."

"Are you clear now?" Bannock teased.

"Am so. What about Hathway? How did that go?"

"As was expected, he's convinced. I damn near convinced myself too. The word will get out, you're dead my friend."

"Ain't never been dead. Feels good." Tyrell smiled as he said that. It was true it did feel good. "I'm glad things went as they did."

"Now it is only a matter of how long you want to stay dead for. You wouldn't have happened to have fed my hogs would you have?" Bannock asked with humour.

"Wouldn't even have known where to start, I'll give you hand though."

"Excellent, let's get to it then." Bannock led his horse over to the corral and set him loose with Pony. "Looks like them two will get along," he said as they watched them for a few seconds.

"For now least wise," Tyrell said as he and Bannock made their way to the hog shed. It took them some time to clean the hogs feed troughs and pen. "You go through this every night?"

"Part of the rearing process Tyrell, it ain't so bad, other than the stink, and it don't take but a few times of doing it, before you get used to it."

"I'm glad it is you and not me." There was a short time lapse of silence as the two of them carried on doing their worked. "Now that I'm dead, Bannock, we have one more loose end to tie-up."

"What's that?" Bannock questioned as he poured the last bucket of slope into the clean hogs troughs.

"This place, once word gets around that I'm dead, which reminds me, how did I die?"

"I said you got yourself shot."

Tyrell chuckled, "I hope that ain't an omen. Anyway, once word gets around that I'm dead, there may be those that might try to force this land into some kind of receivership, or something. Especially if there ain't any Sloans around. My solution is this, we date back a piece of paper that states if anything happens to me, that you have full legal right to be here and that everything here is for your own discretion of which you can utilise any way you see fit. In other words like a will of sorts."

Bannock looked over to Tyrell. "I don't know about that. Ain't sure I'd want something like that on my shoulders."

"What do you mean? It is the only way I figure that I can save this land if for instance, whilst I'm dead something goes awry." Tyrell leaned on the shovel he had been using to clean one of the stalls as he waited for a response.

Bannock sat down on a few sacks of hog feed as he contemplated. "I reckon we'd be doing each other a favour when you say it like that. Still, I don't know. Do you honestly think something like that could happen?"

"I can tell you that I was only a few days early before old granddad was going to lose his land in Red Rock. If I hadn't been there when his brother Bentley showed up, the place would no longer have been in the Sloan name. Bentley told me, grandpa was about to lose the land, because no one related to him had showed up to take it over. I reckon that could happen here as well."

"Humph, alright then, I'll agree to that, if you ever come back we'll burn the note."

"Yeah, of course..." Tyrell replied as he finished cleaning the last stall. His mind flooding with memories of his old man and the land he was about to sign over. He was glad that Bannock agreed to the scheme, it was he knew the safest thing to do under the circumstances.

"One question, how are we going to authenticate the note?"

"We'll back date it to last year before I left. That ain't a big deal, no problem there Bannock."

"I get that, but, I mean authenticate it, you know, make it legal."

"Hell, the date, and our signatures will make it legal. I'll write it out in my own hand writing too of course."

"I should have thought about that, I didn't want to get a Notary involved, is all. Those fellows are pricks, most of them, anyway."

Tyrell nodded. "Yeah a lot of them are; some ain't though, but most is."

"Well, looks like we're done here, I reckon it is time for some coffee." Bannock said as he put the slope bucket away and they exited the hog shed. "I see you found a pair of boots, damn, your old man did do nice work. You

The Missing Years – Part I

ever think about doing that, you know; what your old man did."

"Me, a leather smith," Tyrell laughed. "It never once crossed my mind, ain't got the patience. No sir, that ain't for me. I'd rather raise hogs," he joked.

"Right, I could imagine how that would go," Bannock said as he rolled his eyes at Tyrell.

"Yeah, you're right, not sure I'd want to do that either. I think that might be one of my problems, I ain't sure what I want to be when I grow up."

"You'll have a whole new lease on life soon enough, maybe between now and when you come back to life, you'll have decided." Bannock teased as he opened the door to the house and followed Tyrell inside.

"You have any paper and a writing pen, Bannock?" Tyrell asked as he made his way over to the table, and sat down.

"Yeah, yeah, let me get the coffee on, or you can grab it yourself, there should be an ink well and quill pen over on that old hutch. One of the drawers likely has a pad of paper, least wise I hope so, otherwise, I ain't got any." Bannock said as he stoked the fire and set the coffee pot down.

"Okay," Tyrell stood and made his way over to the hutch, finding the quill pen and ink well, he started thumbing through the drawers looking for paper. "Ah hah, found some. Shit. It ain't lined, you ain't got no lined paper here Bannock?" Tyrell asked in distraught, he really didn't want to write a note of such calibre, which gave Bannock full reign of his estate in case he should die, or in this case was already dead, on unlined paper.

"Paper is paper ain't it?"

"Not really Bannock, not for a note like this." He paused for a moment hoping Bannock would respond, but

The Missing Years – Part I

he never did. "Ah, I'll go have a look see if the old man kept some in his shop."

"Well, if you don't find any, I have a 12 inch straight-edge. You could put down your own lines." Bannock shrugged his shoulders and smiled.

"Jesus, Bannock give me a break." Tyrell shook his head in derision and exited the house. He got lucky as he looked around the old leather smith shop and found a pad of lined paper, blowing the dust off, he continued looking around. He didn't know what he was looking for, or for that matter if he was looking for anything at all. Then he saw it, an old black and white photo, of him and his father. It wasn't something he was looking for, but it surprised him. He stared at it for a few minutes, guessing he was maybe, 12 of 13. He chuckled at how goofy he looked at that age. It was probably the only picture ever taken of the two of them. In fact, he knew that it was, stuffing it into his back pocket as a keepsake, he continued his search for this or that.

His old man had been dead now for six going on seven years, the more he searched through his old man's things the more he wished that he were alive. He missed him enough to have a longing for his voice as he looked through his stuff. Most of it Tyrell knew, he would never have a use for. He could never be his old man. Nor did he want to be a leather smith. *Most of this I reckon, now that I'm dead, might as well get auctioned off, Bannock could keep the proceeds. Maybe then, he could build a proper hog barn, for those damn hogs of his,* Tyrell chuckled as he thought about that. Looking around one last time, he exited his father's shop and returned to the house.

Sitting at the table in deep contemplation they spoke very little as they sipped their evening coffee. Tyrell held the feather quill pen as he looked at the blank piece of

The Missing Years – Part I

paper wondering how he should start the note off. He dated it for August 1, 1889 it was almost six months after that date in all actuality that he headed to Red Rock Canyon. So it had been just over a year since he sat last at that very table, with the same bald headed friend sitting across from him, Tyrell smirked to himself as he proceeded to write the letter, it took four cups of coffee and half a pad of paper to finally get the note right, and to his liking. "Glad I got it right this time, was even getting low on ink." Tyrell chuckled as he signed it and handed it over to Bannock to do the same.

He looked at it and read it as best he could and at times with Tyrell's help. Taking the pen now into his hand, he dipped it in the ink and signed his name. It hadn't even occurred to Tyrell until that time that he didn't even know Bannock's last name, only his first name which he knew was Bane, it was one of the reasons Tyrell assumed that he liked to be called Bannock, that is until he saw Bannock's last name spelled out. "You got to be kidding me, your last name is Nock?"

"Sure is. You didn't know that did you?" Bannock smiled.

"I had no idea, Bane Nock." Tyrell responded as he chuckled. "I guess it makes sense now, why folks call you Bannock. But, what is a matter with Bane. That don't seem to be too bad of a name to me."

"I never once said there was anything wrong with my name. You can call me Bane anytime you want. It's the last name I ain't to fond of, put a 'C' instead of an 'N' and what do you get." They both started laughing uncontrollably and every time Tyrell looked at Bannock, he laughed that much harder. Bannock too was enjoying the play on his name, he was laughing as hard as Tyrell, wiping his eye's he added, "I guess folks would have then called me, Rooster." Again, they burst out into howls of blundering laughter.

Catching his breath, Tyrell cracked another joke. "Just think if your last name was spelled with a 'C'... you have the bald head to match it." There was no stopping the pair as they tossed jokes back and forth. It was indeed a moment in time that neither one would ever forget. Their guts ached from the laughter as they finally ran out of things to joke about. "Jesus, Bane, I ain't ever laughed as hard or for as long, ever," Tyrell commented, as he stood from the table and poured the last of the coffee from their second pot into each of their cups. He sat down with a heavy sigh. "Well, tomorrow I reckon I'm gonna head off. I've gathered most of what I'll need, and sticking around here ain't putting any miles between Tyrell Sloan's life and Travis Sweet's new one."

"Yeah, I figured as much. Gonna hate to see you go, Tyrell."

"Ah," Tyrell waved his hand through the air, "I made my own bed Bannock, and now I got to sleep in it. Who knows Tyrell Sloan, might come back to life sooner or later. I only need some time to figure out what to do next. If there is one bounty hunter looking for Tyrell, you can bet there are more. Only time will tell I guess." He took a drink from his cup. "I was also thinking I ain't got any use for the old man's tools and such, other than what I've already gathered. I want you to know, if you ever need any cash or more space, whatever, feel free to sell, or auction off any of the stuff, except personal memorabilia that I've left behind."

"Why would I ever do a fool thing like that?" Bannock questioned, there was no way that he would ever consider that.

"Like I said, in case you need more room, or whatever."

"I got enough room Tyrell. Besides maybe one day, that stuff you call junk, you might need."

"I doubt that. I'll never be a leather smith, Bannock. It is all useless to me."

"Maybe to you it is, but maybe to Travis Sweet it won't be."

Tyrell chuckled and shook his head. In a sense perhaps, Bannock was right. "Well, if you ever want to get rid of that stuff for any reason you go right ahead and do so."

Bannock stared at him and nodded. "If I ever have a reason to, I will. How is that?" Deep down, he knew that he never would but he also knew if he didn't at least agree, Tyrell would keep harping about it.

"That's good enough for me. I won't mention it again."

"Good, because you know what, you might be dead in a tall tale way, but, I know you're living. I also know that the Tyrell I know will one day make his way back here, like his dog... he always comes back." Bannock chuckled. "I reckon that between now and when you do rise again, some of your old man's stuff might come in handy for you then. If ya ain't got a use for it at that time, you run the auction or sell it. Not me."

Tyrell contemplated for a few seconds maybe Bannock was right. "Like I said old friend, I won't mention it again." Their conversation moved then from that to what was next, *had he* decided on where he was going. *Yes he had,* he decided to head northwest over to the town of Chase, from there north into the Yukon. Eventually, he wanted to end up in Alberta, and the town of Fort Macleod. It was going to take him he knew until mid spring or early

The Missing Years – Part I

summer, there were however a lot of start up townships along the way, he'd stay at them or at least in their vicinities as he travelled, picking up the odd job here or there. *Was he* sure that *he had* all *he* would need and so on. Indeed, he was, and indeed, he had. There was an array of mixed emotions coming from both of them as they conversed into the late evening. One thing was for, certain, their friendship was more of a kinship, they were like brothers, and they always would be.

The morning of October 18th, they shared very little conversation as Tyrell loaded up his gear, and not until he was leaving did either of them say 'good bye'. "I'll see you around Bannock." Tyrell said as he swung onto Pony's back.

Bannock looked on and nodded. "You bet Tyrell. Before you go, I got something for you, hang on minute whilst I get it." Bannock turned and walked into the house, returning a few moments later with a .45-70 Marlin lever action rifle, and three boxes of shells. Clean as it was, Tyrell thought it was brand new, and in-fact it wasn't that old at all. "I reckon you might need this up there in the northern-province, likely need it down east too. It ain't been shot but a couple of times, it is a good rifle and won't let you down." Bannock handed it to him.

"I ain't sure I know what to say, you really hate that little .32-20 I carry that much, that you'd give this beauty away?" Tyrell questioned as he took it and looked at it. It was indeed a nice rifle and, he knew that there wasn't anything it couldn't take down, man or beast.

"I ain't so sure I hate the .32-20, I know that Marlin rifle is what you'll need, and I want for you to have it. I got another."

"You sure about that?"

"Am so. Here are some shells to go with it, I reckon they can also be used in your .45s." he handed the three boxes over, and Tyrell took them.

"Thank you very much, Bannock. I'll take good care of the rifle, you can count on it."

"Shit, Tyrell, it's a rifle. It don't need to be babied, you could probably cave a man's skull in with the butt of it, and it wouldn't be any worse for wear. Use it no differently than that .32-20. It'll take care of itself."

Tyrell nodded and sighed, touched by Bannock's gesture. "Alright, I'll use it no differently. Thanks very much Bannock."

"Ah, it ain't nothing consider it my going away present to you." He waved his hand through the air.

"Well, it is a damn fine one." Tyrell inhaled deeply as he looked westerly. "I guess I best put on some miles." Once more, he nodded his respect and gratitude to Bannock, then, turned Pony in the direction of the gate and the trail that would lead him into the Rocky Mountains, the rivers and lakes that lay ahead.

"Keep away from stray bullets, you hear. I want to see you back here some time. Take care." Bannock called after him. Tyrell turned, tilted his hat in Bannock's direction, and faded into history, taking on the persona of Travis Sweet.

The Missing Years – Part I

Chapter 5

It was October 21st, when the companions experienced the first blast of a fall snowstorm. Tyrell, Pony and Black Dog were a day or two away from the town of Chase. Luckily he noted the storm brewing earlier that day, and managed to throw together a bit of a shelter for himself and Black Dog, a lean-to of sorts made from cedar bows and rope. Pony, was covered up with a couple of woollen blankets, as well as his horse blanket. Tyrell managed to tether him, beneath one of the cedar trees that grew hearty in the area. They weren't too close to the Rockies yet that nothing grew and he was grateful for that. The drooping branches made for a perfect horse shelter, although, it was likely that Pony would have only needed the blankets, Tyrell wanted to be sure that his faithful horse and companion was at least comfortable and out of the whistling wind and blowing wet snow. A fire burned, outside of the lean-to entrance, and he kept it stocked and burning as he and Black Dog huddle close to it.

"We've been on the trail for a whole of three days, Black Dog, and if this weather is an inclination on what we can expect, we better pick up more adequate supplies before too long. This storm here I reckon, ain't going last, but there will be others, might even have to consider getting a packing horse. Pony would probably appreciate that... then, he won't have to pack all the gear we have now." Tyrell spoke as Black Dog lie there lulled by the warmth he was feeling from the flicker flames that he was staring into. "You ain't even listening are you?" Tyrell questioned the dog as he too stared into the flames of the fire only an arm length away.

For one reason or another, his mind drifted to Marissa. She would have been back by now he guessed for almost two months. He wondered as he sat there, what it was she might be doing on an evening such as this, if she was as lonely as he was. He couldn't put her likeness out of his head as he reminisced, and he wondered how she was going to react when the tall tale of his death finally caught up to her and the rest of his friends that he had in Red Rock and in between. *Never thought I'd miss a woman as much as I miss her, but damn it, I do. I have to somehow, shuffle her and all the friends I may never see again into the back of my mind. I have to become Travis Sweet.* He cleared his head, stood from inside the lean-to and stepped out into the darkening night. The snow had slowed down some, and only the odd soft flake fell from the sky. Looking upward, he could see the stars as the dark clouds of the season's first fall snowstorm dissipated into nothingness.

Making his way over to Pony to check up on him, he brought the horse a small amount of grain. "Hey, Pony, looks like the weather is breaking. I see this cedar kept you dry. I didn't expect the storm to last too long. Sure glad it has ended now though, the snow I reckon is an inch or two deep. It'll likely melt away by tomorrow noon. Anyway, here, I brought you some oats." He set the bucket down and Pony neighed and farted, his appreciation. Tyrell chuckled as he leaned against the cedar and waited for him to finish. It didn't take but a few short minutes and once he was done, Tyrell gathered up the bucket, said good night and headed back to his evening lean-to. Tossing a few more sticks onto the fire, he curled up with his bedroll and dozed softly until dawn's early light.

In the opposite direction, Riley Scott was making his way closer to where he found Ed's earlier evening camp, the same place where he noted three horses had been, yet only two left. It bothered him and he couldn't figure out how, that was even possible, how could it be that three horses could be at one spot at the same time yet only two sets of horse tracks left. The obvious solution was that one of the horses died from one thing or the other. If he found a horse carcass, he would then know that Ed had indeed steered him wrong, or in the least lied to him when he asked if he had come across someone with two horses and a dog. Ed told him *'no'* and that he only met up with a fellow who introduced himself as Travis Sweet he had one horse and no dog, according to Ed.

    It seemed fishy to Riley now as he thought on it. Another issue that bothered him was if there was a dead horse near the spot, why hadn't he seen it. Again, there was an obvious solution he, simply had not been looking for one. This time he would spend a few moments looking around a horse carcass shouldn't be hard to miss. The worse part for Riley wasn't the fact that maybe Ed lied to him, but the fact that he'd have to return the $2500 bounty, back to Gabe Roy, after he deducted his expenses. That and the fact that he lost the trail was enough to piss him off, but, he had always been an honest bounty hunter, and working for Gabe would be no different. He had lost his quarry, it was that simple, *getting too old I guess; ten years ago I wouldn't have been fooled so easily,* he thought as he continued on.

    Tyrell slid out from his bedroll, and tossed a few sticks on the cooling embers of his past evening fire and waited for the flames to take. Meanwhile he tore down the lean-to and gathered the rope he used to help build it. It didn't take long and before the sticks burned away to nothing he was done. Black Dog sat nearby waiting for a handout of one thing or another. It seemed as though that Tyrell was taking his time in feeding him, so he darted off and a short time later, while Tyrell was drinking a morning coffee he returned with a rabbit in his jaws. "Found yourself a bush hare eh? Good for you. You eat that up and we'll get. In the meantime, I'm going to enjoy another coffee and bring Pony a handful of oats." He rose from where he was sitting and gathered a feeding of oats for his horse. Pony greeted him in his usual flatulent way, snorting and neighing as he set the bucket of oats down. "Yeah, yeah, good morning to you too, Pony." He chuckled as he swatted the horses behind and made his way back to the fire, leaving Pony alone in his own stink to eat his oats.

With that done and out of the way, he once more sat on a log and sipped his coffee. Black Dog was near enough that he could hear his jaws snap and crack while he crunched the rabbit until all that was left were but a few meagre bone fragments and a rabbit head. "All done?" Tyrell asked with a smile. Black Dog looked at him as though to say that he was and that he wanted to get moving. "Alright then, let me douse the fire and we'll be off." A few minutes later horse and rider and Black Dog were heading in the direction of the town of Chase, which Tyrell estimated was at least fifty or sixty miles away. The trail they were on he knew would eventually lead them the distance, there was no need to rush, so they took their time mostly.

The snow that had fallen the night before as he travelled faded into only a memory, and there was no sign of it at the lower altitudes as he made his way down the mountain slopes. Up in the higher altitudes though, he could see that the snow remained. "Probably a good thing we didn't try to cross into the flatlands, over those mountain passes, we'd be knee deep in snow by now. I wonder if that fellow Ed we met a few days back made it safely to the Fort. I reckon that was a few days almost a week ago, I don't think he'd have got caught up in too much of the white stuff," Tyrell mentioned, if not to the

The Missing Years – Part I

dog and horse at least to himself. The trio were caught by surprise, as another rider approached them. Black Dog darted into the undergrowth and the rider never saw him, it was Black Dog's way of making sure everything was okay. If something were to go wrong, he'd have the advantage of surprise. "Hello there," the man called out, as the two riders approached each other.

"Hello back." Tyrell said as he slowed Pony to a halt.

"I wasn't expecting to see anyone out and about," the man said as he too got his horse to halt.

"Nor was I." Tyrell responded back. "Where are you heading?" he asked in a friendly manner.

"Out doing some buck hunting. Had myself a line on one, a mile or so back. Nice looking buck too, lost him though. And you?" the man asked. "Where are you heading?"

"Into Chase, you know how far that is from here?"

"Two days ride I reckon. I have a cabin not far from here off the main trail. Want some company as you travel onward, I don't think I have a hope in Hell in getting that buck today, I was about to head back anyway."

"Sure I don't mind the company. My name is Travis Sweet, by the way, and you?"

"Mac Rider is my name, pleasure to meet you Travis." He was a lanky sort his hair was as black as coal and his eyes as blue as ice, he wore buckskins and his horse, an obvious mare was an appaloosa. He seemed friendly and cordial. Still Tyrell didn't want to tell him much about anything.

"You too, Mac. So, you been living in these parts long?"

The Missing Years – Part I

"Ten or so years I reckon. Don't see many folk on this trail nowadays, most use the river boats. Where are you coming from if you don't mind me asking?"

"No, not at all, I'm coming from Hells Bottom." Tyrell said as the two men continued on their way.

"Yeah, I get to the Bottom every now and again. Do you live there?"

"No, no, spent a couple days with an old friend."

"Oh, who'd that be. I know a few folks around that area."

"You know Bane?" Tyrell questioned, knowing full well, that nobody knew Bannock as Bane.

"Hmm, nope that don't ring a bell. Ah, it don't matter. So, you're off to Chase, have plans on going into the north-country then?"

"I ain't sure either that or head east." Tyrell shrugged. "I'm only looking for a suitable line of work to get me by, until spring."

"Then where are you heading, I'm sorry if I'm out of line in asking."

"No worries Mac. Friendly conversation don't hurt nobody. I reckon in spring I'll head to Montana."

"Montana? What for? That is a hot and dry place to want to be."

"To see about getting work with one of them, big cattle outfits." Tyrell fibbed.

"So, you work cattle then?"

"Honestly no, I ain't done much work with them, but I know the pay is good, plus most places offer room and board. I'm always up for learning something new."

"Yep, they do. I once worked cattle until I started losing my head, was out on the range too long. That puts a strain on a man's soul; leastwise it did mine. I learnt I weren't no cattleman, that's for sure. I ain't done that kind of work since. I get most of want I need from the land and every now and again I'll head into a town, and repair fences, leaky roofs, you know that type of thing. A handyman of sorts I suppose." Mac chuckled. "I've even done work on the river boats and ferry's in these parts. Thought about working the rails, the thought didn't last more than a few minutes though. You ever thought about working the rails?"

"I can't say as I have. Is the pay good?" Tyrell asked with some interest.

"It ought to be, your life is in danger all the time, from renegades and such. A few trains have been robbed in these parts over the years, but not so often as the ones down south, I guess there are a lot of hoodwinks down that way. Trains is easy pickings on the flat and dusty lands down there." Mac looked at Tyrell. "You ain't one of them train robbing types are you?" he half chuckled. "You did say you wanted to head to Montana."

"No, I ain't no renegade Mac, rest assured. Just a fellow looking for a place to be, is all." Tyrell smiled back.

"Good. I didn't figure you for one of them type, was making a little fun is all."

Tyrell chuckled. They didn't say much to one another after that for a few minutes, that is until Pony reared up, scaring Mac's horse and causing it to also rear up. "Jesus Christ, what was that all about?" Mac asked as Tyrell finally got control of Pony.

"I don't know he gets that way when he gets a whiff of bear or grouse." Tyrell looked around hoping not to see either or.

"Could be a bear is nearby, been seeing them lot's as they head into the high country to den. Ain't seen one in a day or two though, as for grouse there are plenty of them around."

"Well, whatever it was must be gone, he's settled now."

"That's refreshing. What happens when he does see one or the other?" Mac asked.

"Usually he heads toward them, and I always hope I can swing off before he gets there."

"You got to be kidding."

"Nope, that ain't a word of a lie. I have no idea why he's like that, and I'm afraid there ain't a damn thing I can do about it." Tyrell shook his head and smiled. He appreciated Pony, there was no doubt about it, in fact he was the most loyal horse he had ever owned, the only thing he didn't like and wished that he could change was that one little quirk of his. "Maybe all the gear he's packing on this trip convinced him to ignore whatever it may have been. Usually, he doesn't give it a second thought and I have to jump off."

"Shit. Sounds like he is quite the handful."

"He can be, yep."

"Well, we're getting close to my cabin now, not far from here. You want to come visit for a spell? I ain't had many visitors lately and my woman is a Blackfoot and don't speak much English, she's learning though and I could sure use some English speaking conversation. I could have her fix us up some corn bread, and beans. It's almost dinner time I reckon."

"That is a mighty kind invite, Mac. I could use a bit of a rest, are you sure, your woman won't mind. I don't want to be intruding."

"No worries there, I invited you. She won't mind at all. She's one of those type that loves having visitors. Her name is Rosalinda Running Creek. She likes to be called Rose, though. I ain't called her by her full name in a decade or so," Mac chuckled. "She always would give me that look when I used to; that women give you when they don't like something. So, she's been Rose ever since."

"Rose it'll be then." Tyrell responded as they continued onward. It was only a few minutes later when they cut up a trail off the main trail and headed to Mac and Rose's cabin. It was a cosy cabin even from the outside, there was a rail fence that skirted around it, and a few yards away was a horse corral with a young buckskin gelding traipsing around inside. A barn with a few chickens wasn't too far away; a milking cow and a couple of smaller ones were penned separately. Tyrell viewed it all as they approached. "Nice little set up you have here Mac."

"Yep. Got most of everything we need. Don't have any breeding cows though, only that old jersey and the two smaller ones, and that buckskin gelding ain't been trained for a rider yet, but I'll get to that soon enough. The woman needs a horse, I reckon she can have this here old mare, once the gelding gets trained. We tried raising beef up here, but bringing in feed for a dozen or so gets costly. I gave it up. We have eggs daily, milk, cream, and Rose makes butter and has her garden during the growing season, the meat we get from the land. Moose, elk, deer, and on occasion we take a bear or two. We use every part of the animal too, except of course the bigger bones. The smaller ones we store in the cellar and Rose makes soup that type of thing. It is a pretty laidback life style but it ain't easy. Many a time we've gone hungry and had to resort to chopping the heads off a few chickens, but, all in all we get through."

"Well, I reckon the two of you got it figured out. There ain't anything wrong with being self sufficient." Tyrell thought back to the time he spent in Red Rock. Indeed Mac's lifestyle wasn't much different from how he wanted to live, and had lived in the past. The sound of the cabin door opening got their attention as they tethered their horses.

"Hello my love." Mac said as he walked toward Rose. "No deer today, he got away again." He smiled at her and kissed her cheek. "This here is Travis," he began as he pointed toward him. "Met him on the trail earlier and invited him for a visit."

Rose nodded with a smile. "Travis is nice to meet. Come coffee is on."

"Thank you kindly ma'am," he replied as he made his way toward the cabin. Once inside Mac formerly introduced Travis and Rose. "It is a great pleasure to meet you Rose," Tyrell said with sincerity.

"Mac the great hunter, brings no meat today, but brings home friend Travis. It is nice to meet you. Sit." She pointed to a chair at the table. "I will bring coffee." Tyrell nodded his appreciation and sat down tossing his hat on the floor. Rose was a beautiful woman, angelic and shapely. Her green eyes are what stood out most of all, well, those and of course her ample bosom. Her hair was black as night and was in one single braid that grew down to her waist. She too wore a buckskin shirt and pants, and on her feet she wore moccasins. She was a sight of sheer beauty. It took only a few minutes for her to return with coffee and biscuits, and freshly churned butter. "While Mac was out this morning, I found the peace I needed to make biscuits. Please, help yourself."

"Thank you." Tyrell chuckled softly and shook his head.

"What is it? Why you laugh?" Rose questioned as though she had been insulted.

"I'm sorry, I didn't mean to be rude, Mac said you didn't speak English very well, and there you are speaking it better than me or him."

The Missing Years – Part I

Rose reached over and smacked Mac. "He says that, because not every day do I have words to share, he though, mostly never shuts up." She smiled and looked at Tyrell. "Please, eat a biscuit." Tyrell nodded his appreciation and smiled as he helped himself. The three of them shared the enjoyment of being in each other's company as the mid-afternoon faded into evening. Their conversation at times was long winded, but it was apparent they all had a lot in common, and an everlasting friendship developed. It was hard to believe how fast the time went, and by now, it was getting dark outside. Mac and Rose offered him the use of their couch and a supper of venison, garden vegetables, and corn bread. A meal and lodging like that no man would turn down. With gratitude, he accepted their offer.

Afterwards, the two men checked up on the horses and cows, fed the chickens, and sat outside by the fire pit until the chilly fall air turned cold. Retreating inside they drank coffee and shared idle chit-chat. Rose cut pieces of a freshly baked butter cake and joined the men in a few hands of cards. As the evening grew late, he curled up on the couch with his bedroll and Mac and Rose headed to bed. For the first hour or so, his mind drifted as he thought again about Marissa, Red Rock and the life he could have had. It was all gone now and only time would tell if he would ever get it back, he had chosen this road, and to make things right again he had to live through it, to wherever the end would lead.

Riley Scott made the distance to Ed's old evening camp but it was too late to look around, the snow that had fallen erased any visible tracks. Instead, he lit a fire and laid out his bedroll. In the light of dawn, he would search the area looking for a dead horse and prove to himself, that he hadn't been wrong about the three horses, and that indeed Ed wasn't telling the truth about meeting up with the quarry that he had been trailing since Willow Gate. He had never known Ed to lie, and he wondered now as he looked up to the stars why he might have. What he did know as truth was that Ed really had no use for men like Heath Roy, Ollie Johnson, and Heath's father- Gabe Roy. It was because of that reason when he told Ed who it was that he had been trailing that Ed likely lied to him, it was the only thing that made any sense.

Riley wrapped his bedroll around his shoulders as he sat close to the fire with a cup of coffee in his hands. *Even if there is a damn dead horse here about, the truth is I have no choice, but to return to Willow Gate. No matter how I look at it, I've lost this battle,* Riley thought as he stared into the flames. His quarry he knew was long gone by now. Finishing his coffee, he lay next to the fire and closed his eyes, his mind raced with the days he wasted looking for the one man who had killed two.

He thought about what Ed had told him about Gabe, all of it he knew was true. He had followed Gabe Roy's rise to wealth for years, he was a swindler and a shrew. Most of the land, he owned he managed to swindle from righteous and hardworking people. The more Riley pondered this, the less he cared about the bounty or the so-called murder. He decided then, that if he did find a dead horse in the morning, it would only be to prove that he had been right. He would never speak of it to anyone, not even Ed. He would turn over the remainder of cash to Gabe once he made his way back to Willow Gate, and leave it at that. No longer did he have the desire to take on that particular bounty, Gabe would have to hire someone else.

Earlier that same day back at Willow Gate, a hunter reported to the law that he had come across two bodies east of town. The law retrieved the corpses, and the dead men were identified; as, Eli Ferguson and Noble Bathgate, the

The Missing Years – Part I

first two men Gabe had hired to track his son's killer. The law looked at the killing of the two, as callous. Decapitations weren't common and only a cold blooded murderer could be so deranged to slit a man's throat so deeply. What the law knew about Heath, and Ollie's killer was that the man that did the shooting fled in the direction of which Eli and Noble then followed. Putting two, and two, together, the law offered its own reward for the man that killed Heath Roy and Ollie Johnson, and to the list of deaths, they added Eli and Noble's names. The man that shot Heath Roy was now wanted for four killings.

    Gabe, himself, days earlier went over and above the laws reach and sent word to a gunslinger that went by the name of Earl Brubaker. He sent word because of what he heard folks talk about as the days came and went, that the man who shot Heath and Ollie drew his pistol so fast that not even with their guns in their hand's, cocked and ready, did Heath or Ollie, stand a chance. Earl it was said, and Gabe knew it to be true, had the fastest hand in the Canadians, and if what he heard about his son's killer were true then a quick drawing gunslinger was exactly what he needed, to avenge his son's murder. That was the thing about bounty hunters, hired killers, and gunslingers; they always kept looking, hoping to get that next worthwhile bounty, or the cash promised, by those who hired them.

    It was Gabe's hope that Riley might be the one to succeed, but, he hadn't heard from him yet, nor had Brubaker shown up at Gabe's ranch, or for that matter the town of Willow Gate. Gabe knew time was a constraint, and already weeks had passed since Heath's death. The longer it took for a bounty hunter or a gunslinger to bring down the killer, although he would never run out of those, the further away and the colder the trail would grow. Gabe had offered $5000, to Riley and even paid 50% upfront,

Brubaker wouldn't come so cheap, and he knew that. Until he could talk to the man though, he didn't know what he would offer or for that matter what Brubaker would expect.

Gabe sat in his big chair, a whiskey in his hand staring into the unknown, reminiscing about his son Heath, who when he lived was his only living heir. Since Heath's death, he had hired five bounty hunters and two local trackers, both of which were now dead. The bounty hunters, headed in all different directions, they all agreed to take on the bounty of bringing in the killer. He checked their credentials, knew that they were professional, yet, none of them had succeeded in the days that had come and gone. As he sat there with his whiskey in the predawn of morn, he grew flustered. How could it be that one man could out wit, out ride and disappear without so much as leaving any leads on his whereabouts, it was hard for Gabe to fathom. The truth was though, that is exactly what it seemed had happened.

The Missing Years – Part I

Chapter 6

Riley was only a few hours outside of Willow Gate. He hadn't slept for more than a couple of hours and left Ed's camp at 10:00 p.m. because he couldn't sleep and was bothered. Using the moon-lit sky, and fresh carpet of snow to guide him he rode hard and steady right through the night. He would never know whether there was a dead horse at Ed's last camp or not, and he didn't care. The killer of Heath Roy and Ollie Johnson would not be tracked by him.

He felt guilty in a sense, but at the same time, he thought about how guilty he would feel once friends of his that he had known all his life found out that he had brought in the killer. Most folks in Willow Gate despised the Roys and most had reason to do so. It was 6:00 a.m., and the sun was only starting to rise when he rode into Willow Gate. The town itself was void of patrons. There was a time he remembered, not long ago, when Willow Gate even at 6:00 a.m., would have been hopping with people. Today though, those farmers and ranchers who would have been hustling about, were a rare breed. Most had been swindled and run off their land which now belonged to the Roy name. He continued his gaze of the empty streets. *One down, one to go... if only,* he thought.

Making his way over to Emma's Eatery, he tied his horse, and entered, not surprised to see that he was the only customer. Emma and Riley knew each other, and at first, she thought his visit was going to be another grilling by another bounty hunter. So far, she had stuck to her story, regarding Tyrell's description etc., lying to Riley though might not be so easy. She wondered then why it had taken him so long to call upon her. Of all the bounty hunters that

Gabe and the law had hired, Riley was the only one who hadn't shown up until now.

"Hello there Mr. Scott, we haven't seen you around here for a while. How are you?" Emma asked, as she approached.

"Good morning Emma, is Gabby not in today?"

"Sorry, it is her day off," Emma said, as she smiled.

"That's okay. So, how have things been? Are you keeping your head above water?" Riley asked, to make friendly conversation. He knew that she was probably thinking that he was there on business but he wasn't Anything she may or may not know about Heath Roy's killer mattered little to him. He was finished with that bounty.

"Things get slow and things get fast, I'm not making a fortune, but I am keeping Gabe Roy's banker off my back. So, what can I get you Mr. Scott?" Emma asked to change the subject.

"No need for the mister stuff, Emma. I'm not here on business, I've known you for a long time, and the only time you call me mister is when you think I'm here on business." Riley chuckled.

Emma was hesitant for a few moments. Did that mean that, Tyrell had been caught or worse yet killed? She prayed that wasn't the case. Tyrell in her opinion had saved her from what would have likely been a life of abuse and torment. Finally she spoke. "Fair enough, what can I get you Riley?" she asked.

"A coffee is good for now, thanks, Emma," he replied as he looked up to her and smiled. "I have something else to tell you," he started as he gestured for her to sit down. "It might put your mind at ease, I don't expect for you to repeat it though, understood?" He was firm and waited for Emma's response. She nodded that she understood. "Alright, that fellow who killed Heath and Ollie outside your window, he's long gone. I did track him right into Hells Bottom. I'm pretty sure I could have found him, but I didn't. I'm not even going to bother looking anymore. I've had time to think about it, and I think an old friend that I ran into a few days back as I searched, was right. I think the killer, whoever that might be, did Willow Gate and the world a service. Men like Heath Roy, although I know you may harbour feelings for him, eventually they reap what they sow."

"I have no feelings whatsoever for Heath Roy. He never did treat me very well. I was his punching bag on more than one occasion. Whenever he was drunk, he intimidated and abused me. The only sad thing is, it took an outsider to put a stop to his vulgar ways." Emma looked across the table to Riley and smiled. "Thank you for telling me that." She nodded her respect. "Unfortunately, there are others looking for him, there will always be someone, until the Roy's run out of money. Gabe, I know, has no plan on stopping his search. He wants vengeance."

Riley nodded in agreement. It was true he got the same feeling from Gabe when he offered his services. He was indeed out for vengeance and those with money in desperate times like these, brought on by people like him would always be able to buy off the law and desperate men. "I hope it is long in coming, and that Gabe Roy and everybody else, never learn or find out who the killer is, because I know it was more than likely Heath's own personality that got him killed. He simply pulled his .45 on the wrong man, and was beat in the draw. That is my own opinion, Emma. Now, about that coffee..." he smiled at her.

Emma rose and tapped him on the wrist. "Thank you Riley and I mean that with sincerity."

The Missing Years – Part I

"We'll not talk about it again, Emma. What was said has been said, what is done is done." Riley looked out the window into the quiet street, his mind blank and his eyes heavy, he needed to get to Gabe's ranch and refund him, but, that could wait until he rested and had a coffee, he would get to it though and the sooner the better. Emma returned and set his coffee down.

"There you go Riley, this one is on me."

Riley looked at her and winked. "I'll leave a tip." She shook her head with a smile and traipsed away, leaving him alone with his own thoughts. Two coffees later and at 7:00 a.m., Riley approached Gabe's front entrance and knocked. It only took a second for the door to be answered by one of Gabe's house-maids.

"Mr. Scott! Very nice to see you, I will ring Mr. Roy right away, come in." Riley stepped inside and removed his hat. A bell upstairs rang, and a few moments later, a half drunk, Gabe Roy came out onto the foyer.

"Hey, Riley," he slurred, "was thinkin' aboutja not moran a few whishkeys. Ya find my boysh killer?" He was swaying back and forth as, he asked, almost stumbling on occasion.

"We need to talk about that, Gabe. Should I come back at a better time?"

"Ya haven't found my boysh killer, have ya, Riley, you son of a bish? Thought ya was one of 'em provishinawls."

"Look, Gabe, I'll come back in a day or two, get your-self sober in the meantime." Riley said in disgust.

"You take one more fuckin, son of a bishing step, Riley, and I'll... you'll find what the fuckin' Roy name meansh in this shit hole! Now, where ish Heath Roy's killr, I want 'em dead alive."

The Missing Years – Part I

"I ain't gonna talk to you when you're full of whiskey Gabe. I don't do business that way, nor should you."

"Now yer tellin' me how to do bushiness, how does that work? I paid you, I paid them, and not one of you sonsabishess has brought me any results, none, zero, zilch. You know what Riley, if ya ain't any use then, whydja say you could bring my boysh killr in... yer fired, get out of my sight."

Riley chuckled and shook his head. He looked up to Gabe. "This here is $2000 of the $2500 you paid in advance Gabe, I'm keeping $500 for my expenses and to not shoot you. Drunk and stupid as you are right now, you just fired me. This business relationship is now severed, good luck in your endeavours." Riley said as he turned and walked away. He didn't even make it to the door before Gabe, came stumbling down the stairs and charged him.

Riley stepped aside and watched as Gabe regained his composure. "Thatsh fine Riley, I'll shee to it that you never get a bounty contract in theesh parts again. Go on, get the hell from me." Gabe stumbled past and grabbed the money Riley tossed on the desk near the front entrance, and proceeded up the stairs to his office, and more whiskey.

Riley could only shake his head as he exited the Roy residence that morning. He was glad it was over. Naturally, he would have preferred a more cordial encounter, but Gabe kept pressing, and brought the ending on himself. Swinging unto his horse, he headed to the next big bounty.

The rumours of Tyrell's death during the first few days spread like wildfire as expected. Many of Tyrell's friends found themselves visiting with Bannock, who told the same tale he had told Hathway days earlier. The tale never changed whenever it left Bannock's lips, and he would make certain that it never would. How it spread and what was said after that, Bannock cared little, as long as the word of Tyrell's fate made it to the ears of those who knew him, and more importantly to the ears of those who wanted the $5000 dollar bounty, then, all was good.

    He himself wasn't so sure that Tyrell needed to be running at all, there was no clear description of Heath, and Ollie's killer, and as far as he was concerned there could be tens of folks named Tyrell. He did understand Tyrell's concern if he was found guilty of murder, he would hang. There was also the possibility that he could be linked to a few other killings from days passed when the two of them travelled together all those years ago. *Keep the wind to your back my friend,* Bannock thought as he reminisced that morning and looked in the direction Tyrell had travelled days earlier.

The Missing Years – Part I

Chapter 7

The smell and sound of sizzling salt pork, eggs, and pan bread wafted into Tyrell's nostrils. Waking up he saw Rose in the kitchen. "Morning over there." he said as he sat up.

"Good morning, to you too Travis, did the couch help with your sleep?"

"I don't reckon I stirred one bit, it was quite comfortable."

"I am making morning food. Mac should be getting back soon. Would you like fresh coffee, already it is made."

"Thank you, thank you very much Rose, I wouldn't turn down a cup. You said Mac isn't here?" Tyrell asked with curiosity, as he stood up and made his way to the table.

"Yes. He is out and about doing his morning chores."

"He should've woke me, I'd have given him a hand." He sat down at the table as Rose brought him a coffee, nodding his appreciation as he took it from her.

"I have eggs for you and some fried pork, the pan bread will be ready too, soon."

"You didn't have to go through the trouble, the coffee would have sufficed." He took a slurp from his cup as he looked around; to be honest he felt uncomfortable being alone with her. "Maybe I should step out and see if Mac needs any help."

"Mac is fine. You eat, yours is ready."

Tyrell walked into the kitchen and took the plate she was holding as she stood there waiting for him to take it. "Thank you. It smells and looks delicious."

"We Blackfoot have our secrets." She smiled at him and began preparing Mac's food for when he came in.

"I know Little Brown Bear," he started as Rose dropped the eggs she had in her hand. The name Little Brown Bear had been haunting her dreams for years, and they were not good dreams. He was the Blackfoot elder who forced her into acts of perversion. She was young then, and most people who knew him would not have believed such stories. There were other girls too. None, including Rose, ever spoke of the acts he committed. It was the Blackfoot tradition to remain silent about such things. Little Brown Bear was not a good man.

"I'm sorry. I didn't mean to startle you. Are you okay, Rose?" he asked as he stood from the table and helped her clean up the eggs she dropped.

"I am fine, I dropped the eggs accidentally. Go, finish with your morning food."

Tyrell looked deep into her eyes. He could sense the apprehension she was holding back. "Do you know Little Brown Bear?"

Rose turned, and looked out the window as she answered. "I do. He is a bastard."

Tyrell was taken aback as she said that. "What do you mean? Are we talking about the same Little Brown Bear?"

"There is only one. Yes, we are talking about the same man."

"I heard from a friend that he has been getting grumpy in old age. Why did you say he is a bastard?" He knew that perhaps he shouldn't push the issue, but the Little Brow Bear he knew was no bastard.

"It is a long story from my youth. It is nothing. I do not like him much."

"Oh, well, alright, I guess that is all there is to it. But, when I knew him he was no bastard."

"You sound as though you are offended that I said that. Are you?" Rose asked with conviction.

"No, Rose. I don't remember him being anything but cordial on the occasions that I have sat with him. He's a friend." Tyrell shrugged his shoulders. "We all have our own opinions about folks, and that is yours. Mine is different, that's all."

"Yes. That is all." she grabbed more eggs from the bowl on the counter and continued with her cooking.

Tyrell, felt bad that their conversation turned sour. Turning he walked back to the table and finished his meal in silence, never knowing the true reason why Rose felt as she did towards his friend. If he did know the reason, he would certainly have a new outlook and more than likely lose all respect he had for the man, but not knowing, as far as he was concerned Little Brown Bear was his friend. Finishing his food, he brought his empty plate to the kitchen and set it down. "That was very good Rose, I greatly appreciate it. Thank you." He said as he began to walk away.

"Wait, I will tell you why Little Brown Bear to me is a bastard." There was a short pause, as she contemplated. "I have not spoken of this to Mac. Promise me you will not tell him."

"I do, but, if you haven't told him, why would you tell me?" he wanted to know.

"You know him. Mac does not, he has never met him. You say Little Brown Bear is your friend. If he is, then you must be told what kind of man he really is."

Tyrell inhaled deeply having a sense that he was about to be told something that he wasn't sure he wanted to know. At the same time, he felt it was something that she needed to tell him. "I'm listening." He waited for her to respond.

"When I was a young woman, Little Brown Bear often called upon young girls to join him in his 'house of sin'. That is what us young girls began to call it. He told our mothers and fathers that he was teaching us the ways of the Blackfoot and telling tales to us to keep us safe. No one's mother and no one's father asked any more, for they believed Little Brown Bear. It became a weekly ritual, one might say. None of us young girls were safe from him." Rose looked again out the window as she thought about the way it was and how they were all too ashamed to speak of it. She looked at Tyrell. "Do you know why we called it his house of sin?"

"I have an inclination, yes." He nodded his head in concernedness. "That is terrible, Rose. I would have never thought that about him."

"That is why he did it. He is a man with many different faces."

"Is that why you left your people, I mean... well, ah, forget it. I don't want to sound out of line."

"Is that why, I have given myself to a white-man? Is that want you were trying to ask?"

"I probably should have asked in a more cordial way. Let me try again."

She looked at him, "I'm listening." she responded with a weak smile, but a beautiful one at that.

"Is that way you moved away from your people? I always thought the Blackfoot stuck close to their family, and elders and their traditions."

"Yes. That is true the Blackfoot do that. Remember though times are changing. We aren't living in the old ways, the ways my mother and father lived. Some of the men have even left to work alongside the white-man. When

The Missing Years – Part I

I became of age to decide my own fate, I moved to a town and worked as a house cleaner for a very nice family. It was Mac's family." Her face lit up and she smiled. "I can remember when, he first saw me, we stared and smiled at each other for a long time it seemed. Then I went about my house chores. Trying to forget about the handsome man, I witnessed staring at me.

I never could forget it though, Mac, he was so handsome. It was two years later that we finally told everyone that we were leaving. To be clear, we did not marry in the traditional way. We took vows and made promises, that is all, and that is why I do not have his last name." Tyrell felt a little odd hearing that from her, and she noted his confusion.

"Perhaps I shouldn't have said as much. Anyway, we have lived here ever since that time. So, *'no'* it isn't because of what happened to me as a child, that I left my family. It was because I knew there were more opportunities in the white-man's world. I am very glad I left, I would have never known Mac if I hadn't. And I probably would have killed Little Brown Bear." There was the look of sincerity on her face, and in all likelihood, she probably would have killed Little Brown Bear. "What is sad is that I know those weekly visits continue with the new girls that come of age. That is why Little Brown Bear is a bastard." she added.

"I am glad that you found Mac, and that you did leave. Why hasn't anyone confronted Little Brown Bear? If he is doing what you say, he is not anyone I will ever look at as a friend. It is shameful what he does, has done, and continues to do. I won't be seeing him again. Nor will I represent myself as someone who knows him. I am sorry for what he has done to you and the others as well."

"No one has confronted him, because it is hidden. You are the only one I have ever told. The other girls probably have not spoken of it either. We keep it in our own minds."

She turned back to what she was doing earlier, and Tyrell took that as a sign that she no longer wanted to talk about it, and so he left it at that and returned to table. His mind raced with the Little Brown Bear he knew and the one that Rose grew to hate. He was dumbfounded, numb, and could hardly believe it, but he did. Rose's expressions and sincerity are what convinced him. It was around that time that Mac returned from doing the morning chores.

"Morning Mac. You should have woke me. I'd have given you a hand outside." Tyrell said as Mac made his way to the table and sat down.

"No worries. It ain't much work. How did you sleep?"

"Good. Thanks for the use of the couch."

"You're welcome. How was breakfast?" he asked.

"Very good, yours and Rose's hospitality has been appreciated. Thanks for everything." Tyrell said as he took a drink from his coffee, and Rose brought Mac his food. She kissed him, and smiled, and then finally sat down herself for the first time since Tyrell had been awake.

"Thank you hon." Mac said as he took his first mouthful. "It is going to be a warm day today. Good day to do some hunting, care to join me Travis?"

"Ah, I don't know, Mac, I need to put on some miles before the snow falls and stays."

"Yeah about that, Rose and I were talking early this morning I could put a fellow like you to work around here, if you're interested." Mac put another fork full of food into his mouth.

"What kind of work?" Tyrell asked, curious now.

The Missing Years – Part I

"For the past while we have been thinking about clearing some land, and make room for a bigger house, it is time Rose and I start thinking about a family, I ain't getting any younger, nor is she." He winked at Rose sitting across from him. "I figure a fellow like you would be of a great help in getting the work done."

"Shit, excuse the expression." Tyrell said as he offered a look of apology to Rose. "I don't know what to say. How long would this work last, you figure?"

"Depends, I reckon. I have a couple ripsaws, axes, wedges. That type of thing, plus my horse knows how to pull logs. Where this house sits now, it was Rose and I that did the clearing."

"How long did it take the two of you to clear the land?"

"About a year, we lived in a tepee while we did the work. She helped make that too. This house is a bit too small for us now. Want something bigger, and built closer to the creek. It is about five acres I need cleared, or there about. We own near 150 acres in all, but, I have plans on keeping most of it as is, because I like to hunt." Mac smiled as he took a drink of coffee. "I'll use the logs to build it, and of course they'll need to dry for a season. I reckon I could offer you at least work through until spring. What do you say Travis? You did say you were looking for work, well, I have some to offer you."

"I ain't so sure I'd feel comfortable living in here with you folks, and I don't mean any offence, it's that, well, you are a couple. I'd feel a bit awkward." Tyrell responded.

"That's fine. It only takes a couple of hours to set up the tepee. It would get you through the winter and the rainy season. We could do that easily enough, you could even pick out where you want it."

"Well now, what about near the place you want cleared? You said it has a creek, I wouldn't mind being close to where the work is to be done."

"So, do you want the work? I can pay you $50 dollars a month plus we'll throw in the odd meal." Mac chuckled. "Hell, you could eat with us any time you felt like it, ain't that right Rose?"

"It is what we talked about, of course, we can throw in meals. Travis would be welcomed here anytime." Rose confirmed as she replied to Mac.

"See. Your own place to stay, meals, and $50 dollars a month, how is the offer starting to sound now?" Mac hoped it would be enough, he couldn't offer much more, and he did need the help to complete the project by late spring.

"It is a good offer, except I got to tell you something, I ain't any good at building stuff. I don't mind the digging and carrying. I can clear land though. Fifty dollars a month is a lot more than what I'm making now." His mind was made up at that point, it was a good offer and he did need a place to hold up until spring. Mac and Rose's place was far enough off the beaten path that not many folks would pass by. The two of them were decent folk and he liked them both.

"Something else you folks need to know, I have a travelling companion, a dog. I ain't sure you have met him yet, he's a peculiar type, and for one reason or another keeps his eyes on me. He has saved me a few times, in situations that wouldn't have turned out too good for me if he hadn't been there. I call him Black Dog and I won't get rid of him for any work. If I stay, so does he."

"That is fine by me. And *'no'* I have not seen him, but I reckon if you're here he is too, and I still have all my chickens." Mac had no problem with dogs, as long as they didn't hurt his livestock. The ones he and Rose had over the years always seemed to like raw chicken, and he shot them. They never bothered with any more dogs after that. Obviously, Travis's dog didn't have the same desire, otherwise he would have likely gotten into the chickens that past night.

"He's here alright, likely not far from the horse. If you are okay with the fact that you might see a black dog around here every now and again, usually, he won't be around if I ain't, but one never knows. He'll make himself known to you two soon enough, I reckon. You got yourself a hired hand, Mac," Tyrell said as he reached out his hand to make the deal official, and to show his respect.

"That is great. I do appreciate it, Travis. Your dog is welcome too," Mac said with conviction. "We'll finish up our coffee, dig out the old tepee, and get her hauled into place." He was excited that he found someone he trusted enough to offer the work to. There was something about him that made Mac feel comfortable, and he was enthralled that Travis had accepted.

"I'll go round up my horse and gear. I'll wait for you outside." Tyrell said, as he stood from the table. He thanked Rose again for the meal and her hospitality, then exited. He inhaled deeply the scent of the fresh outdoors and mountain air, glad that he would be able to enjoy it for a while longer, and thankful that he was so lucky. A job and a place to live; what more could he have asked for? The offer and the acceptance had made his day.

He smiled as he made the distance to the horse corral. Pony greeted him and so did the grey appaloosa mare; the gelding though stayed a distance away. "I see you two are enjoying each other's company. Good to see you behaving, Pony. Guess what, you can like her a while longer. Mac offered me work that I'm sure you're gonna enjoy."

Tyrell put one foot on the bottom rail and reached out to scratch Pony's ear. "Yep, right through 'til spring least wise, we'll be occupied clearing land. I reckon you could pull logs too." He turned now and looked around hoping to see Black Dog, and sure enough, he saw him prancing toward him. "Good morning Black Dog, got some news to share." He knelt down and waited for the dog to get closer before saying more.

Black Dog licked his face as he made the distance. "Hey now, don't be getting all slobbery." Tyrell chuckled as Black Dog sat and looked at him. "That a boy; good boy Black Dog. We ain't leaving here yet. Got some work lined up with Mac, the fellow who lives here. We met him on the trail yesterday. He and his better half, Rose, have some work they need help with and they offered us the job. That's *Mac* and *Rose,*" Tyrell repeated so that Black Dog would remember their names. "I have accepted. Means we ain't got to leave here. Keep in mind that Mac will put a bullet in you if you bother his animals." Tyrell heard the door open and he looked on as Mac met up with him. Black Dog sat his feet, waiting for the introduction.

"I guess this here is your dog?" he asked as he reached out his hand for the dog to smell.

"Yep. This here is Black Dog."

"He's a nice looking dog. Hello, Black Dog," Mac said as he scratched him behind the ear. "What breed did you say he was again?"

"I didn't, because, I don't know all but one thing about his breed."

"What's that?"

"He's got wolf in him, but he's as gentle as a slow moving creek. Ain't that right, Black Dog?" Black Dog being the ham that he was, rolled over onto his back and panted, waiting for a belly rub. "Good boy, Black Dog. That's enough now," Tyrell said, as he and Mac rose, and Black Dog darted off to the trees.

"The tepee is inside the barn up in the rafters," Mac said, as he opened the gate and they entered the corral. "It's been up there eight or nine years, but there ain't going to be a thing wrong with it. The Blackfoot know how to make them last." Mac led the way as he pulled the barn door open. Looking up to the rafters, he pointed to it. "There it is. It's made the traditional way from buffalo hide. The only things we might need are a few poles if the ones that are with it have dried and cracked too much. I'll get the ladder."

Tyrell stepped into the barn and looked up. "I ain't never lived in a tepee before. It's going to be kind of exciting. You need hand over there, Mac?"

"Nope, not 'til I get up in the rafters. I'll lower it down to you using some rope," he said as he set the ladder in place, and climbed up.

Tyrell held the ladder steady as Mac crawled into the rafters. "You okay?"

"Yep, I got it. Are you ready down there?"

"Sure am. Lower her down." Tyrell watched as Mac slowly lowered the tepee. Grabbing it, he took up some of the weight. "Easy there, Mac, how are you doing?"

"Okay up here. Is she almost o the floor?"

"A couple more feet; shit! she's heavier than I thought," Tyrell said, as he almost lost his grip. "Alright Mac, she's down." he added as he set it on the floor. "Whew. Wasn't expecting it to be so heavy, you all right up there, Mac?"

"No problems. Watch yourself as I toss these poles down." Tyrell stepped clear and watched as Mac tossed out the poles. "There, that's the last one," Mac reported as he looked down to Tyrell. "How many did you count there, Travis?"

"Ten," Tyrell replied.

"That's two more than we need, but that's okay. Okay, coming down." Mac said as Tyrell held onto the ladder. "It won't take us long to set it up."

"How far is it to the work site?" Tyrell asked, as Mac stepped down from the last rung of the ladder.

"Not far at all, but it is secluded. I'd guess two or three miles anyway. Come on, help me get this tepee to the corral. I have a horse cart that we need to dig out to haul it. Don't think Lucy wants to carry it on her back, but she'll have no problem pulling it." The two men picked it up and carried it the short distance to the corral. Setting it on the ground, they gathered the poles and pulled out the cart. It took a few more minutes to load and secure. With that done, Tyrell gathered his gear and he and Mac tossed some of it onto the cart as well, providing less work for Pony, who already seemed to be packing a lot in Mac's opinion.

"That horse can pack that much and haul your ass as well?" he asked Tyrell.

"Easily."

"I didn't realise yesterday how much you actually packed on him."

"Yeah, it is a bit, but Pony don't mind; he's packed more." Tyrell smiled as he swung onto his back. "Well, are we ready to get?"

"Sure are." Mac replied. It took almost an hour to get to the new site. They could hear the sound of the creek as they grew close. "Just up on the other side of that stand of cedar is a real nice spot," Mac said as he pointed.

"I can't believe how beautiful this is up here, Mac."

"I know. I have to warn you though the mosquitoes can be a real nuisance in the late summer, and the bear sometimes ain't so shy. If you have a run in, don't hesitate to fill it with lead. We can always come up with a use for it. You won't have to worry too much about bear at this time of year though. Most are heading into the high country. Same with the mosquitoes; there ain't many of them out and about at this time of year."

"To be able to live in this beauty, I'd live with bear and mosquitoes," Tyrell said, as he continued to look around. "So, you want this entire area cleared out?"

"Not all of it. I'll show you how much once we get you settled," Mac replied, as he pulled his horse to a stop. "This is it. I reckon right over there is the best spot. The trees there will keep your horse dry. That'll be the last place to knock down. By then, we'll have put up a bit of a shelter for him. In this area, there is a lot of cedar and fir; beyond that, we get into birch, all four corners, north, east, south and west. That is where I want to stop clearing, as soon as the birch get thick.

We might knock down some, but very little, I reckon. The cedar and fir is what I need," Mac said, as he swung off Lucy and tethered her. Tyrell followed suit, and a couple hours later after they cleared away some rock and debris from where the tepee was going to sit, it was up and ready for its new occupant.

Mac showed Tyrell how to use the smoke flap at the top. By pulling on a couple of ropes, he could open or close it, and point it in any direction. "Keep it opened away from the direction of the wind, or you might find the tepee filling up with smoke. The buffalo hide floor is an addition, but keeps the dew and frost from getting inside. That cut out circle in the floor that we tacked down with the iron spikes, is for the fire."

"Yeah, I reckon," Tyrell said, as he opened and closed the smoke flap a couple of times. "Going to be interesting living in a tepee," he smiled as they exited.

Standing back, they looked at it. "It looks as good now as it did when Rose and I used her." Mac said as he sat down in some shade. "What do you figure Travis? How does it look to you?"

"Like home," Tyrell responded, as he too sat in some shade. "I reckon it'll work fine. You have any idea when you want to start the work?"

"It won't be today. I'll let you get used to the area first." Rising now, Mac gestured to Tyrell. "I'll show you where that stand of birch on the north-west side is. It won't take but a couple minutes to get there. The creek is in that direction too, and you'll need to know where that is."

"Sure, lead the way," Tyrell said, as he grabbed his big .45-70 rifle and followed Mac. The forest was thick and the further they walked into it the thicker it grew. Crossing the creek, they hiked a few more yards until the stand of birch came into view. "There is the birch I see. So we're gonna clear the rest out to about here somewhere?"

"Yep, right around here I reckon. I don't want to be too close to the creek because that is where we'll be getting our water; yet, I don't want to be too far away either. Before I start building, I'll divert some of it closer to where the house will be, and I don't want to be digging a long trench. As long as I can keep the creek drinkable, then I don't think we'll have a problem with water. Anyway, there you have it. I know it looks like a big job, and for one man it would be. I reckon with two of us working, it won't be so bad. Does your horse pull logs? If he does I'll offer another $10 dollars a month to your pay."

"Oh, he can pull logs all right. I ain't ever had him do it, but, I know he can learn it. I'll tell you what, we'll try him out for a while if he works out I might consider that extra $10. Until then, $50 a month like we talked about will do."

"Are you sure?"

"Yep, no point in paying if he can't do it. Save yourself some money, Mac. I'm quite content with the first offer." The two sat in self-contemplation as they looked around taking in the view of work they were going to commit themselves to do. "You figure by spring we'll have put a dent in the work?"

"Well, it was only Rose and I, like I said earlier, who cleared the area where the house sits now. It's a smaller area I know, but that took us little under a year. I reckon by spring, we'll have come a long way in finishing this here up. Might not be completely finished, but damn close I hope."

"I reckon you're right. Work is work. That is all it is; it never hurt anyone."

"Besides if we ain't finished by then, maybe I could convince you then to stay on a while longer," Mac hinted with a smirk.

"Anything is possible, I suppose," Tyrell returned the smile. "Reckon we should head back? I need to get settled and put my gear away."

"Yep, I reckon you are right." Mac responded as they headed back to the tepee and Tyrell's new tenancy on Mac and Rose's property. "You can go ahead and change anything you want to make the place more liveable. Use whatever deadfall and shit poles you want, for wood and such." Mac said as they made the distance. "I'm going to head back to the house. You got everything you need, Travis?"

The Missing Years – Part I

Tyrell nodded. "For now, yep, sure do," he responded, as he looked up to Mac who was sitting on his mare getting ready to leave.

"If you like, Rose serves dinner around 6:00 p.m., or sundown. You're welcome to stop by."

"Maybe tomorrow, I reckon tonight I want to scout around and get things in perspective as they should be."

"Okay, I'll swing back this way, say, noon tomorrow, and see how things are going. I reckon we'll start the work here in two or three days."

"Sounds good to me, Mac. Give my regards to Rose."

"I will, Travis. See you tomorrow."

"Yep, will so. See you then." He waved as Mac headed back in the direction of his house. "Well, Pony, this here is where we'll settle for the winter. It ain't much right now, but we'll get there." He whistled for Black Dog who came prancing out from some undergrowth.

"I figured you were close. You want to have a look see inside?" he held the entrance flap open. "Well, want to have a look see or not?" Finally Black Dog entered and Tyrell followed him in. "It ain't so bad in here; I can even stand up. The fire goes there," he said, as he pointed to the hole that in buffalo hide floor, which, in itself was an improved added feature. He had been inside a tepee or two before, and could only remember them with dirt floors. Rose and Mac had certainly improved upon that.

There was definitely enough room for all his gear, and then some. "I'll set up my bedroll over there," he pointed. "You can go ahead and lay down wherever you want, when we come in for the day, as long as it is not on my bedroll," he chuckled. "I guess now, we can start stowing the gear. Come on Black Dog, let's get to it."

The Missing Years – Part I

It took a few minutes to get all his gear inside, and to make up his bed. With that all out of the way, he built an outside fire pit and set up a log to sit on. It was looking more and more like home; he was pleased with how it all came together. "There, all done. Home sweet home," he said as he sat down on the log and rested. He had been seated only a short time when he heard the bugle of an elk, and then another. They were a short distance away and north from where he was sitting. *Ain't that something? What a great welcome,* he thought as he continued his gaze.

Sitting in silence, he smiled, pleased, and at peace thinking that he was fortunate to have run into Mac when he did, otherwise he might not have had the same opportunity. Indeed, he was grateful. For the remainder of the day, he stayed close to the tepee as he scouted the area on foot. Finding an old uprooted cedar that left behind a fair sized hole, and as luck would have it not too far from the tepee, he smiled. It was there that he would make his outhouse. It was far enough away from the creek that it would be safe to use for that purpose. He could use a few poles to make a seat, and a few more to throw up some walls and a roof if he found that he needed one. For now, a roof made from cedar boughs was enough to protect him from the sun, snow, or rain when he was doing his business.

As the low-hanging fall sun began its daily descent, he turned back in direction of the tepee and his first night on Rider land. He estimated that it was October 24th. He wasn't sure of the day, a Monday, or a Saturday or anything in between. At that moment it mattered little. With Black Dog trailing close behind, he continued onward watching for landmarks and other things that he could use to find his way back to the tepee, Finally, there it was. He stood back and looked at it as the sun crept behind the western horizon and finally vanished. The tepee now looked ominous in the shadows of night. It was going to be strange sleeping in one.

Tyrell shook his head, *it sure grew dark in a hurry,* he thought as he made his way over to the outside fire pit, and lit a fire there for the first time. Using water from his canteen, he filled the coffee pot and added grounds to the basket. Settling into the warmth of the fire, he waited.

He thought about the work that lay ahead for him and Mac. It wasn't going to be easy. He could expect a handful of blisters during the first few days, but he didn't care; blisters never lasted long, and work never killed a man, that is as long as he was careful. Felling trees, he knew, was as dangerous and maybe more so than most jobs. He knew how to be careful though, and the *'ifs'* and *'buts'*, like what day of the week it was, mattered little. The work and the pay was why he was there. Truthfully, he knew he really didn't need the work so much as he needed a way to disappear.

The scent of freshly perked coffee filled the evening air. It snapped him out of his trance as he reminisced, lulled by the flickering flames. Pouring himself a cup, he listened to the sounds of night as blackness took over all that surrounded him. The only light now was from the fire that once again captivated him. He felt lonely, yet knew he really had no reason to feel that way, Black Dog was nearby and Pony was within viewing distance of the glowing flames; all was well, really. Convincing himself, and to get his mind off how he was feeling, he gathered his shovel and made his way to the center of the tepee's buffalo hide floor. It didn't take long to dig out an area that could handle a comfortable fire. He used the dirt he dug out to build up the fire pit walls. He left about six inches of solid earth between the tepee's hand stitched hemmed alteration, where the floor had been cut out, and the dirt wall of the fire pit.

Although the part of the tepee that was used for fire placement had been tacked to the ground with iron spikes when they set it up, the dirt and a few rocks he now used to complete the seal of earth floor and hide couldn't hurt. It would certainly lessen any chances of an unpleasant wind finding its way into the tepee from beneath the buffalo hide floor. Satisfied, he used a cedar bow to sweep the excess dirt that scattered the floor into the hole. Dark as it was with only the flames from the outside fire flashing light through the tepee entrance, as he did the work it didn't look bad at all. *That was easy enough; she is prepped and ready now,* he thought, as he looked back again and exited.

Leaning his shovel against a pile of wood that he had collected earlier, he strode over to Pony and fed him some oats. "Sure is peaceful, ain't it?" It must have been because not even Pony seemed to want to break the silence. The minutes floated away as Tyrell stood waiting for Pony to finish. He didn't mind standing there, it was refreshing and relaxing in a sense and he felt calm. Noting Pony was finished, he picked up the bucket, and not saying a word, he scratched him behind the ear. Turning, he made his way to the fire, doused it, and headed inside to his awaiting bedroll and the new dawn that was coming.

The Missing Years – Part I

Chapter 8

He slept well that first night, and was surprised at how warm he had been, considering the fact that October was coming to an abrupt end. Finding his way outside that morning before the first bird chirped, he lit a fire. It remained dark as the flames took to life. It was not a black dark that one might associate with evening, but a blue dark that whispered early twilight. In the east, a pale yellow sun slowly rose. Tyrell looked in that direction as he warmed his hands above the flames. His coffee full of fresh creek water began to bubble, and a steady stream of steam rose from the spout like smoke into the sky. Reaching over and removing it from the heat, he poured his first cup of the day. The tin cup warmed his hands as he held it close to his lips and gently blew on it. It was October 25th, what day of the week however was lost to him, *I'll ask Mac what day it is when I see him,* he thought as he slurped the warm brew in his hands.

Setting his coffee down, he added another stick to the fire and mixed up some flapjacks. They were good and doughy the way he liked them and he gobbled down a half dozen. He didn't bother with anything else; the flapjacks had satisfied his morning hunger. The ones that remained in the pan he would nibble on throughout the day, or perhaps hand them out to Black Dog when he finally came to life. Tyrell looked over to where the dog lay and he smiled as he reminisced about the here and now.

Yawning, he stood from the fire and stretched; Pony he knew would want oats. Gathering the bucket, he added a substantial amount and made his way over to him. "Good morning, Pony, I brought you oats." he said as he set the bucket down. "I'll bring you a drink soon, once I get the bucket back. How was your first evening out here in the middle of nowhere?" he asked, as he waited for the horse to finish. Pony answered with a simple neigh. "I slept well, stayed warm enough too. Tonight though, I'll have an inside fire. Until then, I guess we wait and see what the day might bring. Mac said he'd be by some time, so you'll get your chance to see that mare of his again," he chuckled as Pony stopped eating, looked at him, and farted.

"Are you done with the oats now?" He looked into the bucket. "I guess you are, I'll gather you some water, hang tight," he said as he made his way the short distance to the creek and filled the bucket. Making his way back, he set it down and Pony took a long slurp, then as always, shook his head back and forth shaking the water that was on his snout into the air in all directions. "Feel better now?" Tyrell scratched his forehead, as Pony neighed, the answer. "Good. We'll take a ride in a bit, once the sun comes out fully."

It was light enough that he could see, and he looked around at his surroundings. Taking it all in, he inhaled deeply. *I think we'll manage here until spring; we got water, shelter and wood for heat, yep, we'll do just fine,* he thought as he looked to the eastern horizon and watched as the rays from the sun came into full view. It didn't take long for the air to warm up as the sun knocked out the early morning chill, and as it warmed so did he. It was going to be a beautiful day. The deep blue sky and yellow glowing sun proved it to him.

Looking at his pocket watch, he wound it, surprised that it was only 7:00 a.m., he had five hours to kill before Mac would show. To kill the time he saddled up Pony, whistled a wakeup call to Black Dog, and the trio went on a hike. He travelled in the direction he had heard the elk bugling. It didn't take long before he spotted the trampled down grass and six or seven piles of scat. He swung off his horse to study the tracks. The elk travelled north so he looked in that direction. "They headed up that way. Are you two in for a jaunt, we could get lucky and spot them up close," he mentioned to the horse and dog as he swung once more onto Pony's back.

"I say we go have a look see." He heeled Pony's flank. An hour later and off in the distance he could make out the herd. There were, he guessed, two or three bulls and a bunch of cows. "Ain't that something?" He contemplated tethering Pony and hiking a bit further on foot. Maybe he would get a chance to shoot one. Instead, he watched the herd for a while longer, then, turned Pony in the direction of home. *Perhaps another time, I will down one, until that time though, I'll leave them be,* he thought as they made their way closer to home.

The sound of a rushing creek filled his ears and took over the silence of morning. He must have turned a bit too far west. It mattered little, he would follow the creek until he came to familiar ground. If nothing else it would kill a little bit of time; besides, he was enjoying the serenity, and he did need to make himself familiar with his surroundings. It took only an extra hour to come to the stand of birch he and Mac hiked to that past day.

Turning Pony southeast, he crossed the creek and made his way back to the tepee no worse for wear. "Well, we made it, boys." Swinging off the saddle and removing it, he led Pony to a patch of grass to let him graze. "I spotted this yesterday," he said, referring to the grass. "I figured you deserved some roughage, I'll be able to keep my eye on you from the fire. I don't have to tether you do I?" Pony kicked up some grass and dirt then went about grazing. Tyrell chuckled. "I'll take that as a no, but rest assured old boy, the minute you disappear from my view, is the moment that I will tether you. I don't know this area well enough yet, to have to go looking for you, so keep that in mind as you get your fill." He watched the horse up close for a few minutes longer then headed back to the low burning flames of his morning fire.

Adding a few more sticks onto the embers, he warmed up the rest of the coffee and kept his eye on Pony at the same time as his coffee warmed to a drinkable temperature. Black Dog lolled close, and Tyrell tossed him one of the flapjacks, which, the dog snaffled up in a few quick bites. It looked as though the dog wanted more so he tossed him the remaining three. "That will keep you full of poop for a while. We'll cook up some salt pork later, and maybe a can of beans too. We also have a few pounds of jerky left. I figure those four flapjacks that you just ate, will keep you content," Tyrell said, as he slurped from the coffee in his hands.

The sound of a horse approaching got Black Dog's attention and he skittered into the undergrowth. Tyrell stood from the fire and looked in the direction the sound had come from. He was relieved to see Mac and his horse approach, towing behind him was the horse cart. Tyrell brought his hand to his face and scratched his chin. He wasn't expecting Mac yet, and he walked toward him. "What brings you up this way so early Mac?" he asked as he waited for him to get close.

"We have Rose to thank for that."

"What is in the cart?"

"Some wire and posts, axe, ripsaw, sledgehammer, and a post hole bar, I guess there is also a box of fencing staples and hand hammer. Got some land marking tape as well. I reckon that will come in handy up around here."

"You mean that rubber type tape, which you tie around trees and such?" Tyrell wanted to know.

"Yes sir, brought along a couple of rolls actually, a blue and a red I think. Rose figured we should get a corral put up before we start clearing the land, the tape will come in handy for that, I reckon."

"We could have made a corral with some poles."

"I know, but that would have taken a bit more time, time that I don't think is available for us yet. This here won't take as long providing the ground ain't too tough to break through."

"I guess the hope is to pound the post in place, eh?"

"Yep, it won't by any means be a permanent corral, but for now it'll do," Mac said as he swung off his horse. "How was your first night?"

"I ain't got no complaints. That buffalo hide floor is the cat's meow. Whichever one of you two that thought that up sure came up with a good idea."

"That would have been Rose. Most tepees have hides scattered all over the floor, for sitting and sleeping on. This way here is a lot more efficient."

"I wouldn't disagree, it keeps the frost away."

"That it does. You got coffee on?"

"Just finished a small pot, but I'll get another going. Come on let's go have a sit down." The two men made their way to the fire and Pony made his way over to Lucy. "Look at that, the horses seemed to have missed each other," Tyrell said as he gestured toward them.

"Well, Lucy ain't been in the presence of a real horse in a while. And yours hasn't been castrated?"

"No. I couldn't have that done to him. It might change his attitude, and I like his attitude," Tyrell responded, as he made a fresh pot of coffee.

"They might decide to mate up as they get to know one another better, Lucy has only birthed once. That buckskin gelding is hers."

The Missing Years – Part I

"Is that right?"

"Yep, he turned three years old a month or so ago. By now, I should have had him trained for a rider I guess, but time is always a bit of a constraint around here. This winter though when the snow is deep I'll put a saddle on him, less chance of getting bucked off in the snow I reckon."

"Well, it won't hurt as much when he does throw you," Tyrell chuckled.

"Ain't that the truth. You ever broke a horse?" Mac asked.

"Nope, watched the old man do it a time or two. He too waited for the snow. Still, he broke his arm one time. The horse threw him and he fell onto a boulder and smashed his arm. I think that was the last time he ever bothered, bought horses from then on that were already broke." The smell of coffee told them that it was ready, and Tyrell poured each of them a cup.

"Mmm, that is good coffee, Travis. Thank you very much, I didn't get but one cup this morning before Rose was throwing me outside."

"You got at it quite early then?"

"Shortly after 6:00 a.m., or there about," Mac took another swig from his coffee and pulled out his own pocket watch. "It is 11:00 a.m., now. Not doing too bad for time, I reckon. Once we put these coffees down we can unload the cart and figure out the best place to throw up the corral."

"Right over where I tethered Pony last night would suffice. I don't suppose the ground is too hard over there. His hoof prints tell me that story."

"They're sunk in a bit then?"

"Yep."

"Good. That is where we'll put it up then. The softer the better and the easier it'll be." They sat in silence for a few minutes as they finished their cups.

"Oh yeah, before I forget, I heard elk bugling last night, and this morning I tracked a herd down. At that time, they were 3 miles north of here. There were a few bulls that I could see, and a bunch of cows. Thought it might be something you'd be interested in."

"I am so. Maybe we can track them down again after we finish up that corral."

"Sure, it might be worth our effort. I'd be happy to tag along. I reckon, though, that corral ain't gonna build itself, as much as we'd like it too."

"You're right about that. I guess we best get to it." They rose from the fire and Mac led Lucy closer to where they decided to build. It took only a couple of minutes to get the cart unloaded, and then the sound of them pounding in posts, and the odd chatter of them talking and cursing took over the sounds of silence. By the time the sun was as high as it would get that day, they were finished. It hadn't taken too long at all, and now they were sitting in the shade admiring their work. "It don't look too bad does it?"

"It looks pretty damn good, if you ask me." Tyrell responded. "It'll keep the horses contained during the day, and Pony at night. I'd say we did a fine job."

"It is a good spot too with lots of shade and the cedars will keep the snow and rain off them. I ain't so sure there is enough grass though to keep them fed. I have a couple tons of hay, which will get us through. It's only a matter of getting some here. Ah, we'll cross that bridge when the time comes." Mac added. "Well, what do you think, are you up for a quick elk hunt, Travis?"

"That ain't changed since we started. Sure am." Tyrell responded. They had only made their way back to the tepee, when Mac spotted a horse and rider, leading a packing mule.

"Well now, that does seem odd," he said as he gestured toward the bush. "Looks like we have ourselves a visitor, I'll go see what he needs or is looking for." Mac walked in the rider's direction, it was then that Tyrell, thought, he recognised the rider he looked on and squinted.

"Shit," he mumbled beneath his breath. *I think, that is the reverend, I ran into some months back,* he thought as he sat down. It wasn't until he heard the man introduce himself that he knew for sure.

Mac waited some distance away from the rider as he spoke. "Hello there," he began as the rider got close. "Are you lost?"

"Hello back," the man replied. "My name is Reverend Joseph A. Winghauer, and to answer your first question, yes, I seem to have lost the trail I was traveling. I'm on my way to the Chase Wagon Road, I hope I haven't strayed too far off course." The reverend pulled his horse to a halt as Mac approached closer.

"My name is Mac Rider, I own this land. So, you're heading into Chase, then?" Mac wanted to confirm.

"That is the town along the way, indeed. Am I close?"

"Not really, another two days ride. You are about five miles away from the trail that'll get you there."

"And what direction would that be in?" The reverend now looked toward the sole man sitting near the tepee, for a brief moment he too thought he knew the man. "Is that Tyrell Sloan?" He pointed toward Tyrell, who was hoping that the reverend wouldn't get any closer as to be able to recognise him.

The Missing Years – Part I

Mac looked over to Tyrell, and shook his head. "Nope, never heard that name before, that is Travis, my hired hand, he only started here a day or two ago."

"Humph, I thought it was Tyrell Sloan." The reverend was most certain that it was, but he didn't want to pry. "So, in what direction is the trail I need to be on?" he questioned once more.

Mac pointed westerly. "About five miles that way, I'll tell you what reverend, give me a minute to round up my horse and I'll take you there, and get you all straightened out. We were about to go on an elk hunt, but, the elk will wait."

"Oh yes, the elk, I saw them last night. There was a nice bull and few smaller ones, about seven cow elk I think, and three bulls. I wouldn't want to hold you back from a hunt."

Mac waved his hand through the air. "Ah, it isn't a problem, reverend, I'd much rather see a man of the cloth get his bearings straight. Like I said, the elk will wait." Mac walked over to Lucy and swung up onto the saddle. "I'm going to take the reverend down to the trail, that'll get him into Chase. Silly bastard, got himself lost," he said to Tyrell as he chuckled. "Least wise he made it to friendly land."

"Sure, no problem Mac, are you coming back later?"

Mac pulled his pocket watch out and checked the time. "Well, it is getting close to 2:00 p.m., I reckon by the time I get the reverend set straight it'll be close to 4:00 p.m., chances are it'll be getting dark by the time I could get back. I say we'll pick up where we left of tomorrow, the elk won't have got to far away by then, if you happen to see one between now and then go ahead and down one. I'll help you clean it up tomorrow if you get lucky."

Tyrell nodded. "Okay Mac, sounds good."

The Missing Years – Part I

"Oh yeah, a friendly reminder you are welcome to make your way down to the house for dinner if you want."

"I know, you told me that yesterday." Tyrell chuckled, "I reckon though I'll stay put, maybe find the elk again. By the way Mac, what day of the week is it?"

"October 25th, Saturday, I believe. We'll start clearing the land on Monday, that'll be the 27th, I'll tell you what, when I come back tomorrow, I'll bring you a calendar so that you can keep your days and months straight. I'm pretty sure we have a couple of extras."

"Sure, that'd be great. Thanks Mac." Mac turned Lucy toward the reverend's horse, and the two of them headed west. "Whew, that was a little too close. Sure glad you stayed hidden Black Dog. He would have made a liar out of me, and I would've hated to have to explain to Mac why I'm using a different name." He counted his blessings as he sat there waiting for Mac and the reverend to disappear down the trail. When they were out of sight, he stood up and made his way over to Pony, who luckily never got close enough for the reverend to recognise.

"Yep, that was Reverend Joseph A. Winghaur, Pony, I'm sure glad you stayed put you and Black Dog both. Anyway, how do you feel about heading over to where we spotted those elk, this morning? I reckon there is enough daylight left that we might find them again. What do ya say?" Tyrell asked as though Pony would answer, and of course, he did- in his usual way. "Alright then, let's get you saddled up."

Tyrell couldn't know then that his day was about to get even more frantic than it was when he recognised the reverend. A couple of miles north, a grizzly bear, a boar at that, had taken on the scent of the elk that Tyrell, Pony, and Black Dog were going to track down. The grizzly, although not a big one, wanted one last meal, before it returned to its den for a long winter's nap. The scent of *'man'* also wafted up his nostrils every now and again. The bear rose up on his hind legs on a couple of occasion trying to decide which was closer, the man, or the elk. Either way, for Tyrell this spelled trouble. Luckily, the grizzly decided that the elk were closer. Patience, and surprise were his allies, and he cautiously circled the herd, using his sense of smell to decide if any were sick, weak, or very young, but today his sense of smell told him that the herd was healthy.

Tyrell checked over the gear that he packed. He wasn't planning on being gone for too long, but it was always better to be safe than sorry, and so he tossed the roll of red land marking tape into his saddle bags, every now and again he would tie a piece around the odd branch or something as he travelled to the spot. For one reason or another, he even packed the one-hand ripsaw that Mac left behind, as well as an extra length of rope. He made sure that both of his rifles, the .32-20 and his .45-70 levers, were loaded, and that he had a few extra shells for each. His colt .45s around his waist were always ready, pulling one out he spun the cylinder making sure all six shots were live and there were no spent cartridges, he did the same with the other. Slapping the pistol back into place, he was satisfied.

"Well, I reckon we have four maybe five hours give or take, before we'll need to turn back. My guns are loaded," he commented as he swung up into the saddle. Black Dog was already cutting into the bush when he got Pony going, and he followed the dog's trail. "Don't get too far ahead there Black Dog, work our perimeter," Tyrell said loud enough for the dog to hear.

They sauntered onward for close to an hour. He tied pieces of the tape to branches and such leading up to the spot where they had seen the elk earlier, but they had moved on. "Looks like they've taken their grazing

The Missing Years – Part I

somewhere else. Come on, Pony, let's get down to where they were, maybe we can pick up a trail." Pony though didn't budge. It was then that he realised why Pony wasn't moving. Down by his hooves was a pile of fresh bear scat. Pony began bobbing his head up and down and from side to side. "Goddamn it!" Tyrell yelled as he dropped the reins and grabbed the two rifles from either side of the saddle, swinging his right leg over Pony's neck he jumped to the ground.

In one brief show of furry, Pony rose on his hind legs, dug in his hooves and darted into the forest. Tyrell shook his head as he watched Pony vanish into the thick forest, and at his heels, Black Dog trailing close behind. "What a mess this has turned out to be, Jesus Christ anyway." he said, without blame or anger as he shook his head. It was what it was.

Well, guess I follow them. Sure hope they don't run into something that the two of them can't handle. That scat, I reckon, is only a couple hours old. The bear is probably what scared the elk off, he thought as he shrugged his shoulders. Not until, he saw the first track did he grow concerned. *Damn, it is a grizzly. I ain't sure how big; hard to tell by the track.* He looked around for another that would be more definitive, but saw nothing. *I best get moving,* he thought as he struggled into the thick forest, both his hands occupied with a rifle. It was a tough go at first, until he picked up Pony's trail, a clearing up ahead was the perfect spot to get his bearings. He stopped and looked around, the sun was behind him, and so, he knew he was travelling easterly.

"Maybe a little over three hours of daylight left. Sure hope I get this sorted out before then," he said to himself, as he picked up the trail and continued on. He travelled on foot for close to a mile before he stumbled upon Pony. He was standing there as though nothing had taken place. "Man, am I glad to see you, old boy. Thought for sure I wouldn't see you till morn. Where did Black Dog get to?" Tyrell questioned, as he looked around. He was unaware of a bull elk that was hiding in the thicket only sixty or so feet away, which Pony was watching with great intent. Tyrell thought he was simply being Pony, and didn't pay any attention as to why he was standing there so sullenly.

The sound of the growls and snarls not too far away are what finally caught his attention. Running in the direction, he saw Black Dog and the grizzly doing a dance in a clearing. He hollered for the dog to get out of the way and took aim with his .45-70, pulling the trigger at the exact moment that Black Dog pulled far enough away from the bear to be safe from the rifle's slug. The sound of the rifle echoed with sound reflection, as the bullet passed through the bear's body with such a force that the human eye could see where it struck the dirt behind.

The bear staggered, ran a few paces, and fell silent. At that same time the bull elk that held Pony's stare, which Tyrell hadn't seen, punched out of the bush with its head tilted low and rammed into Pony's heavy chest. Luckily, the span of the antlers were wide enough that only a few prongs made contact with Pony. Barely scathed by the elk's attack, Pony stumbled back, raised up on his hind legs and was about to pummel his front hooves down, when suddenly the elk dodged out of his way and made a beeline toward Tyrell.

It was so surreal, Tyrell thought he was in a dream. With very little time to take aim with the rifle, he pulled his right pistol and fired two rounds. Both bullets hit the big bull elk in the chest. In pain and shock, it turned and ran towards the safety of the forest, falling finally before it

The Missing Years – Part I

made the distance. Dumbfounded, Tyrell slapped the pistol back into his holster, and slumped to the ground from the adrenaline rush, where he broke out into nervous laughter. Black Dog now sitting at his side licked his face, while Pony sauntered not too far away. "Holy shit, I can't believe what transpired here Black Dog. Are you okay?" He gave the dog a once over making sure that he was. Looking over to Pony he stood up and walked over to him. Pony hadn't been as lucky as the dog, and he was sporting a few nasty gouges, nothing though Tyrell knew wouldn't heal.

"We all got pretty lucky I reckon. Holy crap, the adrenaline is still pumping too. What a story this will be to tell. I can hardly believe it even took place. Maybe one thing or the other, but certainly not both." He inhaled deeply as he took Pony by the reins. Walking over to the elk, he pulled his knife from his boot sheath, and drew it deeply across the elk's throat. For a few minutes he admired the rack on its head. It was the first elk he ever killed with his .45 pistol, and by the span and length of the elk's antlers, it was also the biggest.

Next, he made his way over to the grizzly and approached it with more caution. He had hoped that Black Dog would have been close, but he was too busy lapping up the fresh elk blood. From a short distance, he poked the bear with a stick that he picked up. Satisfied that it too was dead, he repeated the same tactic, as he did on the elk. However, the bear's fur was so thick that his blade barely made a mark. With more effort now, he stabbed the knife into its throat, and using a sawing motion, he began to cut. Finally, blood spewed out onto his hand, still warm and steaming as he cut through the bear's jugular vein. Sighing in relief he wiped the blood off, and put the knife back into its sheath. *Two kills three bullets,* he thought to himself as he looked on, both amazed, and exhausted from the entire ordeal.

It didn't take him long as, he stood there watching the grizzly bleed out, to make sense of the scenario he happened to come across. It was obvious that the grizzly was hoping for a big elk steak, and the elk was ready for a fight. Pony fixated himself to the elk, while Black Dog tried to discourage the bear. Then along he came almost blowing the entire standoff. He shook his head at how profound it all seemed, but it made perfect sense when he thought about it. He probably wasn't the first person to have something like that happen to him, but, he might be one of only a few who may have survived.

He contemplated on what to do next. Undoubtedly, he was in a bit of a predicament. Leaving the carcasses overnight unguarded wasn't probably the best way to deal with the situation, scavengers would help themselves to parts and pieces and scatter them every which way. Looking east and then at his pocket watch, he estimated that he had only two maybe two and a half hours of decent light left, and maybe an hour after that before the sun set completely. Time was certainly not on his side. It was clear what he had to do. The bear, he noted, was still streaming blood, and so it needed a while longer to bleed out. The elk though he guessed would have bled out by now.

He turned and made his way over to where the elk carcass was. Still leading Pony, he now tethered him. He started the process of gutting and skinning the elk. His boot knife was the perfect size to make quick work of the task. He skinned it up to its neck, not sure exactly how to keep the trophy antlers. He cut the head off leaving the neck hide at a good length. The animals would gnaw on it, and he could come back in the spring and gather the skull and antlers. It seemed like a plan. He tied a piece of red land marking tape around the branch of a sapling near where the elk lay. The guts that he ripped out earlier were already attracting black flies and he swatted at them, as he used the ripsaw to cut and quarter the elk. It wasn't the best job he ever did in prepping an animal, but he didn't have much time, and if he could save only the elk, then all was good. Not far from where he did the butchering he tied a length of rope around two decently thick fir. The worst part for him was climbing the distance up each tree where he felt the meat would be safe enough until morning, and where it was unlikely anything could reach it. Once the rope was in place, stretched out between the two trees, he tied up the four elk quarters. It was not an easy task for one man alone, but he managed. Next, he folded up the hide and stacked rocks onto it to keep it less vulnerable to the elements and any critters that might find it.

He looked now in the direction of the grizzly carcass. There wasn't much he could do to it without a fire for light. *I guess that is what I do next,* he thought as he untied Pony. Choosing to lead him, Tyrell traipsed over to where the grizzly carcass lay and once more tethered the horse, who obviously knew that the grizzly was no longer a threat. "Yeah, he's dead alright, Pony, you ain't got to worry about that any." Tyrell felt no need to rush and he ambled around gathering enough deadfall to keep a fire burning for a few hours. Satisfied now that he had enough he went ahead and got the sticks burning, not too close and not too far away from the butchering task.

As the fire grew brighter, he rested and nibbled on some jerky, and sipped water from his canteen. The short rest and snack improved his strength and wits, and he was slowly getting a second wind. Tossing a bigger piece of wood onto the fire, he waited for the flames to become full and constant, then, went about the task of prepping the

The Missing Years – Part I

grizzly. The only part he himself cared about, as he was never fond of bear meat, was the hide and fur. Mac though he knew would find more uses for the grizzly then simply that, and so he did his best in preserving as much of it as he knew how to.

He went through the same process with the bear meat as he did with the elk, the only difference being each quarter of the bear, weighed, he guessed, 150 pounds. The elk may have weighed half that once the guts were gone. Tired as he was and feeling confident that the meat from both the elk and grizzly bear weren't at risk in being scavenged, he whistled for Black Dog who showed up almost immediately. "It is dark out I know, but the moon will give us some light, Black Dog, and I reckon this evening is going to be a cold one. To be quite honest, I really don't want to be stuck out here. We're going to head for the tepee and make our way back here in the morning. I marked the trail up pretty good with tape and I reckon we could find our way back in a couple of hours."

Black Dog, he knew was indifferent, and as he got Pony moving in the right direction, Black Dog took up the lead and the trio headed for home. He wasn't concerned about the low burning embers of the fire he had used for light. Snow was starting to fall, and the air was chilled. He knew that the fire would go out in no time. An hour later, they were at the place where Pony and Black Dog charged off from him hours earlier, which caused the whole chain reaction of the events that had unfolded. He shook his head, as it ran through his mind once more.

Following the tape as best as he could as they traversed up and down slopes, around bends, and through bramble, he sighed in relief when the landmarks, he remembered finally came into view. Although obscured by darkness, he knew what they were. It took only a few more

The Missing Years – Part I

minutes from that point on to make the distance to the tepee, and then there it was standing out like a beacon against the silver reflection the moon. Black Dog had already made the distance and was making sure the tepee was in the clear from unwanted visitors. Tyrell pulled Pony up to the wire fence corral and removed the saddle and gear the horse had been packing. "I bet that feels a lot better, eh? You're going to feel a lot better tonight too because you ain't got to be tethered." he said as he turned him loose. "I'll be back shortly with some oats and I'll get you some water too, Pony. Hang tight."

    The first thing Tyrell did was spark a fire, so that he could have at least one cup of coffee before turning in. It had been a long day, made even more strenuous by all the work it took to prep his kills. He was home now, and that was all that mattered. Not even the chilly air, nor the weak falling snow, bothered him as the flakes danced to earth. *We made it back just in time, I reckon,* he thought as he stared into the flames, and waited for his coffee. It seemed like an eternity before he was able to pour a cup, and only a few minutes to finish drinking it. Even though, regenerated his strength somehow. Scooping a portion of oats into the bucket for Pony, he made good on his promise. The horse watered and fed now, he turned his attention to bringing a few sticks of wood inside the tepee, and for the first time he lit an inside fire.

    Adjusting the smoke flap, he watched as the smoke funnelled its way up to the opening and billowed out. At that moment, and because of his tired state, the whole process captivated him, and he continued his gaze for a few more minutes. Finally, shaking his head, he looked away. Pulling out his pocket watch, he looked at the time quite surprised that it was 11:30 p.m., and for the last time that night he exited the tepee. The snow was beginning to accumulate, and by now, two fresh inches had fallen. The temperature, he guessed, had dropped by 10 degrees. *The only good I see us getting from shit weather like this, is that the meat might freeze overnight. That's a plus I suppose.* He looked up to the sky and watched as the snowflakes fell and melted against his face as they found their way onto his flesh. Grabbing a few more pieces of wood, he stacked them inside along the left side of the tepee entrance.

    Leaving the entrance flap partially opened for Black Dog's sake, he made his way inside and removed his boots. Next, he undid his holster and set it down near the foot of his bedroll, then turning, he sat crossed-legged next to the fire and stared into the flames, until his senses grew weary, and he could no longer keep his eyes from closing. His bedroll that evening as he curled up into it had never felt so good. With his hands behind his head, he closed his eyes.

Chapter 9

Sunday, October 26th, he rose early and was sitting outside when Mac showed up. Today he rode only his horse, and had with him his hunting rifle, rope, and few other odds, and ends. "Good morning Mac." Tyrell said as he stepped up to him and his horse.

"Morning Travis, snowed heavy up here I see, a couple three or four inches. First snow of the year, I have to admit it has been a warm October, this one. Mind you, we have five days to go, before it ends. She stays like this though, might mean November is going to be wet and cold." Mac commented as he swung off Lucy. "I did forget one thing though."

"What is that?" Tyrell asked.

"A calendar."

"Ah, next time, Mac. I ain't worried about it."

"Was it cold, last night?" Mac questioned out of curiosity.

"Not so bad that I couldn't handle it. Coffee is on." Tyrell turned and they made their way over to the fire. "Got that reverend all straightened out?"

"Sure did. Helluva a nice fellow, preaches perhaps a little too much, but otherwise quite cordial. He told me a few interesting things about a fellow he met near Red Rock, said he travelled with a black dog, and his horse chased bears." Mac was looking at him sullenly. "Said his name was Tyrell Sloan, you ever meet anyone like that?"

There wasn't much Tyrell could say and he swallowed deeply. "Should I gather my gear and get?"

"I never said that. Why would you ask?"

"Well, I reckon you don't want any man working for you that doesn't use his own name. That in itself is likely quite offish for an employer, ain't it?"

"Not necessarily. Maybe you got a good reason. The reverend told me that Tyrell was one of the nicest folk he met in a long time. Said he had good character and was very trustworthy. Sounds like the type of fellow I would trust."

"You would?"

"Why wouldn't I? You have no worries from me. I might be curious to know why a man didn't use his real name, but if I trusted that man and he had a strong character and all I knew about him was the name he offered me, his past wouldn't bother me. Because, I would only know what he tells me."

Tyrell inhaled deeply and looked at Mac, "I reckon that reverend wore off on you Mac, but, I'll tell you why." It took the better part of an hour for him to explain the most relevant pieces of his story and why, he was using the alias.

"I knew it had to be something like that. I'm glad you told me, I haven't spoke a word of this to Rose, and as far as the reverend is concerned you are Travis Sweet, so you don't have to worry that he'll tell anyone that he saw you. And, I reckon since Rose doesn't know, I won't tell her. I'll always address you as Travis, and introduce you the same. I know a little bit about Heath Roy, there are folks even in these parts that have ran into him before. My lips are sealed."

"Again you have been real kind Mac, and I appreciate it." Tyrell said with sincerity and respect.

"We'll leave it at that." Mac said as he took a drink from his coffee. "I have a question, would you want to work with a man that knew that about you?"

Tyrell chuckled. "I guess that would depend on whether or not I trusted that man to keep my secret."

"And if you could?"

"Then I would." Tyrell responded.

The Missing Years – Part I

"Good." Mac said as he nodded his returned respect to Tyrell. "Then I guess we're still working together, Travis."

"Indeed we are Mac. With that out of the way, I downed an elk last night and a boar grizzly."

"Shut up, no you didn't."

"Sure did, let's finish up these coffees and I'll take you to them." Tyrell was grinning for ear to ear, he knew Mac didn't quite believe him, and he knew the story he was about to tell him would only make it sound like more of a fairytale.

"Holy, that is some tale. A grizzly and an elk." Mac was chuckling. "That, my friend is something else. I reckon you got off lucky up there, a bull elk will kill you as quick as grizzly. The way you explained how it all happened, actually makes sense. I reckon it isn't any different if you were to come across a grizzly kill, and the bear was about. We'll certainly make use of the kills. How far up did you say they were again?"

"Five miles, give or take, there is quite a bit of meat to pack out. Four elk quarters and four bear. I spent a few hours cleaning up both. I don't reckon it's the best job I've done on an animal, but, I know it'll do."

"You did all that before heading back this way?" Mac asked with surprise.

"It was the only thing I could do. I didn't want to lose their meat or their hides to scavengers."

"You did the right thing I reckon. It must have been a pain in the ass to do all that alone."

Tyrell shrugged his shoulders. "It was, but, it needed to be done, so I did it. You want another refill of coffee Mac?"

Mac looked at his pocket watch. "It is only 7:00 a.m. I think we have time for one more. Thanks, Travis."

Mac, held out his empty cup, and Tyrell filled it. "I figure it'll take us the majority of the day to gather it all. We can ride up, but we'll have to lead the horses on our return trips. What kind of terrain is up that way?"

"Geez, it is your land Mac, and you don't know what kind of terrain is up that way." Tyrell teased. "I'd think a man, like yourself with all this wilderness, in his backyard would know what kind of terrain his land was on." Tyrell winked at him as he brought his coffee to his lips. Mac sat there shaking his head and stared into the fire, Travis had pulled a funny on him. "It ain't too bad of terrain Mac. I've got the trail already marked." Tyrell added.

"Shit, is there anything you haven't forgot?" Mac smiled at him with recognition.

"You sound as though you are surprised that I thought to mark the trail?" Tyrell was teasing again.

"Not really, you already told me how you cut the quarters, using a rip-saw, most folk wouldn't have thought about that, but, you did."

"I don't know Mac, most folk who go out hunting have a meat-saw of sorts, that they pack with them, or in the least a good Bowie knife. The truth is, neither a rip-saw nor a meat-saw, are much different from one another. Least wise that's my opinion, folks use them differently, and then call them, this or that, so that they can put a name on them and call them something like the, 'incredible stay sharp *'Mac Rider'* meat-saw', and charge a fortune when selling them at the Hudson Company.

Mac started to laugh, that was so true. "Jesus, you're right on the money with that one. Yes sir, when I think about it like that, I see what you are saying and I see it every day, we're all a bunch of fools I think."

The Missing Years – Part I

"Not all of us. Folks like you and Rose, and that Tyrell fellow you mentioned early, have or had the right idea on how to live." He chuckled at the fact that he had used his own name in the example. Looking over to Mac, he realised that Mac, got the gist of it. "Only problem with that is not many folks care. It is all about money and power. The common men that live off the land, raise cattle in a fair market and bust their balls every day to be able to have a can of beans at dinner, can't stand up to the powerful and rich, who either stole what they have, swindled it or simply took it." He paused as he took another swig from his coffee. Inhaling, he carried on.

"Now I know that ain't always the case, a lot of rich men and their families have worked their way to wealth in an honest and dignified way, some might get inheritances or what have you, that sort of thing. It is when those honest men get to the top that they sometimes change." Tyrell looked northerly in the direction they would soon be travelling, and sighed. "Yep, I reckon the world is changing and it isn't going to stop. That would probably be another reason that Tyrell fellow, might also want to slip into obscurity." Rising he dumped out his coffee. "What do you say, Mac? Think we ought to get?"

"The sooner the better I guess. I'm loaded and ready." Mac said as he watched Tyrell walk away in the direction of Pony. He admired Tyrell for being as honest as he had been regarding his alias, and he would always respect him for that. It didn't take him long to saddle Pony up and gather his gear. Whistling for Black Dog, and swinging into the saddle, Tyrell turned him north. "Up this way Mac." Tyrell said as he took the lead

"I'm right behind you." Mac responded as he took up the rear. They spoke very little on that first ride up, their minds drifting as they traipsed onward. Tyrell beat Mac to the first ridge from which he had spotted the elk. He slowed Pony to a halt.

"How you doing, Mac?" he asked as Mac and Lucy rode up to him.

"I'm doing fine, Travis, and yourself?"

"Ain't felt better. I first spotted the elk from here, that day I told you about them. They were grazing down in the gorge." Tyrell pointed to a grassy knoll a few hundred or so feet away. "When I came back up yesterday afternoon, they had moved on a bit east from here. I likely wouldn't have even tracked them then, hadn't it been for the incident." Tyrell took a long swallow from his canteen and wiped his mouth. "It was over yonder that Pony and the dog took off. I had to walk from there, and couldn't mark the trail for the obvious reason, that my saddle bags were on the damn horse, and I never bothered with marking the trail on the way back, because it was too damn dark." Tyrell chuckled. "I know how to get to where were getting to though, hard to forget a hike like that."

"I imagine it would have been a piss off traipsing through all that with both your hands full with rifle."

"To say the least, Mac, to say the least," Tyrell said as he now turned east. "The kills are about a mile maybe a little more, from here." Less than thirty minutes later, they were at the clearing. They both dismounted and removed their horse's saddles. "Which do you figure we ought to pack out first, the hides, or the meat?" Tyrell asked.

"I reckon the meat first we don't want to be packing that out when it cools down, the critters will be out by then." Mac looked up at the tree where the elk hung. "Shit, you got her up there quite high, nicely done." Averting his eyes to the ground, he looked around for the hide and head, shocked when he did finally see them. "You weren't kidding, that is a nice trophy elk. How come you didn't skin the head out?"

"Ain't got a clue on how. I figured I'd leave it whole and let the animals clean it up for me, and come back next spring to claim it." Tyrell shrugged. "The skull and antlers would remain as they are. That's all I want, and even then I ain't sure what I'd do with the damn thing."

"Well, it is your kill you can do whatever you want with the head. Taxidermy ain't one of my favourite things to look at on folks' walls. I'd probably leave it as you said. Let the animals clean it up. I saw it I know how big it was."

"Probably be, a pain in the ass to pack it out anyway with a rack span like." Tyrell said as the two of them now turned their attention to how they were going to pack the elk quarters onto their horses. "What do you think, Mac, think we could pack each horse with a half side? Two quarters each."

"Depends on what they might weigh. Let's get a quarter down and see," Mac said as he walked over to the tree. "You going up or am I?"

"I've been up their once already." Tyrell chortled.

"Yeah, yeah, alright, I'll go up," Mac said as he started to climb. It took under an hour to untie and for Mac to lower all four quarters. Climbing down now, from the opposite tree, he stood on the bottom branch and jumped to the ground. "That wasn't so bad," he said as he caught his breath.

"So then, why are you catching your breath?" Tyrell chuckled.

"Shut up." Mac responded with sarcasm.

"What do you figure each quarter weighs?" Tyrell asked on a more serious note, as he knelt next to one and touched it. "Damn, I thought they might have froze over night."

"They likely did. Probably started to thaw at first light though. I wouldn't say they froze solid, but at least an inch or so of fat did. I ain't sure what they weigh though, hard to tell. What do you think?"

"Ain't got a clue, but if I were to take a leap of faith, I'd say Pony could pack two quarters easily. With nothing else on his back, I don't think it would be a problem. I weigh near 210 pounds, and he can carry me and gear."

"Yeah, I figure Lucy can too, it is a matter of deciding which of our horses gets the hind or front half."

"We'll load Pony up with the two hinds; Lucy can haul the fronts." It took some wrestling and adjusting before they were ready to start their hike down the mountain, and they rested for a few minutes when they finished, talking back and forth as they drank from their canteens. The wind was brisk, and once again, for the second time in as many days in the higher altitudes, it began to snow. The horses had no problem with the weather or even with that first load of the day and all went well for them, even in the snow. Mac and Tyrell though were showing their age. For them the hike had been miserable. The trail was slippery, the wind was cold and at times the blowing snow seemed to blind them. Now back at the tepee, things weren't so bad. It wasn't snowing down there, but it was cold. "Can sure tell it is late October eh, Mac?" Tyrell commented as they unloaded the elk meat and once again strung it up between two trees. It was easy with two people working at it, and they managed to get it done rather quickly.

"That you can, yep. The deep snow ain't going to make it down here for a few weeks though, maybe even a month, but, it is coming." They stood back and looked up to the four elk quarters. "I reckon that will do. They ain't going anywhere," Mac commented as they looked on. Tyrell nodded in agreement, pulled out his watch, and checked the time.

"That round trip took us a little more than five hours, which I reckon ain't so bad considering we hiked on foot back, and the damn snow bit us in the ass. It's close to 1:00 p.m. now, and I imagine the next load and trip ain't going take any less time. We're packing out the grizzly now."

"Yeah, I suppose we should get on with it. You figure the horses could pull a skid along that trail?"

"You mean so we can haul it all out at once? That's a damn good idea, Mac. It wouldn't take much to knock down a few poles and throw something like that together at the top. Why didn't you think about that the first time we we're up there?" Tyrell asked with humour as they walked over to their horses.

"There wouldn't have been any way that we could have got it all, the elk, grizzly and their hides in one load, not even with two horses but, with the elk now out of the way. I think we could do it with one last load."

"We'll have to throw together two skids, I think that would be best. Easier for the horses too I reckon, less chance of them stumbling. I think we will still have to lead them back, mind you, but that's okay. At least we'll be able to bring back the saddles too." The two of them stopped short of their horses.

"Yeah, that's right we have to ride them bareback. Shit, I forgot all about that," Mac said as he shook his head.

Tyrell started to laugh. "Forgot! That is the only thing I've been thinking of since we left them behind," he replied, as he swung up onto Pony's back. Mac swung onto Lucy, and moments later they started up the mountain to gather the grizzly, its hide, and the elk's. It was getting dark by the time they finished at the top and were on their way down. The only thing they left behind was the elk's head. They had everything else. The skid idea worked to both their advantages, and disadvantages. The toughest part was the steep descend into the valley where the tepee was. The weight the horses were pulling hindered them somewhat, and on occasion, they would almost stumble. The snow, though, certainly helped the skid to glide. They cleared the way with an axe when needed, and at times that got hard, dangerous, and time consuming, but they pressed on and worked through it. Other than that, they managed their return, cold, damp, and tired, but otherwise unscathed. It was 10:00 p.m., when they were finally able to sit down at the fire and have a coffee.

"Sure glad that is over with," Mac said, as he took a drink from his cup. "It was getting hectic there near the end."

"Yeah, it is a pretty steep descent into this valley from up there. Sure notice it when you're leading a horse, and the horse is pulling a skid of sorts. Things could have got cockeyed, that is for sure; glad, they didn't. We're done now though, thank God for that," Tyrell replied, as he looked over to where Black Dog was curled up. "Even the dog is pooped, and he don't get pooped easily."

"Well, tomorrow is Monday and I know I said we'd get started with the clearing, but, I figure we'll spend most of it cutting and prepping the meat and getting it stowed away. We can't do much with the hides until spring other than scraping them clean. They'll tan up nicely when the time comes." Mac took the last swallow of his coffee and stood up. "I best get Lucy and me home. Rose might almost be frantic." He chuckled as he said that, "I'll be by tomorrow, but not too early. It was a good day Travis. Tomorrow will only be better." Mac swung up onto Lucy

The Missing Years – Part I

as Tyrell bid him good night. He watched as Mac and his horse headed for home and faded out of sight.

Cold as it was outside at that time, Tyrell grabbed a handful of wood and entered the tepee. Getting a fire going, he slumped to the floor. What he needed inside was a place to sit so that he didn't have to sit cross-legged all the time. It was too late to do anything about it then, but in the days to come he'd rig something up, a small table of sorts and a few blocks of wood would work. Sitting there on the floor and close to the fire, he was impressed with his and Mac's accomplishments that day. They learned a thing or two about each other; they worked together and brought the meat and hides down from the mountain a task he thought wasn't going to be easy, but with Mac's help and ingenuity things turned out well.

He reminisced about their earlier conversation, on why he was using an alias. He knew it would not have been brought up, hadn't the reverend passed by. Still, in a sense, he was glad that it had been. He knew by Mac's sincerity and their shared respect for one another, that Mac would never speak openly about what he had learned. Even as they worked together that day, Mac only ever addressed him as Travis, and he had no reason to believe that would ever change.

Chapter 10

It was shortly after 11:00 a.m., Monday when Mac returned. Tyrell could hear the horse cart as it came around the bend. He could see from where he sat that it was full with something. He ran his fingers over his unshaved face as Mac pulled up. "What is in the cart today, Mac?" Tyrell asked as he stood and walked over to it. "Looks like lumber?"

"It is. I took some measurements this morning of our steam bath. I reckon you're going to need something like that up here. Luckily I had enough lumber on hand. It won't be as big as the one we have. I was short on the lumber lengths, but it'll be big enough for one or two people."

"A steam bath, eh? What a great idea, geez, you're full of them, ain't you?"

"My mind is always thinking about one thing or the other." Mac replied. "I'll get over to the creek and we can unload it," he said as he and Lucy started in the direction. "You could probably hop up on the back there Travis if you like."

"Nah, I'll walk alongside you. The creek ain't that far, and I ain't that old that I'd need a ride," Tyrell chuckled.

Making the distance and finding an appropriate spot, Mac swung off his horse. "Right here is probably as good a spot as any." Tyrell agreed and they unloaded the lumber and box of nails. It took only a few minutes. "I need to bring you up a woodstove and grate so you can heat up the rocks you'll need to use. We should spend some time later to gather a collection, before they all disappear beneath the snow. First things first though, we have to get that meat prepped." Mac took Lucy by the reins, and led her over to the corral and turned her loose with Pony. He walked back to where Tyrell was sitting. "Rose said we shouldn't cut all the meat up, wrapping it in cheese cloth and storing it in chunks helps it last. I figure we'll cut up two elk quarters and one bear quarter. That ought to be enough meat to go around for a couple of weeks. What do you say?"

"Whatever you think is best Mac." Tyrell replied as he poured Mac a coffee and handed it to him.

"Thank you, Travis."

"No problem. I figure we have enough time to put one back."

"Indeed. So, how did last night turn out for you? Getting used to the tepee?"

"Yep, need a table and a couple stools though. I'd like to have a place to sit at. Other than that, the tepee ain't much different from a cabin."

"Nope, other than it can be moved. We had a table and a few chairs inside too, when we used it. Might even have a few of them things, still kicking about in the barn somewhere, I'll take a look when I get back today. Oh yeah," he pulled a calendar out from his jacket and handed it to Tyrell.

"Thanks Mac, I appreciate it." Tyrell said as he looked at it. "Hard to believe 1891 is only a few months away, eh. Man, where did the year go." He set it down on the log they were sitting at. "How long do you figure it'll take to get the meat cut and prepped?"

"No more than a couple of hours. You already did the worst part. The cutting is easy. I brought along a couple of good sharp butchering knives, I'll leave you one." The sun that day was hot as they went about getting the meat cut and loaded into the horse cart, so that Mac could stow it in his and Rose's meat cellar down at their place. They left

The Missing Years – Part I

a portion hanging in the trees for Tyrell's consumption, and when that was gone, he could always get more. Next, they scrapped the hides clean and stretched them out using poles. Standing them up vertically, they braced the hide racks against the wind and elements, using more poles and nearby trees for support. "You leave them like that for now and they'll be safe, until we can get to them. Either in spring or on a warm winter day, when they freeze don't poke and prod them, they could crack." Mac said as they finished. "That grizzly hide when stretched out, sure ain't small is it?"

"You got that right Mac, 6 or 7 feet across easily, might even be closer to 8 or 9."

"Yeah, I'd say 8 or 9, more likely. The elk hide looks small next to it."

"It certainly does. The difference in the thickness of the two catches my eye. Bear are certainly built for cold altitudes, elk, not so much, makes me wonder how they do survive up high."

"They crowd each other, the generated body heat from the entire herd helps with that, I feel sorry for the poor bastards on the outside though, they're the ones that take the brunt of the cold." Mac paused briefly, "their hide makes the best light clothing, bear hide is good for warm clothing, that sort of thing, or plain old rugs. You'll get a lot of use out of both hides. You could make yourself some nice buckskin pants some moccasins, maybe a bear fur coat. The list goes on, Travis. You'll do well with those hides."

"To be honest, Mac, I ain't worked with many hides, I know how to get them to this point." he said referring to how they cleaned and stretched them out. "Mostly, I sold them or traded them, back in the day. I've always had a bit of interest in the process of tanning them and making them soft and pliable, but, that's as far as that goes. As for cutting out clothing pieces, I ain't so sure. I'll tell you what though, you show me the tanning process, and you can keep them. You and Rose will likely have more use for them then I would."

"Alright, that sounds good. We'll do it all right up here, when the time comes. I thought for sure you knew how, I saw a set of buckskins in your gear and assumed you made your own."

"Hell no, those is made and bought. My old man used to fool around making belts and such, the holster I'm wearing is his work, same as with the boots, and I have a couple of belts too. When I was younger I'd bring him the hides cleaned and stretched, and he did the rest. I paid no heed to the process after that. I guess in a way it might have been a business partnership." Tyrell chuckled, "I always had boots and belts," he added. "Come on Mac lets go have another coffee. Before, we get to some rock picking."

"Sure. Might as well, I have to say it turned out warmer today than I expected, the majority of snow has melted." Mac looked up to the mountains, "looks like it stayed up top though."

Tyrell followed Mac's gaze. "Good thing we got done when we did last night, wouldn't want to be up there right now, less it was necessary, looks damn chilly."

"We're not doing to bad today, but in another week, the snow will be staying. Even down here, it won't amount to much though, not until January or there about. By then we should have a good portion of the land cleared."

"Yeah, about that, are the plans to get at it first thing tomorrow morning?" Tyrell wanted to know, he was anxious in a way to get started, and at the same time a bit exhausted. They had done a lot in the past few days.

"More like the day after, on Wednesday. We have a few things we need to do before the work starts. Have to decide on the best place to stack the logs. That steam bath needs to be built and stove put in to it, that might take us half of a day, and then there are the couple pieces of furniture buried in the barn that I'd like for you have up here for the tepee, it'll make it a little more inviting and home like. Might not get to the land clearing until Thursday or Friday, and I reckon if that is the case, then I say, we'll get started next Monday, that would give us a couple days to catch our breaths, after all we have done in these past two days, I kind of want to take a rest." Mac slurped his coffee as he looked around, waiting for Tyrell's response.

"Yeah, me too, okay, so, we'll do the odd thing around here for a few more days that works for me." It was true they both needed a rest, things had moved fast and they kept up, they were both, a little strained. They sat in silence for a few minutes, drinking their coffees and taking in the view. For it being late October, the day was clear and warm.

Setting their empty cups down they wondered around talking about this and that as they gathered enough rocks, to sufficiently fill the rock grate that sat on top of the wood stove once the steam bath, was built, and the stove in place. It didn't take long for the pile to grow as they stacked the rocks for easy access. "That'll do it for the rocks I reckon." Mac looked at his watch, it was past 2:00 p.m., the sun was warm, and there was plenty of daylight left. "We got some time left, and it ain't so bad out right now, what do you say we see how far we can get in building the bath?" Mac asked as he offered his time to Tyrell.

"Sure, why not?" Tyrell shrugged. It didn't take long before the both of them were sawing wood, banging nails, digging dirt, and slashing brush. Three and a half hours later the ground, where the bath would sit, was cleared and levelled and the steam bath frame was in place. They stepped back and looked at it. "I reckon we are a good team Mac. That didn't take long at all."

"No it didn't actually, it looks good too. We'll finish, her up tomorrow, I'll head down to Sanders in the early morning and pick up the stove for it."

Tyrell was looking at him puzzled. "Sanders?" he asked.

"Yeah, Sanders Mercantile, five miles up the trail heading to Chase."

"Really? I didn't know there was a mercantile so close I thought the nearest one would be Chase or Hells Bottom."

"Sanders, has been in this area for a long time. I guess if you have never been up this way or into the town of Chase, you wouldn't know. Sorry, I didn't mention it earlier."

"No need apologising Mac. I'm happy to know now. Maybe, I'll tag along with you."

"Sure, you could do that. It's quite the mercantile, there are a couple of routes that end up there coming from east and west, so they are always well stocked, with most everything one needs. There is a mailing office across the street from it, Sanders runs that too. We could meet at my place at first light, unless of course we get hit with a storm or something. We could make the round trip by mid day. It sometimes gets busy along the trail, though." Mac wanted him to know.

"That don't bother me, ain't no one looking for Travis Sweet, that I know about." Tyrell chuckled. "And I ain't sure anyone knows Tyrell Sloan in these parts either, he's never been up this way."

"Good enough. I say we go have a sit down for a few, and then I'll head for home. We got a lot done again today." Mac mentioned as they walked over to the log and sat down.

"We did so. The meat is all cut, hides scraped and cleaned, and by God if we don't have the frame built for the steam bath. It was a good day undoubtedly." Tyrell said as he tossed a stick onto the coals of his fire. "It won't take long for coffee you care to have some Mac?"

"I could have a cup before I head for home. Thanks Travis. By the way, hand me that calendar, I want to know what next Monday is." Tyrell handed it to him. Mac looked at it and flipped the page. "Monday next week is November 3rd, that will be the day we get started on the land clearing. Best thing to do, is slash away all the small stuff that will get in our way. It'll make it easier for us to fall the trees. So, brush slashing first, we'll make a pile of it over there somewhere," he pointed in the general direction. "Then come spring, we'll have a bon-fire."

"Yeah, I reckon that would be best, don't want to be tripping and stumbling as we cut down trees." Tyrell said as he now poured them a coffee, and handed one to Mac.

"Thanks." Mac took the coffee and slurped. "I have a 6 foot two man rip-saw, the cutting blade is about 4 feet long, the, two handles take up the rest of the length. I don't reckon we'll need anything longer. What do you figure?"

"I wouldn't have a clue. If you say that is all we'll need to knock down the logs, then I guess that is all we need. You have axes and wedges too right?"

"Oh yeah, still, maybe tomorrow when we're at Sanders, we can take a look and see if there is a longer saw. I don't think we'll need anything longer, would be nice to know though if they have longer ones in stock."

"I suppose." Tyrell shrugged and brought his coffee to his lips. "I'm getting excited about that steam bath, ain't been clean in a while, and could sure use a good scrubbing."

"You're welcome to use ours down at the house."

"Nah, I'll wait for this one here to be operational, as long as you don't mind my stink as we work on it." Tyrell chuckled. "Besides, we should have it ready by tomorrow evening."

"Most likely, yep, besides, one more day working alongside you and your stink, ain't going to kill me, I've already worked alongside you for a couple." Mac chortled.

"Yeah, yeah." Tyrell smiled. "So I do stink then?"

"You, ain't no bed of roses." Mac took the last swallow from his coffee. "Anyway, I guess I'll head for home, thanks for the coffee. We'll see you around 6:00 a.m., tomorrow. We'll have breakfast and skedaddle, how does that sound?" Mac stood and Tyrell followed him over to the corral.

"6:00 a.m., it will be my friend, I'm looking forward, to some new scenery." Tyrell commented as Mac led Lucy out of the corral and saddled her.

"Well," Mac started as he swung onto his horse. "I'll see you in the morning, Travis."

"You bet Mac, see you then. I'll try to wash some of the stink off before then. Don't want to offend Rose any."

"It takes a lot to offend her." Mac said as he tilted his hat and sped off in the direction of home. Tyrell walked back to the fire and sat, contemplating on giving his face and arm pits a scrub he gathered a big pot and filled it with water, then set it near the flames to warm it up. While it warmed he stepped inside the tepee and gathered a bar of soap, his shaving brush, straight razor and small shaving mirror, setting them on the tepee floor, he dug around for a cleaner set of clothes. Finding a set, he laid them on the floor as well. He'd simply give himself a sponge bath for now.

He lit the tepee fire to take the chill out of the air. The last thing he wanted was to catch a cold as he scrubbed. Making his way outside he gathered the pot of warm water and went about washing his pits and shaving his face, it didn't take long and before he knew it, he looked respectful and didn't stink as badly as he had, slipping into a cleaner set of clothes he dumped the rancid water, and sat down at the outside fire. He was ready for their trip now and breakfast at Mac and Rose's table, in the morning.

The Missing Years – Part I

Chapter 11

As the first birds of morning began their constant song, Tyrell, rolled out of bed. His pocket watch read 5:00 a.m. It would take him less than an hour to make the distance to Mac and Rose's. He stretched and yawned, then slipped into his clothes. Looking through his saddlebags, he pulled out his money satchel. He had $200 dollars, more than he would need to pick a few things up at Sanders. He didn't need much, maybe a few cans of beans, coffee, sugar, that sort of thing. Pulling on his boots and holstering his .45s, he stepped outside, and inhaled deeply the cool fresh air of late October. He didn't bother with a fire or coffee. Instead, he saddled up Pony and headed to Mac's place, Black Dog trailing close behind.

The trail was easy to follow and he made the distance before the sun crested the eastern horizon. He could tell that both Rose and Mac were already awake, and he gently knocked on their door. "Good morning, Travis," Rose said as she answered. "Please, come in. I will get coffee for you. Are you ready for the trip to Sanders?" she asked as she stepped aside and gesture for him to sit.

"Sure am, Rose. Thanks," he replied as he made his way to the table and sat across from Mac. "Good morning Mac."

"Good morning to you too, Travis, I wasn't sure you would be up by now."

"Oh, I'm always up by this time."

"Yeah, us too. We'll get on our way soon. Would you like some flap jacks, eggs, and bacon, before we head out?"

"Sure would; that'd be great." Tyrell removed his hat and set it across his lap, as Rose brought him a coffee. "Thank you, Rose."

"Yes, you are welcome. I will bring your breakfast shortly. Please, enjoy the coffee while you wait."

"I will." Tyrell took a long slurp. "The weather looks good today, warm like yesterday I hope."

"I think so. We should be back before we know it. Then we'll finish up that steam bath of yours," Mac said, as Rose now brought Tyrell his plate of food.

"Mmm, that looks and smells good. Thank you kindly, Rose." They sat in silence as he ate, speaking every now and again about how they hoped the day would turn out. Finally, after another coffee and scraping his plate clean, Tyrell rose from the table and the two men exited into the early light of predawn. It took Mac a few minutes to hook Lucy up to the horse cart, and then they headed off down the trail. Tyrell commanded Black Dog to stay and to take care of the place. The dog sat and watched as Mac and Tyrell headed out, then he found a comfortable place on Mac's stoop, and waited. It took another 15 minutes to get to the main trail, and in that time they spoke sporadically, choosing instead to listen to the forest as it came awake.

"It is a nice trip, to Sanders, especially on a day like this; you will enjoy it," Mac said as they made the distance to the main trail.

"So far that has all been true. There ain't nothing like a brisk ride in the early morning, makes a man feel alive."

"Yeah, that is true. Usually I don't leave as early, but, today is an exception, because we need to get back long before the sun sets."

"Five miles ain't that long. A ten mile round trip could probably be walked before the sun sets." Tyrell responded.

"You might end up with blistered feet though," Mac chuckled.

The Missing Years – Part I

"Blisters heal," Tyrell said as they continued on, again in silence. He took in all the views and landmarks making, himself familiar with the area and the trail. "So, you said yesterday there are a few routes heading east and west from the mercantile, I reckon one heads due north too, into Chase don't it?"

"Yep, the Chase Wagon Road, actually takes you south down to the Pacific, or north to the Yukon. I have only ever been to Chase. For a start up town, it isn't as small as one might think. There are a few hotels and saloons, a mercantile, a barber shop, and a train station; and if a man wanted to find trouble there he could."

"Yeah, that is the way most start up towns are, there always seems to be that one person who is bent on making your stay or visit as miserable as they can. Funny how that works actually; lack of law I reckon."

"Well, Chase has a Mounted Police station, but not many Mounted Police, so, your reasoning on why is probably true. They do what they can, I guess, even though sometimes it isn't enough. That's when folks have to take matters into their own hands and deal with the trouble on their own. A couple of ranchers up in the area I once heard, strung up a cattle rustler, they were judge, jury and executioners. The law never gave them much flack for that."

"Sometimes, that is the way it has to be though," Tyrell said, as he reminisced about Heath Roy and Ollie Johnson. The two of them were perfect examples of swift justice, being served, although, his decision to run wasn't probably the best decision he could have made. The decision to fight back as far as he was concerned was, and many folks living in Willow Gate would agree.

"Different situations require different means too, sometimes it is better to let those folks live in their own

The Missing Years – Part I

misery. Folks that cause problems for others for no apparent reason are likely so miserable with their own lives, that we're sometime better off leaving them to wallow in their own self-pity," Mac commented, as they travelled onward. Time slipped by and before they knew it they were getting close to Sanders. "Another mile and we'll be at our destination, Travis. Not much longer at all."

"It has been a nice trip so far, hope the return is the same," Tyrell responded.

"As long as the weather doesn't take a turn, I don't imagine the return trip will be any less pleasant. Indeed it has been a nice ride so far." Finally, the trail opened up and they could see the mercantile. "There it is, Sanders Mercantile. Looks kind of odd out here in the middle of nowhere, doesn't it?"

"Oh, I don't know, most mercantiles I've run across are always out in the middle of nowhere; seems appropriate that Sanders is too." They pulled their horse up to the horse pole outside the store, dismounted and made their way inside.

"Hello there Mac, how are things going back at the farm, keeping busy?" Hank Sanders asked as Mac and Tyrell approached the counter.

"As busy as a man can be, I reckon. This here is Travis Sweet." Mac said as he introduced him to Hank. "He's giving me a hand in finally clearing that top five acres that I've been trying to get done."

"You've been trying to get that done for years now," Hank mentioned as he reached out his hand to shake Tyrell's, "Nice to meet you Travis."

"Likewise, Hank, was it?"

"Yep, Hank the old crank, some call me. So, what brings you today, Mac, anything I can help you fellows with?"

The Missing Years – Part I

"I need a woodstove, and stove pipe, some roofing paper, the good kind that don't leak, a bucket of tar, plus a wash tub to sit on top of the stove."

"Making a steam bath I'm guessing?"

"That we are Hank, going to need the rock grid too."

"Yeah, I have all you need. Swing your horse and cart around back, and I'll get the things you'll need."

"Thanks Hank. I think Travis here is looking for a few odds and ends too."

"Sure no problem, have a look around Travis, I'll get Mac squared away."

"You sure you don't need a hand?" Tyrell asked.

"The wood stove ain't that heavy, nor is the pipe. Thanks for asking though," Hank replied, as he stepped out from the counter and opened the loading door, leaving Tyrell to look for the things he needed. It didn't take long for the two men to get their needs and load them into the cart. The cost for the woodstove, rock grate, roofing paper and tar, as well as Tyrell's few items came to $40 dollars and Mac offered to pay for the works.

"Thanks Mac, but, I reckon I'll pay for my own stuff. No offence, I would feel better if I paid for those few items out of my own pocket."

"No offence taken, Travis, I understand," Mac responded. Hank did a quick calculation and added Tyrell's stuff separate.

"Okay," Hank started, "Mac's stuff comes to $32.50, Mr. Travis' stuff comes to $7.50," Hank said as Mac, and Tyrell dug into their pockets and paid. "Thank you," Hank said as he took their money and tossed it into the cash register. "Is there anything else you fellows might need?" he asked.

"I don't think so. Anything more you need, Travis?"

"Not presently, Mac, I'm good. Got what I need."

"All right then. Oh yeah, I was going to ask you Hank, do you carry tree rip-saws, and what is the longest one you got?"

"I do, and I think the longest one I have in stock is an eight foot, six foot of blade, and the rest handle. Think you'll need something that long? The six foot ones seem to be the ones that most folk use for clearing land. I can also order you in a ten foot, but, I don't reckon there are any trees up your way that are that big at the base."

"No probably not, was only inquiring. Good to know if we need, we can get an eight foot saw. By the way, do you know if Maggie is cooking today over at the eatery?"

"She is as far as I know."

"Okay, well, Hank, nice seeing you again and thanks for your help in loading me up. I think I'll treat Travis to a cup of coffee and a bowl of soup, before we head back."

"She does make the best soup." Hank smiled and waved as Mac and Tyrell exited.

"So, do you want a cup of coffee and a bowl of soup, Travis? My treat."

"Sure, I'd never turn down a bowl of soup."

A few minutes later, they were sitting in the eatery at the side of the mercantile building. It wasn't big at all with only four tables and a counter with a couple of stools. "Huh, ain't this quaint," Tyrell said as he looked around and tossed his hat to the floor. "It certainly smells good in here." He inhaled the scent of cooking and fresh brewed coffee.

"Always smells the same," Mac said as Maggie approached. "Afternoon, Maggie. How is business?" he asked.

The Missing Years – Part I

"Same as always Mac, what can I get you fellows?"

"Soup and coffee please," Mac answered.

"Will have it to you shortly, I'll get you coffees now." She turned and grab a couple of cups and the pot of coffee. "Who is you friend, Mac?" she asked as she poured the two cups.

"My name is Travis, Maggie. Mac here is putting me to work up on his farm," Tyrell said as he took drink from his coffee.

"Well, very nice to meet you Travis." she looked at Mac. "Decided to hire some help to clear that land, eh?"

"Yep," Mac said, as he too now took a drink from his coffee.

"I'll bet Rose is happy about that."

"I reckon. She's been wanting, me to get to it for a while. Finally got the opportunity, and so it shall be."

Maggie chuckled as she went back to get their soup. "Well it has been years in coming." It took her a few more minutes to return with their soup and biscuits. "Here you go," she said as she set the bowls down. "Today it is minestrone. Enjoy."

"Thank you Maggie, we will," Mac replied, as she went back to her kitchen. "Sure smells good, don't it?"

"I wouldn't disagree," Tyrell said, as he dunked his biscuit and began to eat. It was true what they said about Maggie. It was some of the best soup he ever tasted, and he finished it up without out stopping. Mopping up the last few drops with his biscuit, he ordered another bowl. Mac too took seconds as well as coffee and a piece of pie. Finished now, they thanked Maggie for the service, the great soup, and toothsome pie. Mac paid the bill and off again they started heading for home.

When they pulled up to Mac's place a few hours later, it was 1:30 p.m. Black Dog greeted their return wagging his tail as he approached. "Good boy, Black Dog, glad you stuck around. I hope you stayed out of trouble," Tyrell teased, as he swung off Pony. "You gonna stop off here for a bit Mac, to let Rose know you're back?" Tyrell asked as he scratched the dog behind the ear.

"Yep, won't take long. I'll be back in a jiffy, Travis," Mac replied, as he swung off Lucy's back and entered the house. "Rose! Travis and I made it back." He called out as she came around the corner from the kitchen.

"Okay, are you heading up to the tepee without coffee?" she asked.

"I reckon. We had a bite to eat at Maggie's."

"Oh, how is she?" Rose wondered.

"Same as always, not too talkative but friendly," Mac answered. "I'll probably be back home before it gets dark. We ain't got much left to do to the steam bath, other than finishing it," Mac smiled as he kissed her cheek.

"It won't take long?"

"A few hours, three maybe four, give or take. The hard part is done. The frame is already in place, so, yeah, I don't think it'll take too long."

"Do you need food for up there, a snack, or something?" Rose asked.

Mac rubbed his stomach. "Nope I'm full from the soup. I'll be wanting a big man-sized dinner when I get back though."

"I will make stew then."

"Sounds good to me. Alright then, now that you know we are back from Sanders, I guess I best get at it. Talk to you when I get back from the top five, Rose." Mac turned and exited the house.

"Bye, Mac. Be safe. Dinner will be hot when you come home." She blew him a kiss as he looked back and winked at her, closing the door he swung back onto his horse and he and Tyrell headed for the tepee. It was shortly past 2:00 p.m., when they finally arrived, and 2:30 p.m., when they were unloaded. Tyrell lit a fire and set the bucket of tar next to it to warm up so that they could use it when the time came. With the tar now heating up, they started putting up the walls and roof. It didn't take long to bang it all together, and the eight foot by eight foot steam bath was finally standing. All that was left was tarring the roof and laying down the black roofing paper. With that done, they sat and rested for a few minutes and chatted. Next, they installed the wood stove, and rock grid. It was getting dark when they finished, but there it was in all its glory.

"There you go, my friend. That ought to keep you happy and clean," Mac said, as he leaned up against the horse cart and looked on.

"Yep, it sure is going to be nice to wash away the filth tonight," Tyrell said, as he stood next to Mac and looked at their newest accomplishment. "Just have to fill the tub with water, start the fire, and wait." He smiled as he looked at Mac and each grabbed a bucket and started hauling water filling up the tub. Tyrell lit the fire and they exited closing the door behind them. "How long do you figure for the water to get hot, Mac?"

"An hour maybe. It's going to be hot inside, so make sure you bring in a bucket of cold water too, otherwise you might find the water is hot enough to scald. Every now and again, give the rocks a good soaking and stand back because the steam will surely knock you on your ass," Mac chuckled. "I know, because it has happened to me. But, I'll tell you there ain't nothing like a hot steam bath on a cold winter day to clean out your pores, relax your aches and pains, and wash away dirt."

The Missing Years – Part I

Tyrell agreed with a nod. "So, do you have time for a coffee? It won't take long to get a pot going?"

"Always have time for a coffee, Travis." Mac smiled as they made their way to the fire and sat down on the log. At 7:00 p.m., after a couple cups of coffee, Mac was ready to head for home. "I'll be back sometime tomorrow with those few bits of furniture I have in the barn. We'll get this place like home for you in no time. Have a good steam bath, Travis and I'll see you tomorrow," Mac said.

"See you then, Mac." Tyrell made his way over to the steam bath and checked the water. It was as Mac said, very hot inside, but the tub of water needed a few more minutes to be warm enough for him to wash up. He added another stick of wood and exited, returning to the tepee he grabbed his bar of soap, his hairbrush, and his oil lantern. With his only towel in hand, he made his way back to the steam bath, set the lantern on the floor and lit it. The lantern filled the little room with light casting his shadow on the wall behind him.

He slipped out of his clothes and hung them on the door hook, and for the first time in a week or so, he washed his hair and crotch, scrubbed his face and poured warm water over his head. The dirt and sweat now washed away, he sat on the bench and soaked up the steam. *Boy, does this ever feel nice,* he thought. The fire and hissing rocks now filled the room with a soft and caressing sound, as he sat there in quiet contemplation. Another day of living tucked into his belt.

When he stepped out of the steam bath, a brisk and cold wind blew down the valley. Although he had been hot, the cold air sucked his body heat away. Shivering he made his way to the tepee. The fire outside was low but he didn't bother adding any wood; instead, he lit the fire inside and sat on the floor. The fire warmed the tepee in a comfortable sense, and he no longer felt the chill in his bones. Outside the wind continued to blow, and as he looked up through the smoke flap, he could see that it started to snow. *Damn, I hope it don't accumulate; looks like it is going to be heavy,* he thought. He looked at his pocket watch and seeing that it was getting late, he decided that he would check on Pony and Black Dog, then curl up in his bedroll. There was nothing more, he wanted to do until tomorrow. All that needed doing on that day had been done, and now sleep beckoned him.

The Missing Years – Part I

Chapter 12

He woke up to 6 inches of snow that Wednesday. It was a heavy snow due to the chilled temperatures from the night. It would melt as the day progressed. The sun was already warming things up, and the snow that stayed on the branches of the trees was already beginning to melt and fall to the ground, as the branches warmed, causing the snow to slide from them. He wiped the log where he sat clear of snow. The coals from the past night's fire no longer held a spark so he gathered some dry birch bark, chopped some kindling, and relit the fire. It didn't take long for it burn hot and for him to be able to make coffee. Black Dog was nearby and he scratched him behind the ear.

"This month sure came and went fast, didn't it? Hard to believe actually how far you, Pony, and I have travelled. Hard to believe I'm even sitting here, with you and Pony, and with winter work lined up to boot. I would never have thought we'd be so lucky," Tyrell said, as he looked around. "I reckon it could and will get cold up here, but we have shelter, and lots to do to keep busy." The scent of fresh coffee now tantalized his sense of smell, and he poured a cup, reminiscing about the turn of events that brought him where he was sitting, right now at that moment. *Yep, we got lucky,* he thought as he drank his coffee.

He pitter-pattered for a few hours, bringing feed and water to Pony and gathered more wood for the fires. He even checked on the hides stretched out not far from the tepee. All was well. The few big chunks of both bear and elk meat that he and Mac left behind for his consumption, strung up in a tree, remained intact. No critters had bothered it. He sliced off a piece from each, his knife luckily sharp enough to cut through the partially frozen

The Missing Years – Part I

meat. The meat, he knew, would thaw by the time dinner rolled around, and he would indulge in a meat fest. He was glad that he made the trip to Sanders Mercantile with Mac. The few things he bought would certainly complement the meal, when the time came. Putting the frozen meat onto a plate, he set the plate on top of his inside woodpile to thaw.

Mac showed up shortly thereafter. The horse cart was loaded with furniture and a few other odds and ends. There was a fire-spit in the mix built especially for the tepee, made from iron, there were three pieces to it, the two 'Y' shape pieces that stuck in the ground and the cross piece with a handle on one end and a sharp point on the other for skewering meat. Along with that, Mac brought a fire grill that looked like a stool with four legs and a metal grid to set pots and pans on for cooking. The table was wood and so were the two chairs, which Mac and Rose cut and carved from one block each. They were as solid as the block of wood they were carved from. At the front of the cart was a wood box with a lid and latch for storing clothing, dry goods or what have you.

"Wasn't expecting all this, Mac, that's quite a load of 'this and that's'," Tyrell said as he looked inside.

"Well, it ain't being used in my barn; might as well put it to use up here. Besides, everything in there you'll need. There might even be a few pots and pans inside that dry box, in fact, I'm most certain there is. You'll find a use for it all." Mac responded as he leaned against the cart. He commented on how much it snowed and how fast it was melting as he looked around. They talked back and forth for a few minutes then went about unloading the cart and getting everything placed inside the tepee. The tepee looked good now and Tyrell was please with its decor.

The Missing Years – Part I

"It looks good in here now, Mac. Thanks for bringing it all to me. I appreciate it," Tyrell said, as he looked around. "You could use a standing shelf, I think, to store canned goods and stuff. There is probably enough left over lumber from the steam bath that would work, so, if you decide, go ahead and use it, for whatever you want. There is a hammer, a wood saw, and a few nails in the box I left behind yesterday. I'll leave them here for you, I got extra at home."

"Yeah, I suppose a shelf of sorts would be handy. For now, though, I'm content. Sounds, like you are in a bit of a rush today, Mac."

"A little bit, yep. Have some things to catch up on. I have time for a coffee though, got any made?"

"Won't take but a jiffy to get some started. I'll get fresh water and set a pot to perk," Tyrell said, as they exited. A few minutes later, they were drinking a cup and discussing Monday's work plan. Although it was five days away, Mac wouldn't be back that way until Saturday, leaving Tyrell to fend for himself. He didn't mind one bit, he could use the break and so could Mac, they had both been hard at it for the past few days, and neither one wanted to be worn-out when Monday rolled around. They would work from sun up until sundown from Monday to Friday once they started. Saturdays, and Sundays, would be recoup days. The work would not be easy but they were both committed and anxious. With their coffee finished now, Mac swung onto his horse and reminded Tyrell that, he would be back on Saturday to check up on him, and in the meantime, he was welcome down at the farm anytime.

"I know, but I can find a lot to do up here, Mac. Thanks again, though, for the invite. I'll see you on Saturday," Tyrell replied with a nod.

The Missing Years – Part I

"Yep, see you on Saturday," Mac said, as he and Lucy headed for home. The reason for Mac's haste that day was because he and Rose had a bit of a quarrel the night before, and he had spent the night on the couch. Waking in the morning he headed outside and cleaned up the barn as he loaded the cart with the furnishings and whatnots. He hadn't even spoke to Rose yet, and he was feeling a need to do exactly that, an apology to her was definitely needed. They rarely battled and when they did, it was always over something trivial, like last night's quarrel. Mac shook his head as he and Lucy traipsed along.

Early as it was, Tyrell retreated inside and Black Dog followed. Sitting at the table for the first time, he made himself comfortable, putting his feet up he stretched out with his hands behind his head. The few things Mac brought him certainly improved both the look of the tepee and his comfort. "Looks good in here now, doesn't it?" he questioned Black Dog who was lying close to the entrance. Tyrell chuckled. "I know if you could talk you would agree." Smiling, he rested his eyes, as he listened to the chatter of a nearby squirrel. He must have dozed off though, because the next thing, he heard were the low warning growls of Black Dog letting him know, that something wasn't right.

He stood from the table, arming himself with his .32-20 rifle as he cautiously stuck his head out of the tepee entrance. In the distance, he could see a man approaching, Black Dog was on full alert his nose raised into the wind as he tried to scent the oncoming visitor. Stepping out, Tyrell could see that the man was dressed in Blackfoot garb, and on his head was a flat top cowboy hat, the style that most young native men in the area that had lived amongst the white man chose to wear. Tyrell held steadfast as the man approached, commanding Black Dog to sit and behave he

The Missing Years – Part I

waited for the Blackfoot brave to make the distance, his rifle in his left hand, and his right hand ready to draw. Now in closer proximity, Tyrell could see that he wasn't that old, perhaps in his late twenties. His long jet black hair was in two braids and wasn't as long as one might expect. "Hello," Tyrell said, as the man now stopped his horse and looked at him.

"Is this Mac Rider land?" the young brave asked.

"Who wants to know?" Tyrell answered with evasiveness, not sure, he should answer with a 'yes'.

"My name is Half Moon Running Creek, I bring news to my sister Rosalinda Running Creek about the death of our father. I saw your tepee from afar. It is of Blackfoot design. That is why I approach."

At that moment, Tyrell knew that his only answer to the young Blackfoot's question would have to be yes. "This is Mac's land, I am sorry to hear about your father. Mac and Rose live down the trail a ways." Tyrell pointed. "If you give me a minute, I'll saddle up my horse and take you there."

Half Moon observed the dog, and Tyrell's horse. A man he met as he travelled asked him if he had seen ever seen anyone that rode a big horse and travelled side by side with a dog. He wondered now if only for a moment, although he didn't care, if this was the man that the traveller spoke of. For now though, it mattered little.

"Thank you. I have travelled far, across the prairie and Rocky Mountains. The snow up high is close to my horse's belly. I am tired but can now sigh in relief that I have found my sister's home," Half Moon replied, with a sigh of relief.

"Yes, you can," Tyrell said as he saddled up Pony. "It won't take us long to get there." He reined Pony in the direction of Mac and Rose's place, and the two started off.

The Missing Years – Part I

"How long have you been travelling?" Tyrell asked to make friendly conversation.

"Seven days and have only rested for one."

"That is quite a ride."

"It was important. More important than how fatigued I felt as I travelled," Half Moon replied, as they carried on.

"By the way, I ain't sure I introduced myself, Half Moon, and I'm sorry about that, got caught up in the moment, feeling your need and importance to talk with Rose. Anyway, my name is Travis Sweet, nice to meet you Half Moon." Tyrell smiled and nodded his recognition.

"In your world, I have grown accustom to Joe," Half Moon smiled weakly. "You can call me Joe."

"That's fair enough, but what is wrong with Half Moon?"

"Nothing, but, I have found that the white man have simple names, and that they never can remember our native names, or they stumble with their English when they try to address us. It is easier for them to say Joe."

Tyrell chuckled softly, the statement Half Moon made seemed funny because of how true it was. "As true as that might be, I prefer Half Moon." Tyrell said.

"I prefer it too. I appreciate your effort. Now, enough talk. I must prepare myself for how badly Rosalinda is going to take the news I bring her." Half Moon sped up his horse a few paces ahead and Tyrell hung back, wondering if he had said something wrong, or if Half Moon was simply tired of his babbling. *I guess I can understand where he is coming from. He's been on the trail for a while carrying a burden that not even I would like to carry,* he thought, as he carried onward. Half Moon finally slowed his horse to a halt, and waited, realising himself, that the man he met who went by the name of Travis was only trying to be polite.

"I am sorry for my ignorance for showing little interest in idle talk. I mean not to be impolite," Half Moon said, as Tyrell pulled up next to him.

"No worries. I understand your need to get to Rose. It ain't far from here, maybe another ten minutes," Tyrell replied as he heeled Pony's flank and the two riders carried on. They rode in silence for a few minutes, both content with the simple ride. It was Half Moon who now felt the need for conversation.

"How long have you known my sister?"

"Not long at all. Mac hired me to help with clearing some land up near the tepee. I've only met Rose on a couple of occasions but have known Mac for almost as long as you have been on the trail."

"It is a very short time. Rosalinda left our people at a young age, ten years ago. I have only seen her once in that time. I moved to a city and worked after that. I don't like cities. I moved back to our land two years ago have been there since." By now, they could see Mac and Rose's house.

Tyrell pointed. "Mac and Rose live there. I'm going to turn back and let you folks grieve your loss. It was a pleasure meeting you, Half Moon. I look forward to when we meet again," Tyrell said with sincerity as he reined Pony to a halt.

"Thank you for showing me the way to my sister's house. We will meet again Travis." Half Moon tilted his hat in respect and rode off in the direction of Mac and Rose's. Tyrell turned and headed back the way he came. Making the distance to the front door, Half Moon dismounted and knocked. It was Rose who answered, her jaw dropped and she stood back in awe, there before her was her younger brother, it could only mean one thing: something terrible had happened.

"Half Moon, my brother," she started, as she threw her arms around his neck and hugged him. "It has been a long time," she said as tears welled up in her eyes. "Something has happened, hasn't it?"

"I am afraid so," he replied, as he removed his hat. "Father has been killed by Little Brown Bear. He took captive two young girls and fled with five of our braves."

"Oh my God!" Rose wailed. "What happened?"

"Father saw some things. Little Brown Bear killed him for what he saw."

Rose knew exactly what their father must have seen. "Little Brown Bear and his perversions, yes?"

"Yes. Father confronted him. Little Brown Bear stabbed him in his heart, then fled. They headed deep into the flat lands, renegades all of them. Little Brown Bear must pay."

"I am saddened. And mother, how is she?" Rose questioned.

"Mother is strong, her weeping is over, now she sits alone and waits for Little Brown Bear. She wants vengeance, and she will have it."

"You can't go alone, Little Brown Bear is ruthless. Come sit at our table and rest." Rose gestured toward the kitchen and the table, her eyes wet with tears. Mac heard their conversation and he met them as they made their way into the kitchen.

"Hello, Half Moon. It is nice to finally meet you up close. This news you bring is devastating. When did this happen?"

"Eight days ago." Half Moon sat at the table exhausted and weary. "I have travelled seven days, long and hard to bring this news to my sister. Soon I must make

The Missing Years – Part I

the journey back, and gather men from our tribe to hunt down and kill this menace who at one time we all held in great regard. He is now a renegade and a murderer. He must die, for the death of our father and for the pain and humiliation he has brought to our young women."

"For now Half Moon, you must rest, gain back your strength. I will travel back with you to sit with mother, and pay my respect to our departed father, Great Eagle."

Rose sat down next to him and cupped her hand over his. Together, they chanted and prayed, as Mac stood back and listened. He knew they needed to be alone, so he turned and made his way outside. He would leave the two of them to grieve for now. There was no way he was going to let Rose travel back with her brother alone. He would go too, and give his respect to Great Eagle Running Water, and his condolences to his wife White Bird. Finding someone to look after their farm wouldn't be too difficult, their neighbour Ben Westcott came to mind, he lived less than a mile away and had looked after their farm before. Old as he was he was always willing to help.

Although he had only met Great Eagle and White Bird once, he respected them both with great admiration. He too was saddened at the news, and wanted nothing more than to hold Rose close and comfort her as she grieved but he knew it wasn't his place yet. Rose and Half Moon firstly had to finish with their prayers. He sat down on a chair on the front porch and looked toward the east and the mountains they would have to cross to get to Rose and Half Moon's people.

It had taken Half Moon seven days and chances were he didn't stop. For the three of them to make the same distance, Mac knew it would take longer, perhaps ten days. Sitting in contemplation, he planned their journey inside his head. *It may be better and safer,* he thought, *to travel the*

The Missing Years – Part I

eastern trail from Sanders Mercantile. The eastern wagon trail would be easier but might take longer. The mountains up high would be dangerous, and unrelenting; the eastern wagon trail was down low. It was a safer and better route than Half Moon had taken. Perhaps, he and Half Moon would be able to follow his route back, but, not with Rose, he would never put her safety in such peril.

The door to the house opened and he looked up to see a tearing Rose. He stood and held her tightly, cooing her with his gentle caress and whispering condolences. "I am sorry for your family's loss Rose, it is indeed a tragedy. We will go to your people together and grieve with them." He rubbed her back as she snuggled deeper into his chest and wept.

"My brother, Half Moon, wants to leave at first light tomorrow, but he is too weak and tired. He must rest and eat. I will convince him to stay for a day or two. Father is dead and we cannot do anything for him now, but I can certainly do something for my brother and offer him rest and food."

"Yes, Rose, it'll be better for him to travel after he is full and well rested," Mac said as he gently held her in a warm embrace as she continued to weep. "Come, let's go back inside, and sit with Half Moon." He opened the door for her and followed her inside. "I'll make us coffee, go sit with your brother, I'll be there shortly," Mac said as he turned into the kitchen and placed the coffee pot on the wood cooking stove. He leaned against the counter and looked out at the darkening sky as evening approached. The fight he and Rose had the night before, for which they were apologising to each other, was nothing more, than a distant memory. The news that Half Moon brought was more important than any simple argument. The coffee now done, he brought it over to the table along with three cups.

Pouring each of them a cup, he sat down with a sigh. "I will travel back with you and Rose, in the coming days, Half Moon. I feel as though I owe your father that respect and I owe your mother my condolences. I will ride over to our neighbour's place after we speak with Travis and ask him to look after the farm while we are away," Mac said as he took a drink from his coffee.

"Travelling with Rose though, I will not allow for her to travel over the Rockies. We will take the east wagon road, which is only a few miles from here. It'll take us through the mountains and to your people in ten days."

"In ten days, Little Brown Bear and his followers will be miles away and hard to follow. How can I seek vengeance, if he is not to be found?" Half Moon questioned as he looked into Mac's eyes.

Mac inhaled deeply. "I understand your point, Half Moon, but I can't allow us to take any other route. It would put us all in peril. I will help look for Little Brown Bear and his band of thugs. I can help and I will," he assured.

"It could take weeks to track him down. Your friend Travis, who guided me here, tells me that you two have work. Is this work not important?"

"It isn't as important as travelling with Rose and you back to your people. The work will wait. Travis, may even join us. He is good with a gun and knows how to track."

"Two white man accompanying Blackfoot braves may spell trouble for all of us. Your way in bringing justice is not the Blackfoot way. Little Brown Bear must die, and so must those that followed him into this abyss of eternal damnation. He has raped our women, his own women, and has killed Great Eagle, our father."

The Missing Years – Part I

"To kill or not to kill him, will be left up to you and your people; and to be clear Half Moon, I am not afraid to kill in the honour of my wife's family."

Half Moon could hear the sincerity in Mac's voice as he said that. "Alright then, we will travel the east wagon trail you speak of. We will rally some of my people and together we will find Great Eagle's killer." Half Moon brought his cup of coffee to his lips and swallowed a drink. "You, Mac Rider, are a friend of mine. You have taken good care of my sister and I trust your judgement. I am sorry for how I, and my people reacted when you took Rosalinda's hand in vow. I see now though that she is happy and has met a good man."

"Thank you for that, brother. Mac is all that you have said. And yes, I am happy," Rose reassured her brother.

"I thank you too Half Moon. I am relieved that we can now share respect for each other and that you have accepted Rose and my vows. It is appreciated. Thank you," Mac repeated as he took a drink from his coffee. "I will head up to Travis' in the morning and tell him what has happened, and that Rose and I are heading back with you. I'll let him decide if he wants to join us. Ultimately it will be up to him."

"I will ride with you to his place. I would like to thank him again, for guiding me here, he was very accommodating."

Mac nodded his head. "You would be more then welcome to tag along, Half Moon. I would enjoy the company." They sat in silence for a few moments as they drank their coffee, each of them in self-contemplation. Rose was wondering if she should mention that in her younger days she was also a victim of Little Brown Bear, or for that matter that Travis said he knew him. She decided now wasn't the time. Perhaps when it was all over, she would be able to talk about it without fear of retaliation that her father faced when he discovered Little Brown Bear's deviousness. Half Moon, on the other hand, was thinking about how he was going to kill Little Brown Bear, if he ever got the chance. Mac, was thinking about all the trouble he may have signed up for, but, to defend Rose's family and to help bring home the young women that Little Brown Bear had taken captive outweighed any feeling of doubt he might have. The blood and death that might follow was all part of the dilemma in doing the right thing in the eyes of the Blackfoot, which ultimately meant death to Little Brown Bear and his followers.

Meanwhile Tyrell was sitting at his own table, wondering how things were going down at Mac's. It was sad to know Rose's father had passed, how he passed, he didn't know. It mattered little then, death was death, men lived and men died. He didn't pry as he led Half Moon to Mac and Rose's, so he could only assume that Rose and Half Moon's father had died from old age or sickness. He would have never guessed that their father died at the hands of his once old friend Little Brown Bear. That alone would certainly put a lump in his throat and anger him even more when he found out why.

He now stirred the coals of his fire, and skewered the pieces of meat that he cut earlier that day onto the skewer. Then, he set the skewer in place on the spit. Opening a can of beans, he set the can onto the cooking grate and waited for his meal to cook. The tepee filled with the scents of cooking, and the flames hissed and grew brighter each time fat from the succulent meat dripped into them. He stirred his beans, and set them to the side away from the direct flames to keep warm, while he watched with anticipation as the tantalizing elk and bear meat

The Missing Years – Part I

slowly cooked. It took only a while longer for it to be ready and now he sat at his table with a plate of beans and meat. He ate only his beans and elk meat. The bear meat when it cooled found its way into Black Dog's dish, Tyrell never did have a taste for it. He finished his evening off with a pot of coffee as he settled in for the night. Black Dog lolled near the inside fire next to the table where Tyrell sat, quite content in gnawing the bear meat. "I'm glad I didn't have to waste that, you can have the rest that is up in that tree too," he said, as he took a swig from his coffee. "I haven't got a taste for that greasy stuff; it's too damn gamey and it stinks too."

Back at Mac and Rose's, the three of them came to terms with the news that Half Moon brought, they cried together, and laughed together, and were feeling better, although, still saddened deeply and angered on why it happened at all. They realised that there was nothing they could do. They could not turn back time, only move ahead and move ahead they would. Rose warmed up left over stew for their supper that night and baked fresh corn bread biscuits. Full now, they sat together as families do and conversed about the here and now.

Before they headed to bed that night, Mac and Half Moon led his horse, a beautiful painted stallion, into the corral and turned him loose with Lucy and the buckskin gelding. They watched the three horses for a short time as they played and showed off to one another. Then with heavy sighs and yawns, they headed back inside. Rose had cleaned up their supper dishes by then and a pot of tea, something Mac rarely drank, along with three pieces of cake sat on the table for their bedtime snack. Finally, the solemn and dreary night ended, and off to bed they went.

The news they brought to Tyrell that following morning about how and why Rose and Half Moon's father,

The Missing Years – Part I

Great Eagle, had died angered him. "I knew Little Brown Bear," he started as he looked at Mac. "I met him a couple of different times as I drifted when I was young. I don't think, he was that way then, but I could be wrong. I never met any of his kin nor did he ever invite me to his tribe. He was always alone. He did take me and a friend to a place of refuge one time. He said that he often went there to get away. Told us, only he knew about it; that he had never brought anyone else there. If he is running, it could be that place where he has gone," Tyrell suggested as a possibility. "I feel the same way as Half Moon does. He needs to be found before he hurts the girls more than he already likely has. Men like Little Brown Bear are dangerous." Tyrell averted his eyes as he reminisced. "Those that chose to follow him are only following his example."

"This place that you speak of where he has taken you, can you remember?" Half Moon asked.

"I think I could. It isn't near the prairies though. It is in the Rockies and hidden quite well; and I reckon by now, would take a lot of determination to get to. If Little Brown Bear has a bit of the man I knew him as still in him, then I know he's got determination and will be quite the adversary," Tyrell answered with informative concern.

"We will rally some of my people, more than those he has with him now, and we will be more of an adversary to him than he will be to us."

"To be quite honest, Half Moon, the more men that head into the Rockies, the greater chance he and his men have to get away. Little Brown Bear isn't stupid, out of the five men you say are with him, you can bet that two of them will be scouting, all day, every day. They will be on the lookout for anything unusual, and ten or so men heading into the Rockies will be unusual."

"You figure it is best to have fewer men?" Mac asked afraid to hear the answer.

"I do. That is exactly what I figure."

Mac shook his head. "I don't know, Travis. How do fewer men have an advantage?"

"Less chance of looking unusual, Mac; think about it. There are, as far as we know, only Little Brown Bear and five men. That's six men. Six men taken by surprise have a smaller chance of retaliating than six men lying in wait; seems logical to me," Tyrell shrugged. "Three or four men might go unnoticed. More men in my book equals a greater chance of being noticed especially at this time of year. The snow gives away secrets it also hides them."

"By that you mean their tracks that may have been left behind as they travelled, to this place in the Rockies, that is, if they did at all, are by now hidden, but ours will be visible." Half Moon contemplated as he nodded in agreement with Tyrell. "Yes, that does make sense."

"Humph, yeah, I see the point now too," Mac said as he looked up at the mountains. "I reckon we're going to need to be prepared. Do you have a guess on how long it might take?"

"From here, not a clue, but from the southeast side of the Rockies, three or four days would be a good educated guess. If we calculate the time it'll take us to get to Blackfoot territory and a day with their people, we should be able to be on top of Little Brown Bear in eleven or twelve days from when we leave. If he ain't in that area, then who knows, he might never be found. I guess what I'm trying to say, is that if he ain't where I think he might be, then it will be pointless to even try and look for him. He'll have twenty or more days on us, and could be as far away as the south Dakotas."

The Missing Years – Part I

The air grew still as the three of them contemplated all possibilities. Their only chance, it would seem, was if Little Brown Bear and his men were as Tyrell suspected at a secret spot only he knew how to get to, or if by chance they happened to come across him sooner than later.

Was it even worth the effort was now the big question. There was a slim chance that Tyrell was right, but there was also a chance that he wasn't, in which case the amount of time they would need to spend looking, would be time enough for Little Brown Bear to get into the Dakotas, or for that matter almost any other southern state. Tyrell finally broke the silence. "Now I have a question," he began as he looked at Mac. "If the two of us, are going to do this, Mac, who is going to look after your farm, and the bits and pieces up here?"

"Old Ben Westcott is our closest neighbour. He's looked after the place before, lives only a mile or so west of us. I ain't asked him yet, but, I'm pretty sure he will. If not, then I'll have to ask Sanders to send down one of his boys, to live on site until we get back. Friends and neighbours may be few and far between, but finding someone to look after what is yours, most will do it around here, if you ask," Mac replied with confidence.

"Okay, so that part is covered. I guess now we have to decide if we're going to do this. We know the possibilities, and we've discussed a few facts."

"Well, if we do, this work here will have to be put off for another month, cause that is about how long it'll take for us to get there, check the Rockies, and get back." Mac looked over to Tyrell, who was looking back and nodding.

"Yep, that's what I figure too. On a personal point of view, I have no problem checking the place out. We are talking human life; the two women that bastard has taken

The Missing Years – Part I

from the Blackfoot people need to be brought home safe. It will be worth our efforts if things pan out; it'll be waste of time if it doesn't." Again, silence and thought took over as the three of them sat.

"I have a question now," Half Moon started. "I met up with a man as I travelled here he asked if I have ever seen a man with a big horse, who travelled with a dog." Half Moon looked around to Pony, and then to Black Dog. "He introduced himself to me as," he fell silent as he tried to remember the name. "Ah, yes, Brubaker, I think. Do you know him?"

Tyrell's mind raced. That was the last name he wanted to hear. Indeed, he did know Brubaker. He was a hired gun. He didn't know him personally, only knew his reputation. If Brubaker was looking for him, then he needed to grow eyes on the back of his head. Brubaker was quick on the draw, but he also killed many by shooting them in the back. It didn't matter to him how he collected his pay whether in a fair fight or an ambush. He would be a formidable opponent, in a straight-out gunfight. Tyrell knew that much for certain, "Hmm, nope, can say as I have ever heard that name before," he fibbed as shook his head. "Which way was this fellow heading when you came across him?"

"He was going east over the Rockies, while I travelled west to here. Yesterday, when I arrived at this place, I noticed your dog and your horse, I thought maybe he was looking for you. Perhaps he was a friend I thought, that is why I asked now. Curious." Half Moon responded as he shrugged his shoulders.

"Nope, I don't know anyone that goes by that name. I imagine though, there are a few folks in the area, that might have a dog and big horse. I can't be the only one," he chuckled, as he looked over to Mac and then back to Half

The Missing Years – Part I

Moon. Things were going sideways now. A fellow like Brubaker looking for him, who happened to be heading east, the direction they would have to travel if they decided to hunt down Little Brown Bear, made Tyrell feel a little nervous. He wonder now how many more hired guns and killers, not to mention bounty hunters, were actually looking for him. He decided then that if they did try to track down Little Brown Bear, Black Dog would have to stay put at the tepee and Mac's farm. He was a dead giveaway for now. "Anyway, Mac, Half Moon, what do you guys figure. Are we going to track down Little Brown Bear?"

"I'm contemplating all the ifs, and buts, Travis. As you said, it could be a waste of a great deal of time. Could be we get lucky and set things right. To be honest, I ain't sure now. What about you Half Moon?"

"The Blackfoot will hunt him down with or without your counselling. He is a menace, a disgrace to the Blackfoot. We will not let him be until he is dead and our women are returned to their homes where they belong. I understand both yours and Travis's apprehension now. With all that we have talked about, I will not condemn either of you if your decision is no," Half Moon responded with conviction.

Mac removed his hat and fiddled with the brim as he contemplated. "Great Eagle was your and Rose's father. He was murdered by a coward whom Great Eagle was going to have expelled from the Blackfoot tribe for unorthodox conduct and perversion. That is how I understand it. Travis, already said that he is a dangerous man. He will only grow more so if he isn't stopped. I am already going to travel back with you for Rose's sake and to pay respect to Great Eagle, and condolences to your mother White Bird. I reckon since I'm already going to be there that my responsibility won't end there. I'll help track him down for as long as I can, a month might be fair to say."

"Well then, it is settled. I'm with you, Mac. I'll commit. I guess we're going to be heading into Blackfoot territory and a little bit of fun," Tyrell smiled.

"I'm not so sure it will be fun," Mac started as he looked at Tyrell. "But, I'll commit too." He now looked over to Half Moon. "You have our help, my friend."

Half Moon nodded with appreciation. "I am glad. The three of us," he said as he pointed at himself and then to Mac and Tyrell, "and Thunder Cloud, a friend of mine, will head into the Rockies. I will rally others to spread out to all four corners in small groups."

And, so it was, and so it would be. Mac and Half Moon left Tyrell's camp a short time later. Mac needed to make his way over to Ben's place to ask him to watch over the farm and the tepee, northeast of the farm, where the work was supposed to take place. Half Moon stayed behind with Rose and the two of them caught up on their lives since her marriage to Mac.

Mac returned later that day with good news. Ben had agreed to look after their place while they were gone.

Two days later in the early predawn, the entourage headed east. Before they left, Tyrell made it clear to Black Dog that this time his duty was to keep intruders and the animals away from both Mac's farm and the tepee. It was a simple task for Black Dog and he understood everything Tyrell told him. He wagged his tail and watched as Tyrell left him that morning, promising to come back as soon as possible.

Ben agreed that he would leave scraps out for the dog down at Mac's place, so there were no worries that the dog would go hungry. They picked up two canvas tents

The Missing Years – Part I

from Sanders as they passed, and some other gear as well to help make the trip as comfortable and safe as they could. They loaded the gear into Mac and Rose's horse cart, which as Mac said, was better than any wagon. It was both light and versatile, plus, there were skids for it so that it could traverse through snow. It floated as well which was another advantage. The only truly disadvantage was that it seated only two and couldn't haul a lot of weight. Other than that, it was Mac's preferred way of travel when travelling with Rose. Alone, he simply used a packing horse.

    The trail they travelled was scattered with the odd homestead and a stagecoach depot, which didn't operate through November to February because of the depth of the snow. It opened again in March, and at that time, only sporadic trips were made both east and west to other nearby outposts. The stagecoach ran full-time from June until November. It was closed now, but there was always a caretaker on duty. They knew that if they ran into any trouble they could seek help from homesteaders or the caretaker if need be. Surprisingly, they made the distance to Blackfoot territory in eight days, not the ten Mac had first thought. The trip in fact had been without incident. Now at the Blackfoot village, Rose's reunion with her mother, White Bird, and the mourning for her father, Great Eagle began.

The Missing Years – Part I

Chapter 13

The first night that they spent at the village turned out to be a celebration and a wake for Great Eagle. The fire that burned in the center of the village was big enough that its flames lit up the entire village. As it burned, Blackfoot braves and Blackfoot women danced into the wee hours of dawn, chanting prayer and hymns. Blackfoot elders told stories and buffalo hide drums and tam tams echoed across the prairie. It was quite the show of the solidarity and honour by which the Blackfoot lived.

Tyrell, Mac, Half Moon, and Thunder Cloud left for the Rockies the day after the festivities. Half Moon managed to rally together a few groups of Blackfoot braves, five in each group, and the groups spread out across the land, looking for any signs of Little Brown Bear and his band of Blackfoot renegades. It was decided that the groups would return to the village in five days, with or without Little Brown Bear, and wait for Half Moon and his group to return.

On the second day Half Moon's group made the distance to the shadows of the Rockies as the weather began to change. It grew cold quickly; wind and ice pellets forced them to seek shelter. For a day and a half, they were held hostage by the gruelling weather.

Finally, they were able to move on. The accumulated snow made traveling slow and dangerous. They tried to stay in the mountain scrub and bramble both for cover and to make the journey less perilous. The snow wasn't as deep in those areas, but there seemed to be more rock and steep terrain then cover. Above them and to the west, they could see where the evergreens met up with rock. Beyond that, Tyrell knew, was Little Big Bear's hideout. They couldn't tell if he and his men were there, and so far they hadn't found any clues that suggested they were, but that was to be expected. Any evidence would have disappeared by then due to the snow and the time that had passed since Little Brown Bear and his men fled. Half Moon and his fellow searchers wouldn't know one way or the other until they made the distance to the tree line above them a few miles away, and even after that there were two or three miles of bush bashing that lay ahead before they were close enough to do a thorough search on foot.

They rested the horses often whenever there was adequate cover. It was no easy feat. Not even their zigzagging technique made it any easier. On one occasion they led the horses and used rope to pull up their gear. Ever so slowly, they trudged on making their way up. It took the better part of a day before they were able to find suitable cover. They spent more time out in the open then they wanted as they traversed the rock bluffs and steep open field terrain of the mountain. Now, hidden from any possible view from above on a plateau that had a clump of thick fir trees, they rested. The horses, were no worse for wear, but they themselves were beat up some.

"Whew, that was certainly a pain in the ass," Tyrell said as he took a drink from his canteen, and looked down from whence they came.

"I feel good about this search. This is exactly the terrain I see Little Brown Bear heading into. He would know up here not many would want to follow," Thunder Cloud said, as he too looked down the mountain to the last ridge they stood on. "We have come up a long way since then," he added as he pointed.

"Yeah, we have," Mac said as he sighed. "I take it we have a way to go, eh Travis?"

Tyrell looked up at the tree line and nodded. "Yep, once we get up there, we need to cut northwest and travel another couple miles or so, until we come to a basin. Most of it is forest and the snow won't be as deep as it is out in the open," he pointed out. "If Little Brown Bear is up there, we'll be able to see his encampment or his fire at night from this side of it. There is enough cover that we can stay hidden."

"The tree line above is another two miles I would guess," Half Moon mentioned as the four continued their gaze looking up.

"Might even be further. Regardless though, that is where we need to go," Tyrell commented, as he looked around hoping to find an easier route.

"Are we going to continue on from here or set up for the night?" Mac questioned. "It is going to be dark soon," he added.

"Yes. That is a good point. I agree with you." Thunder Cloud said as he looked to the sky. "Soon, the weather might change. It may snow again tonight. That would be good; it would cover our tracks."

"This is a good place to set up an evening camp. We have cover and cannot be seen from above or from below," Half Moon mentioned.

"Yeah, I'd say so. Let's get the horses tethered and ourselves dug in. If bad weather is coming, then we better set up our tents or slap together a lean-to or *two*," Tyrell chuckled at his own joke, as they swung off their horses and tied them to trees. An hour later, the tents were in place out of the wind and view hidden by the clump of trees that grew on the plateau. "Might even get away with a little fire," Tyrell said as he looked at the tents. "I don't think the flames could be spotted, and smoke can't be seen too well at night from a small fire."

"Perhaps visually it would be hard to notice, but, what about scent?" Half Moon questioned.

The Missing Years – Part I

"I reckon if Little Brown Bear is up here, and he could smell smoke from a fire at three or four miles away, and on the other side of the mountain, then, I reckon he'd already know we're here." Tyrell answered as he smiled and shook his head. "A small fire will be okay, Half Moon. I assure you. We will use it for heat only and we will eat our beans cold. How does that sound?"

"I suppose you are right. Little Brown Bear might be a Blackfoot, a bear he is not. So, there is no reason to eat our beans cold, either," Half Moon said as he chuckled.

The four of them spanned out gathering fuel for the fire. Dry scrub was easy enough to find in and amongst the trees and in only a short time, they had enough sticks to start a fire once it got dark, and enough to keep it fuelled for a few hours. They set their saddles on their horse blankets that they tossed in a circle close to where the fire would be, so that they could have something to sit on rather than the partially snow-covered ground. The camp was as comfortable as they could get it, and so they sat and conversed.

During those moments when they grew silent and reminisced, the only sounds heard were the odd noises that their horses made. No fire burned, no coffee perked as smoke at that time of day would be noticeable. It was a simple precaution. The clothes they wore for now were sufficient to fight off the cooling temperatures at that altitude. Once it grew dark though, the ambient heat from a fire would indeed improve their comfort. For now, it was what it was.

In the time that Tyrell, Mac and Rose had been gone, Black Dog and old Ben had grown accustomed to each other and had quite a rapport. Ben kept him fed and Black Dog kept Ben safe and amused. Every morning at 6:00 a.m., Black Dog left the tepee and spent time down at

The Missing Years – Part I

Mac's, waiting and watching for old Ben to show, and every day Ben and his horse showed. He always brought with him any leftovers he had or could spare, and he laid them out for the dog while he checked on the young gelding, the few cows, and Mac's chickens. Every day when he left he always thanked the dog for cleaning his dishes, then with a smile he would prance off home.

That day though, Ben and his horse didn't show. Black Dog waited patiently on the porch for the entire day until it grew dark and then he headed back to the tepee. In the morning he would return, until then though, he knew his duty was to stay at the tepee. He whined and whimpered as he curled up on the tepee floor, anxious, concerned, and maybe even a little lonely. He found himself making his way back to the farm and the comfort of the animals that lived there.

He crawled through the rails of the corral and curled up in some hay that had been scattered and was next to the barn. The buckskin gelding it seemed was lonely too, and it made its way over to Black Dog and stood near him. The cows in the next pen over were not lonely. They had each other; however their stomachs were empty, and they mooed every now and again. The chickens, hungry as they were, but less lonely because there were more chickens then there were cows, squabbled, and clucked causing as much of a ruckus as they could. Black Dog inhaled deeply, curled up tighter, and fell asleep.

As it was now dark up on the mountain, Tyrell lit the fire. They melted snow to make coffee and to water the horses. Half Moon cooked Indian bread, and Mac worked on the beans, while Tyrell and Thunder Cloud tended to the horses.

"I was wondering, what breed is your horse?" Thunder Cloud asked.

The Missing Years – Part I

"I ain't sure to be honest. Some have suggested Hanoverian and Percheron cross. That is only speculation though. There ain't no way to know for sure."

"I have not heard of such a breed. We use prairie Mustang. They are swift and agile. They cannot carry as much weight as a horse as big as yours can."

"Yep, he can haul weight. He can pull stuff too. There are a lot of things about him that make him special," Tyrell smiled as he reminisced. "There were a few things I had to grow accustomed to, but I did. He too had to learn a thing or two about me as well, and had to learn how to cope them. We have an understanding."

Thunder Cloud chuckled. "Yes, I had to learn about my horse too."

"That is the thing about horses I suppose. We learn as we go." Tyrell nodded his head and smiled. "Well, I figure they have been fed and watered enough for now, let's get some eats into us." More than food though, Tyrell wanted a coffee. The food was a bonus.

"Yes. Good idea," Thunder Cloud responded as the two turned and made their way to the fire.

"We got beans and bread, and fresh coffee is brewing," Mac said as Tyrell and Thunder Cloud walked up to the fire and sat down on their saddles.

"I'll take a cup of coffee right off the get go," Tyrell said as he reached for the pot and poured himself one. Holding the pot, he asked if anyone else wanted one and filled their cups too. Mac scooped out beans and handed the plates around. The bread that Half Moon cooked was on a separate plate sitting next to the fire, and they helped themselves to it. As they ate, in the distance timber wolves began their evening choir, their howls answered by their own echoes. At times, it sounded as though the wolves were close and other times distant.

"The howl of a wolf, it is said, brings good luck to travellers. This the Blackfoot truly believe," Half Moon said. "Their voice keeps unwanted visitors away, visitors from both this world and the world beyond. We will be safe as we sleep tonight." The four sat there mesmerized by the wolves' howls and the gentle flames of the small fire that burned. They drank coffee and nibbled on bread reminiscing mostly on why they were there. There was no guaranteed outcome on how their confrontation with Little Brown Bear and his band of renegades, if indeed they were up there, would end up. Any of them could die. Perhaps the wolves that howled that night would be the last they ever heard.

Tyrell yawned and stretched, dumping what was left of his coffee onto the ground he stood up. "I'm heading to bed. It's been a long day, and I reckon tomorrow ain't going to be any shorter. Goodnight," he said, as he made his way over to his and Mac's tent crawled inside and curled up in his bedroll.

"Yeah, I think I'm going to follow Travis's example. See you in the morning, fellows," Mac said, as he crawled inside the tent and curled up in his own bedroll. "Reckon we'll make the distance to the top tomorrow, Travis?" Mac asked, as he made himself comfortable.

"Sure hope so, Mac," Tyrell replied as he stared up at the tent ceiling with his hands behind his head. "Only tomorrow knows, I reckon."

"I suppose you are right," Mac said as he rolled over and faced the tent wall. "Good night Travis."

"Goodnight Mac."

Half Moon and Thunder Cloud eventually found their way into their own tent as well, and as the four men slept that night, a cold wind outside began to moan bringing with it another early winter snowfall.

Chapter 14

The snow continued to fall as Tyrell rolled out of bed early the next morning and exited the tent. The first to rise, he shivered as he looked around. Six or more inches of fresh snow covered the ground. It was a dry snow, not wet, due to the abnormally dry and cold temperature.

To the east the sun did appear to be rising, and maybe in an hour or two things would warm up. Now though, as he stood relieving himself even his piss froze as it hit the ground.

"Damn, is it ever cold," he said as he zipped up his fly. Rubbing his hands together in hopes of warming them, he made his way over to the horses. They seemed to have survived. A little bit of frost covered their backs, but the tree branches had protected them against the dump of snow.

"Morning fellows," he began. "Must have been brutal for you guys out here last night, I heard the wind, but didn't bother to see if it were snowing. It did though, by God, near six inches maybe more. I'll gather you some grain, hang on," he said, as he retrieved grain and fed them.

Mac was up by now and he stretched as he inhaled the cool fresh air. "Shit, it snowed again last night didn't it?"

"You noticed that eh?' Tyrell joked, as he made his way over to where Mac stood. "It's damn awful cold too. The sun though, I reckon, will warm things up in a bit. We best get them Blackfoot woken up." He walked over to their tent and pulled out a peg so the top fell in. He could here Half Moon and Thunder Cloud rustling inside and cursing. "Rise and shine," he chuckled as Half Moon stuck his head out and cursed him.

"Could you not have simply woke us up?" Half Moon questioned, as he crawled out, followed by Thunder Cloud.

"I could have, but that was more fun," Tyrell smiled as he walked away and sat down.

"White man is crazy," Thunder Cloud said, as he stood beside Half Moon and rubbed his eyes. Less than an hour later, the foursome were packed up, and moving up the slope to the tree line. It was cold and their hands felt as though they were freezing. "Soon the sun will take away the chill in our hands. I hope," Thunder Cloud mentioned, as they stopped for a moment to let the horses rest.

Down on Mac's farm, Black Dog as usual sat on Mac's porch that morning waiting for the man and his horse to show. It seemed like forever. Finally, curiosity and concern led him in the direction Ben and his horse always came from. He wagged his tail in excitement and relief when he finally saw the man and horse coming around the corner. "What's a matter there dog? I ain't forgot about you, I missed a day though. The colder the weather gets, the slower I roll out of bed," Ben chuckled. "Still, I try to get done in a day, what I need to get done. Yesterday though, I had a pressing concern that I was getting low on supplies, so I had to go to the mercantile. I'm here now and brought you some leftovers," he said as he sped his horse up. Black Dog trailed behind, his nose in the air, trying to scent what Ben might have for him.

Ben slowed his horse down and swung off. He led him to the horse pole and tethered him. Black Dog sat near wagging his tail and waited. Finally, Ben pulled out the lard can from his saddlebag that he used to put leftovers in. "I brought you stew today, my friend." He set the can down for the dog. "You go ahead and eat that all up, and I'll get on with the chores. Not sure what I'm supposed to do with

The Missing Years – Part I

all the eggs I've been gathering, but I'm taking a dozen with me today," he said as he strolled off and carried on with the chores. It took a few minutes and when he was done, he sat on the porch with Black Dog.

"All is well here, my friend. The cows are fed, and watered; so are the chickens, and that gelding too, they are all happy now. I shouldn't be late again," he started as he looked around making sure he didn't forget anything. "Yep, it won't be long before Mac and Rose return. Then you might not see me as often, but, I do come around every now and again and when I do, I'll expect to see you from time to time." He stood up and untied his horse, "I'll see you in the morning. Stay warm. My bones tell me that tonight is going to be cold." Turning his horse, he set off for home. Black Dog stuck around for a few minutes longer and as the sun began to shine, he made his way back to the tepee, marking his territory here and there. He walked the perimeter making sure everything and every scent was as it were when he left. Satisfied, he made his way in through the tepee entrance and curled up for a morning nap. *Loneliness.*

By now Tyrell, Mac, Half Moon, and Thunder Cloud were less than a quarter of a mile away from the tree line they needed to reach. The sun was bright and yellow making the snow a blinding issue. Thunder Cloud found a birch tree and peeled a few pieces bark off, cutting eye slits into them. He handed them out. "Tie these around your eyes. It will help prevent snow blindness. Snow like this and sun like that will hurt your eyes." He tied his around his head and the others followed suit. It worked like a damn and Tyrell was impressed.

"That is quite the thing. Thanks for showing this to me, damn. Least now we can carry on without having to squint. Can see everything now," he commented as he looked around. "Yep, I'll remember this little trick."

The Missing Years – Part I

"White men are used to snow glasses, I think. Blackfoot, though, they use what nature provides," Thunder Cloud said with a smile, as he now removed the birch bark tied around his head, and removed from his saddlebag a pair of dark glasses. "I only had one pair, so those who forget what snow can do to the eyes, use birch bark like that."

"Now where did you pick those up, Thunder Cloud? I thought you said you were a Blackfoot?" Tyrell chortled.

"I am, but I am not stupid."

"Nor am I, but I ain't got a nothing like that. You buy those in a store, or what?"

"Not so much," Thunder Cloud responded.

"You made them then."

"Nope."

"Well if you didn't buy them in a store and you didn't make them, you must have stolen them," Tyrell teased.

"A man who crossed me had them on. When he died, I took them. Not stolen, reused." He looked at Tyrell and smiled. All Tyrell could do was look back at him and shake his head. Even with his usual quick wit, he was witless.

"Killed a man for glasses eh, humph, and you said us white men are crazy." That was all Tyrell could come up with, he chuckled as they continued onward. A more serious tone now enveloped them as they crested the last plateau before the tree line. Tyrell slowed Pony to a halt and waited for the others to pull up next to him. "All right, from here we go up one rider and horse at a time, and keep our voices low. I'll head up first, once I get Pony settled I'll come to where you'll be able to see me," he pointed to where he would stand. "Right there I reckon, I'll have a good view of you and you'll be able to see me."

"Why one-rider at a time?" Mac asked.

"If by chance Little Brown Bear is up here, and if by chance, there is a scout out right now, they might hear sixteen sets of horse hooves trudging up. One rider won't be as noisy as four." Tyrell replied, as he and Pony headed up. The three of them remained on their horses as they watched Tyrell crest the plateau, it took a few minutes for him to return on foot and signal for the next rider to come up. The process took some time and when they were all together at the top, and their horses tethered, the four huddled close and discussed their approach as they took a deserved rest.

From there on, they would need to lead their horses, or leave them tethered. Tyrell had overestimated the distance to the basin, but not until he made it to the top where they sat now, did he realise that they were closer than he originally thought. They would have to hike on foot for a couple hundred feet before they could determine that Little Brown Bear and his men were in the area. Satisfied with the plan to do some scouting, they spread out and headed west keeping each other in constant view. It didn't take long for the story to unfold. In the distance they could see smoke rising. Tyrell signalled for them to head back to the horses.

It took a few minutes to get back, but once they did, they decided at first sign of dusk they would make their move. Their plan was that one of them would get the women safe and out of harm's way before they went in with guns blazing. The hope was they could pull it off without anyone knowing. Once the women were safe, it would be open season. If they were caught or otherwise noticed, then whoever was closest to the women would work on getting them out; and the others would fight tooth

The Missing Years – Part I

and nail and do their best to keep whoever that might be and the women covered, killing the renegades regardless.

It would be safer, they knew, if all four could be fighting the same battle and the women were safe beforehand, but sometimes plans didn't always pan out. They would keep two of the horses as well so the women could ride out. The terrain they were in was not made for doubling. The other horses they would shoo away. As for the dead, well, as far as they were concerned the animals could have their way, with one exception; Little Brown Bear's head, Half Moon wanted that on a pike. Although Mac and Tyrell cringed at the thought, they weren't going to try and sway him otherwise. He was quite adamant so they left it at that. It was what it was.

With their plan in place, the long wait for dusk began. Tyrell pulled out his pocket watch and looked at the time it was 11:00 a.m., they had six hours to sit and wait. "Might as well get comfortable, we got a long wait till dusk," he said almost silently, but loud enough for the others to hear. They were hidden from prying eyes, but they could see an approach by anyone that may be out and about looking around.

"I'm certainly glad that the sun is warm, six hours would be a long wait in the cold." Tyrell kicked away snow as he tossed his horse blanket on the ground next to a tree. He set his saddle on the blanket and sat. The others followed his example and they were soon all seated their backs to trees.

The distance between them wasn't that far and when they spoke they spoke quietly. When they didn't speak, they sat and contemplated, each of them wondering if they would even make it off the mountain. Six men against four was a slight disadvantage for them, but they had the element of surprise. As far as they knew no one had seen them, and their advantage was they knew someone other than themselves were up there and that they were not far from where the four of them now sat in wait.

"Is it not wise for one of us to go have a closer look?" Thunder Cloud asked.

"It might be. Problem is Little Brown Bear knows three of us, and if he saw either you or Half Moon, he would know your reasons for being here. If he saw me, he might wonder the same. The only one that he don't know by sight is Mac, and I'm sure Mac, don't want to be skulking through the bush alone. Not even I would want to do that. Little Brown Bear as I have said before, and you should know, ain't stupid. If he happened to see Mac and for a moment thought that Mac might be a threat, Mac would die. I say we wait. It is safer that we head that way at dusk, side by each. That way, we can keep each other covered. I don't know about you Thunder Cloud, but I still like to think I have something worth living for."

"Yes. Okay, white man. We wait."

"Yep, I reckon, that be best," Tyrell said, as he tilted his hat over his eyes and rested. What the four of them couldn't know is that Little Brown Bear and the five Blackfoot braves, had already been taken care of. They weren't dead. They were tied and tethered to trees. The two women waited patiently for the opportunity to pounce and when it came, they pounced. The men tied now for three days sat in their own filth. Only the trees gave them shelter when it snowed, and their only source of heat was the fire that the women kept burning near where the six of them sat. They tried to struggle loose on a few occasions, and every time they did, the women tied them tighter. There was no escape. Unarmed and immobile all they could do is sit and wait for whatever the outcome may be.

The Missing Years – Part I

What they were going to do with the men, the women weren't certain, but they did discuss the possibility of trudging out of the mountains with them in tow. The only problem was, they were two horses short of the eight they would need to make the distance safely. Instead, they would wait for better weather and one would head back to the Blackfoot village and get help. Until then, they had shelter, food and weapons. They were by no means in dire need of anything; everything they needed was already there. In fact, they could hold out until spring with all that they did have. Over the years, Little Brown Bear stowed enough food for that. The men however would die long before then, and if it did turn out that way, the women would simply drag them, one by one, as they died, deep into the mountain and let their corpses feed the animals. What the women had no way of knowing was that less than a quarter of a mile away a search and rescue team lay in wait, and at dusk, they would approach.

For now, the women, Willow-Bow and Light Feather, went about their daily routine, checking on their prisoners, feeding the horses and prepping for night. The threats from the men went unnoticed, it was all talk. There was nothing they could do to the two of them. They were tied and tethered and not a threat at all.

"You speak as though your words of anger and insult will frighten us. They do not. We, Light Feather and I, do not fear you. Keep that in mind as you try to fight what it is that you do not like," Willow-Bow said, as she traipsed by checking the knots that bind them. "You are pathetic weak men," she said conclusively. The men grew silent with rage and hatred. Willow-Bow was right there was nothing they could do.

Light Feather stood beside Willow-Bow now. "You six will face Tribal Counsel. You will be branded and

The Missing Years – Part I

exiled by the Blackfoot elders. That is your fate. Try to escape and you will die at the hands of women. The spirit world would then laugh at you for eternity, for there is no honour in dying at the hands of meagre women. However, meagre, we are not; you six are," she said, as the two of them now turned and made their way back to the warming glow of their own fire that burned near the cabin that Little Brown Bear built up over the years. Built into the west slope of the basin the cabin was barely noticeable unless one knew it was there.

Inside was a wood stove that he had hiked in years earlier. There were a few chairs and a small table, built from poles that he gathered over the course of time that it took him to build the shelter. It was built to withstand the coldest winter weather and the hottest summer temperatures. It was his refuge, but it no longer served him, it served women. Tied to a tree and left out in the elements, sitting in his own bodily waste, he half-wished he would die. Anything was better than the humiliation of sitting in his own filth or being forced to face a Tribal Counsel for his ungodly deeds. Worse yet, he had been relieved of his power by two women, that fooled him and his men. Death in his mind would be a godsend. He looked up to the yellow sun and let its warmth caress his face, as he prayed for death.

As the day progressed, Tyrell and the others rested lazily, and mingled. They spoke sporadically in low voices, their conversation nothing more than a way to pass time. The sun was at its warmest now and they sat beneath its rays alert and ready for any confrontation from a renegade Blackfoot scout that may spring out at them, but none came. The only thing that alerted them was the dead calm that shrouded the mountain. That seemed odd to them. Other than the movement from a small herd of elk that they had been watching were the only things moving on the mountain. "I would have thought that by now we would have had a run in with a scout. Little Brown Bear, if it is indeed him over yonder, has for one reason or another let his guard down I think. It don't seem right to me," Tyrell said with uneasiness.

Mac looked to the west. Smoke continued to rise and so whoever it was that had a fire burning was still there. "Maybe he thinks that he has been here long enough already that he doesn't need a scout running around. It has been well over twenty days since the incident."

"Could be that is true," Tyrell stated as he too now looked west. "Where there is smoke there are folk. Who them folk might be, we ain't going to know for a bit."

"Perhaps, a scout has already seen us, and they are planning an attack," Thunder Cloud brought to their attention.

Half Moon looked at Thunder Cloud and countered. "I have kept my eyes and senses alert to all sounds. The four of us, I would think would have been alerted after all four sets of eyes are watching, and we have been hidden. Not even the elk know we are here."

"Yes. That is true," Thunder Cloud admitted. "But there are some hours left in the day, anything could happen before dusk."

"My watch reads, 4:00 p.m.; maybe an hour left before dusk," Mac said as he looked back at them. "I reckon we should go over our plan one more time, check our weapon's and prepare for what is to come. We ain't decided which of us is going to enter the encampment and look for the women. We need to get them to safety, and like we talked about before, once that is out of the way, we simply go in shooting and eradicate the dirt that is down there," Mac said, referring to Little Brown Bear and his men.

"That is about the gist of it, yep." Tyrell responded. "I reckon the women would be more inclined to follow instruction from Half Moon or Thunder Cloud." He looked at them both. "So which of you wants the task?"

"I will do it," Half Moon said. "Thunder Cloud is good with rifle. I am good with knife."

"We'll all approach at the same time, but, once we have a visual, you go ahead Half Moon and the three of us will encircle them in a half moon shape," Tyrell chuckled. "I didn't mean nothing by that, but it sure came out as though I were making a funny. That isn't the case though, what I meant is we can't be on either side of the encampment and open fire we'd end up shooting ourselves in the cross fire." He paused for a moment as he caught his breath. "I'll take center course, Mac and Thunder Cloud on either side a distance apart, and we'll wait for it to be clear, once you get the women to safety make your way back to where we'll be, and we'll finish what it is that we came here to do." All in agreement, they sat in silence as they checked their weapons. Loaded and ready they slowly made their way to the basin. It was turning to dusk when they finally made the distance, getting in position, Tyrell signalled for Half Moon to descend upon the camp. He watched as Half Moon, disappeared into the bramble, and then bobbed up his head, as he got closer. He had a clear view of the camp now, but only saw the two women. Looking back in Tyrell's direction, he shrugged. Then once more disappeared from Tyrell's view, Tyrell never saw him again until he snuck up behind him.

"Only the women, I saw." Half Moon said beneath his breath in a whisper.

"No men?"

"None I could see, from where I stood." He looked over to where Thunder Cloud was, who was signalling him that he had visual of the men, and smiling. Half Moon nudged Tyrell and pointed. Tyrell looked and then signalled for Thunder Cloud to come over, to fill them in. Mac held point and watched this from his vantage point. He saw neither the men nor the women, only the smoke from two fires. He waited and watched as Thunder Cloud now approached Tyrell and Half Moon.

Thunder Cloud was chuckling quietly as he made the distance to where Tyrell and Half Moon were crouched.

"What is so funny?" Tyrell asked as Thunder Cloud came within whispering distance.

"The men, Little Brown Bear, and the five others, are tied to trees." He was still chuckling as he said that.

"What? Tied to trees?" Now all three of them began to chuckle as Tyrell signalled for Mac to come down to where they were and they filled him in on what Thunder Cloud saw.

"Jesus Christ, that is funny ain't it?" he concluded in a whisper as he too now laughed quietly. "I can't wait to find out how that happened. Shit, I guess Little Brown Bear and his men ain't so astute after all." He added as he looked up to Tyrell and the others who were crouching there looking behind him as though they had seen a ghost. Mac slowly turned around to be face to face with the bore of a rifle. The women holding it smiled.

"Thunder Cloud and Half Moon, it took you long enough," she said as she lowered the rifle.

"Light Feather, it is good to see you," Half Moon said, as he stood and the others followed suit. "These are my friends." He pointed at Mac. "He is the one that took vow with my sister; his name is Mac, and this is Travis, he works for Mac."

"It is a pleasure to meet you," Light Feather said as she shook their hands. "How did you know to look here?" she asked.

"Travis knew Little Brown Bear years ago. He travelled here once before with him. That is all I know," Half Moon answered.

Light Feather looked at Travis. "You were friends with Little Brown Bear?"

"Maybe at one time perhaps; not anymore, it was a long time ago."

"I see. Willow-Bow, come out. It is safe."

Willow-Bow slid around to the front of the tree that she had been hiding behind. "Yes, I see now it is Thunder Cloud and Half Moon, with two white men. Come, the fire is warm." She said as she turned and walked back to the camp, the others following close behind.

Approaching the camp Half Moon walked briskly to where he could see then men were tied, Tyrell on his heels. Removing his machete, he looked into Little Brown Bear's eyes. "Since the death of my father Great Eagle, I have waited for this day."

Tyrell by now was standing only a few paces away, he locked eyes with Little Brown Bear, who was about to say something, but, in one fatal swing Half Moon decapitated him with such voracity the blade of his machete hit the tree behind with a thud and stuck there. Little Brown Bear's head fell from his shoulders as blood spewed up from the grotesque wound and rolled down an incline to Tyrell's feet coming to halt as it hit his boots.

Tyrell jumped back. "Really? Did that just happen? Holy Christ, Half Moon! Couldn't you have at least waited until I was out of the way?" Tyrell questioned in both shock and awe at the brutality.

The five other men started to chant the Blackfoot death chant waiting for the same fate. Half Moon turned and walked away, grabbing Little Brown Bear's bodiless head. "I have my trophy now. The Blackfoot will be safe from this menace. The five of you," he started, "will not leave this mountain with us. The trees you are tied to are your fate." The five Blackfoot braves continued with their chant hoping for a quick death, but none would come. They would die from the elements and starvation. That is what they had to look forward to.

"What?" Mac asked. "Are we going to leave them here?"

"Half Moon is right," Thunder Cloud interjected. "They do not deserve anything more."

"What about Tribal Counsel and suitable justice?" Mac questioned. He wasn't sure he liked the idea of leaving them there to die.

"This is suitable justice, Mac." Tyrell replied. "Whether we like the idea or not, in the eyes of the Blackfoot, they sealed their fate when they chose to flee with Little Brown Bear. Besides, we were going to kill them anyway. You knew that."

"Yeah, but that was when we thought they were armed and would be shooting back. I think there is a difference, since, they are tied and tethered."

"We could always give them a gun, and then shoot them," Thunder Cloud said, with a smile.

"Shit. I think the whole lot of you are crazy," Mac half chuckled, "but I guess if this is how it is going to be, then I ain't going to argue on their behalf." He turned and walked away over to the fire where the women stood looking on. Sitting with a heavy sigh, he warmed his hands. Meanwhile, Half Moon gathered two of the six horses and tethered them, then removing the reins and bridals from the

The Missing Years – Part I

remaining four he shooed them off, they would make their own way back to the Blackfoot village if they decided, or herd up with the other mustangs down on the prairie. Either way, he cared little, the horses were no longer their problem. They were free to do whatever it is they wanted.

The four men and the two women congregated near the fire, a pot of stew cooking over the flames. "It is too late to leave tonight, but there is plenty of room inside for us all." Willow-Bow pointed out. "You men must be hungry. Eat stew and rest now; the ordeal you have put yourselves through to come to this place I think has made you weary."

"That about sums it up for me," Tyrell said. "And that stew does look tantalising. We'll rest tonight and head back in the morning." He looked around. "Little Brown Bear has done a lot of work here it looks like."

"Yes, but before we leave this place, we will tear it all down and burn it, leaving nothing for those five, if they manage to release themselves," Light Feather said, as she set the rifle she was holding up against the cabin wall. For Mac, it all seemed like a waste, but he wasn't about to make a case out of it. He already knew how that would turn out. Light Feather now sat down and warmed her own hands above the fire. "You took vow with Rosalinda Running Creek, yes?" she questioned to confirm and to make conversation.

"That I did," Mac replied.

"She has been gone from here for a long time. I was young when she left, but I knew her. It will be nice to see her again. You though, seem withdrawn."

"Naturally, Great Eagle was Rose's father, and I just watched her brother cut the head off one of his own people. That, and the fact that it has been decided that those five who keep chanting that awful chant ain't going nowhere, and that they will die right there, kind of puts me in a saddened mood."

"It shouldn't. They deserve what they have coming. They have ravished many of us women and have killed your woman's father."

"I suppose you are right, and maybe I am over reacting. It doesn't seem right, that's all."

"I think you are a man with a kind heart, but for today, let it go."

Mac looked at her and nodded. "I'll do my best, but I don't condone it."

"That is fine," Light Feather replied. "Do not condemn our ways either. They may be different from yours, but we all live under the same principles of life, or principles that closely resemble those by which we live. The Blackfoot say this; 'Do not disrespect your mother or father. Do not take what you do not need. Share with the less fortunate the good fortune that you may have. Fight with honour for truth and justice. Do not practice corruption, incest or rape. Protect women and children from bad men. Kill before getting killed'." She averted her eyes and looked at Travis, now as well. "Those are the words I want to offer to you both." Again, she paused as they all sat there and mulled over what she had said.

Mac understood all the lines. Rose had said the same thing on occasion. Perhaps a few lines were added here or there, but it all meant the same thing; that much he knew. Tyrell, understood them too. They were the basic life values that each culture taught their children and lived by. He nodded his acknowledgement to Light Feather's words. "Now that I have said what I felt I needed to say. I hope you can understand the importance of not condemning our ways. Those five men did not live by those words. They

The Missing Years – Part I

participated willingly in Little Brown Bear's perversions, corruption, and dishonour. Have no remorse for them."

Mac inhaled deeply as he removed his hat and wiped his brow. "When you say it like that, Light Feather, I understand completely. I will not be regretful for whatever happens to them."

"Good. Now let's eat stew and talk about happier things," Willow-Bow spoke out.

"I'm with you on that," Tyrell commented as Willow-Bow slopped out a bowlful and handed it to him. Taking it from her, he nodded his thanks. Bringing the steaming bowl up to his nose, he inhaled the heavenly scent. Sitting again, he began to eat while Willow-Bow handed out more to the others; and so the evening progressed.

At the crack-of-dawn, they tore down Little Brown Bear's cabin. They piled up all the debris, and with the coals from their past evening's fire, they torched the pile. The five Blackfoot braves, now sick with fever and hunger, could only watch as Half Moon and the others left the area, leaving them tied and tethered. This was their fate. Before Half Moon and the others made the distance back to the Blackfoot village four days later, with Little Brown Bear's head in a sack, the five braves perished. They had been given a slow and agonizing death. Frozen and starved, and tied to trees, their bodies now fed the animals.

Half Moon and Thunder Cloud received great honours from the Blackfoot chief and Blackfoot elders for the success of their journey to find their captive women and to bring Little Brown Bear and his followers to justice. Thanks was also given to Tyrell and Mac, and their names would always be held in great regard by the Blackfoot people. Mac not satisfied with how they left the five Blackfoot braves and Little Brown Bear tied to trees, sought counsel with Chief Red Water, and pled his case. Red Water agreed that the Blackfoot would return to the place and retrieve any remains when the snows melted and fields of green once more grew. Chief Red Water made it clear that the five, as well as the headless body of Little Brown Bear; would not be buried the traditional way of the Blackfoot. Instead, they would be buried without religious ritual, and only a simple cross would mark their bones final resting place, in the area where they died.

The Missing Years – Part I

Chapter 15

Rose's mother, White Bird, finally gave Rose and Mac her blessing. The Blackfoot held a mock wedding in the traditional manner of their tribe. Although Mac and Rose had taken their vows years earlier, they now took them in the marriage circle of the Blackfoot. On November 14th, Tyrell, Mac, and Rose left the Blackfoot village and headed west arriving home on November 22nd.

"There it is, there's home," Mac said as their house came into view. "I can hardly wait to sleep in my own bed."

"I can hardly wait for the same, plus, I need to see Black Dog. Hard to believe I missed him," Tyrell chuckled. "I'll help get you unloaded, and then head to the tepee. Sure hope it is still standing. Looks like we've had quite the weather change around here. The snow is really deep," Tyrell said as he swung off Pony. As soon as he dismounted along came Black Dog bounding to his side, wagging his tail and jumping all over the place. "Hey, Black Dog, sure nice to see you. How you been faring? Looks like Ben has been keeping you well fed," Tyrell said, as he knelt down and wrapped his arms around Black Dog's shoulders giving him an *'I sure missed you,'* hug. Black Dog licked his face and ran in circles chasing his tail, showing Tyrell how much he too missed him. "Things feel good already, Mac. Sure nice to be back here," Tyrell said, as he now helped Mac unload the gear.

"Yeah, it sure does feel good. Quite the journey both ways. I'm glad it is over, in more ways than one," Mac said, as he handed Tyrell another armload of gear.

Rose, by now, had the woodstove lit inside and was making coffee. She looked through the house making sure all was good. Other than the build up of mouse poop and dust, the place was no worse for wear. "Yuk," she said, as she looked at the droppings. "We need a cat, I think. Disgusting little vermin," she said, referring to the mice that were obviously quite busy while they were gone. She quickly cleaned the mess, straightening up the rest of the house as she went. She was glad to be home.

With all the gear unloaded and stacked on the porch, Mac led Lucy to the corral and turned her loose. The gelding met her, snorting and neighing as it welcomed her back. Mac and Tyrell watched for a few minutes as the two horses bucked and snorted. Lucy too, was glad to be home. "I reckon Rose has coffee on. Care to join us for one? It's been a long trip."

"Well, I see Black Dog is lying on the porch, and seems content. Sure, I'll have a quick cup," Tyrell answered.

A few minutes later they were sitting at the table, drinking coffee and talking about their journey and things that went on. "I tell you Travis, I don't ever want to have to go through all that again. I can't believe half of what I saw. The way Half Moon reacted to Little Brown Bear and those five others, I reckon that'll be in my dreams for a while."

"Forget about it, Mac. The Blackfoot have their ways as we have ours," Rose said, as she took a drink from her coffee.

"Yeah, I agree with Rose, Mac. Forget about it. We hang our hoodlums and that is a type of punishment. The Blackfoot do it differently. Get it out of your head, my friend."

"I know. Our way, I suppose, seems a little bit more civilised, that's all."

"Civilised it might be, but it is still death. I remember how Little Brown Bear's head rolled into my boot, with that dead look of shock on his face. I'll always

The Missing Years – Part I

remember that. I saw a hanging one time which wasn't as quick as the death Half Moon offered Little Brown Bear, so I ask myself which way is more humane, to be hung or beheaded? I reckon they're both terrible ways to go, but with the same results." Tyrell finished the last of his coffee and set his empty cup down. "Anyway, Mac, Rose, I'm going to head out. There is likely an array of things I need to do up at the tepee, and Mac, forget about it." Tyrell said referring to the death of Little Brown Bear and the five others.

"Not sure I'll ever forget, but I don't see much point to talk about it anymore." He waved his hand through the air, "I won't mention it again."

"Yeah, alright, neither will I. Anyway, I guess I should get."

"Okay, Travis. I'll swing up in a day or two, once I get things in order again down here. We still got land to clear," Mac said, with a smile.

Tyrell nodded. "Yep, we do." Donning his hat, he bid them *'good night'* and headed for his own little piece of paradise.

The tepee was a welcoming sight as it came into view. Considering the length of time he had been gone, he was quite surprised that it was still standing. Dismounting, he led Pony to his own corral and turned him loose. Even Pony was glad to be home. Tyrell looked around at the amount it had snowed since he had been gone. It gave a different look and feel to the place. The snow made everything look so clean and untouched. It was beautiful in a sense and at the same time ominous. The big cedar trees added a splash of green to the white background of the glistening snow, and the bright rays of the sun made it look like millions of diamonds were scattered across the virgin surface of the untouched winter beauty. There was no doubt the snow was there to stay. He inhaled deeply. *Sure missed being here, and am sure glad to be back,* he thought, as he made his way over to the tepee, half-expecting to find vermin inside, but the place wasn't much different from when he left, and he sighed in relief.

Walking over to the table, he removed his holster and set it down, pulling up a chair he sat and rested before the task of unloading his gear. Black Dog made his way inside and lay on the floor at Tyrell's side. In only a few minutes, he was fast asleep, having the best sleep he had since Tyrell had been gone. Looking at his pocket watch Tyrell wound the dial. It was 2:00 p.m. There was plenty of time to unload, gather wood and light the wood stove for the steam bath, which he desperately wanted to have.

First, though, he wanted to do a quick walk around outside and check on the elk meat that hung in the tree. The cold weather, he hoped, kept it edible. Lowering the rope it hung by, he looked the meat over. It didn't look nor did it smell bad and he cut a chunk off. He strung it back up and lowered the bear meat and repeated the same process. Once it thawed, he would have a better idea if it were safe for his consumption, or if it was Black Dog's now. He set the two pieces on a plate and set the plate on the table inside his tepee. Gathering wood, he lit a fire inside, then made his way over to the steam bath. Filling the tub with clean water after chopping through the ice that covered the creek, he lit the wood stove. Looking towards the mountains, he could see the grey clouds that shrouded them, and high in the trees he could see their tops swaying in the wind. More snow, he knew, was on its way.

By the time his steam bath was ready, he could see his breath in the air as he made his way to it. *Going to be cold this evening, I reckon,* he thought, as he opened the door and stepped inside. The instant heat was gratifying.

He removed his clothes, and sat on the bench and sweated. Pouring water over the rocks, he let the steam encase him in a warm embrace. Dumping water over his head, he scrubbed his skin with soap and washed his hair. Wiping the condensation off his shaving mirror, he looked into it and studied his face. For a brief moment in time, his mind filled with memories of Marissa, and he felt a tear well up in his eye. *What could have been, may still someday be,* he thought, as he now lathered his face with shaving soap, and spent a few minutes having a shave. Clean now and relaxed, he dressed and walked back to the tepee.

Black Dog hadn't moved and as he pulled up a chair and sat at the table, he smiled. *The only thing missing is Marissa. Shit, I got to quick thinking about her, but every time I see a woman, I see her...* he reminisced. *I blame those two idiots, Heath and Ollie, sons-of-bitches should never have pulled their pistols on me, I would have spent some time in Hells Bottom and would have likely returned to Red Rock by now, if only to see Marissa one more time. Damn, life sometimes sure goes awry. I wonder if she ever thinks about me as often as I think about her.*

Indeed Marissa did. In fact, at the same time he was thinking about her, she was thinking about him. Her five month baby bump made her think of him more often than Tyrell would ever know.

As he sat there in contemplation the sound of heavy snow falling on the tepee became more audible than the low burning fire. He looked up through the smoke flap and watched as the flakes danced their way to earth. They weren't small fluttering flakes but more like large wet balls of cotton. The clouds in the sky were black-grey and they floated across the surface as though they were in a race to collide with one another. It was the high wind that blew, that pushed them forcing them to mash into one big cloud

The Missing Years – Part I

of darkness and snow. He tossed another stick on the fire and set his coffee pot to brew.

The meat on the table had thawed by now and he brought the plate up to his nose and smelled it. As far as he was concerned, it was as fit for human consumption as it was on the day he left. Skewering it, he set it on the spit to cook. It didn't take long for the smell of cooking meat and perking coffee to fill the tepee with its tantalizing scents of home. The bear meat he put on a separate plate and waited for it to cool before handing it off to Black Dog, who by now had woken up, refreshed, revived, and happy that he hadn't been dreaming about Tyrell's return. Finishing with his last swallow of both coffee and elk meat, Tyrell rose from the table and ventured outside. It was getting dark and the air was cold, the wind now blew down low and the trees around his camp swayed back and forth.

His hat flew off his head and skidded across the snow, finally stopping a few feet away. Picking it up he put it back on his head and pulled it down tight. Making his way over to Pony, he brought him some grain and waited as the horse finished. "Sure windy out, eh Pony?" he said, above the howling wind. "Going to be a cold one tonight I think. I'll put a couple of blankets on you, as soon as you finish up there with them oats. Good thing you have these cedars for protection, they'll keep the snow off." He looked around, squinting. His eyes stung as the wind and snow blasted his face. The forest surrounding his place was dark and frozen, and he sighed as he took the empty bucket from Pony and set it with the grain, noting he was running low. *Going to have to get some hay up here soon, I reckon,* he thought as he set the bucket down and covered the sack with a tarp.

Retrieving a couple of horse blankets, he fitted them across Pony's back and tied them around his stomach.

"There, that ought to keep the heat in. I don't reckon the weather is going to stay like this, but I bet it will for a day or two. Once it clears off, I'll see if Mac has some more old lumber and I'll toss up a bit of a shelter or wind break for you. For now, I reckon the blankets will have to do." He rubbed Pony's head with his knuckles, then bade him good night. "I'll see you in the morning Pony. I got to get wood inside, and unload my gear still. Stay dry," he said as he made his way over to the woodpile and stowed a few more pieces inside.

Next, he made his way over to his saddlebags that sat on the floor of the tepee and removed his bedroll and the few pieces of gear he carried with him when they headed to the Blackfoot village. Rolling his bedroll out and putting the gear away, he sat down at the table and poured another coffee. Looking at his watched, he noted the time to be 7:00 p.m. It was early, and he wasn't ready for bed. He pulled out his deck of cards and played some solitaire to pass time. A ruckus outside caught both his and Black Dogs attention, and he listened intently. Black Dog perked up his ears and tilted his head. Obviously it wasn't something, he was concerned with and so Tyrell knew it wasn't a threat, but nonetheless, he strapped on his holster and grabbed his .45-70 rifle and exited.

Looking this way and that, he saw nothing. Then he heard it again and he looked in the direction of the sound, surprised to see a bull moose and two cows in a full run. They were obviously in a hurry as they crashed through the bramble and up the slope out of sight. Cautiously, Tyrell looked in the direction they were coming from and was startled to see a pack of wolves hot on the moose's trail. He grabbed Black Dog who wanted to go see what was going on. "No, no, Black Dog, those wolves must be hungry if they're chasing moose. You best sit and stay with me," he commanded, as Black Dog sat obediently and Tyrell cocked his rifle. If the wolves turned around, he wanted to be ready.

The two stood out in the dark and cold for a few minutes longer waiting, but the wolves didn't return. "I reckon the moose took them far enough away from here, I think they're gone. Come on, let's get back inside." Once they were inside, Tyrell tied the tepee entrance flap closed, in case the hungry wolves decided that he was an easier meal. Before he sat down, he tossed another stick of wood onto the fire and went back to his game of cards.

He was playing his third hand when Black Dog sat up abruptly and started to growl. "What's a matter?" Tyrell questioned as Black Dog made a beeline for the entrance. Then, all Hell broke loose! The wolves had returned and they were pawing at the flap as they snapped and fought outside, trying to decide which of the four was going to be the first one inside. Black Dog barked and growled at the wolves as the first one pawed its way in. The fight was on!

Tyrell stood up quickly and pulling out his pistol, he shot at the first one. The sound of the .45 pistol seemed loud inside the tepee making his ears ring. He had only wounded it, he realised, as the wolf backed out and darted off. The second wolf wasn't as lucky and Black Dog had it by the throat and slammed it to the ground. Piercing the wolf's throat in a death grip, he shook the life out of it. The three remaining wolves, including the one that Tyrell wounded, knowing now that their opponents were not such an easy kill after all, tried desperately to get away. Black Dog made quick work of another as he broke its back when he pounced on it from behind and smashed it into the snow-covered ground. It yelped, then fell silent.

The first wolf, the one that Tyrell wounded, found the lead from his .45 on his second shot at it and it ran a short distance before it stumbled and fell. It took only one clean shot to knock the fourth and final wolf down. Tyrell ran over to where Black Dog was, making sure that the dog was okay. Thank God, he was. Then he walked over to the third wolf, the one he had wounded with the first shot. Not even his second shot killed it and he shot it for the third time, putting the wolf out of its misery. Checking on the fourth, he could see it was dead. His shot had been true, and the bullet had pierced both its lungs.

"Wow. That was quite the ordeal, Black Dog. Holy crap," Tyrell said, as he caught his breath and holstered his .45. "I guess we have four dead wolves to clean up. I reckon their fur is worth something, somewhere. We'll gather them and string them up, I ain't in the mood right now to do any skinning. I'll wait until morning to do that. Damn, sure wish they had kept right on running. I only ever shot one wolf in my time, and now I've killed three counting these two. How you ever managed to take down two on your own is beyond me. I thought for sure things were going to turn out badly for you, old boy. You got awful lucky. I think we both did actually," Tyrell said, as Black Dog now sniffed the wolf that lay at Tyrell's feet. "Yeah, he's dead. No worries Black Dog. Come on, let's get them strung up, somewhere."

Finding rope and using his lantern for light, Tyrell tied the four wolves by their hind legs and strung them up onto a thick cedar branch. "There, that's done," he sighed as he looked at them hanging from the tree. He felt remorseful that it had to be as it was, but it was either them or the wolves. He was glad that neither he nor Black Dog suffered any physical wounds. "I tell you Black Dog, I ain't ever seen wolves attack a dwelling. Could see them attacking if we were out and about, but for them to do what they tried to do, don't make any sense whatsoever," Tyrell said, as he spit to the ground. "I haven't had as many damn run-ins with critters as I've had here. I ain't even been here that long. I sure hope it ain't an omen. Come on, I'm done for the evening," he said with regret, as they made their way back inside.

Adding more wood to the fire, he slumped into his chair. The thought of what took place bounced around in his mind. Why were the wolves so brazen? The only thing that made sense was either rabies or starvation, the latter, he hoped. There was no way of knowing either way, unless in the next couple of days Black Dog got sick. How he hoped that wouldn't be the case. The possibility he would have to put him down did not sit well with him. Standing, he walked over to where Black Dog lay and looked him over for any ragged and open wounds. Luckily, he didn't find any. How Black Dog managed to get away unscathed amazed him, but somehow he did. "I think you are alright, Black Dog. You managed to get away without so much as a scratch. Damn impressive old boy, damn impressive," he repeated as he now stood and made his way back to the table and sat down again.

He pulled his .45 pistol out and removed the spent cartridges, replacing them with live rounds. He slapped it back into his holster, unbuckled it and placed it on the table. No sooner had he done that when he heard a horse approach. Dark as it was outside, he wondered who would be out at this time. Once more, he strapped his holster on, grabbed his rifle, and exited the tepee. It was Mac.

"We heard some shooting while we were having our steam bath. Is everything okay?" he asked, as he swung off Lucy.

"It's all fine now; had a run in with some wolves. At first they were chasing after a few moose that took off up the slope. I thought for sure they were gone. Next thing I know they're back. I got them strung up over yonder," Tyrell pointed. "They tried digging their way inside. Damndest thing I ever saw from wolves."

"Jesus Christ, that is something new. I ain't ever heard of that either. You don't suppose they had the rabies, do you?" Mac asked, with concern.

"I sure hope not. The dog killed two on his own, but he doesn't seem to have any wounds that I could find. I reckon he got lucky. I'm hoping the wolves were just hungry," Tyrell shrugged.

"Could be they were scouting this place out over the last little while that we were gone, and figured out that the dog was alone. I could see them attempting to break in if that is what they thought," Mac suggested.

"That is a good point, Mac. I didn't even think about that. Maybe that is why. It would make sense. They did seem some surprised that the dog wasn't alone. That makes me feel better already, and even better that we made it back here when we did; otherwise I might be coming home to a dead dog."

"Well, I'm glad that ain't the situation. So, you're all right, then?"

"Yep, a little taken back at the whole ordeal, but I'll get over it as long as the dog don't get sick."

"Let's hope not," Mac said, as he swung back onto Lucy. "I'll come by tomorrow and we'll have a closer look at the wolves. Incidentally, there is a high market for wolf skin."

"I figured as much. You know anyone that will want to buy them?" Tyrell asked out of curiosity. "I ain't got any use for wolf skin."

"Yeah, Sanders buys them and ships them off to God only knows where. Rose don't use them, nor do I. Selling them though, I ain't got a problem with. I think I have only ever seen them in these parts on a few occasions. Usually they stay away. Or I ain't been looking. They ever made their way into my yard though and caused grief, I wouldn't hesitate to shoot. Don't feel bad about it. They are vermin."

"Vermin or not, it don't sit well with me that I had to go to the extreme of killing them. I reckon though, if I hadn't, Black Dog would have done his best."

"Least wise the two of you are okay. I guess I'll head back, got to finish with the steam bath. I'll talk to you tomorrow, Travis." Mac turned Lucy in the direction of home and headed off.

"See you tomorrow, Mac. Don't make it too damn early. I need to have a good night's sleep," Tyrell chuckled, "and I don't want to be bothered before the sun is up."

"Yeah, yeah, me neither," Mac replied, as he and Lucy faded into the darkness.

Tyrell stood outside for a few minutes, noting that the snow had stopped. He could still see the crimson blood-soaked ground from where the dead wolves had lain. *Wish it hadn't stopped before that was all covered, damn snow anyway,* he thought, as he looked on. It was what it was. Turning he made his way inside, unbuckled his holster and tossed it on the table for the third time that night. He crouched next to the fire and warmed his hand. Stoking the fire, he blew out the lantern and curled up in his bedroll to sleep.

The Missing Years – Part I

Chapter 16

On November 23rd, he slept well for the first time in days. Rested and raring to get something done, Tyrell stepped outside. The sun was shining brightly and the cool morning was refreshing. The only thing that took away the beauty of the day was the four frozen blood pools from the night before when he killed the wolves. He walked over to each spot and kicked snow over the crimson coloured ground. *Don't need to be reminded about that,* he thought, as he made his way over to his outside fire pit and got some sticks burning. Gathering water from the hole he had cut through the ice the night before, he filled his coffee pot and a bucket for Pony. The fire snapped and crackled as billows of smoke swirled into the sky. Setting his coffee pot on the flames, he took Pony the bucket of water.

"Turned out to be a nice morning after the crappy night we had last night, eh? The sky is as blue as a jay and the sun as bright as a nugget of gold," he said, as he visited with Pony while the horse slurped at the water. "I guess you won't have a need for these blankets wrapped around you on such a beautiful day like this." He removed them and put them away for the next time.

The beautiful day though was about to change. Down at Mac and Rose's a stranger had trod in. Mac was already gone, running errands over at Ben's house and he wasn't around. The stranger swung off his horse and looked around. It was a nice little place; there was no doubt about it. Knocking on the door, he waited for a response. Rose opened the door a short time later and as soon as she did, the man had his pistol drawn and pointing at her. She tried to slam the door shut, but the stranger stuck his foot in the doorway to prevent it. The man forced his way in, pushing her to the floor, his pistol pointing at her.

The Missing Years – Part I

"I'm looking for a fellow named Tyrell. I have reason to believe that you know who I'm talking about." He was threatening her with the pistol.

"I, I, I don't know anyone by that name," Rose said, as she tried to stand up, but the man only swatted her to the ground, leaving her nose and lips bloodied and swollen.

"Bullshit! Start talking, woman, or never speak again." He cocked his pistol.

"I have already told you, I know no one named Tyrell." Rose repeated, as she began to sob. How she wished Mac were there. This wouldn't be happening then.

The man slapped her again this time harder. "Tell me why are there tracks outside your door that say there is a man around here who has a dog and a horse, which I've been following for weeks now." The man was getting madder with every breath he took.

"There is only Travis, he has a dog."

"Travis what? What's his last name?" the man asked, "and where is he now?"

"He works for us, up the trail to the east."

"What do you mean works for you?"

"My husband Mac hired him to help do some land clearing."

"Hired eh, and when might that have been?" the man snarled.

"Early, fall. Why is that important to you? His name isn't Tyrell," Rose pleaded.

"Where is your husband? I need to have words with him too, I think, so where is he?"

"Not far, he should be coming through that door any minute," Rose lied.

"Maybe I should wait, huh, and ask him some questions as well."

"He will kill you for what you have done."

The Missing Years – Part I

"I doubt that lady," the man said as he slammed the butt of his pistol into Rose's head and knocked her out cold. Rising, he looked around the inside of the house and helped himself to some food that was on a plate on the table. Exiting, he headed east looking for a trail. It didn't take long and he swung off his horse and studied the tracks. *Yep, a big horse, and a dog, I sense a payday,* he thought, as he swung back onto his horses and followed the trail.

Rose was coming to by the time the man had disappeared, and she wept loudly from the pain and the fear of what had taken place. Sitting now, she prayed for Mac to return in case the man came back. Too fearful to move, she lowered her head into her hands and continued to sob. Finally, catching her breath, she stood up and grabbed one of Mac's rifles and set it on the table. If the man came back before Mac, she would simply shoot him. No ifs and no buts about it. With eager determination, she waited her eyes pinned to the door.

In the distance down the trail that led to Mac and Rose's place, Tyrell saw a rider approach. He knew it wasn't Mac and he prepared himself for the intrusion. *Wonder who that might be,* he thought, as he made his way to the tepee and grabbed his rifle. He watched armed and ready as the newcomer approached.

"You Tyrell?" the man asked, as he drew near. Tyrell knew then that it was Earl Brubaker, the hired gun.

"Nope, name is Travis Sweet. What can I do for you?"

"That squaw down the trail some said the same thing, even while I slapped her around a bit."

"Excuse me." Tyrell replied with conviction. "If you laid a hand on Mac and Rose, then I don't think you'll be getting far from here."

The Missing Years – Part I

"Never saw any man, just that squaw. Wouldn't have mattered much if the man was there or not. Besides, what are you going to do about it? I think your name is Tyrell and I've been tracking you for some time. Seems you committed murder in a place called Willow Gate. You killed two men, Heath Roy and Ollie Johnson, and I've been paid to find you and take you in or kill you. Which will it be?"

"Already told you mister, my name is Travis Sweet. That woman and man down the trail are friends of mine. If you have hurt either one, then I'll repeat myself. You ain't going to get far from here." Tyrell was ready. He knew Brubaker had a lighting fast draw from stories he had heard about the man. It was said that there was no one living that could beat him. Today though, Brubaker may have met the one man who could.

"You know who I am?" Brubaker asked.

"Nope, but I reckon you are looking for someone that ain't here. Which puts you, I would guess, in the category of a bounty hunter," Tyrell answered. He was more ready now than ever to pull his pistol, as he stared at Brubaker not showing any fear whatsoever. He had met men like Brubaker before. Perhaps none were as menacing or as quick with a gun, but they were still men who thought they could beat him. He looked at Brubaker the same way as he looked at all the men that came before him. Either he won or Brubaker killed him. He was ready.

"On the contrary, I'm more of a threat than any bounty hunter. My name is Earl Brubaker. I'm the man folks hire to track down killers when the bounty hunters can't. The man I'm looking for is standing right in front of me. The question is, do you admit it or do I shoot you anyway?"

"I guess then you'd be committing murder. Wouldn't that make you no different from this fellow named Tyrell, who you keep talking about?" He never once averted his eyes from the face of the man called Brubaker. He studied him and watched his facial expressions as they taunted each other. The face never lied, and when a man was about to pull his pistol the face had always told him. He waited.

Brubaker chuckled. "You seem pretty confident. Think you could out draw me, Tyrell?" Brubaker taunted. "You better, think on that for a minute."

"I'm done thinking," Tyrell responded. "And I'll tell you again, my name is Travis Sweet. I don't know anyone named Tyrell, nor have I heard that name before."

It was at that instant Brubaker's face contorted ever so slightly, and it was at the exact same moment that he reached for his pistol. He was fast there was no doubt about it. Tyrell though, at the speed of a wink pulled his faster and fired. The bullet echoed in the silence as it ripped through Brubaker's body, knocking him clean off his horse. Still clutching his pistol, Brubaker gasped in shock and pain at his defeat. Blood from the quarter-sized wound spilled out onto the snow-covered ground. Even with his gun cocked and his finger on the trigger he didn't have a second chance to fire, as Tyrell shot him once more through the heart from a few paces away.

"That is for ruining my day, and for any harm you have caused Rose," Tyrell said, as he checked Brubaker's vitals for any sign of life. Brubaker, though, was stone-cold dead. "Weren't quick enough today, were you, Earl," Tyrell said, as he slapped his pistol back into his holster. He wasted no time swinging up onto Brubaker's horse and headed for Mac and Rose's. It didn't take him long to make the distance; he kept Brubaker's horse going at a full run.

The Missing Years – Part I

Pulling up to the house he swung off the horse and made haste for the front door. He could see that Lucy wasn't around, and so he knew Mac was away. He didn't bother to knock on the door. He swung it open and was able to side step by only a few inches as the bullet fired by Rose whizzed by.

"Rose, Rose. It's me, Travis," he said, as he peeked around the corner, to see Rose sitting there her face all bloodied and bruised.

"Travis!" she exclaimed in relief. "I'm, I'm so sorry. I thought you were that man that was here earlier. I didn't shoot you, did I?" she asked as she now stood up and ran to him.

He wrapped his arms around her to comfort her. "No, I'm okay Rose. I came as fast as I could once I put lead in that fellow. He's dead now, Rose. Are you okay?"

"I am now that I'm not alone. I was so scared. He broke in here and started asking questions about someone he was following. I think he said he was following someone named Tyrell who had a dog."

"I know, I know. Come on let's get you seated. It's okay now. Where is Mac?"

"He is over at Ben's place, paying him for watching our place." She looked at him, "You're not Tyrell are you?"

"Hell no, I haven't even heard that name before. The only reason that fellow thought I was is because I have a dog," Tyrell lied, not knowing what else to say.

"That man is dead, the one that was here?" she asked to confirm, still in shock from the ordeal.

"He is. I killed him, and for what he did to you he deserved both ounces of lead," Tyrell said, as he now sat across from her. "When is Mac expected back Rose?"

"Soon, I think. He left at 8:00 a.m. What time is it now, Travis?"

The Missing Years – Part I

Tyrell looked at his watch. "Almost 10:00 a.m."

"Yes, he should be back soon. You will stay until he gets back, won't you?"

"Of course I will. I wouldn't leave you alone, Rose. I'll wait." He stood from the table and gathered some water and a cloth, then gently wiped away the blood on Rose's face. "You'll be okay, Rose. He didn't hurt you any other way did he?"

"No, only hurt my face. Yes, I'll be okay. Thank you Travis."

"Is there anything I can get you, coffee, tea, anything like that?" Tyrell asked.

"I am fine, thank you."

Tyrell nodded as he continued swabbing her face with the damp cloth. She had a busted lip and black eye, and on the side of her head where Brubaker slammed his pistol, a goose egg was forming and trickled blood. She would live though; she was a strong woman. Things could have been a lot worse for her.

Finally, Mac returned. Noting the odd horse, he was cautious as he entered the house. Rose stood from the table and ran into his arms. "Oh Mac, hold me," she said, as she began to cry.

"What, what happened Rose?" he asked, as he looked at her.

"A man broke in her asking about someone named Tyrell. I told him I knew of nobody by that name and he hit me. Then he said he had been following someone with a dog. He kept hitting me, and I told him only person I knew with a dog was Travis. Oh Mac, I was so afraid. I don't know what happened after that, but when I woke up he was gone. Travis has said that he has killed this man."

The Missing Years – Part I

"It is true, Mac. He's dead, and as I told Rose he deserved the two ounces of lead I wasted on him," Tyrell said, as he looked into Mac's eyes.

Mac walked Rose back to the table and sat down with her and Tyrell. "If the ground weren't froze, I would say bury him. Since it is though, we're gonna have to get the body over to Sanders' place. The law can pick it up there. Who was this man?" Mac asked, as he looked at Tyrell.

"Said his name was Earl Brubaker."

"Earl Brubaker? Shit, Travis, do you know who that is?"

Tyrell nodded. "I do so."

"Wait, no more speaking. Who is Earl Brubaker?" Rose wanted to know.

"He's a hired gun; said to be one of the best." Mac answered.

"Hired gun? You mean a man that gets paid to kill?"

"Yep, he's a different breed of bounty hunter, Rose." Mac said as he looked at her. "Enough of that for now though, I'm more concerned with you Rose."

"I am now okay." Rose offered a weak smile, but it was sincere. "I will heal. If there is no more threat, you and Travis must go and take that man's body to Sanders'. He may not be a good man, but he may have family. They have a right to know he is dead. It is the Christian thing to do, yes."

"It is, but any man that can do what he did to you Rose, doesn't deserve your forgiveness. Christian, he likely ain't; family, he might have, and that is the only reason other than the ground being froze that I'd bring him to Sanders' place. Otherwise, I'd bury him," Mac responded with hate for the man who had hurt his Rose.

The Missing Years – Part I

"Not while you are my Mac, you wouldn't," Rose said with conviction. She was feeling better with every passing minute as the three of them sat. The man was dead and Mac was home. She felt safe and secure.

"I'll tell you what," Tyrell stated, as he looked at Mac and Rose. Knowing their need to be alone at that point was important, he'd leave it up to Mac to tell her or not who he really was. "I'll head back, get the skid we used to pull the game off the mountain dug out of the snow, and get it tied to Brubaker's horse. I'll get his body on there as well, and the wolf carcasses too. I figure we might as well get rid of them at Sanders at the same time we bring the body in. I'll get them loaded and head back this way. You two need to be alone for a bit, I reckon, because of what took place here today." Tyrell stood from the table and nodded as he exited.

Swinging onto Brubaker's horse, he headed to the tepee that he called home, Black Dog nipping at the horse's heels. Two hours later the wolf carcasses as well as the body of Earl Brubaker were loaded up and ready for transport to Sanders' place. Tyrell wasn't sure what he was going to say about Brubaker's death. There were a lot of things that could go wrong. People like Brubaker with reputations such as he had, didn't get shot by people named Travis Sweet.

There would be questions and he needed to have the answers. Did it mean more lies and deceit, or would he tell the truth? He contemplated as he saddled up Pony, Grabbing Brubaker's horse by the reins, he led him in the direction of Mac and Rose's, the body of Earl Brubaker secured to the skid.

By the time he made the distance to Mac and Rose's, Mac had Lucy harnessed to the cart. He wondered why, until Mac and Rose met him outside. "We're ready to

The Missing Years – Part I

get. I ain't leaving Rose behind. Besides, she is the witness to what took place. She has the scars to show what that bastard did." Mac said, as he looked at the dead body. "So that is him, eh; the great and mighty Earl Brubaker?" Mac shook his head and kicked the skid. "He sure doesn't look like much now. Come on, let's make tracks," he said, as he helped Rose into the cart and they set off.

"What we know to be law, Travis, is that Brubaker broke the homesteaders law and about as many other laws as I had in eggs this morning. Self-defence is what it boils down to. You have no worries, once Rose tells those that need to know how he broke into a private dwelling and slapped her around, and how you killed him for doing so. Earl was having a bad day and you simply beat him at the draw. That is all the law will need to know. It'll end there, I assure you, Travis." Mac nodded his head and winked at him.

"I sure hope so. I only wonder how many more folks might think I'm this Tyrell fellow only because I have a dog."

"I wouldn't worry about it, once folks see that you also have one, they'll know that whoever that Tyrell fellow is, isn't the only one that has one. It is a big world, Travis. Tyrell can't be the only one with a dog."

"That is somewhat comforting, Mac, thanks." It was true there had to be others that had dogs. At 6:00 p.m., they made the distance to Sanders'. Travis was paid $96.00 for the wolves' carcasses, a fair price for them not being skinned, which Sanders put in his books as a credit to Travis Sweet. By 7:00 p.m., the story had been told on who and why, and the single Mounted Police constable that was in the area sent them on their way, none the wiser as to who Travis Sweet really was, other than the man who beat Earl Brubaker to the draw. Truth was that, in itself, might be as much of a headache as using an alias. It was quite dark as they made their return to Mac and Rose's place, the only things that guided them were Lucy and Pony and the moonlit sky that enhanced the snow-covered trail so they could see it. Tyrell stayed behind long enough at Mac's to help with his evening chores. They conversed about the possibility that others may come looking for him, and maybe it was best that he moved on. The last thing he wanted was to put Mac and Rose in jeopardy. "It has happened once Mac, it could happen again."

"I know it could, but I might get hit by lightning too. I ain't worried Travis; it only means we have to be a little more vigilant, and there ain't nothing wrong being a little bit more so, especially in these times. We've lived here for over ten years. Today was the first time anything happened like this. Folks around here have been getting lazy and this is a wakeup call."

"I'm the reason why it happened, Mac."

"Nope, the only reason it happened was because my hired hand has a dog, and some dimwit thought you were someone they was tracking. Assumption, that's all that is. You, leave from here now though, you'll only be confirming that you are that person that folks might be trailing. By staying, you're proving that you aren't. Do you understand what I mean, Travis?"

"In a sense I do, and I thank you for saying it."

"No thanks needed," Mac said, as he tossed the horses their hay. "Well, that's all done. How are you set for hay and grain? I think the last time I was there I noticed you were running low."

"Yeah, could likely use some."

"All right then, lets load up the horse cart and harness up your horse," Mac said, without question or hesitation as he entered the hay shed. Tyrell followed behind and in a few minutes, they had four bales of hay and a fifty-pound sack of grain loaded.

"That'll do Mac. Thanks," Tyrell said, as he led Pony over to the cart and looked at the harness contraption. It took him a moment or two to figure out how the cart and harness worked, but he figured it out, with Mac's help.

"Thanks for that Mac, you made it look easy."

"After you do it once or twice, it'll be a snap. The log harnesses work almost the same, without, of course, the cart," Mac chuckled.

"Yeah about that, with all that has happened in the past while, we sure are behind, Mac. We should get to it." Tyrell mentioned.

"Yep, I know. It isn't going to happen tomorrow though."

Tyrell chuckled, "I didn't expect that it would, but we better get on it soon."

"I don't disagree. Sometimes though, other things take a precedence. It weren't how I planned it, but plans don't always go as one may want."

"What day is it, Mac?" Tyrell asked not sure exactly.

"Near the end of the month, I reckon. Think it is November 23rd, Sunday, I think."

"Well then, if we ain't gonna start tomorrow, how about Tuesday?"

"Yeah, we'll get that day's rest one way or the other. Okay, Tuesday it will be."

"All right then, if I don't see you tomorrow, Mac, I'll see you at first light Tuesday, November 25th."

"Will to, Travis. I'll see you then."

"Yep, I'll be waiting," Tyrell said, as he got Pony moving. Two hours later, the horse cart was unloaded, and

The Missing Years – Part I

he was sitting inside the tepee. It had been a long and troubling day, and now all he wanted was rest.

The Missing Years – Part I

Chapter 17

On Tuesday, November 25th, 1890, their work started. As they discussed, they worked hard and steadily right through until January. Surprisingly, for that entire time no one came snooping around looking for the man named Tyrell. All was good, and for the first time in months, he felt at ease with his anonymity. His efforts were now concentrated on working with Mac. The land was slowly opening up and piles of logs scattered the landing near the tepee. Cut to lengths and limbed, they waited for the hot sun of spring to cure them. It turned quite cold in the latter days of January 1891, and that was when their work slowed.

They stood beside one another now as they took their first break of the day. It was January 22nd, 1891. Looking at their accomplishments for that day as they rested near the fire at Tyrell's tepee, they slurped coffee. Their breath was like mist when they spoke.

"We've done good Travis; still have a way to go, but we'll get there. This cold weather isn't going to make things easy on us or the horses. Last thing I want is frost bit fingers and toes. What do you figure? Should break for a few days and see if the weather warms a bit?"

Tyrell rubbed his hands together above the fire as he looked on. "You're the boss, Mac. I still have all my fingers and toes, but yeah, it is bloody cold out. We have come a long way since late November; hard to believe actually how far. I don't reckon we want it to warm yet. Come spring thaw there will be a greater chance for mishaps with the horses. The way it is now, the logs ain't too hard for them to pull. The tie-ons around their hooves with the one inch spikes work good now. When it gets muddy, that'll be a different story."

The Missing Years – Part I

"That ain't going to happen for a few months. I figure we deserve a break and then we'll get back to it," Mac responded.

Tyrell nodded. "Well, I ain't going to turn down a few days of rest and recovery. You, I and the horses probably could use it."

"Alright, we'll finish off today and break till Monday the 26th," Mac said, as they finished the last of their coffee. Making their way over to their horses, they snapped the reins of the harnesses and went over to the next set of logs to be pulled out. One or two was the most each horse could pull at a time, depending on length and circumference. By the end of the day, they managed to pull out and stack ten logs. It had been a slower process than other days due to the penetrating wind and biting cold, but they worked through it. Now they were seated inside the tepee and a warming fire burned as their after-work coffee perked. "Sure has been a miserable and cold one today, Travis," Mac said, as Tyrell handed him a coffee.

"Yep, you got that right. Hot coffee and some heat though, goes a long way in taking the damn chill away." They conversed back and forth for a few minutes longer until Mac finished his coffee and warmed up enough to head home. Tyrell walked outside with him and helped him remove Lucy's harness and hoof tie-ons. Then, after tossing the saddle on, Mac headed for home.

"We'll see you Monday, Travis. If you get too damn cold up here, you know where to go," Mac said, as he heeled Lucy's flank and headed off down the trail.

"If it gets too cold you can count on it. See you Monday, Mac," Tyrell called after him. He watched as Mac and Lucy sauntered on and disappeared around the bend. Ducking into the tepee, he added wood to the fire and sat at the table. Pulling out his pocket watch, he noted the time to

The Missing Years – Part I

be 5:45 p.m. He looked over to where Black Dog lay. "What do you suppose we should do for the next four days Black Dog?" he asked, as though the dog would answer. "One thing is for certain, if it stays cold out like this we won't be doing much. We might take some time to pitter-patter around the landing, clean up some more brush, that type of thing, I have a feeling though for the next couple of days we'll be indoors more than we'll be out," Tyrell smiled. "That's okay though, I got my cards." Truth was, he was already bored, four days of nothing was still nothing, and he hated not keeping busy. *I'll have to find something to do,* he thought as he took the last swallow of his coffee.

Over the past few months the name, Travis Sweet, was gaining momentum and spreading far- and- wide as the name of the man who shot and killed Earl Brubaker. There was no plus side to this other than the fact that Earl Brubaker's death was self-defence. All the same, there were those men that heard the name Travis Sweet and the story of how he beat Brubaker's draw, that made some curious and want to try Travis Sweet's hand, and nothing but death could ever come of that. He was caught between two worlds now: the world of Travis Sweet and the world of Tyrell Sloan, although one and the same, Tyrell was wanted for murder; Travis Sweet was a man that would make you famous. There were bounty hunters looking for Tyrell, and there were gunslingers waiting for the day that they would meet up with Travis Sweet.

When word reached Gabe Roy that Earl Brubaker was dead, and the man who killed him was Travis Sweet, he wanted nothing more than to meet that man. He wanted to put Travis Sweet on his payroll. Maybe he could bring in his son's killer. Gabe sent two men, Buck Ainsworth, and Tanner McBride to look for and bring Travis Sweet to him.

The Missing Years – Part I

Both McBride and Ainsworth were amateur bounty hunters desperate for a gig. Amateur as they were, both had a couple of successful bounty's under their belts. Ainsworth had brought in a fellow by the name of Lance Krueger, a hired gun who had gone astray and killed four men for no apparent reason other than for the joy of doing it. Buck Ainsworth was a medium sized man, with golden hair and eyes of blue. He was in early forties, had travelled most of the territories and was no slouch. He knew how to handle both a pistol and a rifle, and was somewhat a survivalist. Standing six foot plus a few inches, he was an eager yet calm man until pushed.

McBride had brought in a Ktunax Indian named Running Bird, wanted for countless murders and rapes. He had been running from the law for almost five years before McBride got lucky and found him. A renegade most of his life, he spent time behind iron bars down south, only to be let go due to legal technicalities. His crimes, as petty as they were, would have made him see a year or two in prison had he been convicted. Again, luck was on his side. He ventured into Canada where he spent time at a few Christian missions helping those of the cloth in building their places of worship. At age thirty-five, he changed his ways and began working for the law as an informer, somewhat well-liked by those he knew. He stood six foot. He had long brown hair that went below his shoulders, his eyes were brown as the shit that he sometimes shovelled as a stable hand. He was quick on the draw, although that didn't always save him from being shot. Hot lead found its way into him on a few different occasions, but he was always lucky.

Ainsworth and McBride knew one thing, that Travis Sweet was working for a fellow by the name of Mac Rider, who lived close to the town of Chase. The two men left

The Missing Years – Part I

Willow Gate with a wad of cash paid to them by Gabe Roy and headed north to track down and make Travis Sweet an offer, he couldn't refuse. That was on December 15th, 1890, and although sidetracked a few different times they were getting closer to the answer that awaited them.

"You know what, Buck?" Tanner asked. He was sitting on his horse the reins slipped over the saddle horn so his hands could be free while he looked at a map by the light of the few lanterns that hung from poles along the street as their two horses sauntered on slowly making their way through the town of Hells Bottom.

"What's that Tanner?"

"According to this map, the town of Chase is close to a hundred miles away. That is about another weeks travel. Shit, I thought we were closer than that."

"A hundred miles ain't that bad," Buck answered.

"It may not be, but, this damn cold weather is going to slow us down a bit, I would think."

"I've been in colder weather than this, Tanner. We just have to keep moving, rest when the horses get tired, and make shelter if it gets too damn cold. I'm starting to think, you might slow this operation down."

"Bullshit, we'll keep moving, Buck, but the smell of food is wafting up my nose. We might want to stop here in town and have a bite to eat, maybe a whiskey or two. What do you say?"

Buck slowed his horse to a stop and waited for Tanner to pull up alongside. "How long you figure we've been trying to make the distance, Tanner?"

"I ain't got a clue. It's been a few weeks, I think."

"So you ain't got a clue on how many days we've been trying to get where it is we need to get. Do you even know what day it is today?"

The Missing Years – Part I

Tanner shrugged his shoulders. "Nope, do you?" he asked with a sneer.

"I do, today is January 22nd. The Goddamn New Year has come since we've been on the trail. The only reason it has taken this damn long is because of your need to stop off at every little piss ant township to have a whiskey. Shit, some of the places were out of our way, but at your insistence we always stopped," Buck informed him. "Now you want to stop here?"

"Jesus Christ, Buck. A man sometimes needs to let loose and get some relaxing in. There ain't no rush. That Travis fellow ain't going to vanish. Besides, Gabe never gave us a timeline. He said *'get it done'*, and we will. Let's stop here, have a bite to eat. I'll skip the whiskey as a compromise."

Buck shook his head. He had been travelling with Tanner for a while now and knew he wouldn't relent. If they didn't stop, Tanner would likely harp about it for days to come. "Fine, we ain't going to make much more distance tonight, but we ain't going to stay here either. We'll have some hot food and continue on another few miles up the trail."

"All right. That makes me happy, Buck. We'll eat and then we'll leave," Tanner said, as the two of them pulled up to the wooden walkway and tethered their horses. "Saw an establishment down the way a bit."

"I saw it too. Come on let's get on with it," Buck replied, as they walked the short distance to the Maple Leaf eatery. The clock on the wall read 7:00 p.m., he noticed as they sat down. It didn't take long for the woman behind the counter to come by.

"Evening gentleman, there isn't much on the menu at this time of night. The kitchen has been closed for a couple of hours."

The Missing Years – Part I

"Is there coffee?" Tanner asked.

"That and maybe beans." The woman said as she shrugged apologetically.

"That works for me, beans and coffee. I'll have some of that," Buck responded.

"Make that two rounds. Bread would be nice, too," Tanner added.

"Sure, coffee, beans and a plate of bread. I'll get that for you," the women answered as she darted off into the kitchen.

"Was hoping for steak and spuds myself," Tanner said as they waited and talked amongst themselves. "By the time we get out of here, might be too dark to travel."

"You know what you can do with those words, Tanner?" Buck looked at him sternly. "We're gonna eat our beans, have a coffee, and put a few miles on before we break tonight, whether you like it or not. We agreed on a quick meal which we're going to eat and then we're going to get."

"Yeah, yeah. You know what your problem is, Buck. You're more concerned with the job than all the splendours that might come with it. Shit, this is a paid trip across the southwest and northeast corners of this great province. Enjoy it a little bit would you. We're paid messengers and we're making a lot more than the Pony Express. That makes me smile everyday that you and I ride together. This ain't no bounty job. This is a business venture to talk with a fellow by the name of Travis Sweet," Tanner commented in response.

The woman that served them was making her way back to their table and she overheard a word or two. She set their plates down and smiled at them. "Are you fellows bounty hunters?" she asked with curiosity, as she now poured them a coffee from the pot she had with her.

"What makes you ask that?" Buck replied as he nodded his thanks.

"Oh, I thought I heard your friend say something about a bounty or something like that. No worries, it probably isn't any of my business." She waved her hand through the air in a *'forget about it'* gesture, as she turned and walked away.

"What is so wrong about being bounty hunters, Buck? You seemed to have answered her question with evasiveness. You ashamed of being a bounty hunter?"

"Not nearly ashamed as sitting with you at times," Buck chuckled. "Eat up and let's get out of here and back on the trail." They sat in silence as they ate their food, scraping the last of their beans onto bread and swallowing the last of their coffee. Tanner tossed a dollar bill and a couple of coins on the table. Buck paid the same amount up at the counter as Tanner exited. "Thanks for the meal ma'am, the beans were quite good." Buck nodded as he too now exited. Outside the wind seemed to have picked up some, and there were a few frost flakes in the air. Buck pulled his coat collar up and around his ears. "We'll head out of town a few miles and set up for the evening. Might need a tarp shelter tonight," he said as he met up with Tanner and the two of them climbed onto their horses.

"Might? Hell yeah, the wind I'm sure ain't going to last long, but the snow and cold ain't going to stop tonight, I don't reckon," Tanner answered as they headed out of the town of Hells Bottom.

Crossing the Stagway river bridge, north of town some five miles, they spotted a campsite that was on the far side and off the trail a short distance. It was already set up with a fire pit and a stack of wood. Although buried by snow, the woodpile was noticeable. The camp was recently used they could tell. They pulled their horses up to it, dismounted, and tethered them. Buck removed the rolled up canvas tarp he had and they made their evening shelter. Satisfied, they lit a fire and settled in for the evening. Full as they were from their recent meal, they shared some jerky and passed a half bottle of whiskey back and forth as they reminisced and conversed. "Hey, Buck, did you know that fellow Brubaker?" Tanner asked as he took another swig from the whiskey bottle, and handed it back.

"Nope," Buck replied, as he took the whiskey bottle from Tanner. "All I know of him is what I've heard. Some might be true, some maybe not. I heard he was supposed to be quick on the draw; heard also he didn't care who got in his way, man or woman. He'd walk through most that got in his way."

"I heard about as much. I saw him from a distance one time in a saloon. Can't remember where exactly. Down south, I think. Anyway, he was throwing his weight around, that is for sure. I half wanted to take him out back and test his draw. I left shortly after that."

"Why didn't you test his draw, Tanner?"

"I don't know. Maybe I believed the stories a little too much and maybe thought it was a bad idea." Tanner smiled. "I ain't stupid, Buck." He paused as he contemplated. "Now though, makes me wonder if he was as good as most said. I mean, I ain't ever heard the name Travis Sweet, until he beat Brubaker's draw. Now folk's is saying he's the man to beat."

"If you believe what you have heard about Brubaker, then Travis Sweet is the man to beat. Well, him and that fellow Tyrell that laid Heath Roy and Ollie to rest. A man has to be pretty quick to drop two men with guns already drawn." Buck took a swig from the bottle. "Here's something else you need to think on. Who is to say this

Travis fellow did beat Brubaker in a fair draw, and if he did, could be he might have only got lucky."

"Could be," Tanner agreed, as he nodded. It was true he himself had gotten lucky in a few gunfights going against those said to be quicker on the draw. The thing was, Tyrell Sloan, aka Travis Sweet, was that quick, and in fact did beat Brubaker in a fair draw. Neither Tanner nor Buck could know that, not yet, at least. "It don't matter either way I suppose. We ain't hunting the man down to pick a fight, only offering him a business proposition offered by Gabe Roy. That is where our job ends."

"Yep, that is correct," Buck stared into the fire as the flames danced this way and that. "Gabe is going to be hard pressed when we return and tell him this Travis fellow turned down his monetary offer and gain," he added with absolution as he tossed another piece of wood into the fire.

"What makes you think he'll turn the offer down? Working for Gabe Roy always means money," Tanner pointed out.

"I ain't saying it don't, but I know people like Travis. They much rather live simply without the constant harassment and stupid men that want to make a name for themselves. What do you think he cares about a fellow named Heath Roy, a name, which, he probably ain't ever heard. I think Gabe was off his rocker to assume that a simple man living so far off the beaten path would even consider a salary to look for his son's killer. It is absurd, don't you think, Tanner?"

"Shit when you point it out like that, it does raise a few questions. What are we supposed to do if he does turn it down?"

"Do?" Buck asked, as he raised an eyebrow. "We do nothing, except turn around and go back with the news. That is all I got from the conversation when we made the

The Missing Years – Part I

deal. Gabe paid you and me $1000 dollars cash apiece to offer this fellow named Travis a proposition; that is all."

"True enough. Old Gabe though won't like news like that."

Buck chuckled. "You're right he'll climb the walls, which will be a payoff in itself." Silence enveloped them as they both stared into the fire, absorbing the little bit of warmth it produced. "Snowing like a bugger outside still," Buck said as he looked out past the fire through the opening. "I guess we might as well get the bedrolls." Buck rose from where he was sitting and stepped outside into the falling snow. Making his way over to his horse, he removed his bedroll and brushed the snow off as he looked around. The evening, although cold and breezy, was well worth the little amount of time that he stood out there and observed the serenity.

"Hey, Buck want to grab mine too?" Tanner hollered from the shelter.

"What is a matter with your legs?"

"Ain't nothing wrong with my legs. Thought since you were out there, you might as well grab mine too."

"Get your own damn gear, Tanner. I ain't your maid nor your damn mother," Buck said, as he stumbled inside and rolled out his bedroll next to the fire.

"Alright, I could probably take a whiz anyway," Tanner said, as he went and gathered his own bedding. A few minutes later, the two were snoring in a half-whiskey-drunk state. It snowed through the night and remained cold, but neither Buck nor Tanner noticed. The whiskey kept them warm. Now, as they loaded up their gear and tore down the tarp while their morning coffee perked, they were feeling a little less rambunctious than the day and night before. "Should never have finished off that whiskey last night, Buck. Now we ain't got nothing for tonight," Tanner joked.

"I have another, but, I ain't touching it for a day or two. So, don't even ask," Buck replied.

"Ask not I will."

"Good. Let's get to our coffee so we can make tracks."

"Again, you're rushing me, Buck. It ain't even quite sunup yet."

"It don't matter. The sooner we get, the sooner we'll start to feel better. I think that bottle of whiskey was sour. It left a bad gurgle in my gut." Sitting down on a piece of wood, he poured a coffee. "Damn, that is good," he said as he took his first swallow. "There is nothing like a hot cup of black coffee and smoke from a fire to make a fellow come around from a night of whiskey."

"What about a woman lying in your bed after a night of drinking whiskey?" Tanner chortled as he poured his own cup of coffee.

"That might trump it. Out here though its black coffee and fire," Buck responded, as he took another drink, not wanting to discuss women with Tanner. It was inappropriate at that time as far as he was concerned.

"I won't argue because this coffee is good," Tanner agreed. They conversed through another cup each, then kicking snow into the embers, Buck and Tanner saddled up and once more headed north toward the town of Chase. "Looks like some better weather might be on the way; suns coming up and the sky is blue," Tanner mentioned, as he looked to the east while they travelled onward.

"Could be that is true, and I wouldn't complain one bit. The only problem is the brighter the sun, the brighter the fresh snow. It could hurt our eyes."

"Just have to tilt the hat, I suppose. Besides, looks like the trail heads into the bush not far from here. The trees will keep us shaded and cool, I reckon. Enjoy the sun while you can, Buck," Tanner added, as they rode on.

Three miles further along the trail, they came upon a homestead that sat off the trail some sixty or so feet, close enough that passerby's could carry on with a conversation from anyone who lived there and happened to be out at the same time. The two riders took note of the place as well as the fellow that stood on the porch, looking at them. The man on the porch knew by their look alone the type of men they were. "Bounty hunters," he murmured beneath his breath as he looked on, *that can't be good,* he thought. *Sure hope they ain't looking to be sociable.* He stood there looking on and they looked back with the same stare.

"Morning," Buck said, as he nodded and acknowledged the man.

"Morning to you too," the man on the porch responded, hoping that would be the end of their brief conversation.

"You by chance know how far we are from Chase?" Tanner spoke out.

The man on the porch lowered his head and sighed, *shit,* he thought before he replied. "Do so, ninety-five or so more miles north by west, would be a good guess. You're on the right trail, if that is your next question."

"Thank you kindly, for that." Buck responded as he slowed his horse more, as the man now approached, wanting to get a closer look and maybe a name for future reference. He likely wouldn't have wasted his time hadn't the riders started the conversation. Now, he was curious.

"You folks heading to Chase then?" Bannock questioned as he drew close.

"Near that area, we're looking for Mac Rider's land. Got some business with him. You ever hear that name?" Tanner questioned with friendliness.

Bannock stepped closer up to the rail fence that skirted the house and leaned against it. "Nope, never heard that name before," Truly he hadn't.

"Just the same I reckon. You have a nice piece of land here," Buck responded.

"Yep, good place to raise hogs." He stepped away from the fence and walked through gate the opening. "Name is Bannock." He reached out his hand.

"I'm Buck Ainsworth, this here," he pointed to Tanner, "is Tanner McBride."

Bannock nodded. He would remember those names. "Well nice to meet you folks. I have to admit though, seems like a bad time of year, to be heading to Chase. This trail don't get used much in the winter. Saw only one other fellow a few days back going this way," he mentioned.

"I was under the impression that it was the easiest route to Chase."

"It is the shortest, but at this time of year, I ain't so sure it is the easiest." Bannock averted his eyes up the trail. "Be careful up there on the mountain. It'll crest into a nice valley, but between here and there the terrain can get deadly."

"How deadly, exactly?" Tanner questioned.

"Avalanches tend to happen, every now and again. Just keep your wits about you as you travel through the pass. You'll be okay, I reckon, once that is behind you. You'll come into a nice valley after that as I mentioned, and the terrain ain't so hilly."

"Avalanches, eh? Anything else we might need to know?"

"Might be the odd pole cat or wolf in the valley. Mostly they'll take off long before you'll see them. You might see their tracks though." Bannock wasn't bluffing. It was true avalanches and pole cats were a concern in the area.

"Not much different from travelling the northern Yukon, I reckon." Buck said, as he looked up the trail. "We don't want to take up anymore of your time, Bannock. But we do thank you for the heads up."

"No problem, Buck." Bannock responded as the two riders tilted their hats and set off. He watched them for a few short moments, then turned and made his way back to the house. He scribbled their names and a brief description of each of them onto a piece of paper. He didn't know why he did that, but he did. Besides, who could say that in the future it wouldn't be of some use. They were definitely bounty hunters that much he knew.

"That fellow seemed friendly enough, eh?"

"I suppose; was chatty that is for sure," Buck replied, as they now entered the overgrown trail that would lead them over a pass and into a valley. It grew cold as they traversed along the trail. The sun, mostly blocked now by the trees that skirted the mountain and the trail contributed to the trail's icy surface. The horses on a few occasions almost lost their grip. "Whoa! Easy there, Clyde," Buck said to his horse, as Clyde for the third time in only a few minutes slipped forward, but luckily was able to keep his footing. "Be careful in that spot, Tanner," Buck said, as he looked back and pointed.

"Yeah, I saw that. Might have to lead them if it keeps up like this. We can't afford a lame horse out here." Tanner slowly inched his horse over the ice patch that spread the distance across the trail.

The Missing Years – Part I

"It could turn out to be like that," Buck stated as he turned the bend and saw the remnants of an old avalanche. "Well now. Would you look at that," he slowed his horse to a stop and waited for Tanner. "We have an old avalanche to cross."

"I guess our boy back a few miles wasn't joking," Tanner said, as he pulled up next to Buck.

"There'd be no reason for a man to lie about something like that, Tanner."

Tanner nodded. "I suppose not. How you want to approach this dilemma? Can't imagine we can cross that on the horses' backs."

"Only choices are to go around through the scrub or lead the horses. I vote for leading them. Probably less likely to break something than to make trail around," Buck responded, as he sighed and looked on.

"Once we get closer we can make a better judgement. Might be a trail going across already." Tanner shrugged his shoulders. "Let's get," he said, as he slowly took the lead.

"Right behind you." It took only a few paces for them to make the distance and get a better view. "It don't look like anyone has crossed over, but there is a game trail." Buck pointed to the left of the trail. "It looks as though it goes around."

"Our horses are bigger than anything that went through there," Tanner pointed out. "It can't be any easier than making our own damn way around, Buck. I say we lead them."

Buck contemplated for a few moments as he looked around. Tanner, although most times a bit of a nuisance had made a good point. Now that he looked closer to the game trail, he saw that only deer had been using it. "I think you are right, Tanner. I think you are right," Buck responded with a sigh. "All right then, I guess we lead them." Buck swung off his horse and Tanner followed suit. "You first or me?" he asked, knowing it would be less dangerous for each of them to cross separately.

"Let's do a dry draw," Tanner suggested half jokingly.

"What is a dry draw?"

"We see who can draw out their pistol fastest. The loser goes first."

"Shit, that there is a kid's game, Tanner. I'll lead," Buck said with annoyance, as he took Clyde by the reins. "I'll signal you from the other side."

"Hey, Buck!" Tanner exclaimed, as he waited for Buck to turn and look at him. At that very instant, he pulled his pistol and so did Buck. Neither one was faster than the other. "Shit, that's pretty good, Buck, I think I might have had you by the short ones, though," he chuckled.

"Bullshit, Tanner. I would have sent lead your way long before you pulled the trigger," Buck responded, not at all impressed with Tanner's idea of a joke.

"Come on, lighten up Buck, was only trying to break the monotony. I'm getting bored sitting here and waiting for you to get to the other side."

"I'd have been halfway across by now if you weren't insisting on playing kids' games. Smarten up and let me get on with it." Buck turned as he slapped his pistol into his holster and carried on. It took a few minutes of careful trail busting as Buck and Clyde made the distance. He looked across and waved to Tanner to proceed. Neither one was about to holler, they knew what the ramifications could be in an area with a recent avalanche. Tanner made the distance nearly as quickly as Buck. Now, safely on the other side, they rested for a few minutes. "That's done," Buck said, as they gazed across.

The Missing Years – Part I

"Yep, damn deep in the middle. I sank up to my knees before I hit packed snow. Rancho and I dragged our asses a few times," Tanner replied, referring to his horse. "Maybe next time might be safer to go around something like this."

"I don't know. We might still be following that game trail if we used it. Now at least we're back on the main trail. Better than fighting scrub and bramble, I think." Buck swung onto his horse's back and waited for Tanner to do the same. "Guess we best make tracks," he said, as Tanner adjusted his saddle and swung up. "I reckon we'll make the valley soon. The trail seems to head down from here."

"Are we going to break for coffee once we get there? I could use a coffee," Tanner suggested.

"Depends how far along we get, I suppose." Buck looked at his watch. "It's only 11:00 a.m., now. Let's see how far we get by midday. We're going to be riding into some sun soon. Might just decide to travel 'til dusk."

"Yeah... all right," Tanner said, with little enthusiasm as they travelled on, able now to travel side by each. At 3:00 p.m., that day they reached the valley. "Well, there it is I reckon," Tanner said, as they looked down the last slope and into the valley below.

"The descent might be a little hairy. Looks like quite the incline," Buck pointed out as they approached, and, with caution, slowly descended into the valley. Stopping at the bottom, they looked back the way they came. "Shit, looks steep from this end too."

"And to think in a few days or a week we'll be going up." Tanner mentioned. "Anyway, we're here now, I say we spark a fire and brew some coffee and maybe chew on some jerky. I'm a little tired; could use a rest."

The Missing Years – Part I

"I suppose. Another couple of hours and it'll be getting dark. A quick rest and a coffee sounds good to me," Buck responded as they looked around for the best spot to rest. Gesturing with his chin, he pointed to an area where the sun still shone. "Right over there will be best, I reckon," he said, as he motioned for his horse to move over to the spot. Stopping, they dismounted and gathered dry wood from some deadfall. A few minutes later they were sunning it up. "Sure is peaceful eh, Tanner?" Buck questioned as he looked around and admired their surroundings. The valley stretched on for a distance, and skirting it were evergreen trees and birch that made the valley look even more spectacular, with the snow covered rock bluffs up high and the never-ending sea of snow that covered the valley floor.

"I imagine it could change nasty cold in a heartbeat, especially with the Rocky Mountains so close. For now though, yeah, I'd say it is peaceful." Tanner looked to the east and the peaks of Rockies that looked so close one could reach out and touch them. "I do admit the view is worth remembering." They fell silent for a time as they warmed their hands above the flames of the fire, and waited for their coffee to finish.

"You know what, Tanner? I might get convinced to set up a camp here for the evening," Buck said, as he looked around. "It is a nice place. I like it here, we already have wood gathered, and it wouldn't take much to set up a shelter. What do you say?" Buck picked up his tin cup and poured a coffee.

"We wouldn't get much further then we already are before dusk. I reckon this place is as good as any, I suppose. Sure, let's set up here for the evening. We could even have a hot and decent meal too." Both in agreement they went about preparing their evening camp. It didn't take long to set it up and before it turned cold they were whipping up some canned stew and biscuits. They conversed as their meal cooked and slurped on coffee, talking about this and that and sometimes nothing at all. As darkness settled in so did they. Tired as they were, it didn't take long before they were snoring.

The Missing Years – Part I

Chapter 18

January 24th, wasn't much different from the day before. Buck added a couple of sticks to the cooling embers of their past evening fire; he melted snow for coffee, and they nibbled on leftover biscuits as they went about dismantling their shelter and gathering their gear. With the horses loaded and saddled, they spent a few minutes in the glory of predawn as they finished their meagre breakfast and morning coffee. "Slept well last night, Tanner. How about you?" Buck asked, as he looked to the east and rising sun.

"I don't have any complaints. I got cold for a little bit, but other than that I'd say I slept well." Tanner took a swallow of his coffee as he averted his eyes in the direction Buck was looking. "Sun is going to be hot again today, looks like."

"That it is, I think. It'll make for a good day of riding. I'm rested and feel good."

"I feel damn good too, Buck, I certainly do. Was a good thing we stopped when we did yesterday. It gave us a few extra hours of rest and believe me, I will admit I needed those few extra hours."

"Yeah, I reckon so. It was the damn crossing of that avalanche and the slipping and a sliding the horses did as we travelled. That kind of stuff can wear on a man's bones. That and the chill wore me down too. I would have liked to have put a few miles more behind us than we did, but all in all, I reckon we did okay. I don't imagine Chase being more than two days ride. What does your map say, Tanner?" Buck wanted to know. It took Tanner a few moments to find it.

"If this is the valley we're in that I see here," he pointed to an area of the map as he showed it to Buck.

The Missing Years – Part I

"Then it looks like we might have between seventy and eighty miles to go. I don't think we can do that in two days, three maybe."

"Shit, I thought we were closer than that. We would have been too if we carried on a bit further last night." Buck shrugged. "We'll have to put on some hard miles today, I guess."

Yeah, steady," Tanner looked at the map once more as he contemplated the distance. The trail they were on according to the map lead to a lake, then, cut east and north again as it circled around. "We go hard until dark, we could likely end up here." He pointed again to an area of the map. "That there is Yellow Lake. Chances are it'll be frozen solid. We could cut off a few miles of trail if we cross it."

"I ain't crossing no lake, froze or otherwise. I can't swim, Tanner. I ain't swum a day in my life. Forget about crossing some froze lake."

"It was only a suggestion, Buck. Either way we get to the lake and we'll have travelled near thirty miles. As long as the trail ain't in bad shape, I reckon we could do thirty miles. We wouldn't have a snowballs chance in Hell to do that if we weren't on a cleared trail; ten miles a day then, maybe cutting through brush and bramble. Our advantage is the trail."

"Yeah, and our hope is the trail is good straight through. If it is, then I reckon thirty miles is doable." Dumping out the last of his coffee, he stood and made his way over to his horse. "Are ya coming Tanner, or are you gonna stare at that map all day? Come on, let's get." Buck swung onto his horses and waited again for Tanner to put some poop into his step.

"You're in a damn rush again, Buck."

"Never mind the belly aching, Tanner; daylight is a wasting."

The Missing Years – Part I

"Wasting? I reckon it is only 6:00 a.m. It ain't even daylight yet. How can it be wasting?" Tanner asked as he put the map away and jumped onto his horse. "We'll make near five miles before the first rays will even lighten our way. Jesus Christ, Buck, you have two cups of coffee and you're wound up like a wagon spring." He shook his head and chuckled as they turned their horses and side by each proceeded northward. The sun that day was warm, raising the late January temperatures to that of an early spring day.

They travelled for about six hours, talking sporadically between themselves. The trail remained clear of avalanches and ice patches making their journey safe and tolerable. "I can feel spring in the air, Tanner, I think we're going to have a hot one this year," Buck said to start a conversation.

"Still have a few months of winter, I think. Today though, is a nice one. I'll give you that. In fact, I think its the nicest one since starting this trip. The wind ain't even that bad and it feels kind of good after the sun has been beating down on you. Spring it ain't though, Buck. Spring it ain't." he repeated as they continued onward. Four hours later, Yellow Lake came into view. The lake itself wasn't that big and the hot sun that bore down that day caused the ice along the shore to recede. "Look at that, Buck. The damn lake ain't even froze. You'd figure one that small in size would freeze solid," Tanner pointed out.

"Could be there is a hot spring that bleeds into it. I've heard there are a few around this area."

"That likely explains it. Might as well let the horses have a drink, and fill our canteens. You don't suppose that the water will be bad, do you?" Tanner asked, as the two men slid off their horses and led them to the shore for a drink.

"It won't bother the horses if it is, but might give us a belly ache. To be safe we'll boil it for our consumption," Buck responded, as he looked out across the scantily ice covered lake. "So, according to the map, the trail circles around, eh?"

"Yep, if we were able to cut straight north here and cross the lake we'd cut off maybe four or five miles of trail."

"For that amount of a gain, even if it were frozen, I still wouldn't cross."

"Nah, probably wouldn't make much of a difference. Reckon we should set up camp here for the night?"

Buck shrugged. "Depends on what time it is, I suppose." He looked at his watch. "We're pushing 4:30 p.m., won't be long till dusk, two or three hours at tops. We could carry on."

"All right then, maybe we could get around the lake to the other side before then. I'm up for it. It's been easy going so far today. I don't reckon that'll change before dusk."

"You never know. It could, but I'm with you on the fact that it likely won't." They waited a few minutes as their horses finished slurping up some lake water, then once more set off. The trail around the lake was as good as the trail that led up to it and so they made the distance to the other side by 6:00 p.m. Near the shore they found another well-used camp and made it their own that night. With the tarp shelter set up and a fire burning, they sat and contemplated their day of travel. It had been a good day and they guessed that they put behind them another thirty-five miles and were that much closer to their destination. "Take a gander at that map now, Tanner. By this time

The Missing Years – Part I

tomorrow we ought to be damn close," Buck assumed, as he waited for Tanner to find it.

Finding it, Tanner opened it up and looked. "We're getting there. If we can put on as many miles as we did today we might make the distance early the following day after tomorrow."

"It might take us a day to find Mac Rider, and to get the answer from that fellow Travis. Means we'll make it back to Willow Gate sometime in late February or early March, and that is only if we don't run into any problems on our return trip."

"You say today is the 24th, of January. We left Willow Gate, ummm, shit I can't remember. Do you?" Tanner asked, as he tried to think back.

"We left Willow Gate on the December 15th. We've been on the trail for well over a month, and that of course is due to some lollygagging, and whiskey drinking," Buck answered. "To get where we are now has taken near forty days. That's a long time on the trail, Tanner. Should have asked Gabe for more money. A quick calculation in my mind means the son of a bitch is paying us a little more than $12 a day each for this trip and that is return. That ain't very much in my mind."

"We didn't have clue on how long it would take, but, yeah if its eighty days return then he ain't paying us much more than the $12 a day. Hopefully he'll buck up, Buck." Tanner chuckled at his own joke. Buck only shook his head and smiled.

"You know Gabe. He ain't gonna reward us anymore than what we accepted. It is part our fault, I reckon. We should have thought it through and maybe did some calculations before we agreed on the $1000 dollars apiece. Live and learn I guess, eh Tanner?"

The Missing Years – Part I

"You have to admit, Buck, it ain't been so bad. I think I've only spent $50 since we left, and that includes the whiskey we drank here or there and the few times we spent in hotel saloons and the food we bought."

"I ain't complaining, Tanner, just pointing out that I think we got short-changed. The job itself ain't really the issue; it's the peril we put ourselves in. I figure my life is worth more than $12 a day to go scooting across the land in mid winter."

"Well, Buck, like you said, live and learn. Next time we'll ask for $20 a day."

"I ain't sure that would even be enough. Shit, Gabe is offering that Travis fellow $300 a week to track down Tyrell. That is a wee bit more than $40 a day. I do admit there is more risk involved or, at least, risk that may include gunfire." Buck paused for a moment as he contemplated. "That is another thing that makes me wonder. How is anyone supposed to find anybody, when all they have is a first name and no description whatsoever. Not even the law knows who Tyrell is, yet Gabe will offer some fellow $300 a week to try and find him, and pay a bounty hunter the reward to do the same. It seems quite senseless to me, Tanner. I don't reckon anyone living today will ever solve that mystery of who Tyrell is."

"I hear you, Buck. That is probably one of the main reasons Riley Scott turned down the bounty. He knew it was pointless to try and track down a ghost," Tanner chuckled. "I figure Gabe has more money than common sense, but his money sure feels good in a man's pocket." he added with a smirk. There was one thing that, Tanner, hadn't shared with anyone, and the chances were he never would. He had a dirty little secret in his back pocket. The dirty little secret he kept was that back in his younger days he rode with a fellow named Tyrell Sloan. In fact, the two

The Missing Years – Part I

of them were good friends, separated only by the few months Tanner had spent in prison. When he was released, Tyrell Sloan had left the south. Never again did they lay eyes upon each other. Tyrell Sloan, he knew, was able to disappear quickly. Even back in the days they rode together, he had that ability. Tanner, being the educated hoodwink that he was, knew right from the beginning that in all probability, the Tyrell that so many were so frantically looking for, was likely his old friend. He often wondered what he would do if he ever came across him.

The $5000 dollar reward that was offered certainly wasn't enough for Tanner to turn him in. Chances were, in fact, no amount would be. Sometimes, though, things changed. He remembered the gunfights that Tyrell had been in and that he had witnessed brought on by ego, jealousy, and senseless arguments. Most times it wasn't even Tyrell's fault. He was only a target by those who wanted to see if they could beat him. None ever did. Tanner remembered him to be honest and forthright, not much different than himself, and it was likely due to the same mannerisms they shared that they got along so well. He also knew the death of Heath Roy and Ollie Johnson wasn't murder. That was pure ridicule.

Whether it was the Tyrell he knew or some other Tyrell from God knows where, the entire fiasco in his mind was self-defence, and Heath Roy and Ollie Johnson got what they deserved. Although that was becoming the view of more and more people, there would always be those who wanted the reward, and even more as the reward grew as time went by. All rewards worked that way. It was a vicious circle. Tanner looked across the fire to Buck, who was transfixed by the flames, his eyes weary. "Hey, Buck, you alive over there?"

The Missing Years – Part I

"Am so. Was thinking a little too much Tanner, that's all, I reckon," Buck answered, as he looked over to Tanner.

"Well, stop it. You ain't said two words in the last while."

"Ain't got nothing to say. You ain't been so vocal either, Tanner. Shit, sometimes a man simply runs out of things to say." The two of them sighed in unison, knowing that was fact. Both of them now gazed into the fire, their minds adrift, to the here and now, yesterday, beyond, and forthcoming. One thing was for certain, the realisation on how far they actually travelled and what they descended, and ascended, was beginning to wear on them. The thought alone of having to go through it all over again made both of their bodies ache, fit as both were. The weather they would have to endure, the food they would have to eat, and the distance they'd have to travel again made them nauseous. "You ever think of doing something a little less aggravating than what we do now?" Buck questioned, without rhyme or reason.

"I don't know, Buck. It is all I've ever done on the honest side of things and made a living at. There ain't much out there. Either you are born rich or born not so. Those born not so, have to do what they can. For me, this is what I *'can'*, that's my philosophy." Something caught Tanner's eye as he said that and he glanced into the distance. "Shit, got company approaching."

"Who would be out here other than you and me?"

"Only one rider is all I see. Ain't no point in getting all anxious, Buck. Likely a simple passerby no different than ourselves. Besides, it is only one rider," Tanner shrugged.

The Missing Years – Part I

"I'm more curious than anxious, Tanner." They could hear the horse now and they both stood to meet whoever it was that came their way.

"Evening gentlemen," the rider said, as he approached. "My name is Ben Westcott." He tilted his hat to them with regard.

Both Buck and Tanner were quite shocked at how old the man looked. "Howdy, Ben, I'm Buck Ainsworth, this here is Tanner McBride. It's kind of late to be out and about, ain't it?" Buck asked with concern.

"Oh, I suppose. I saw your fire from a distance and thought I'd make myself noticed."

"And noticed you are," Tanner said, as he stepped forward and offered a handshake. "You might as well get off your horse and join us."

"That is kind of you. Thank you," Ben said, as he swung off his horse and tethered him near. "We don't usually get folks around here at this time of year. Are you fellows lost?" the old codger asked.

Buck almost started to laugh. "Lost? No sir. Were heading into Chase, and yourself?"

"Heading to Hells Bottom, best time of year to be there is early February, that's when the Bottom wakes up," Ben chuckled.

"Wakes up?" Tanner questioned with curiosity.

"That's what I said. The big gamblers from down south come up for the big Hells Bottom poker tournaments. Happens every year, from February 6th, through to the 16th, ten days of wins and losses. Some of them gamblers have very pretty wives," Ben snickered, as he sat next to the fire.

Buck looked at him and smiled. "You're a gambler, Ben?"

The Missing Years – Part I

"Only when I win. When I lose I feel more like a jackass." The three of them chuckled.

"So, Hells Bottom gets lively in February. I had no idea." Tanner looked over to Buck. "Maybe we can find some time to spend there when we head back. I wouldn't mind getting into some poker. What kind of stakes are we talking, Ben?"

"There is most certainly money to be won, but remember for it to be won, someone loses. It can get ghastly dire. Sometimes I sit on the sidelines and take in the sights and sounds. There are all kinds of food and expensive drink, bells and whistles. It is a grand time to be honest." It was easy to tell that Ben was excited about the whole thing.

"You go there every year, Ben?"

Ben looked at him and nodded. "Every year I can afford, sometimes not."

"You must live around here then?"

"I do and not far from here actually."

"Do you by chance know Mac Rider?" Tanner asked in a friendly tone.

"Yes, yes I do. Who wants to know?" Ben responded evasively.

"It ain't him we're so much looking for, we're looking for Travis Sweet he is said to work with Mac. No harm will come to them. We've been hired by a fellow down in Willow Gate who wants to offer him a job," Buck made clear.

"That is comforting. I know his work with Mac cannot last forever..."

Tanner cut him off there. "So, you know Travis as well as Mac?"

"Yes, I've already said that. I've only know Travis for a short period. I can't say I know him personally. Mac, on the other hand, I've known for more than a few years, likely ten. Travis is helping him with some horse logging on his property. He and Rose, that's Mac's wife of sorts, want to build a bigger house. What I know of Travis is very little, except that Mac hired him some time back a few months ago if I recall. Mac seems to like him, says he works hard and is a pleasure to be around in general," Ben stated. He felt no threat from the men the two of them seemed honest and cordial. There was nothing to fear from them. Truly there wasn't.

Buck scratched his chin wondering if he should even ask the next question. He didn't want Ben to feel as though he were being interrogated. It was important though and since Ben had already shared as much, he went ahead and asked. "You have a guess on how far Mac's place is from here?"

"Fifteen miles," Ben offered up freely. "The trail is pretty good too from here on. Follow my tracks, 'til you come to another trail on the right of the main trail. Hard to miss, actually. Anyway you follow that trail straight up to Mac's place, maybe a mile from the main trail. Be kind to the lady behind the door," Ben both warned and made aware. "Also ignore the sign which reads 'Rider Land Keep Left' that is the one you'll see going this way, coming from the other way it reads 'Rider Land Keep Right'. Funny, those two signs are. A lot of folks get confused by them and I reckon that is why Mac put them there," he chuckled.

"So, folks carry right on by, wondering where Mac lives, eh? That is damn funny," Buck chuckled. "Thanks for sharing that, Ben. I'm glad to know we're close. We've travelled a long way. Thought we'd have to work our way back from Chase."

"Chase is another forty-five maybe fifty miles north of Mac's. Indeed you are closer than you thought."

The Missing Years – Part I

Tanner poured Ben a cup of coffee and handed it to him. "Thank you, umm, Tanner it was, yes," Ben wanted to confirm.

"Is too. Thought you might want a cup, kind of rude not to have offered you one sooner. Sorry about that, Ben," Tanner replied, apologetically.

"That's okay, the questions were more important and I'm glad I could help," Ben responded, as he took a swallow from his coffee. The relief that Buck and Tanner were feeling, knowing that they would make the distance to Mac's house in less than day, made up for how they were feeling earlier. Soon, they could turn around and head for home. Soon, it would all be over, and they could take on the next dirty job that perhaps some other bigwig would offer. The life of a bounty hunter, at the best of times, was pretty exhausting and troublesome. "You make very good camp coffee," Ben said, to whichever one made it, as he nodded his appreciation.

"Thanks. We're about to cook up some food and you are welcome to join us," Buck added.

"That would be grand. Thank you again, Buck, correct?" Ben wanted to be clear, he wasn't always so good with names, but once he learned your name, he never forgot it.

"That's right, I'm Buck and that is Tanner," Buck responded, as he gestured with his chin in the direction of which Tanner sat.

"Good, I'm clear now." Ben took another swig of his coffee while Tanner opened a couple cans of beans and tossed together some biscuit dough. A pot of coffee later, the three of them shared the meal. Full and satisfied, Buck made another pot, and the three of them shared tales and jokes as they sat huddled near the fire. The weather turned again as they sat there, and the wind from the north blew hard and cold, making their tarp shelter flap and ripple in the wind. Snow drifts piled here and there as the wind skidded across the land, unrelenting. "Damn," Ben started. "Lately we've been getting that cold wind up around here. Sure makes for unpleasant days. How was the weather down southerly, from which you travelled?" Ben asked.

"Mostly cold, a biting cold actually. There was some wind, but there were also some days that were spring-like," Buck answered.

"Humph, around here it has been the same. Not as much snow this year as last."

"Shit, the snow's probably been blown away. With wind like this, sure makes for a chilly evening," Tanner said as he added his own thoughts to the conversation.

"We had some rather cold days. The first one I remember this year which was intolerable was the 20th." Ben paused, as he reminisced how cold it had been. The wind during the day back then didn't only blow at night. There were a few days where it blew straight through both night and day for two entire days, bringing with it the cold temperature from high on the Rockies, that surrounded the area. It chilled his bones as he thought about. "It is starting to get better, I think, except, of course, for the wind, but that never lasts long and then the sun shines. It is unpredictable, the weather is, this year."

"Maybe we'll have an early spring and hot summer. That wouldn't hurt my feelings."

"I think late February, and early March, will be one of two things 'hot' or 'cold'." Ben chuckled.

Buck shook his head and joined Ben in a chuckle. "I wouldn't argue that Ben, it can only be one or the other." The wind finally settled after an hour or so, and the evening temperature did get colder. They wrapped themselves up in their bedrolls and remained huddled around the fire for most of the night keeping amused with idle chit-chat. At 11:00 p.m., agreeing to take turns adding wood to the fire throughout the night, they made up their beds and fell asleep.

The Missing Years – Part I

Chapter 19

It started to snow in the early twilight of predawn, and by the time they woke that morning another boot-top depth of powdered snow had accumulated. "Snowed again last night," Buck pointed out, as he came in from gathering more wood. "Just above the boots. It is powder though, fluffy as cotton. It'll melt, or like you said last night, Tanner, it'll blow away." He added another stick to the fire and tried pouring water into the coffee pot from his canteen but it was frozen solid. He set it closer to the fire and waited for it to thaw before he was able to make any. Finally, Tanner and Ben forced their asses out of bed.

"Shit, snowed again you say?" Tanner questioned as he sat up and rubbed his eyes.

"Yeah, it's all powder though."

"That ain't so bad then, I reckon. It is a lot better than if it were wet and heavy. That stuff always makes things miserable. The cold, though, keeps the snow dry. Once the sun hits it, it'll lower in depth."

Ben crawled out of his bedroll and pulled on his woollen pants. "Well, Buck and Tanner, was nice to have met each of you, but, I need to put on some miles today. An early start is always best." He rolled up his bedding and tied the leather lace around it. "Let Mac know for me that my cows need hay at 4:00 p.m., every day until I get back. Was in such a rush for one reason or another, I totally forgot to ask him. The mind is good most times, but sometimes it shows its age."

"We'll let him know Ben, no problem. You ain't going to stay for a morning coffee?" Tanner asked.

Ben hummed and hawed for a moment then finally agreed on a quick cup. "I suppose I could have one." He

The Missing Years – Part I

looked at his watch. "It is only 6:00 a.m.; it couldn't hurt I guess."

"Good, I'm glad you decided." Buck poured Ben a cup and handed it to him, then poured another for himself and Tanner. Coffees in hand, they stepped outside and looked around, as the cool morning air revived their senses, and woke them up. "A little cold still this morning. I reckon it'll warm up though as the sun crests the Rockies."

"The sky isn't as blue as yesterday; might get more snow." Ben took a swig from his coffee as he roped both his hands around the hot tin of the cup to warm them against the chill. He shrugged. "One never knows though. You could be right, Buck, and it might turn out warm."

"Warm or not, things need doing and we'll carry on." Tanner said, as he set his cup down and found a bush to relieve himself. "Once we finish with our coffees we might as well head off too, Buck. The sooner we get gone and meet up with Mac and Travis, the sooner we can turn around and head back. I'm kind of looking forward to stopping off in Hells Bottom and see what I can see, and play a hand or two." Tanner buttoned up his fly and returned to his cup of coffee. "You said the 6th of February, didn't you, Ben?"

"That is the first day of festivities, yep. Today, I believe is the 25th it will take me about five days to get there, so the 30th. I'll have a week to secure funds, get a good room and spoil myself a wee bit, before all the noise starts."

"If things go as planned with us, we'll probably catch up with you on the 1st, or shortly thereafter." Buck did a quick calculation in his head. "Geez, that does leave a lot of time before the tournaments start, don't it?" Buck pointed out. "Ain't sure I want to hang out that long, would rather get on with business. We will stop though when we

The Missing Years – Part I

turn back that way." He looked over to Tanner. "I don't know if it'll be worth our while to stick around in the Bottom though, Tanner."

"You're always putting out my spark, you know that, Buck. It'll only be a few days of waiting."

"That is a few days we can put behind us which brings us that much closer to Willow Gate."

"I know you're right. Still, a little fun to celebrate wouldn't hurt my feelings any." Tanner took the last swallow from his coffee. "Anyway, let's tear down camp and get on with it."

"Yes, I should be getting on the trail now as well," Ben said, as he loaded up his gear and swung onto his horse. "Don't forget to give that message to Mac for me about my cows. Otherwise, they'll be a mite skinny when I get back. It was a pleasure meeting you both and good luck in your endeavours, if I don't lay eyes on you again."

"No worries there Ben, we'll let him know. It was nice meeting you too by the way, and we'll see if we can't find you once we get back to Hells Bottom. Keep your eyes peeled for any signs of avalanches." Tanner responded as Ben turned his horse and heeled its flank.

"Will do, Tanner, will do. We'll see you two when you get to the Bottom." Ben hollered as he and his horse headed in the direction of Hells Bottom a five-day ride away. Buck and Tanner watched as he headed off. Then they went about dismantling and cleaning up their camp. Their gear loaded now, they headed off in the opposite direction. Today they would get their answer from the man they were hired to find. Today their job would be complete.

They followed the trail as Ben had suggested and by mid-day they turned off the main trail and headed easterly toward Mac's place. It was easy going for the pair. They could see smoke rising from the chimney of the small house, as they grew closer. "This must be Mac's place, I reckon." Buck said, as they pulled up to the outside stoop. "I'll do the knocking." Buck dismounted and made his way to the door while Tanner stayed in his saddle. Knocking he waited a few moments and then knocked again.

Rose cocked the rifle as she slowly approached the door. Standing far enough away to have a clear shot, at anyone who decided to simply bust in, she questioned. "Who is it and what do you want?"

"My name is Buck Ainsworth. I don't mean you no harm, ma'am. My partner and I are looking for Mac Rider. Is this his place?" Buck responded from the other side of the closed door.

"What do you want with Mac?" Rose answered back as she slowly opened the door a crack, the rifle beneath her arm she peeked through the opening. She saw the man standing there and waited for his response to her question.

"We have a job offer for the man that works with Mac. Goes by the name of Travis Sweet," Buck answered with honesty.

"I'm going to open the door now, mister. My rifle is loaded and I can shoot, so don't try anything that will get you killed." Rose opened the door and held the rifle steady. "What is that you said about a job?"

Buck removed his hat nervously as he looked down the barrel of the rifle the women held on him. He took a step back raising his hands to show that he wasn't there to cause any harm to her, Mac or Travis. "Easy ma'am, I ain't here to die. We're looking for Travis Sweet, heard he works for Mac Rider. Is this his land?" Buck repeated.

"It is. He isn't here right now though, as you can see."

"When will he be back?"

The Missing Years – Part I

"Soon, but, if you say you're here to find Travis, he and Mac are up at the top five. You can find them there."

"Where exactly is that, ma'am?"

Rose gestured with the barrel of her rifle. "Follow the trail up, you'll find them."

Buck looked in the direction Rose was pointing. "All right. Thank you very much, ma'am. We'll be off now." Buck put his hat back on as he slowly stepped away and mounted his horse. Rose watched as the two riders turned up the trail and disappeared around the first bend, before she closed the door and returned to her baking.

"That was a little bit odd. Weren't that a squaw woman?" Tanner asked. It seemed odd to him to see one living civil and amongst the white man.

"It was, indeed. Pretty little thing too she was," Buck said, as they continued onward. Twenty minutes later, they were close enough to the top five that they could see the two men working. "I reckon that be them up ahead," Buck said, as he and Tanner now came in view of the men.

"Got visitors, Mac," Tyrell said, as he slowed Pony to halt from pulling a couple of cedars out of the bush. He gestured for Black Dog to hide and to be ready if there was trouble. "Hope they are friendly," he added as he and Mac looked on.

"Hello there!" Mac called out as they approached closer. Right off the bat, Tanner recognised Tyrell Sloan, and Tyrell knew he was looking at Tanner McBride.

Shit, he thought as Tanner pulled up beside the two men. Not Tanner, nor Tyrell, said anything to one another, they just looked at each other. Tanner took that as a sign not to mention that they knew each other. It all made sense to him now.

"Hello there. We're looking for Mac Rider." Tanner said as he slowed his horse to a halt.

The Missing Years – Part I

"I'm Mac, and who might you be?"

"I'm Tanner McBride, and this is Buck Ainsworth. I guess if you are Mac, then you must be Travis Sweet." Tanner responded as, he looked deep into Tyrell's eyes.

"That is correct. What is this about?" Tyrell questioned. He knew Tanner had made him and he showed him his appreciation for not spoiling the fib in the way he looked at Tanner.

"You ever heard of Gabe Roy, lives down in Willow Gate?" Tanner asked. For a moment Tyrell wasn't sure how he should respond. If Tanner and Buck were there to get the bounty, there was going to be trouble.

"That name don't ring a bell. Can't say I have, nope," Tyrell responded, as he shrugged. "What does that have to do with anything?" he asked, as he tilted his head.

"You're the fellow who sent Earl Brubaker on a one way trip to Hell, ain't you?" Buck asked, with a smile. "That is what has been said, leastwise."

"I might be that man. Again, what does that have to do with anything?" He was ready to draw if he had to, and by the look of Mac, so was he.

"Gabe Roy asked us to come all the way up here and offer you a business proposal. If you're the man that beat Earl Brubaker, Gabe has a good offer for you. Are you that man?"

"What did you say you name was again?" Mac asked of Buck.

"I'm Buck Ainsworth and this is Tanner McBride," Buck responded with clarity.

"Are you two working for this fellow named Gabe?" Tyrell questioned.

"Not in a permanent sense. He offered us a $1000 apiece to find the man that beat Brubaker to the draw." Tanner looked at both Mac and Tyrell.

"Well, you did find him," Tyrell answered. "What does he want from me?"

"A few months back, his son Heath was murdered. Gabe wanted to know if you'd like to be put on a payroll and help track down his son's killer."

"No sir, I ain't interested in anything like that. That is what they have bounty hunters for, and I ain't one."

"He told us to tell you he'll pay you $300 a week," Buck added.

Tyrell only shook his head as he looked around. "That is a nice sum, but I have work here. You can tell that Gabe fellow I ain't interested."

Buck nodded. "Yeah, I figured that would be your answer. It is a tidy sum though."

"It is indeed. Except that ain't what I do. I reckon this all came about because of what he may or may not have heard about the killing of that Brubaker fellow. Ain't that right?"

"Any man that can beat a fellow like Brubaker is going to get a lot of requests and offers. That goes without saying."

"That might be true except I ain't for hire. Tell me Buck, what have you heard about it. What is the story that has made this Gabe fellow so interested?" Tyrell wanted to know.

"Only told us that you beat Brubaker's hand and that you worked with, Mac Rider. Told us where the incident took place and where we could find Mac. Then he sent us on our merry way to fetch you."

"Hearsay, that is all that is. I did beat his hand, but it took two slugs of lead to kill him. Does that sound to you like, maybe I got lucky?" Tyrell knew that wasn't the case. Brubaker was quick, and it took two slugs because he had to side-step a possible ounce of lead himself, and his aim

The Missing Years – Part I

was a bit off; but he did beat him before Brubaker could pull the trigger.

"I guess it really don't matter. You don't want the job and that is the end of it." Tanner looked over to Buck. "I say our job here is done, Buck. I reckon we should let Mac and Travis to get back to their work. It was nice to meet you both," Tanner nodded. "Come on, Buck, let's head back." Tanner began to turn his horse.

"No use rushing off. You two are quite welcome to join us in a coffee, we're about to break for one." Mac said invitingly, as he looked at Travis.

Tyrell agreed. "Yeah, what do you say? Want to join us for a coffee?" His hope was that they would, so, that he might get a moment to talk to Tanner out of earshot of the others. He thought, *how odd it was that after all these years, they were face to face again.* His mind raced with the memories he and Tanner had shared back in the day. It was good to see him, as long as he wasn't there to pull his pistol. Tyrell was most certain that he wouldn't, and he knew by the way Tanner looked at him, that he wasn't going to spill beans about who he really was. It was a simple understanding that they shared even back in the day. It kept most people guessing if they were even acquainted. It also saved them a time or two from the law, as well as those that wanted to test their pistol speed and the like. Deep down they both knew this was one of those times as well.

"That is mighty kind of you, Travis. What do you figure, Tanner? Want to join Mac and Travis for a coffee before we head off?"

Tanner turned his horse again to face them. "Sure, that'd be a nice gesture. Thank you fellows." he said as he swung off the saddle and Buck followed suit. "So, how long have the two of you been at this horse logging?"

The Missing Years – Part I

Tanner asked to make friendly conversation, as the four of them made their way over to the fire that gently burned.

"Since late November, we took a few days off a couple of days ago. The weather turned cold and blusterous. Today is our first day back." Mac paused as they finally made the distance to the fire and sat down. "I imagine the two of you have been on the trail for quite a spell, eh? Willow Gate ain't that close."

"That isn't a word of a lie, Mac. We left there on December 15th or there about. Likely would have made the distance here in a shorter bit of time if we never stopped off as often as we did. Plus the weather did slow us down," Buck pointed out.

"The weather has been a bit odd, that is for sure," Tyrell said as he set the coffee pot full of snow next to the fire so they could make coffee. "That'll take a few minutes to melt down. Could have got fresh water I suppose, but, snow works too. So, Buck, Tanner, what kind of place is Willow Gate, I ain't never been there, I don't think," Tyrell fibbed.

Tanner looked at him and smiled. "It ain't much different than Hells Bottom, I don't suspect. The town is mostly, run by the Roy family or should I say Gabe Roy, since, he is the only Roy breathing. There are a few other rich folk too that seem to run things. Gabe has a brother too, but, he lives way down south from what I know," Tanner shrugged. "Most folks stay out of Gabe's business. He does what he wants when he wants."

"He's the mayor then, or what?"

"He ain't no mayor; don't think Willow Gate even has one of those. Things would be different then I think."

"So, Gabe is a rich man that throws his weight around, I suspect."

"That would be the marrow of it."

The Missing Years – Part I

"Yeah, I figured that right off the get go, as soon as you told me he wanted a hired gun," Tyrell said, as he averted his eyes to the fire. "Folks like that, I have no use for. What happened to his son by the way. You said earlier it was murder?"

"That's only what Gabe wants to believe. To be honest, Travis, Heath got what was coming to him, so did his friend," Buck answered.

"A friend of his got killed too?"

"Yep Ollie Johnson. He wasn't much better than Heath. The two of them were a bit unruly and in my opinion simply pulled the heavy on the fellow who killed them."

"What was that fellow's name. I ain't sure you mentioned that yet?"

"The only name that anyone knows is Tyrell. Shit, they don't even have a description that is any good. The law has a few wanted posters around Willow Gate and few other places. Not even they have a clue on who the shooter was. Likely no one will ever know, unless the man turns himself in."

"This Tyrell fellow is wanted for the murder of two men, then? Humph, sounds like self-defence in a sense, don't it?"

"The law claims to have four murders to pin on him: Heath Roy, Ollie Johnson, and two other folk, who went after the killer shortly after the incident. There ain't much said about those two, though. Most are simply interested in the bounty Gabe has offered. It's twice the amount of the laws."

Tyrell was shocked to hear that. He hadn't killed anyone except Heath and Ollie. He kept his composure as they continued to converse. "Really, four murders? How do

The Missing Years – Part I

they come to that conclusion?" Tyrell was curious to know more. "Some fellow found the bodies east of Willow Gate, the direction the killer was said to be travelling. From what I've heard, is they were almost decapitated. It didn't sound to me like it was the same guy that killed Heath and Ollie, but, that is only my own educated guess." Tanner wanted to make clear. "I don't think someone who shoots someone in self-defence would cut the heads off two other men. What would be the point of that?"

The first name that came to Tyrell's mind was, Dr. Harold Pike, the same man that tried to slit his throat. If that were the case, then Dr. Pike was amongst the living, and likely more of a threat than Tyrell ever could be. "I think I'd agree with you on that, Tanner. It doesn't make sense at all. But, who is to say, maybe that is what happened."

"Nah, if I were the law, I wouldn't even suspect that. I'd be looking more into a close confrontation. Maybe they ran into a few Ktunax, or Cree. That sounds more probable to me. Anyone running from the law for whatever reason ain't going to leave a trail of bodies. That'd be too damn obvious."

Tyrell nodded in simple agreement as he dumped some grounds into the coffee pot that was now shooting steam. "Ahh, it don't matter I suppose. Maybe one day that Tyrell fellow will get caught. Who knows?" Tyrell shrugged. "It don't matter to me either way."

"Yeah, nor I really, like Buck said. Heath and Ollie made their own bed and are now forced to sleep in it with the worms and all." Tanner looked to the mountains, as the four of them contemplated the conversation and a few minutes of awkwardness followed as they sat in silence.

The Missing Years – Part I

Finally, the scent of fresh perked coffee enveloped them, and Tyrell inhaled deeply. "The coffee is done, fellows." He handed out cups and poured one for Mac, then the others and himself. "Here's to a good day, and new acquaintances." he said, as he took a swallow.

"I'll drink to that," Buck said, as he brought his cup to his lips and took a drink. "Camp coffee always tastes best in the company of friends."

"What time is it getting on to be, Buck?" Tanner asked as Buck dug into his pocket and pulled out his watch.

"Almost 2:00 p.m., we have a bit of time left before it turns dark. Sounds to me, like, you're the one, in a rush now, Tanner." Buck looked over to Travis. "He's always harping on how much of a rush I'm in." He chuckled. "But, we had a job to do then, now it's done, and he's wetting himself to get going."

"You won't get to far down the trail before it turns dark. If the two of you want to set up here for the night, feel free." Mac said. "We ain't got but another load each to pull out of the bramble. Then we'll be done for the day. No use in rushing off if it ain't necessary." Mac was always that way with weary travellers, and he could tell that both Buck and Tanner were weary.

"Again, that is awful nice of you, Mac. Either of you two whiskey drinkers?" Buck question in good cheer.

"I ain't touched it in a while. You got a bottle then, Buck?"

"I do. Been saving it actually, but, I reckon now is as good a time as any to crack it open. We'll wait, of course, 'til you gather your last logs. We'll set up for the evening whilst you go about that; if it's okay with Tanner, that is." Buck looked over to Tanner. "What do you say Tanner?"

The Missing Years – Part I

He was nodding his head. "Yeah, I reckon, sure, why not."

"In that case," Mac started. "The logs can wait 'til morrow. We'll get our horses put away and have a whiskey. How does that sound to you, Travis?"

"Yeah, I'd be okay with that, I ain't touched whiskey in a while either. Sure." Tyrell said, as he and Mac went about getting their horses squared away, while Buck and Tanner wrestled with the tarp. A half-hour later, the four of them were sitting around the fire sipping whiskey and telling tall tales. It was during this time that Tanner and Tyrell were able to get together out of earshot from Buck and Mac. "So, Tanner," Tyrell started. "How have you been? It sure is good to see you. Last, I heard, you were behind bars down in Washington, what happened?"

"Got caught up in some legalities, but nothing ever came of it. Spent thirty days proving my innocence to the state Marshall. The bastard claimed I had broke the peace. When I found myself being cheated at cards, the fellow doing the cheating figured he'd have a go at me. It didn't last long, he threw some punches, I threw some punches, and in the end he was a bundle of beat up," Tanner chuckled. "My turn to ask a question, why are you using an alias? You're that Tyrell fellow, folks is looking for ain't you?"

"I imagine you already know that answer. It was a blatant case of self-defence, Tanner. Whatever has been said, ain't likely what happened. Heath and Ollie drew on me first, whilst I was enjoying a cup of coffee with a woman who went by the name of Emma. You probably already know that part of the story. Anyway, those two clowns showed up and tossed a bucket through her eatery's window, then started yipping and a hollering, threatening her and me."

The Missing Years – Part I

Tyrell sighed and then continued. "I guess Heath and Emma were once an item. It ended that night though, when she came prancing into the saloon, a few of us were playing five card stud. She pulled Heath's knife from his waistband sheath and gave him a quick nick on the face, and started calling him out on the fact that he had taken advantage of her sister.

Heath slapped her to the ground, split her lip and everything, and called her a bunch of names. She left after that, and I tossed my hand in. Felt bad that it happened. Anyway, I went over to the eatery across the street that is where I saw her next. The rest is history. Heath stormed in his pistol a blazing only thing I could do was slap leather and came up shooting myself. Then Ollie fired at me. He was a better shot than Heath by the way and the bullet grazed me."

Tyrell paused for a moment as he caught his breath. "After that, Emma whisked me into a back room bandaged me up and told me who Heath was and that his old man would want vengeance and take it any way he could get it. I guess now that is all true. Never saw the men that were supposedly trailing me. I ain't sure how their deaths came about." He had an idea on what might have transpired, but it was only conjecture, there was no point in bringing it up. "Not good news knowing the law wants to pin that on me as well. I'll hang for sure, Tanner," Tyrell made clear.

"I figured it was something like that. In fact when I heard the name Tyrell, it was you I conjured up. Anyway, Tyrell, you don't have to worry about me, I ain't gonna say a peep one way or the other. Does, Mac know? Or does he assume you are really a fellow named Travis?"

"He wouldn't have known, but, yeah he does now. He ain't going to say any different either. In fact, he calls me and introduces me as Travis as you've already heard.

The Missing Years – Part I

His wife, as far as I know, don't know any different either. I'd appreciate it if you'd do the same, Tanner."

"Of course, I'll follow Mac's example. My lips are sealed, Tyrell," Tanner said with conviction. "Besides, I don't reckon we'll be seeing each other in the next while. I have a business relationship with Buck. It sometimes takes us a distance away. I can say one thing, old friend. It sure has been nice seeing you. I'm glad you're alive and well."

"Yeah, it has been nice seeing you too, Tanner. Well, I guess we ought to make our way back to the whiskey, before Buck and Mac finish it off. By the way, thanks for helping with feeding the horses." Tyrell winked at him.

"You bet, Travis."

Making the distance back, they pulled up to where they were sitting earlier, before feeding the horses. "They're fed and watered, how you doing there, Mac?" Tyrell asked noticing Mac's droopy eyes and blurred vision.

"Well I think I drank a bit more then I wanted. Damn dark almost already, Rose is probably pulling her hair out." Mac slurred with some guilt.

"I'll set the pot back on and you can have a couple cups of coffee, that'll fix you up. It's only 4:00 p.m., Mac. I'll sober you up." Tyrell chuckled as he made a stronger half pot of coffee for Mac and anyone else that wanted one. He, on the other hand, poured another whiskey for himself, Buck and Tanner. They kicked it back and then another, and another and so on, until the coffee was done. Both Buck and Mac by then wanted nothing more than to throw up, but coffee would suffice. Meanwhile, Tyrell and Tanner kept on with the whiskey, until they too were as drunk as Mac and Buck before they stopped with the whiskey and began slurping coffee. Good strong black coffee, always fixed up a drunken state after it wasn't fun to be drunk anymore.

It was shortly after 6:30 p.m., when Mac finally felt sober enough to head for home. The four of them walked and stumbled the short distance to the corral with him. "Ain't sure how I'm going to be feeling tomorrow, Travis, if I ain't here by dawn, I ain't coming. If you can muster the strength, feel free to pull in the four or five logs we didn't get to," Mac said, as he saddled up Lucy. "Buck, Tanner, was a real pleasure meeting up with you. If you're ever in the area again, whiskey will be on me."

"Was nice meeting you too, Mac, you've been real cordial," Buck responded, as he looked over to Tanner who obviously couldn't get the words out of his mouth due to being drunk. Buck chuckled. "I reckon I speak for Tanner too." Then it dawned on him they had forgotten all about Ben's cows, and the message the old codger wanted them to relay to Mac. "Hang on a second Mac," Buck began as Mac looked at him. "We forgot to mention that we came across a fellow named Ben was on his way to the great Hells Bottom poker tourney. He said his cows need feed at 4:00 p.m. every day until he gets back."

"Shit," Mac responded. "I guess they go hungry for today. Can't believe he's headed that way already; that ain't happening for a while. Anyway, thanks for letting me know." Mac tilted his hat in regards, still feeling the booze himself. "Keep the peace, eh," he said, as he trod off. Tanner, Buck, and Tyrell looked on as he and Lucy coursed their way out of sight.

"Good thing Lucy knows the way," Travis said, with a smile. Drunk as he was, he felt like playing cards and invited Tanner and Buck inside the tepee. "You two want to shuffle through a hand or two of cards?"

"Some five card stud?" Buck asked.

"Sure. We going to put anything up for a stake or just win lose?" Tyrell asked as he led them inside and lit the fire.

"I wouldn't want to take advantage of you and Tanner," Buck joked as he looked around. "I ain't been in one of these for a while. Quite cosy this one is." Buck and Tanner made their way to the table and sat down. "The buffalo hide floor is a fine idea."

"Yeah, one of the best features actually; keeps the wind and dew away. So, about stakes, are we going to play for stakes or what?" Tyrell asked again. "Shit, we could make it simple and play for bullets."

"Bullets? That ain't a bad idea, sure, I'll play for bullets, what about you Buck?" Tanner asked, as he looked over to him.

"Depends I guess what calibre are we talking?"

"Forty-five, I reckon, is most common," Tyrell said, as he sat down on a block of un-split wood, and shuffled the cards.

"Yeah, okay. I'm game," Buck responded, and so their evening went, playing five-card stud for bullets.

Mac got into a little bit of hot water when he finally made it home after stopping three or four times to vomit along the trail. Rose could smell the whiskey and sourness on his breath as he stumbled through the door. "Sorry, I'm a little late, met some folk. Nice fellows they were, I had a few drinks with them and Travis."

"Really, like I couldn't notice, my Mac? You stink of the fire-water, and have spittle on your shirt. Sit now and I'll bring you dinner and coffee." She was not impressed. "Those men came here today. They are Travis' friends I assume?" Rose asked from the kitchen as she scooped out food for Mac and poured him coffee.

"Umm, not really. They were sent up this way by that ass Gabe Roy. I guess he heard the tale about Travis killing that fellow Brubaker. He sent the two of them up here to offer Travis a payroll position, $300 dollars a week, to help look for his son Heath's killer."

"That is hired gun work, is it not?"

"It is and that's why Travis said he wasn't interested. He is a good man that Travis is. There is more honour in making a fair wage and getting blisters from hard work. That was his point of view I think, and he is right you know? He didn't even bat an eye at the amount Gabe was willing to pay."

"Yes. Travis is good mannered and trust worthy. The Blackfoot and I, as well as you my Mac, will always have respect for him." Rose made her way back to the table and set some food and coffee down for Mac. He had his head in his hands and his elbows on the table. She slapped the one closest to her out from his head and he slumped in that direction. "Eat. You are still drunk and need coffee," Rose said, as she waited for him to snap out of it. Finally, he shook his head and looked at her.

"Yeah, you're right my love. Thank you very much. Now sit with your husband. Come on, sit down with me, Rose," Mac coaxed. "I ain't saw you all day, and missed you." Mac took a drink from his coffee as she sat down. "There, now I can look at you. Anyway, back to what we were talking about. Those two fellows, Buck and Tanner are staying up at the top five with Travis for the night. They seemed weary from all the damn travelling they've been doing. Buck had whiskey and well...you can see the results." Mac's head fell forward as he passed out face first into his dinner.

"Ahh, stupid man. You know better than to drink until you are sick." Rose helped him up and wiped the food

The Missing Years – Part I

off his face. "Tonight, you sleep on the couch." She said sternly as she led him to it. He slumped into it and Rose removed his boots and holster. Then, tossing a blanket over him, she grabbed a bucket and set it on the floor next to his head. "The bucket is on the floor. Use it if you have to, Mac. Do I make clear?" she questioned. His response told her that he understood. "All right, I will clean up now." She pranced away and cleared the table of Mac's plate and his spilled cup of coffee. "Men, drinking whiskey and acting like asses, I'm sure. He'll pay tomorrow. No work will get done," she muttered to herself as she headed back into the kitchen. It was 8:00 p.m. before she could finally sit down to a cup of tea. She looked over to Mac snoring and shook her head. Not ready for sleep herself she poured another tea, noticing through the kitchen window Lucy staring in on her. Startled, she jumped and squealed spilling her own tea all over her blouse. "Now I'm mad!" She stormed outside and led Lucy to the corral.

"That stupid Mac forgot all about you, poor Lucy. I'll fetch you hay." She opened the corral gate and set her loose. Making her way to the barn entrance, she grabbed a leaf of hay and tossed it over the rails. "There you go, Lucy; you and the gelding eat up." Rose watched the two of them for a few minutes. *Need to train that gelding,* she thought with a smile. *I will make Mac do that tomorrow. That will fix him for getting so drunk, and he better not argue either, I want a ride-able horse.* Turning now, she made her way back inside. To her surprise, Mac had fallen off the couch. She stood there and looked at the spectacle for a moment, then angry as she was, she helped him back up and once again tossed the blanket over him, tucking in the long part that hung over the couch beneath the cushions that Mac lay on. "There, tied in," she said, as she walked away. At 10:00 p.m., she made her way to their bedroom and closed the door so she wouldn't be forced to listen to Mac's annoying snores. Setting the lantern she carried with her onto the bedside table, she blew out the flame, curled up and went to sleep.

Up at the top five, things were coming to an end as well. So far, Tyrell was up a half dozen bullets and Buck near as much. Tanner was the big loser, but it had all been in fun. They were happy with their winnings and their losses. "You going to the Bottom for the poker tourney, Travis?" Buck asked.

Tyrell shook his head. "I don't think so. Too much work around here. Besides, I ain't got a lot of money to lose. I wouldn't mind winning some, but don't want to lose any," he chuckled. "What about you, Buck? You and Tanner going to stop in on the way back?" he asked Buck directly. Tanner was too drunk to hear much of anything. Tyrell smiled, as he remembered how Tanner never could hold his booze.

"Tanner seems to think so. Myself, I ain't got much use for festivities like that. I think I'd rather continue on to Willow Gate than spend too much time in the Bottom."

"Yeah, I ain't too keen on stuff like that myself."

Buck looked over to Tanner and decided it was time to hit the sack. "I guess, I'll get Tanner put away and hit the sack myself," Buck said, as he stood up and helped Tanner to his feet. "All right, Travis, we'll see you in the morning."

"Yeah, yes you will, Buck. You need any help with Tanner?"

"Nope, it ain't the first time nor will it be the last that I've had to carry his ass off," Buck chuckled, as he began to sing some drunk and annoying song as he exited. Tyrell heard him singing it for a few minutes and he chuckled at the stupid song. Tossing another piece of wood

The Missing Years – Part I

on the fire, he made his way over to his bed, blew out the lantern, and was snoring before he removed his boots.

Chapter 20

The following morning, hung over as they were, the three of them were chipper. Tyrell added wood to the outside fire and gently blew on the coals to get the wood to take a flame. Buck, hearing the noise, sat up and looked through the opening. Noticing Tyrell sitting on the log, he rubbed his eyes and yawned. "How are you feeling this morning, Travis?" Buck asked, as he crawled out of his bedding and dressed.

"A little fuzzy upstairs, but that will pass as soon as I get some coffee. Looks like it is going to be another warm day today. That helps make me feel better. How about yourself Buck, how are you feeling?"

"Probably not much different. I quit drinking earlier than you and Tanner, so I've had a longer period of sobriety." He chuckled as he made his way over to the fire. "That coffee smells good. We have some flour and whatnot. Want me to throw together some hot cakes?"

"Sure. I'll toss some elk meat into a pan as well. We'll have a hearty breakfast, some hot coffee and bullshit a bit more. I reckon you and Tanner are heading back to Willow Gate sometime today, eh?" Tyrell asked, as he stood up and stretched.

"Sometime today yep, depending, of course, on how Tanner might be feeling," Buck said, as he rummaged through his gear to find the flour. Tyrell walked around behind the tepee and cut off some of the elk meat that surprisingly was still frozen. He brought the pieces up to his nose and smelled them. He shrugged. "Smells good enough to me," he said quietly to himself as he walked back to the fire. Around this time, Black Dog came out from somewhere and walked alongside Tyrell. "Morning, Black Dog, I didn't expect you to hide all night." Tyrell shook his head as he knelt down and handed him a piece of the partially frozen elk meat. "I don't think you have met our visitors. Come on, I'll introduce you." A few moments later, he made the distance back, Black Dog at his side.

"Is that your dog?" Buck asked with surprise. "I was wondering last night when I started seeing tracks if you had a dog or if it were wolf tracks I was seeing."

"This here is Black Dog, and, yeah, he's mine. Black Dog, this here is Buck. Buck this is Black Dog." Black Dog wagged his tail as he lay next to the fire and chewed on the elk meat Tyrell had given him.

"Where was he last night? He wasn't around then, was he?" Buck was a bit confused until Tyrell explained to him that the dog travelled here and there and showed up whenever he felt the need. "He's a nice looking fellow." Buck responded as he reached down and scratched the dog behind the ear.

"He is a little quirky but, a great companion, especially up here in the woods." Tyrell set a cast iron pan onto the flames and waited for it to heat up. Buck was busy stirring up pancake dough when Tanner finally sat up and looked outside.

"What time is it, fellows?" he asked in a tired voice as he scratched his eyes.

"Time to get up and at it; the sun is rising. How are you feeling, Tanner?'

"I ain't sure, Buck. Is there coffee?"

"Yep, coffee and pancakes, and Travis is going to burn us some elk meat."

Tanner slid out of his bedroll, slipped on his boots and holster and met Tyrell and Buck at the fire. He didn't even notice Black Dog yet, groggy as he still was. "Is that coffee ready? I desperately need one. Holy shit!" he said, as he noticed Black Dog lying near the fire. "Is that your dog, Travis?"

"That there is Black Dog. He comes and goes, but I like to think he's mine." Tyrell answered, as he threw the chunks of elk meat into the hot pan. The meat sizzled and crackled as he flipped it. "That smells good don't it?"

"Yeah. You say it's elk?"

"Yep, fresh off the tree." He chuckled as he flipped it again.

"Tree elk, eh?" Tanner said, as though tree elk were a species. "That and some pancakes and camp coffee ought to get my head on straight." He looked over to Black Dog. "Where was the dog last night?"

"Ain't sure. Hadn't seen him all day, actually," Tyrell fibbed. "He showed up here this morning. Must have been out chasing rabbits." He stood and entered the tepee. Grabbing three plates, he tossed a hefty chunk of the meat onto each plate. He handed them to Buck who added a few hot cakes. With their breakfast in hand, they talked about the past night, the weather, the dog, and last, but not least, their return trip to Willow Gate. It was easy to tell neither Buck nor Tanner were looking forward to it. "Yeah, I reckon I wouldn't want to do that trip more than once. It's a long haul."

"It is at that." Tanner yawned. "Have to do it, though. We have an obligation to Gabe. Can hardly wait until it's over actually. I ain't sure what might be in store for us once we tell Gabe that you ain't interested in his offer. At this point though, I don't care. What about you, Buck; do you care?" Tanner finished the last of his food on his plate as he waited for a response.

"To be honest, not really, but, like you said we do have an obligation, and once he's been told and we're done with it, I ain't never going to take him up on any work like this again."

"I don't reckon so either." Tanner took a drink of coffee as he looked at Tyrell. "I don't think though that Gabe will ever stop hounding you, Travis. He'll likely send someone else to try and convince you otherwise."

"He can send whoever he wants, I still ain't going to budge. Besides, come spring, I ain't likely going to be here. Once the work is done I'll be off. Ain't sure to where, but he won't find me in these parts."

"You think you and Mac will have it all done by then? There is a lot of work here, according to what he mentioned to me last night."

"Not sure Buck. I hope so. I really don't want to put all my eggs in one basket. There is a big world out there waiting for me. Was thinking on heading up north to the Yukon territories. Maybe find some work in a mine or something. I hear that type of job pays good."

"You ever think about bounty hunting? Not as a hired gun but for plain old bounties on your own terms."

"It might have crossed my mind a time or two, but I never really thought on it seriously enough to make a decision in that regard. Listening to the two of you and the shit you have to go through, I'm more inclined to say *'no'*, but things change." He poured himself another coffee as he contemplated the idea. He knew he could do the job. He had already been offered a position with Ed McCoy and had told Ed that he'd make his way to Fort Macleod in late spring early summer. He may have blown smoke up Ed's ass, but hey, there always was that chance that he would follow up on Ed's offer. Only time would tell. For now, he was content with the work he was doing for Mac, and if it did turn out that Mac still needed him in spring, he wouldn't turn him down.

The Missing Years – Part I

At 9:00 a.m., that morning January 26th, 1891 when the sun was hot, he bid Tanner and Buck farewell as they headed back to Willow Gate and a life that waited for them, wherever it was they would go and do next. In a sense he was saddened. He and Tanner had a past, and although it was long ago, it was heart wrenching to watch him leave, knowing that they may never lay eyes on each other again. *The past is the past. Friends come and go, but memories are forever,* he thought, as he said his final good bye to them both. Sitting alone now at the fire with Black Dog at his side, he reminisced. In time, he knew, others would come to try their hand in beating the draw of the man that beat Earl Brubaker. Until then all that mattered was living.

He looked over to Black Dog. "You know what, Black Dog, I never wanted this life. It gets too damn lonely and frustrating at times. I wish more than ever that we never left Red Rock. We could have made a life there, I think. Now look at us. We left it all behind and are now living as fugitives. We made, or should I say, I made one mistake and that was running after that incident with those two knuckleheads, Heath and Ollie. Now I've been accused of killing two more men that I never even saw. One mistake, Black Dog; that is all it took."

Black Dog made his way over to Tyrell, noting how down he seemed and licked his face as if to assure him that no matter what, he would always be by his side through thick and thin. "You know exactly how I'm feeling, don't you? You are a great friend and companion, Black Dog, indeed, you are, and I'm damn grateful to have you around. I know I need to snap out of this slump I seem to put myself into every time I start thinking about this and that. After all it is what it is, ain't it?" It was at that time that he saw two more riders coming up the trail. He squinted as he focused on the riders. "Shit, it's Mac and Rose, and Mac is

The Missing Years – Part I

riding that gelding of his. Come on, Black Dog. Let's look alive, a lady is coming to visit." Standing he walked toward them, Black Dog following close behind. "Morning Mac, Rose, what a pleasant surprise," he said as they approached. "Got the gelding trained I see. When did that happen?"

"It was either that or take a horsewhipping. Damn woman," Mac replied with annoyance.

"Mac thought today he could sleep from all the whiskey he drank, but I had him up before dawn and told him I wanted that horse trained," Rose said, as Tyrell took Lucy's reins and helped her off. "For three years that horse has waited to be saddle trained. Mac hasn't even named him yet. Stupid man," she said, as she looked around, while Mac slowly slid off the geldings back.

"Geez, Mac you ain't looking too healthy."

Mac looked at him, unimpressed because he had been coerced into training the gelding while being hung over.

"So, what are you going to name him, 'Three Years Without a Name'," Tyrell teased.

"Shut up. You have coffee on, Travis?" Mac asked as he slowly made his way to the fire and sat down. Rose, was walking around looking at all the work the two of them had done.

"I'll get a fresh pot going. So, how many times did the gelding throw you?"

"I ain't sure, a couple, but I fell off a few times too due to the damn hangover I seem to have, which is why we won't be doing any work up here today. Tanner and Buck stopped on their way out to give us their good-byes. Nice fellows the two of them."

"They seemed that way, yep. I feel sorry for them. That is a long way to travel to ask a simple question. I guess that is the type of work they do." Tyrell shrugged as though what they did made little sense. "It ain't bounty hunting. It is something in between, I reckon."

"It is bounty hunting. I think the business has changed over the years. Today they take whatever they can get. The reason for that is because there are so damn many of them, nowadays. Too many of one thing such as Bounty Hunters lessen the workload, which, leaves a bunch of them without work. They have to scratch and claw to make a few bucks or get hired by men like Gabe Roy." Mac sighed. "I haven't felt this ill in a long while, Travis. I think that whiskey Buck poured for us last night was poisonous," he half chuckled, although he did wonder.

"He didn't pour it for us, Mac. We took it upon ourselves to drink it. I know how you are feeling, leastwise hangover wise. Geez, that was a lot of wises," Tyrell smiled. He knew he had thrown Mac for a loop with that sentence. The coffee pot was steaming and gurgling. Removing it from the flames, he set it on the ground, close enough to stay warm and not so close that it would continue to boil. He rinsed out the coffee cups by wiping them inside and out with snow. It was good enough for him and it did clean them.

Pouring the first cup he handed it to Mac, who desperately took it. He had only been able to swig back one that morning at 5:00 a.m., before Rose was kicking him outside to saddle train the gelding. How he worshipped that second cup. He looked over to the gelding and smiled. He honestly thought he would never get around to it, but Rose had pushed him, and now as he looked at that horse he was glad she had. Averting his eyes, he watched Rose, look over the work that had been done. Next, she checked out the steam bath, then the corral and so on. As she wandered about, he didn't once take his eyes off her. *That is my Rose,* he thought as he gazed. Tyrell noticing this smiled to himself. He envied Mac in a way, but he also understood how a woman made a man feel by her presence alone. It was a special feeling. One only a man and woman could share. He watched as Rose made her way to the fire.

"So, what do you think, Rose? How is it looking up here?" Tyrell asked, as she made the distance.

"My Mac and you have done good work here. Is the tepee keeping you warm?" she asked as Tyrell poured her a coffee and handed it to her. Taking it from him, she thanked him.

"The tepee hasn't caused me any discomfort. It stays warm once you get it to that point. Mac tells me it was your idea for a buffalo hide floor. That is the selling point, keeps the frost and wind out. It is a great idea, I think."

"The Blackfoot have the same thing, only it is not sewn or tied into place, and only lies on the ground. Rocks or family possessions and other heavy stuff keep the floor from slipping. They use the floor only during cold and winter months. It is an old idea made better. I think that too." The three of them conversed over another coffee, and since Mac was feeling better by then, they walked around with Rose, answering her questions and discussing ideas and hopeful outcomes. They spent two hours and gave Rose the full tour. It was 2:00 p.m., when they sat down again. The sun's brilliance and warmth caressed their faces as the soft gentle breeze blew smoke from the fire this way and that. In their silent contemplation, if they listened closely they could hear as the snow literally melting from the bows of the cedar trees that surrounded them. "It is very peaceful up here, my Mac. We will build amongst this beauty one day."

"Yes we will, Rose. Things may look different by then though. Now that we have a second horse, there ain't

The Missing Years – Part I

nothing stopping you from checking up as we go. It can get hard explaining what it is we're doing up here without you seeing it for yourself."

"I will visit as you two go along, maybe bring picnic too. Do not fall all the trees. Take only what you need to make the land useable for building house. The trees are what make it so enchanted and beautiful. Keep for shade too."

"No worries there, Rose. I ain't going to tear down the forest, only going to clear enough land to build on, and cut enough trees to use for the building of a house, barn that type of thing. We have more than we'll need so not all of them will be felled." Mac looked around. Rose was right and he knew it to be true. The serenity, and peace up there at the top five was nothing less than magnificent. Their house would improve the area when he finally built it in a year or two.

He already had a visual in his mind on how he wanted it to look. His visual, he knew, was Rose's too. They would build it with three bedrooms and possibly two floors with a large kitchen, and maybe even a veranda on the second floor that would over look the forest. With the tall birch in the back and mammoth cedars in the front, it would be spectacular. He guessed it would take three years to complete, less time if he hired someone to help when the time to build finally came. For now, and before he could even start building, the land needed to be cleared, the logs peeled and dried. He shook his head as visions of his ultimate dream danced in his head. It was 4:00 p.m., when Mac and Rose headed for home. Tyrell waved as he watched them disappear around the bend.

Lonely as he was after his company left, he fired up the wood stove to heat up a steam bath, something he desperately needed. As it warmed, he tossed some hay in the corral for Pony and gave him water. "Been a couple of interesting days hasn't it old boy. The weather sure has turned nice. Ain't sure how long it will last, but I hope for a while. It makes the work a little less aggravating and difficult. Compared to last week, this week is like spring. The sun has been hot and the snow has stayed up high in the mountains. Ain't sure that is a good thing or not. Might make for a drier than usual summer." Pony, finished now with the bucket of water, Tyrell left him to leisurely feed on the hay.

"I'll swing back in a bit with more water, Pony. Right now I think my steam bath is ready." Tyrell grabbed the empty bucket as he made his way back to the tepee and set it down. Entering, he fished through his gear for a change of clothes, some soap, the lantern, and his straight razor. The steam bath felt good. It revived him and even helped clear his head from the annoying thumping he had been feeling all day. Whiskey always did that to him and he wondered why he bothered drinking the stuff. Sure, things were fun while he drank, but the outcome to that was never really worth it. The head ache, the sick feeling and in some cases even guilt would plague him. It was the same every time. Yet, on occasion, he would do it all over again. It was stupid. That was the easiest way to explain it.

As the weeks and months came and went, Tyrell and Mac worked day in and day out, taking only a few days off every second week or so. On those days of rest, Mac taught him how to tan the elk and bear hide, as he had promised after Tyrell had killed the two.

The horse logging continued through snow, rain, and the biting cold that came and went as spring approached. During this time, no incidents of bounty hunters, gunslingers, or hired killers came around looking for a fellow named Tyrell or Travis Sweet. It was a time of peace and tranquility and Tyrell was beginning to think that the witch-hunt for Heath Roy's and Ollie Johnson's killer was over, or at the least interest in finding the killer had faded. What lay ahead for his alias Travis Sweet he had no idea, only time would tell. Only time would tell if there was a reprieve for the fellow named Tyrell. Until he knew for certain, he would continue on as Travis Sweet. In all honesty, he was beginning to like that persona. The name Travis Sweet was legendary and only because of one simple encounter with the man named Earl Brubaker, who on the day that he died, pulled his pistol on the wrong man, the man known as Travis Sweet.

On April 15th, 1891, the horse logging ended. Enough land was clear to build on, and by Mac's calculations, he had plenty of logs to build with. They spent the rest of April and May peeling the logs and restacking them with poles between each layer to help with the drying process. They stacked them five wide and two high and when it was all done they had eight full stacks. "I reckon eighty logs is a good start, Travis. Might even be enough to build the house," Mac said, as the two of them now rested each sitting on a stump. "I'll let them sit all summer and maybe by next spring they'll be cured enough to use." Although that part of the job was finished and he was happy for that reason, there was a bit of sadness in his voice as they conversed. In the back of his mind, he knew the time had come where Travis would soon be on his way. He wondered as they sat there looking on at all that they had accomplished if there would ever be a time when he and Travis would ever meet again.

"I figure by next spring they'll be dry, Mac. In another year or so, you'll have your house built and you and Rose will be able to look out your windows every day at all the beauty this place holds."

The Missing Years – Part I

"Yep, and I'll always know it was you and I that made it so. You worked hard Travis, and if I could convince you stick around, I would, but I know you want to get on with your next leg of this journey." Mac inhaled deeply as he averted his eyes to the east and gazed at the Rocky Mountains.

"Don't get all teary eyed Mac, I'll be back this way one day. I ain't sure when, but, I will check in on you." Tyrell wasn't so sure about that, but he smiled at the possibility as he too now looked to the mountains. He felt sad himself. He had grown to like Mac and Rose, and he too wondered if they ever would meet again. On May 30th, 1891, Tyrell picked up his last pay from Mac and bid him and Rose farewell. He and Black Dog headed north, destination unknown. He had $300 dollars of earned pay in his pocket and $150 dollars left from the original $500 dollars he had when he left Willow Gate that past September.

Forth Coming: "The Missing Years-Part II"
"Tyrell Sloan aka Travis Sweet, Bounty Hunter"
A Tyrell Sloan Western Adventure.

The Missing Years – Part I

Other Books by Brian T. Seifrit

A Bloodstained Hammer (with Alison Townsend MacNicol)

This is the story of a hog-farming family, the Townsends, living in the Kootenays in British Columbia, Canada in the late 1950's and later years. The story describes the hard life for the farmer who has to work at a nearby mine and smelter in order to support his farm work. The story is a fictionalized description based on the actual events that occurred. Of course, the conversations, thoughts expressed and activities are the product of the authors' imaginations. The fact that the events are still so clearly remembered fifty years later is significant, indicating the depth to which the events affected the family.

Family day-to-day life is described. The need for hired help is satisfied when a young man answers their advertisement. He joins the family, works hard, learns the ropes of hog farming and butchering. The hired man, called Hudulak in the story, has a number of problems related to his limited intelligence, his sexual desires and his drinking to excess on the few occasions he goes out on the town. These problems are not noted especially by the Townsend family, although the eight year old daughter Emily is unhappy with the way he leers at her.

Hudulak goes on a drinking binge with a neighbor and ends up in Mrs. Townsend's bedroom in the middle of the night. Mr. Townsend is working the night shift. Unfortunately, the confrontation in the bedroom leads to the death of both Mrs. Townsend and Emily, the eight year old. Hudulak cleans up a little and drives away in the family car.

The Missing Years – Part I

Although he is caught within a few hours, he is able to convince the authorities that he is insane and his only punishment is a life of leisure in a mental hospital for 18 years. Eventually, he is given a complete release, marries and lives a normal life.

In the meantime, life goes on for the remnants of the Townsend family. The effect of this crime on the family is described, and the frustration felt by the family members by the ineffective way in which the crimes were handled is lamented. The Townsends believe that the Canadian Justice system failed and believe that Hudulak simply fooled all the authorities.

Based on a true story, the authors get inside the minds of the characters, describing the thoughts and feelings of a murderer and his victims.

A free workbook for the use of ESL students and teachers to aid in studying the text is available on the Publisher's website. The student will have the opportunity to correct the grammar.

Due to the descriptions of the sexually explicit thoughts of the hired hand, the story is unsuitable for public school children.

Although the insanity defence is still in vogue today, the Townsends believe that today's psychiatrists and prosecutors would not be quite so lenient as they were in the 1960's in a remote area in the interior of British Columbia. Interestingly, in 2012, a mental patient in Quebec who killed his children and was found not guilty by reason of insanity, was given a full discharge after only two years of treatment. This story will shine some light on the impact these crimes have on the victims.

The Coalition of Purgatory

The Missing Years – Part I

A ruthless land developer threatens the land of the Grizzly bear and the sacred land of the Ktunaxa people. Bryce Ellwood, a nationally renowned freelance journalist, an orphaned grizzly cub, a man with a shaded past, an Indian guide and his granddaughter, form a Coalition to prevent any further destruction of the Purgatory Mountains. Love, pain, hate, and sorrow are entwined together in an absorbing tale of a reality that someday may exist for British Columbia's wildlife.

Red Rock Canyon

Tyrell Sloan is the heir to his Grandfather's estate, which consists of an old ramshackle cabin, and over three hundred and twenty acres of red shale, pasture, and forest. During the journey to Red Rock Canyon, he encounters a slew of unforgettable characters. He hears some unusual tales about his Grandfather and wrestles with the day-to-day survival of solitude, as he tries to make a life for himself. He learns that three of the richest gold claims in the Columbia Kootenay are on Sloan land, but all that gold, he realizes, is not worth the burden.

Return to Red Rock

Six years after leaving behind his inheritance, Tyrell Sloan returns to familiar ground. In 1890, he was the heir to the estate of his Grandfather, John Henry Sloan Sr. consisting of 300 acres of red shale, forest, and pasture. Near the homestead, and less than an hour's ride up stream of the Hudu Creek, were three gold claims, the Sloan 1, 2 and 3. At the time of his departure, the claims were contracted for a two-year term with the Wake Up Jake, a mining company.

When he left, he wrote a letter that he stashed in the sacks of gold put in Grandma Heddy's care. Tyrell

The Missing Years – Part I

bequeathed the gold to Grandma, and his share of whatever the Wake Up Jake produced during the term of the contract. To Marissa, he left the homestead, all 300 acres. With plans to head north to his hometown of Hell's Bottom, he was side tracked. A recurring dream of his Grandfather's death and the men who killed him, as well as the face-to-face encounter with the villainous men of his dream, took over the next six years of his life.

With the possibility of being captured and hanged, Tyrell returns to Red Rock Canyon to live his life in obscurity. To his surprise, Marissa, his onetime true love continues to reside there. It isn't long before the two are once more reacquainted, and their adventure begins as Tyrell tries to right his wrongs from days gone past.

Voracity

Voracity follows a team of researchers and field assassins that work for the elite K.A.T. (Kuru Assault Team) Agency, as they search for a cure for a disease derived from the Kuru virus. A young neurologist, Trent Sweet discovered it. Papers he wrote and submitted to medical magazines and health organisations were dismissed as fiction. Trent died a gruesome death for the cause in 1994. The circumstances would always haunt his brother Blain.

The Agency has a purpose that Blain endorses so he continues on, building up the Agency to what it is today. So secret is the K.A.T Agency that few in the Canadian Government or law enforcement agencies know of its existence.

Blain is the Agency's finest and most elite assassin. He is assigned to do some field research, a part of his job that he detests. During this research, he discovers there is more to K-15 then anyone had expected.

The Missing Years – Part I

A Biography of Brian T. Seifrit

Brian is a seven-time published author. In September 1988-December-1989, he attended Columbia Academy of Radio, Television & Recording Arts, in Calgary, AB, where he majored in Broadcast Journalism. Following that, and ten years later, he attended Selkirk College in Castlegar BC, from September 1999-April 2001 where he was Enrolled in UT Courses – English History, Philosophy, Creative Writing, and Canadian Literature and majored in Print Journalism.

He has been happily married for 27 years and counting. He has four children, two from previous relationships, and two with his current wife. He grew up on a small hobby farm outside of Fruitvale BC.

In 2000, he wrote for the Source a community newspaper in Fruitvale BC, and since then has done freelance writing of human interest for the Trail Daily Times.

When he writes for himself, he tries not to stay in only one genre, He finds that one genre gets stale after a while. Instead he chooses to write in as many genres as he can. Imagination and creativity are wonderful tools, and he uses them both. From the list of the titles and brief descriptions above, you will undoubtedly agree that Brian is a multi-faceted writer with a vivid imagination.

Brian lives in the Kootenays in the British Columbia interior in a wild part of Canada.

Any communications with Brian can be emailed to:

tbseifrit@gmail.com

William Jenkins, Publisher

This publishing activity was established in 2014 for the purpose of self-publishing the stories by William Jenkins. These stories are supplementary reading for elementary school students (about Grade 5).

He also edits and publishes stories submitted to him upon request.

Mr. Jenkins can be contacted at:

williamhenryjenkins@gmail.com

Previously. Mr. Jenkins published under the corporation Your ESL Story Publishers Ltd. That corporation is/was dissolved as of December 31, 2014.

Made in the USA
Charleston, SC
15 February 2017